Kathy REICHS & Brendan Reichs

EXPOSURE

Published by Young Arrow in 2014

2 4 6 8 10 9 7 5 3 1

Published by arrangement with the original publisher, G.P. Putnam's Son's, an imprint of Penguin Inc.

Young Arrow
The Random House Group Limited
20 Vauxhall Bridge Road, London, SW1V 2SA

www.randomhouse.co.uk

Addresses for companies within The Random House Group Limited can be found at:
www.randomhouse.co.uk/offices.htm

The Random House Group Limited Reg. No. 954009

A CIP catalogue record for this book
is available from the British Library

HB ISBN 9780099567240
TPB ISBN 9780099568056

The Random House Group Limited supports the Forest Stewardship Council® (FSC®), the leading international forest-certification organisation. Our books carrying the FSC label are printed on FSC®-certified paper. FSC is the only forest-certification scheme supported by the leading environmental organisations, including Greenpeace. Our paper procurement policy can be found at: www.randomhouse.co.uk/environment

Printed and bound by Clays Ltd, St Ives plc

Brendan Reichs would like to dedicate this book
to his mind-blowingly wonderful new daughter, Alice.
You are the cutest baby in the world, and that's a fact.

Kathy Reichs would like to dedicate this book
to her fantabulous agent Jennifer Rudolph Walsh.
This one makes twenty!

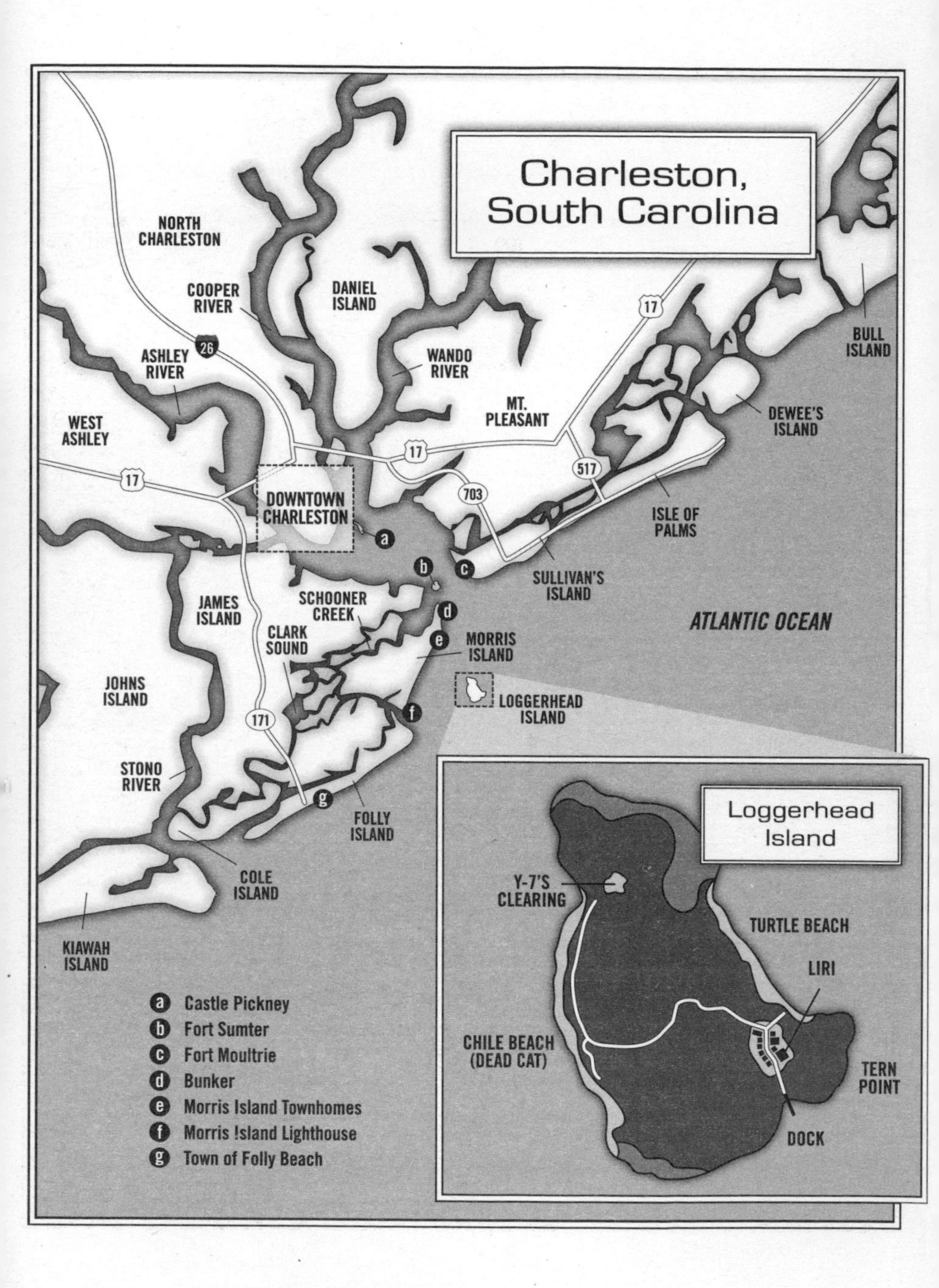
Charleston, South Carolina
NORTH CHARLESTON
COOPER RIVER
DANIEL ISLAND
WANDO RIVER
ASHLEY RIVER
WEST ASHLEY
MT. PLEASANT
DOWNTOWN CHARLESTON
BULL ISLAND
DEWEE'S ISLAND
ISLE OF PALMS
SULLIVAN'S ISLAND
JAMES ISLAND
SCHOONER CREEK
CLARK SOUND
MORRIS ISLAND
ATLANTIC OCEAN
JOHNS ISLAND
LOGGERHEAD ISLAND
STONO RIVER
FOLLY ISLAND
COLE ISLAND
KIAWAH ISLAND
26
17
17
17
17
517
703
171
a Castle Pickney
b Fort Sumter
c Fort Moultrie
d Bunker
e Morris Island Townhomes
f Morris !sland Lighthouse
g Town of Folly Beach
Loggerhead Island
Y-7'S CLEARING
TURTLE BEACH
LIRI
CHILE BEACH (DEAD CAT)
TERN POINT
DOCK

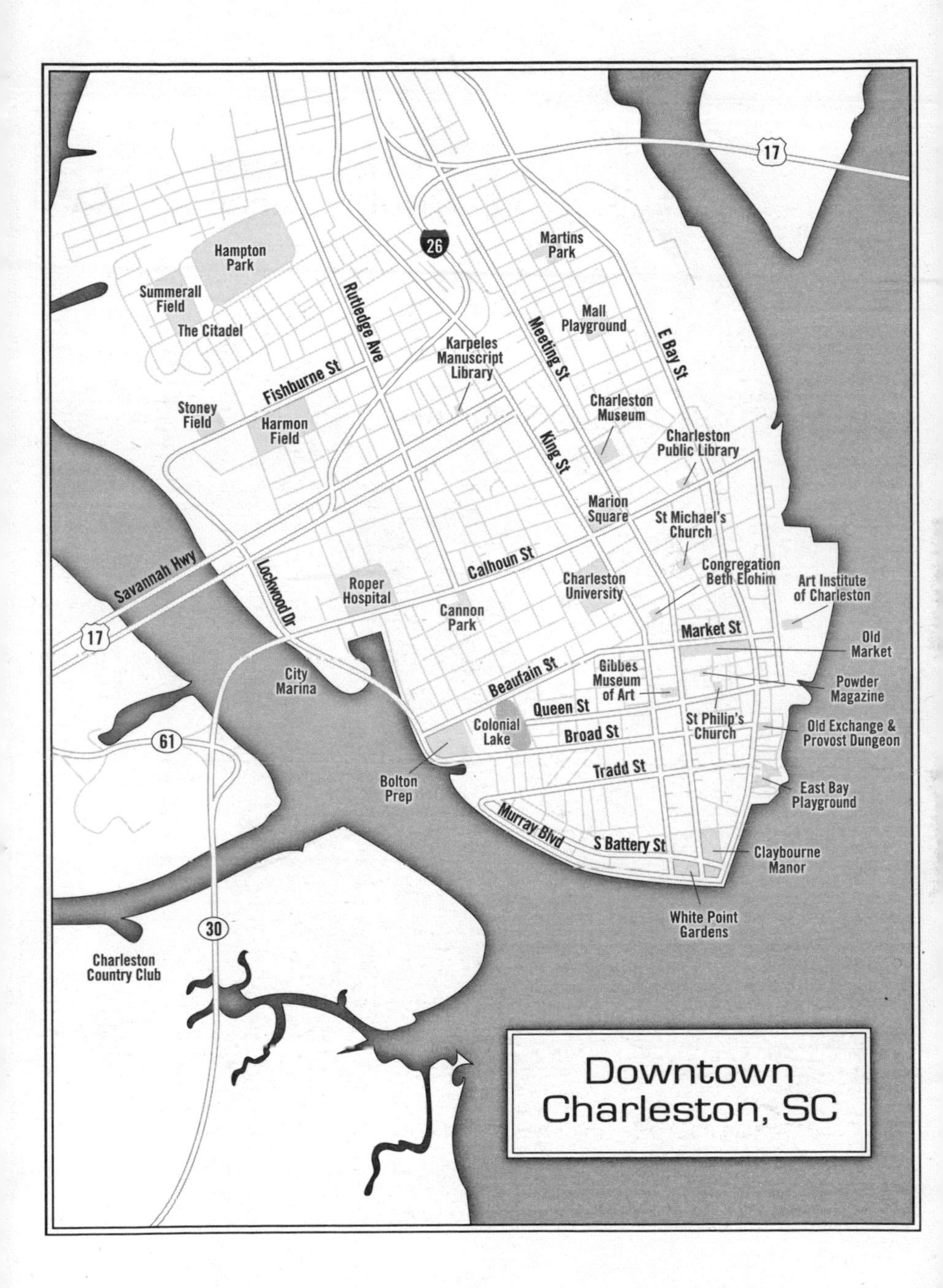
17
26
Martins Park
Hampton Park
Summerall Field
The Citadel
Rutledge Ave
Mall Playground
Meeting St
E Bay St
Karpeles Manuscript Library
Fishburne St
Stoney Field
Harmon Field
Charleston Museum
King St
Charleston Public Library
Marion Square
St Michael's Church
Savannah Hwy
Lockwood Dr
Calhoun St
Congregation Beth Elohim
Art Institute of Charleston
Roper Hospital
Charleston University
Cannon Park
17
Market St
Old Market
Beaufain St
Gibbes Museum of Art
Powder Magazine
City Marina
Queen St
St Philip's Church
Old Exchange & Provost Dungeon
Colonial Lake
Broad St
61
Tradd St
Bolton Prep
East Bay Playground
Murray Blvd
S Battery St
Claybourne Manor
White Point Gardens
30
Charleston Country Club
Downtown Charleston, SC

PROLOGUE

Beads of water tumbled from the darkness above.

Drip. Drip. Drip.

The girl shifted, angling her pale face away from the cascade. Sodden blond hair hung lank to her shoulders, filthy with grime and debris.

The boy rose from where he crouched. Ushered the girl across the narrow stone chamber. Silently took her place. Dirty rivulets began rolling down his cheeks, gathering at the chin before dropping to the earthen floor. He took no notice. There were no dry places.

Outside the dim, moldy cell, beyond a line of rusty steel bars, a red light glowed. Steady. Unblinking. Their sole companion.

Shivers racked the girl's body. She began to whimper.

The boy reached without looking and squeezed her shoulder. The crying ceased, replaced by a smattering of snotty hiccups.

The red light watched. Fixed. Indifferent.

Time passed, unmarked by any further movement.

The whimpers soon returned. This time, the boy didn't bother to reach.

Suddenly, a loud bang broke the stillness.

Two pairs of eyes darted, nervously probing the impenetrable gloom.

The noise repeated, followed by a shriek of metal.

Instinctually, the boy and girl drew closer together.

The rasping clatter grew, echoing off the ancient stone walls.

A shadow, blacker than the surrounding dark, materialized overhead. Descended.

The boy and girl watched, breathless, their fingers interlocked.

The shadow took form—a bucket. Wooden, bound with frayed rope, and splintered along its sides. It lowered steadily on a thick metal chain.

The bucket lurched to a stop. Dangled five feet from the floor.

The boy stood. Cautiously peered over the rim.

Inside was a hunk of stale bread, already wilting in the damp, fetid air.

The prisoners attacked the loaf ravenously. Devoured the paltry meal in seconds.

"I'm still hungry," the girl whispered.

The boy shook his head.

With a squeal, the pail began to ascend. Angrily, the boy lashed out with both fists, sending the bucket arcing and spinning as it rose.

"What do you want with us!?" the boy bellowed. "Let us out of here!"

A chuckle echoed from somewhere high above.

The girl began to weep.

The bucket swung its way skyward. Disappeared into the gloom.

Water fell.

The red light gleamed.

In moments, all was dark and silent once more.

PART ONE

JUSTICE

CHAPTER 1

Monday

"What I'd like from you is the truth, Miss Brennan."

The defense attorney's gravelly voice boomed inside the courtroom.

A jolt of adrenaline tore through me.

My mind had wandered. Impossible, I know, given the circumstances. But a second hour of questioning was taking its toll.

And this pompous toolbag showed no signs of winding down.

I cleared my throat. Shifted on the witness stand.

"Could you repeat the question, sir?" Stalling for time.

Parrish sighed dramatically. "Again?"

I nodded.

Parrish sneered, doubling his already abundant collection of chins. No doubt he thought me rattled.

Honestly, I was just tired. Tired, and incredibly on edge.

I had to watch every single word.

"Do you need a break, Miss Brennan?" Crossing his arms, Parrish nodded toward the district attorney's table. "Perhaps a chance to get your story straight with counsel?"

"Objection!" Nell Harris shot to her feet, suit jacket flapping, her ice-blue eyes radiating anger. "Mr. Parrish is impugning the witness before the jury! His false, incendiary comment must be stricken from—"

Judge Felix DeMerit raised a placating hand. "Sustained, Ms. Harris."

Afternoon sunlight slanted through the tall windows behind his lofty bench, reflecting from his liver-spotted scalp.

"Watch yourself, Counsel." DeMerit glared at Parrish over the rims of his old-fangled reading glasses. "Miss Brennan is a minor, and not the party on trial here. Make your case, but she *shall* be accorded proper treatment. Am I understood?"

"Of course, Your Honor." Stroking his scraggly beard, Parrish aimed for contrite. Aimed, and failed. "My sincerest apologies to both Miss Brennan and the Court."

Whispers swirled inside the cavernous room, Charleston's largest chamber of justice. Though camera crews had been barred from the chamber—due to the presence of minors as witnesses—dozens of other media members packed the gallery. The remaining seats were filled by government officials, police functionaries, members of the Bar, and the city's elite. Armed bailiffs lined the aisles and walls, and double-manned every door.

Charleston hadn't seen a trial like this in years, nor dealt with a crime remotely as sensational. Everyone with enough pull to wrangle access had squeezed onto one of the long wooden benches.

To watch *me.*

The fourteen-year-old schoolgirl who'd outsmarted a psychopath.

It was Monday, the first day of the year's fourth month.

A local blogger had already dubbed me "April Fool."

Blargh.

"The jury shall disregard the last comment made by Mr. Parrish."

Judge DeMerit swiveled to face me. "*Do* you need a short break, Miss Brennan? This isn't an endurance contest, it's a court of law."

"I'm fine."

I wasn't. Not even close. But I wanted this nightmare over ASAP.

Despite the courtroom's subarctic temperature, my sweat glands were starting to churn full tilt. I was thankful my Bolton Prep blazer was a deep navy blue.

Pit stains do not increase credibility.

I fiddled with my ponytail before remembering Harris's advice: *Don't fidget. Sit up straight. Address your answers directly to the jury. Try not to lose your cool.*

So far, I was struggling on all counts.

I hoped my face wasn't paler than my usual Irish white. And that freckles didn't really multiply when you lied, as my mother had warned when I was little.

If true, I'd soon be covered head to foot.

A quick glance at the jury. All twelve were eyeballing me.

Was that pity in their eyes? Skepticism? Boredom?

I couldn't tell. Wasn't sure I wanted to know.

Just get through this. Ben did. So can I.

My gaze flicked to the gallery, though I knew Ben wasn't there. Couldn't be. By rule, one witness can't be present for the testimony of another. To avoid collusion, I think, though it's a stupid rule—if people want to lie, they're going to lie. Period.

Because Ben and I were definitely lying. Some.

There was no way around it.

We *couldn't* tell the whole truth. Not without exposing what we were. Revealing the hidden powers we possessed. Announcing our warped DNA to the public.

Putting our lives at risk.

Not gonna happen.

Inadvertently, my eyes drifted to the one spot I'd avoided since taking the stand.

Another set was staring back.

No welcome there.

Only anger. Oh yes, plenty of that.

The Gamemaster beamed pure hatred from his seat at defense counsel's table. He wore a cheap gray suit and a pair of "innocent man" glasses. But the fake plastic lenses failed to mask his palpable rage. I nearly gasped at its intensity.

Had he been glaring at me the whole time? Couldn't *everyone* see he was crazy?

I tore my eyes away, searched for a more comfortable landing spot.

There. Kit.

My father manned the first seat of the front row, his mop of curly brown hair disheveled by constant worrying with his fingers. Kit looked equal parts incensed, fretful, and supportive. Catching my eye, he gave me a firm nod and flashed a thumbs-up.

I exhaled slowly. At least one person was in my corner.

I knew this day was killing him—Kit had made it *abundantly* clear that he didn't like my being called as a witness. He didn't want me in the same room as that monster.

But Harris had been adamant—Ben and I were the keys to a conviction. Uncomfortable as testifying might be, I had no intention of letting the Gamemaster go free.

Side note. I wasn't speaking to Ben. Hadn't since the hurricane.

Not now. Focus.

I spotted Hi and Shelton, sitting beside Kit. Relaxed a fraction more.

Those two had been spared this ordeal—Harris thought two eyewitnesses were sufficient, and Ben and I were the obvious choices. Shelton had nearly passed out in relief, but I suspect Hi was disappointed. That boy loves a show.

They sat side by side, wearing matching Bolton uniforms—white button-up shirts, maroon ties, tan pants, and navy sport jackets adorned with griffin crests. Hi was wearing his blazer properly, rather than his usual inside out.

Even Hiram Stolowitski was taking this seriously.

Noticing my glance, Shelton nodded encouragement, his thick, black-framed glasses bouncing on his nose.

Hi winked. Raised and shook both fists. Then beat his flabby chest like a gorilla.

Okay, maybe not *too* seriously.

"I'll try again." Parrish adopted an expression of long-suffering patience, tossing a quick glance at the jury to measure the effect of his performance.

Dirtbag.

"You *claim* that five of you—" Parrish turned to squint at Hi and Shelton, before returning his gaze to me, "—were lured to and trapped inside a basement by my client. Correct?"

"Yes."

"This group included Mr. Benjamin Blue?"

"It did."

Parrish pivoted to face the jury. "That would be the *same* Ben Blue who has already admitted complicity in these crimes."

I sat up straighter. "Ben only helped *before* The Game turned dangerous. He didn't know what the Gamemaster really had planned. Once Ben did, he tried to stop—"

"So he claims," Parrish interrupted. "How very convenient for him. And for his deal with the prosecution."

"Objection!" Harris popped up once more, looking daggers at Parrish.

"Withdrawn." Parrish crossed to his table and picked up a thick file marked Exhibit B. "Miss Brennan, in a statement to police you asserted that a massive steel grate trapped your group inside a ventilation room."

Not a question. I didn't respond.

Parrish smirked at my small defiance. "Yet when police arrived three days later, they found the way clear, and the metal grate lying *broken and to the side.* The report described its condition—thick steel bars, twisted, with some pieces snapped clear in half."

My perspiration waterfall resumed its flow.

Parrish adopted a quizzical expression. "Can you explain that?"

"Explain what?" Lame response, even to my partial ears.

"You *claim* that this grate was a sinister trap, designed and constructed by my client." Parrish moved in closer, like a buzzard circling a carcass. "So how did it end up mangled on the basement floor?"

"We managed to escape." I couldn't look at the jury.

"You managed to escape?" Parrish's brows rose theatrically. "This inescapable prison? How, pray tell?"

I swallowed. "We dislodged the grate from the wall."

"You dislodged it?" His eyes widened with exaggerated wonder. "A five-hundred-pound metal barrier, composed of interlinking steel bars?"

"That's right." Curtly spoken. His habit of repeating my answers was beyond irritating. "There were four of us pounding on the thing. It was stressful. We must've had enough adrenaline pumping to pull it off."

Parrish snorted. "That's pretty darn impressive, to snap steel bars like matchsticks."

I felt blood rush to my face. Hoped the jurors didn't notice.

My explanation sounded sketchy, even to me. But I couldn't reveal how we'd really done it. Couldn't tell the jury we have freaking superpowers.

You see, fellow citizens, my friends and I were recently exposed to a canine supervirus, and have developed tremendous physical and supersensory capabilities as a result. We ripped that grate from the wall by unlocking wolf-like powers hidden in our DNA.

I wasn't sure which would happen first—the Gamemaster's acquittal, or my committal.

The jury stirred. I saw doubt creep onto several faces.

Parrish moved in for the kill. "Isn't it *more* likely that you found that big ol' grate already lying on the ground? Where it'd been resting, broken, for years? That your friend Ben Blue took you straight to it, as part of his dangerous prank?"

"Of course not!"

Parrish's voice sharpened, his drawl disappearing. "You were never trapped in that room, were you, Miss Brennan?"

Enough defense. Play offense.

"Maybe the bolts were poorly seated," I said firmly.

Parrish paused, assessing my words. The Gamemaster shifted in his seat.

I pushed ahead. "Police investigators found three-inch steel bolts scattered on the electrical room floor. Look in that report you're holding—they matched a series of drill holes surrounding the ventilation room's doorframe. Keep reading, and you'll see where CPD confirmed that those holes were newly excavated, and that the runners flanking the doorway had recently been greased."

Parrish held up an index finger. "That's neither here nor—"

I cut him off. "CPD also confirmed that the quarter-inch screws securing the steel bars were purchased locally, only a month before the incident. Same with the grate's track-locking mechanism. And please reread the statement of Max Fuller, a freelance welder in Myrtle Beach. He recalls building the wheel assembly just six months ago. The DA sent you that one, correct?"

Parrish's face purpled. "Listen here, missy. *I'll* ask the questions."

"I thought you wanted a response?" I shot back. "Evidence proves the grate was recently constructed and attached to the basement wall. It slid down from the ceiling and locked us in. As its maker intended."

Parrish struggled for words. He waved a hand weakly, attempting to regain control of the exchange. I declined to let him.

"Why did the grate fail?" I shrugged, then turned my most earnest face on the jury. "I honestly can't say for sure, but my friends and I are only alive because it did. It was a gift from God. And for that reason, I don't question my good fortune."

Smiles. Nods. I noticed the Gamemaster seething in his chair.

"Who knows?" I met his glare directly. "Maybe the whole apparatus was poorly constructed."

"Liar!" The Gamemaster slammed both fists on the defense table. "I built it perfectly!"

The courtroom froze in stunned silence.

"The Game was *flawless*!" Spittle flew from the Gamemaster's mouth as he suddenly sprang up and vaulted over the table. "You *cheated*! You had *help* somehow!"

Screams. Breaking glass. The sound of chairs overturning.

The Gamemaster bounded toward the witness stand, madness in his eyes.

Two strides.

Something stirred deep within me.

No! Not here!

Then a crush of bodies swarmed the Gamemaster. He disappeared under a pile of tan bailiffs' uniforms, still struggling to reach me.

The gallery erupted in chaos.

Judge DeMerit pounded his gavel, but no one paid any attention. Mayhem engulfed the courtroom as more guards entered the well and flung themselves atop the enraged defendant.

Slowly, the officers regained control. Multiple sets of handcuffs appeared and were applied. Bailiffs began peeling off the dog-pile like layers of an onion.

And there, at the bottom of the scrum, was Kit.

Oh, Dad.

He was panting like a marathoner, arms still wrapping the Gamemaster's legs in a death grip. He'd clearly been first to react.

"This Court is in recess!" Judge DeMerit bellowed, still hammering away. "The witness is dismissed. Bailiffs, remove the jury and remand the defendant into custody."

As some officers hustled the jurors from the room, more guards marched the now-silent Gamemaster through a rear door.

Harris sped to the stand and grabbed my hand, her short blond bob now as mussed as an abandoned bird's nest. "Are you okay, Tory?"

I nodded, still too shaken to speak. Harris escorted me over to Kit, who was seated at the prosecution table, holding a napkin to his nose.

"Nice tackle." Unsure what to do, I squeezed his shoulder.

"Missed my calling." Kit rubbed the side of his face. "I'm a born linebacker."

Shelton and Hi appeared at my side.

"Oh, man!" Shelton had both hands on his dome. He seemed winded, despite not having moved during the attack. "Things just got real in here."

"I've said it before, Tory." Hi shook his head in wonder. "You have a natural gift for pissing people off. And not just *kinda* mad. Like, lose-your-freaking-mind, rush-the-stand-in-open-court bonkers."

My eyes rolled. "Thanks."

Harris smoothed her suit with trembling hands. "We need to clear the courtroom." Despite everything, I detected an undercurrent of excitement in her voice. "I'll walk you out."

I cast a final look back at the stand. Judge DeMerit stood frozen behind his bench, gavel in hand, a stunned expression on his face.

I hear that.

Kit gathered me with one arm and we hustled from the chamber.

CHAPTER 2

Shelton pulled the portal shut behind us.

My heartbeat finally slowed.

I sank into a chair beside our bunker's circular worktable.

What a day.

"I still can't believe he came at you like that!" Hi, for the third time. He dropped into the space-age super-chair attached to our computer workstation. "That was a pure psycho move right there. What a loon."

Hiram can be described as husky or chubby, depending on your generosity. A funny kid, with twinkling brown eyes and wavy brown hair, Hi has quick wits and a razor-sharp tongue. He's also a science nut, and loves setting up complex experiments.

Hiram had ditched his school uniform, and was now sporting faded brown cargo shorts and a red *Gremlins* tee. He was obsessed with retro gear—half the time, I'd never even heard of the subjects.

Hi was always happy to explain. At length.

"Sorry I froze in there, Tor." Shelton frowned as he shirt-wiped his glasses. "Not exactly my 'One Shining Moment,' huh?"

I waved off his apology. I knew Shelton hated how skittish he could be.

"Hey, *I* froze, too." My skin crawled at the memory. "Let's just hope the jury got a good look. And that Parrish doesn't find some way to spin it. That man is a snake."

"True story." Shelton had changed into Bermuda shorts and a yellow polo. Both hung loosely on his skinny frame. Shelton's dark chocolate skin mirrors that of his father, Nelson, but he'd inherited the soft facial features of his Japanese mother, Lorelei.

Our computer ace—a cyber-hacker extraordinaire—Shelton's equally adept with codes and puzzles. An expert lock picker, too. He's not, however, much of a thrill seeker. Shelton's list of phobias is a mile long.

Shelton had turned sixteen in November, the second Viral to clear that lofty bar. He'd gotten his driver's license just after Christmas, and now spent countless hours searching used-car websites, hunting the perfect ride.

I'd celebrated my *fifteenth* birthday six weeks before the trial. We'd kept the festivities low key—just Shelton and Hi, Kit and Whitney, a few gifts, and a three-course meal at Husk. I'd been more than satisfied, though why Hiram thought I'd want an Angry Birds T-shirt was still a mystery.

No Bolton Prep kids had been invited, not even Jason.

He'd understood. The last thing I wanted was to broadcast how young I was. How I'd skipped a grade, and was "so smart." That hadn't worked out for me in the past.

Maybe next year.

Ben hadn't been invited to my birthday, either. That was harder.

But facts were facts: Ben had worked with the Gamemaster.

He'd known who that lunatic was, all along, and said nothing.

I hadn't seen Ben much since his confession the night of the hurricane. Not that I'd wanted to see him. He'd turned seventeen in December, and I'd been invited to a celebratory dinner—along with Hi and Shelton—but didn't attend.

How could I?

"You have to admit," Hi said suddenly, "that wacko is pretty agile. He got, what, halfway to strangling you? Not a bad effort."

Shelton blew out a breath. "When the Gamemaster started moving, I just couldn't believe it. His lawyer must be going *crazy* right now."

"He'll have nightmares about Kit diving for his knees," Hi added. "I'm pretty sure that was an illegal tackle. Chop block. Something."

I was replaying the courtroom madness in my head when something brushed against my kneecaps. I glanced down. Spotted Cooper's giant head poking from beneath the table.

The wolfdog pawed at my lap, his deep blue eyes locking onto mine. He could usually sense when I was feeling troubled.

Part of our unique bond? Or just a pet's intuition? Who knew.

"Hello, dog face." I scratched behind his gray-brown ears.

The four of us were holed up inside our clubhouse, an ancient Civil War bunker at the northern tip of Morris Island, the middle-of-nowhere barrier isle on which our families lived. Hidden deep inside a sand hill overlooking the Atlantic, the remote dugout was practically invisible to the outside world.

I felt safe there. Mainly because no one else knew the bunker existed.

Except Ben, of course.

I pushed the thought away.

Morris Island is essentially off the grid, an empty stretch of hills, fields, and cattail-covered dunes that forms the southern half of the entrance to the Charleston Harbor. The entire four square miles is one parcel, owned by the Loggerhead Trust, which preserves it in a mostly undeveloped state.

Only one modern structure exists on Morris—the small townhouse complex where we all live. A single road connects our neighborhood to the outside world—a one-lane, unmarked strip of blacktop winding south through grassy meadows before crossing to Folly Island.

Our tiny community is one of the most isolated in the Lowcountry. We live in virtual exile from the rest of Charleston. Even most *locals* think Morris is uninhabited.

The Loggerhead Trust also owns the townhouse complex, and leases its ten identical units to employees working at the Loggerhead Island Research Institute, one of the most advanced veterinary research facilities on the planet.

Kit and I have one. Which makes sense, since Kit is not only LIRI's director, but also the founder and manager of the trust.

The Stolowitski and Devers clans each have a unit—Hi's dad is the institute's chief lab technician; Shelton's dad is IT director, while his mother is a vet tech working in Lab One. Ben's father, Tom Blue, operates the institute's shuttle boat, *Hugo,* and lives in the last unit on the right. Ben splits time between there and his mother's place across the bay in Mount Pleasant.

"Has anyone cycled the batteries lately?" Shelton asked.

"Yeppers." Hi was booting the iMac. "Did it yesterday. We're good to go."

Once a key outpost protecting the city from naval attack, our bunker had been forgotten by the world. At least, until my friends and I discovered it while tracking down a stray Frisbee.

Things had changed quite a bit since that day.

At first the dugout had been little more than a dark, drafty hill cave, empty but for a dangerous mine entrance and a splintery wooden bench. But as a result of our adventure chasing the legendary she-pirate Anne Bonny, we'd acquired some funds and put them to good use.

Cash—and backbreaking effort—had transformed the bunker into something special. Meticulously up-fitted, and jammed with the latest technology, our clubhouse now had enough juice to land a space shuttle.

Indoor-outdoor carpet covered the floor, and a clever retractable window sealed the wall-length cannon slit overlooking the ocean. The interior was decorated with sleek modular furniture—circular drafting table, matching chairs, cabinet, bookshelf, and our totally kick-ass computer workstation.

Hi had demanded and received a mini-fridge. The old wooden bench still ran beneath the window, but had been sanded, polished, and stained. A quartet of cheery floor lamps manned the corners.

Our largest purchase, by far, had been a solar-powered generator. Getting the bulky-yet-delicate gadget delivered—and hauled out, undetected—had been a nightmare. But we'd somehow pulled it off, installing the four-panel array in the scrub grass just above the bunker's entrance.

"Stupid wireless is on the fritz." Hi rose and stepped into the bunker's second chamber. Fumbled for the light. That room was always dark—we'd permanently sealed the cannon slit and boarded over the collapsed mineshaft snaking from its rear.

Bundled cables dangled from metal shelves against the wall, each packed with hardware. Wireless routers. Servers. Blade drives. AV equipment. A dozen other high-tech components. The bottom rack housed a row of industrial-sized rechargeable batteries.

Coop followed Hi, eyes alert to his every move. The room's far corner doubled as the wolfdog's private lounge: Kong doggie bed, food and water dispensers, and a half-dozen antlers, bones, and slobber-covered chew toys scattered on the floor.

"Relax, Cujo." Hi reset a power strip on the upper shelf. "Just tripping the modem. Your kingdom remains undisturbed."

Coop walked to his bed, circled twice, then curled up and went to sleep.

Hi returned to the main room and plopped back into his chair.

"What was the problem?" I asked.

"Network was out of whack." He avoided my eye. "Ben might've stopped by and tried surfing the net. He always forgets the password. I fixed it."

Shelton walked to the window and peered down. "The mooring ropes have been moved. He probably came by yesterday."

I didn't comment.

Outside our hideout, a narrow path knifed down the hillside to a tiny cove hidden among the rocks. Shielded by a pair of rugged stone outcroppings, both path and cove were hidden from view by sea. Within the bay was an ancient sunken post, perfect for mooring a vessel away from prying eyes.

Ships passed night and day, entering and exiting the harbor, their occupants never imagining that a high-tech nerve center was tucked away inside that hill.

Our secret.

The remodel had taken weeks, cost thousands, and stretched the limits of our abilities at subterfuge. But the results were worth it.

And, thankfully, Hurricane Katelyn had spared our lair.

I'd been a nervous wreck while riding out the storm at my great-aunt Tempe's house in Charlotte. A full week had passed before we could finally return.

Katelyn had pummeled Charleston with sustained winds of over 130 mph. Our island had gotten shellacked—the storm even knocked out the small bridge to Folly.

With less than thirty residents on Morris, fixing that particular span wasn't high on the county's priority list. In the end, Kit elected to have the repairs done privately, with LIRI funds. Anything to get us all home.

We'd weatherproofed the bunker as best we could, dismantling the solar array and hauling it inside—a backbreaking process I hoped never to repeat. But we'd had no clue whether the centuries-old hill cave would survive a Category 4 tempest.

But the gods had been kind—the townhouses were mostly unharmed, and our hideout had survived with nothing more than some mild flooding.

"Is the trial almost over?" Hi's question brought me back. "This drama-in-real-life is cutting into my TV time."

I shrugged. "The DA isn't sure *what* Parrish will do next. I mean, his client just went psycho in front of the jury. Harris is worried the judge might declare a mistrial."

"Mistrial? So you'd have to do it all over again?" Shelton's eyes widened as he took the seat across from me. "But the Gamemaster practically confessed! What a nightmare."

Couldn't have said it better myself.

"Ben will *freak* if he has to testify twice," Hi said. "Parrish was way harder on him than you, Tor. He tried to make it look like *Ben* was responsible for everything."

I glanced at the window bench. Where Ben always sat.

Had always sat.

Before he betrayed us.

My eyes jerked away. I didn't like thinking about it.

Hi and Shelton had forgiven Ben almost immediately, but I couldn't. To me, his betrayal was still too raw. Ran too deep.

Plus, I wasn't ready to deal with the other stuff between us.

He'd confessed something else that night. A secret I kept to myself, even now.

Ben had done it all to impress me. He wanted to be more than just friends.

Even five months later, I didn't know how to feel about that. About *any* of it.

So I did what I do best when it comes to boys—avoid the topic.

Hi must've read my thoughts.

"Ben didn't know what was going to happen," he said quietly. "Not the bad parts. He wouldn't have done that to us, Tory. You know that."

I didn't respond.

Maybe I agreed, but it didn't change how I felt.

How can I ever trust him again?

Ben, one of my closest friends. The boy I'd gone to school with every day, and hung out with for hours afterward. A member of my pack. A Viral.

Ben, who was practically family. In some ways, even closer.

No longer.

Ben had been kicked out of Bolton Prep for his role in the Gamemaster scandal. That's why he mostly stayed with his mother now. Myra's Mount Pleasant apartment is much closer to Ben's new school, Wando High.

Ben's expulsion wasn't fair. Even I could admit that. But when is life fair?

There was nothing fair about Mom getting killed.

Enough.

Ben was gone, and we couldn't change it.

Closing my eyes, I tried to banish the topic.

And felt a tingle in the corner of my mind. A slight . . . pull. Barely perceptible, like a mild ocean current. A gentle breeze of Viral awareness, tickling the recesses of my brain even though my powers were switched off.

I'd experienced it a half-dozen times since the hurricane. Most recently in court that morning. The sensation came and went without warning—I could neither summon it, nor capture it once it surfaced.

And lately, the effect was getting stronger.

Which worried me.

Was this some lingering psychological remnant? Post-traumatic stress? A harmless echo of the measures we'd taken while fighting the Gamemaster, soon to fade?

Or was it the harbinger of a more serious, permanent change in my psyche? The first symptom of opening a door that, once unlocked, can never be fully closed again.

The feeling escalated, taunting my conscious mind. It was maddening, being right on the cusp, yet unable to grasp it at all. I nearly ground my teeth in frustration.

Calm down. Let it come to you.

"Tory?" Shelton was eyeing me strangely. "You okay?"

Hi waved a hand before my face. "Anyone home? Got that bad mojo working?"

Ignoring them both, I slowed my breathing. Closed my eyes, and tried to wrap my mind in the strange sensation. Delve into its essence. Keep the slippery vibe from fading away.

There.

Something slid into focus.

Suddenly, I could *feel* Coop's presence, though he was sprawled on his doggie bed in the other room. A similar awareness extended toward Shelton and Hi. It went beyond merely sensing their locations. The vibe felt like . . . kinship. A strange knowing.

I could sense the Virals in a way I can't explain.

Hi. Shelton. Coop. Even Ben, far away.

My pack.

But you're not flaring.

How was that possible?

By now, you're probably wondering what I'm talking about. Here's the deal.

Last year, my friends and I were infected by a supervirus, a vicious little pathogen created by Dr. Marcus Karsten, the former director of LIRI and my dad's old boss. Hoping to strike it rich with a new vaccine, Karsten combined DNA from two different strains of parvovirus, accidentally creating a third.

Major problem: This newborn germ was contagious to humans. My friends and I caught it while rescuing Cooper, whom Karsten was using as a test subject.

Once inside us, the ruthless bug rewrote our genetic code, slipping canine sequences into our human double helixes.

The sickness struck first. Headaches. Fevers. Nightmares. Blackouts.

Strange transformations followed, as the microscopic invader shuffled chromosomes like playing cards.

We evolved, or regressed. Became something new, yet ancient.

The wolf became a part of us. And something more.

We learned how to *flare.*

I still can't describe it very well. My mind warps and snaps. Powerful forces rack my body. Primal instincts resonate in my subconscious.

Then my powers unleash.

Every sense blasts into hyperdrive. Hearing. Sight. Scent. Touch. Taste. Each becomes sharper than humanly possible. My muscles pulse with canine speed and agility. I practically smolder with energy. And my eyes blaze with golden light—an unfortunate side effect we have to conceal.

After nearly a year, the effects don't seem to be fading. Quite the opposite.

The wolf now lives inside our cellular blueprint. Welding us into a pack.

We're Viral. Genetic freaks. A brand-new species.

And we don't have the slightest idea what to do about it.

What if the sickness returns? Or the mutations grow more extreme? Could the powers simply vanish one day? Or will they become too intense, our wolf traits overcoming their human counterparts?

With Karsten gone, I'd thought any chance of finding answers had vanished along with him. Then we discovered his flash drive. A lifeline in the dark.

Small problem: We can't access the information on it. The stupid files are encrypted.

"What's goin' on, Tory?" Shelton's voice dragged me back to the present. He was tugging an earlobe, a nervous habit. "Did it happen again?"

The sensation wavered. Began to slip away.

"Explain what you're feeling," Hi suggested. "Talk it out."

"I can't explain. I wish I could. Ever since the storm, this odd sensitivity randomly comes and goes, like a memory just out of reach. Or a song lyric I can't place."

Hi snorted. "Too bad we can't Shazam your head."

"You get this vibe *without* flaring?" Shelton pressed. "Just out of the blue?"

I nodded.

Then, on impulse, I tried something.

SNAP.

Power burned through me.

Fire in my veins. Ice down my spine. A thousand sparking needles, tattooing my skin.

The flare burst to life like a supernova, kicking my senses into overdrive.

Vitality poured into my muscles. The wolf came out to play.

"Hey, I'm in." Molten gold exploded in Hiram's eyes. His chest heaved as he struggled to catch his breath.

"Playing with fire," Shelton muttered, but in seconds the same glow ignited behind his irises. Hands shaking, he removed his glasses and set them on the table—while flaring, Shelton's vision was as sharp as a laser.

Though our eyes gleamed with equal intensity, our powers weren't uniform. The mutations varied slightly with each of us. Why? Who knows. Add it to the list of things we don't understand.

Hiram can see with spectacular precision, far outstripping the rest of us. Shelton has the best ears. Ben becomes strongest and fastest. Me? A little weirder.

When flaring, my nose can sniff out almost anything, even other people's emotions. Anger. Fear. Panic. Worry. Envy. Each has a specific odor, if you can catch the scent and know what to look for.

My theory involves hormones and pheromones, but, in truth, I'm not sure. My brain just makes these leaps, and I've learned not to question them.

It *does* work. After the events of the last year, I no longer doubt my instincts.

But that's not the apex of what Virals can do.

When in close proximity, our powers become extrasensory.

Telepathic. Psychic. Whatever term you prefer.

During the hurricane, somehow, I shattered the mental walls separating us, allowing the Virals to share thoughts as easily as words. No: more than that. We could communicate *without* words, tapping into one another's senses, and sending fully formed ideas, images, and emotions. Even seeing through one another's eyes.

In those singular moments, our minds had melded.

Five beings, blending to form one unified consciousness. Completely. Seamlessly. The pack became whole. Our powers, fully unleashed.

So—bonded, hearts and minds—we'd gone hunting. And bagged our prey.

The feeling was amazing. Breathtaking. And, honestly, terrifying.

Since that day in the storm, however, I'd been unable to duplicate the complete telepathic effect. No matter how many flares I burned, or how hard I tried with Hi and Shelton, even Coop, I couldn't force the same perfect union. I was stuck.

You need Ben. The pack must be whole.

I shoved the thought away. Though I knew it was true.

These special talents have saved our lives more than once, but we struggle to control them. Every time I think I've mastered my abilities, I discover how little I really know.

As my flare unfolded, I tested boundaries, seeking the strange sensation I'd felt moments before.

Coop fired through the doorway, fur bristling.

Our eyes met. He settled on his haunches, watching me.

Hello, I sent.

Sister-friend, Coop responded.

Something skipped inside my brain. The connection wavered. I tried to focus my concentration, but the tenuous link refused to solidify.

Ben. He's too far away. Our pack is fractured.

No. More than that.

Lately, my powers had seemed . . . off. Out of sync, as if they'd somehow slipped from their usual groove. Tiny disturbances had been cropping up for weeks.

I closed my eyes. Tried to focus.

Suddenly, pressure built inside my chest. The air leaked from my lungs. As I struggled to catch my breath, an electric shiver crawled along my spine.

What in the world?

SNUP.

My flare blipped from existence. The room spun at its abrupt departure.

Coop whined, cocked his head.

"What was that?" The light vanished from Shelton's eyes. "My flare just snuffed out like a candle. And things . . . things don't feel right."

"Same here." I blinked rapidly, steadying my head with shaking hands. "I didn't release my flare, either. It felt like a fridge was dropped on me, then my powers just . . . disappeared."

"Ditto." Hi was red-faced, his flare gone. "*No es bueno.*"

My brow furrowed. "Something seems wrong. Like the powers have changed somehow."

Shelton slipped his glasses onto his nose. "Changed how?"

"I don't know. But we'd better figure it out. Quickly."

"Rain check?" Hi nodded toward the clock. "As much as I love making myself dizzy, we've got a fun-filled day coming up tomorrow. School should be a blast."

I winced. "I'd been blocking that out."

"Unhealthy." Hi dug a string cheese from the mini-fridge. "Gotta face your fans."

Since foiling the Gamemaster, we Morris Islanders had become something of a sensation at Bolton Prep. The trial had reignited the hysteria, and today's events were sure to be front-page news. I wasn't looking forward to another day of being gawked at in the halls.

"I can't wait for this to be over." Gathering my things. "I hate the spotlight."

"You said it," Shelton agreed. "Invisibility is *way* better than notoriety."

"You two are nuts." Hi raised the roof. "Go big or go home, I say."

"Sure, Hi." I whistled for Coop to follow. "Right now, let's just go home."

CHAPTER 3

I halted at the steps to my townhouse.

"I have to go in, don't I?" My shoulders slumped at the prospect.

"You can crash in my garage," Hi offered. "There's a pop-tent in there somewhere. Heads up, though—our cat uses it as his emergency litter box. It smells pretty bad."

My nose crinkled. "Charming."

The last rays of daylight were fading as the sun melted into Schooner Creek. The air remained sticky and warm, one of those classic spring nights in the Lowcountry. I'd probably sleep with my window open, if the bullfrogs weren't croaking too loudly. So different from the still-frigid gloom of my native Massachusetts.

The walk back from the bunker had taken twenty minutes, mainly because we hadn't hurried. It's an easy stroll down the beach, and you can't get lost. Our block is the only building for miles.

Kit had recently dubbed our neighborhood Exile Acres. The name stuck.

"Later, peeps." Hi fumbled for keys as he climbed to his front door. "I'm gonna watch *Battleship* at nine if you guys wanna live chat. Fair warning though—it looks absolutely terrible. Like, shockingly, horrifically bad." With that, he disappeared inside.

"Bye." I didn't move.

A gentle breeze swept off the Atlantic, carrying the bitter tang of sea salt and stirring the azaleas Mrs. Stolowitski had planted along the front walkway. Out over the dunes, fireflies bobbed and winked like floating candles, as a legion of crickets began their nightly serenade.

On Morris, you could close your eyes and pretend the civilized world didn't exist.

So peaceful. Like a land out of time.

Coop nudged my leg. I reached down and absently stroked his back.

I can't stand out here forever. Or can I?

"That bad, huh?" Shelton had paused to watch me from his stoop. "I thought ya'll worked things out?"

"It's horrible," I grumbled. "I can stand Whitney in small doses, but suddenly I've got a lifetime supply. The hits never stop."

"Good luck with that." Shelton waved once, and was gone.

More seconds ticked by.

Coop yipped. Danced a circle. He took a few steps toward the dock, turned, and barked twice.

"I hear ya, dog breath." Shaking my head. "But we're already late. Hiding will only make it worse."

With a piteous sigh, I trudged up to the front door.

Slipping inside, I climbed the three steps to the main level. Before me stretched our living room, dining room, kitchen and breakfast nook, all lined up in a row. To my left, a narrow staircase descended to Kit's tiny home office and a single-car garage.

Up one flight were two bedrooms, each with its own bathroom. Thank God.

The top floor, once Kit's awesome man cave, had recently been transformed into a formal sitting room. Don't get me started. Double doors opened onto a spacious roof deck with a spectacular ocean view.

Nice digs, if you can handle all the stairs.

Though I barely recognized the place anymore.

Our furniture *used* to be strictly Ikea. Simple, durable catalog gear to make any yuppie proud. Those days were over.

Delicate antiques now dominated the common areas. Gilded mahogany side tables. Lacquered chests and brazilwood bureaus. A tassel-trimmed silk ottoman. Pointy, upholstered chairs.

At times, I wasn't sure where I should sit, or what I could touch.

The fancy pieces looked so . . . uncomfortable. Breakable. The bizarrely asymmetrical coffee table seemed destined to collapse at any moment. A pair of living room lamps resembled medieval torture devices.

Worst of all, I'd been evicted from the bedroom facing the ocean. It was the larger chamber of the two—okay, fine, it was the master—but I'd been its sole tenant since joining Kit on Morris. It was mine.

No longer. As Kit explained, the bigger bedroom was better suited to handle a double occupancy. And, with the back room all to myself, I'd still have the most space out of anyone.

Blah blah blah.

I'd been unceremoniously bumped to Kit's smaller, rear-facing cell. Thanks so much.

Why all the changes?

The reason was sashaying around my kitchen at that very moment.

Whitney Blanche DuBois. My father's ditzy gal-pal.

The blond bombshell had become a permanent resident at Casa de Kit.

My own private nightmare.

Hurricane Katelyn had shown less mercy to Whitney's property than to ours. A massive oak had reorganized her kitchen, after crashing through the two stories above it. Pouring rain and gale-force winds had done the rest.

Homeless, Whitney had moved in with us while her place underwent repairs.

Five months later, she showed no signs of ever leaving.

“Tory, darling!” Whitney cooed in her sugary Southern drawl. “I thought we’d discussed being home *before* sunset. It’s not safe for a girl to wander alone after dark.”

Coop slunk past me and beelined for his food dish. Whitney tracked him from the corner of her eye.

Make no mistake—wolfdog and bimbo did *not* get along.

Whitney considered Coop a wild animal infesting the property. Coop considered Whitney a meddling interloper disturbing the peace. I backed the wolfdog’s take.

“Sorry,” I mumbled. “Lost track of time.”

“Don’t talk to your shoes, sweetheart.” Whitney *tsk*ed. “A proper lady prides herself on making firm eye contact.”

I fought an urge to flip her the bird. “Thanks for the tip.”

Whitney desperately wanted for us to be friends. But her personality and priorities made it all but impossible. I’d tried my hardest to like her. And failed. Repeatedly.

It is what it is. The woman doesn’t get me, and I can’t fathom her.

But Kit adored his Barbie girl, so I kept those thoughts to myself. As far as he knew, the bimbo and I were getting along okay.

Oh, sure. Everything’s just hunky-dory.

Kit’s an outstanding marine biologist, and a good dad, but he’s not the most perceptive guy on the planet. Or even top half. A fact I’d used to my advantage more than once.

You’re probably wondering about that.

I'd been living with Christopher "Kit" Howard for over a year, ever since my mother was killed in car accident. Broadside. Drunk driver. Mom never stood a chance.

The pain still surfaces unexpectedly. I'll hear a Rolling Stones song, or see a ratty yellow futon, and *boom,* it all comes rushing back. A raw wound that never quite heals.

I try to hide the eruptions, but the guys can always tell. They do their best to support me even though it makes them uncomfortable. It's very sweet, but teenage boys make lousy grief counselors. Same with Kit, though he's getting better at it.

I'm working things out on my own. Seems easier that way.

If the accident hadn't happened, I'd likely never have met my father.

A sad thought.

Kit and I got off to a rocky start. He'd had zero idea how to deal with the shattered, weepy teenage girl who'd dropped into his life like an H-bomb. But slowly, we'd learned to trust each other. To peacefully coexist, and even enjoy each other's company.

We'll never have a "normal" father-daughter relationship—I call him Kit, and decided to keep my last name—but we weren't strangers anymore. Real progress had been made since those first awkward weeks.

Until he'd added the ditz to our household, anyway.

And Whitney's dreadful presence wasn't the only change.

As if making up for prior negligence, Kit now watched me like a hawk. That'll happen when your teenage daughter manages to get stalked, attacked, shot at, or arrested every few months.

What can I say? Being Viral is like golfing in a thunderstorm.

Trouble seems to find me.

"That you, sport?" Kit emerged from the kitchen wearing an apron that said "Hail to the Chef." The mind weeps. "Good walk?"

"Yes." I swept past Whitney. "It's getting really nice outside."

Kit knew my friends and I had a secret clubhouse, but he didn't pry. Which was fortunate. The bunker's true scope would blow his mind.

Tossing my bag onto one of the awful chairs, I flopped on the living room couch, the lone piece of furniture to survive *Extreme Makeover: Whitney Edition.*

I pretended not to notice as Whitney retrieved my bag and hung it by the door.

Grrrrr.

Whitney was a compulsive straightener. I don't know why it bugged me, but it did.

Whitney walked over and kissed Kit's cheek. "I was just telling Tory how it's not wise to walk alone after nightfall."

"I learned a lot." Straight-faced.

"Okay, who's hungry?" Kit forced a smile. "Tory, set the table. Now, please."

Sometimes I pitied my dad—he often walked on eggshells around the two women in his life.

You brought her here, pal. We were doing just fine before.

I laid out the flatware and took my usual seat. Whitney began distributing her latest masterpiece: chicken-fried steak, okra, mashed potatoes, and butter beans, everything slathered in thick, beefy gravy.

One point I'll concede—Whitney is a phenomenal cook. Lights out. I can't imagine how she maintained her figure, eating like that, but I was happy to be along for the ride. Her culinary prowess was the sole perk of sharing a roof.

"Tory!" Whitney flashed synthetically whitened teeth. "Now that you've debuted, have you thought about how you'd like to give back to the community? We'll need to get you admitted first, but there are several interesting committee openings in the Mag League."

I froze, mid-bite. "The what?"

"The Magnolia League." Mascaraed lashes fluttered in surprise. "Surely you've heard?"

"Can't say that I have." Voice flat. I didn't like where this was going.

Whitney turned disbelieving eyes on Kit. "The Magnolia League of Charleston is *only* the most exclusive young women's service organization in the South. I'm sure all of your debutante friends have already joined."

"My debutante friends? Who would they be, exactly?"

"I don't understand." Whitney cocked her head like a sparrow. "I'm referring to the wonderful group of young ladies with whom you shared your introduction. Why, you're practically *sisters* now! Members of a debutante class are lifelong friends. You girls will be grouped together when you join the League."

Blargh.

I'd thought this nonsense dead and buried. Apparently my debut was merely a prelude to a life sentence.

I tried to be diplomatic. "I'm not sure that's a good fit for—"

"It's a *perfect* fit. Tory, this is simply *what you do* as a member of polite society. It's also a tremendous honor. Only daughters of the finest families are even *considered* for admission." Whitney's lips thinned. "Frankly, you're lucky to still be invited, after this nasty court business."

My jaw clenched. I fought an impulse to say something I'd regret. Whitney describing the Gamemaster's trial as some kind of embarrassing inconvenience drove me bonkers.

"It's completely up to you." Kit gave me a hopeful look. "Might be fun?"

"You simply *must* continue with your charitable work." Whitney practically whined.

"I'll think about it." Changing the subject. "Everything good at work, Kit?"

"What?" Kit lowered a forkful of mashed potatoes. "Oh, fine, fine.

Business as usual. The hurricane damage has been repaired, and the monkeys seem unaffected. Overall, we were very lucky."

"We need to pay better attention to the social side of things." Whitney folded her napkin and placed in on her lap. "Your employees need diversions, living out here in the sticks."

Meaning you *do, you harridan.*

"There's much more to do in the city," I said innocently. "When is your place due to be finished?"

"Not for weeks yet," Whitney murmured.

Kit dodged my eye. "What diversions did you have in mind, Whitney?"

She perked up. Had been waiting for the question.

"We should host a block party. Right outside, on the front lawn. We could rent a white pavilion, tables and chairs, and serve barbeque and iced tea. Maybe have some games. Croquet. Or even badminton! And door prizes, of course."

"Oh, of course," I repeated.

Kit gave me a warning look.

Whitney clapped her hands, delighted by her own idea. "Doesn't that sound wonderful? And LIRI should cover the entire cost. A gesture like that would show the neighbors how much you care about their well-being."

"Great idea," Kit said automatically. "You should organize it."

Whitney positively beamed. "I'd be *honored.* Tory, you can help!"

"Fantastic."

Double blargh.

CHAPTER 4

Tuesday

I braced myself for the coming storm.

Downtown. Tuesday morning. 7:00 a.m.

Time to face the music.

Shelton, Hi, and I stepped off *Hugo,* exited the marina onto Lockwood Drive, and walked south to Broad Street. Moments later we reached Bolton Preparatory Academy's majestic front gates.

I stopped. "Ugh."

"Yep." Hi adjusted his backpack. With no court appearance that morning, he was back to the inside-out jacket, with the blue lining exposed. "Gonna be wild."

Shelton snorted. "By wild, you mean horribly awful, right?"

Bolton Prep is Charleston's oldest and most prestigious private school. For well over a century, admission to its hallowed halls has been a coveted and expensive status symbol. Most students hail from the city's wealthy elite.

My crew couldn't have been more out of place.

As an incentive for LIRI employees living out on Morris Island, the institute provides tuition for their children to attend Bolton. Otherwise, we'd never set foot inside. And since the drive to campus takes over an hour, LIRI also provides Tom Blue's daily shuttle service. All in all, not a bad deal.

Hi, Shelton, and I were on the backstretch of our sophomore year, my second at the academy. Our time there hadn't been easy.

To most of our classmates we were aliens—unknowable foreign beings, dropped from the sky to spoil their lavish party. For a few, our presence was actually offensive. We had no place in their indulgent, privileged world.

Everyone knew we attended on scholarships. We'd been called "island refugees," "boat kids," even "peasants." Rarely had a day passed without one of us getting picked on.

The three of us had identical schedules that year, so we watched one another's backs.

"Safety in numbers" is a real thing.

Our course load was nearly all AP classes, which drew students from across Bolton's different grade levels. The previous semester Ben had been in half our classes, too, despite being a junior. Obviously, he was no longer around. Sometimes it felt like a limb was missing.

For a group of middle-class, unapologetic science geeks, Bolton was a social minefield. The mocking began the first time I opened my locker, and found a Barbie doll dressed like a homeless woman. And when those same jokesters discovered that the "snotty ginger genius" was also the baby of the class, the sniping turned uglier.

Freshman year had been brutal. No other way to describe it. Only my Morris Island buddies had kept me from demanding a transfer. Depressingly, sophomore year hadn't started much better.

But that was all out the window.

The Morris Island Three. That's what they called us now.

Since the events of last fall, we'd practically become celebrities.

The Gamemaster saga had been headline news for months. Every infinitesimal detail of the case had been examined, debated, printed, broadcast, and blogged. There were seven Tumblr accounts dedicated to the trial alone.

Our classmates had learned what almost happened at the debutante ball. Most had been there that night, or had friends or family who'd attended. They'd learned that the "boat kids" had stopped a murderous psychopath. That those dirty "peasants" had saved their upper-class asses.

The effect was shocking.

Former tormentors now regarded us with something close to awe. Dozens of wide-eyed classmates—many who'd never glanced our way before—had personally thanked us for what we'd done. A few seemed too intimidated to even approach.

Sometimes the world flips upside down, then forgets to right itself.

Suddenly, every day at Bolton felt like that.

Which isn't to say we'd become popular. The majority still avoided us, unable to bridge the gap from grudging respect to actual friendship. But the taunting had stopped. The pranks had been discontinued.

Fine by me.

Being left in peace was enough.

Our classmates' change in attitude didn't extend to Ben, however. They took his expulsion as irrefutable confirmation of his complicity in the Gamemaster's schemes. Nothing could convince them otherwise. I'd stopped trying.

Shelton checked his watch. "Bell in five."

"All right, you jackals." Hi squared his shoulders. "Come and get some Hiram."

They both looked to me. I nodded.

Hi pounded his chest—once, twice—then strode through the

archway. Shelton and I followed him down the cobblestone path. Circling a cherub-capped fountain, we entered the quad and made for the mammoth granite lions flanking the school's front steps.

Students filled the courtyard, chatting in groups among the benches and delicate rock gardens, soaking in the morning sunlight before first bell. The usual morning scene.

Maybe no one will care.

As we crossed the flower-lined plaza, conversation stopped.

Heads turned. Eyes followed. Whispers flew behind cupped hands.

Crap. The local TMZ was tuned in to us.

Hi's head whipped this way and that. "They're staring like we're buck naked."

"Keep moving," Shelton hissed. "This is excruciating."

"Just follow me." Ignoring the gawkers, I hurried to the giant wooden doors and slipped inside. A deep breath. Then, face set to neutral, I fired down the hallway. AP Calculus was first period. I needed my book.

Rounding the first corner, my heart sank.

Jason Taylor was idling by my locker. Pretending not to be.

"Tory!" Jason flashed a grin. "I heard you did great yesterday. Did that guy really pull a knife on you?"

"Knife? What?" *Argh.* Worse than I thought.

"That's the rumor outside. Didn't sound too likely."

Jason had the whole Nordic thing going. Ice-blue eyes. Pale skin. White-blond hair. His body was Thor-sized, too. Captain of our lacrosse team, Jason was a sick athlete.

He was also infatuated with me.

A problem that appeared to be getting worse.

These days, Jason seemed to pop up everywhere I went. I worried he'd planted a tracking chip on me, like a prized Labrador.

Don't get me wrong—Jason's a fantastic guy, and a true friend, one of the few non-Virals I could count on in a jam. He'd been instrumental in thwarting the Gamemaster, risking his life to help save others. That's not something you forget.

Romantically, however, he just didn't do it for me.

No tingle. No spark. Chemistry fail. I didn't understand why, but there it was.

Jason spoke as I shuffled my books. "Did you know Chance was there?"

My hands froze. "Where? In court?"

Jason nodded. "He sat in back. Saw the whole thing. It must've been banana pants in that room. You sure like causing a stir."

Jason went on, but I was barely listening.

Chance Claybourne. In the gallery. Watching me.

I wasn't sure what it meant. What I *wanted* it to mean.

Make no mistake, Chance was a problem. A fabulously gorgeous problem.

Chance had graduated from Bolton the previous semester. Though only eighteen, he'd gained access to a large portion of his inheritance, making him one of the richest men in Charleston. Son of former state senator and pharmaceutical magnate Hollis Claybourne, and heir to the staggering Claybourne family fortune, he was also the city's most eligible bachelor.

Chance kept turning up in my life.

Twice in the last year he'd witnessed our flare powers unleashed. He'd seen our enhanced speed and strength, and glimpsed our glowing eyes.

The first time shocked him so badly, he'd ended up in a mental hospital. The second time convinced him to return for more treatment.

I encouraged those fears, selfishly protecting the pack at his expense.

Guilt still dogged me, but I'd done what was necessary.

Protecting our secret came first. Always.

When Chance resurfaced, he'd been a different person. His playful side had mostly disappeared. The current version was more bitter, with harder edges. And that man was intensely suspicious of me and my friends.

Chance had also helped stop the Gamemaster—saving our butts along the way—but those events had convinced him we were hiding a secret. I had to stop him from learning how right he was.

Abruptly, I realized Jason had stopped talking.

One pale eyebrow rose. "You're sure everything's okay?"

"I'm fine." Closing my locker and shouldering my pack. "People are making a bigger deal out of it than it was."

"Just another day for the Morris Island Three." Jason smiled to show he was kidding. "I'm sure you dazzled them, like you do everybody else."

Hi and Shelton reappeared, saving me from having to respond.

They greeted Jason with exaggerated head nods—those two had accepted his friendship completely, and seemed to revel in his attention. I understood. It was nice being friends with one of the cool kids.

Heels clicked on the hardwood behind me.

My eyes squeezed shut.

Of course.

I turned to find the Tripod of Bitch standing in formation.

Their positions had shuffled, but the components remained the same.

Ashley Bodford was now front leg. She had dark eyes, glossy black hair, and perfect teeth. Pretty, but in a cold, *mean* way, if that makes sense. She wore the same uniform I did—white blouse, plaid skirt, black knee socks and shoes, and navy blazer—but somehow *she* made it look stylish. No idea.

Courtney Holt stood a half pace behind Ashley. Tall and thin, with a model-perfect physique, she was the stereotypical embodiment of pure blond vacancy. She was sporting her "go-to" look—a white Bolton

Griffins cheerleading uniform, two sizes too small. Upon discovering that particular dress code loophole, she'd purchased five sets so she could wear one every day.

Those two were awful in their own right—though, truthfully, Courtney was more stupid than mean. Just standing close to them made my skin crawl. But it was the coven's third member that caused me sleepless nights.

Madison Dunkle cowered behind Ashley, color flooding her cheeks as she dodged my eye. With exquisite makeup, machine-tanned skin, and a new arrangement of perfectly highlighted auburn hair, Madison was a study in manufactured beauty. Our uniforms matched, but Madison's anklet could've put me through college.

Formerly the Tripod's leader, Madison had been dethroned by Ashley.

The most likely cause? Her palpable fear of me.

Last summer, in a fit of anger, I'd flashed my flare eyes at Madison. She'd nearly fainted. And if that wasn't bad enough, a few months later I'd tried to . . . well . . . read her thoughts.

I know.

She'd sensed me poking around. And freaked. Hard.

The experience had shaken Maddy Dunkle badly. She seemed to verge on a panic attack every time we crossed paths. Only I knew why.

Ashley didn't care. Pouncing on her frenemy's weakness, she'd taken over the clique. I quickly realized that Ashley had always been the nastiest of the three, a pit viper with a venomous tongue. Madison was a classic bully. Ashley *smiled* while cutting you to pieces.

But like everyone else at Bolton, the Tripod had changed.

"Hey, Tory." Ashley flashed her shark-like smile. I tried not to flinch. "We heard about the attack in court yesterday. How awful!"

"Did that schizo *really* have a gun?" Courtney blinked, wide-eyed.

Not a candidate for Mensa. "They shouldn't let him have one in prison."

"It was nothing." Searching for a quick escape. "The bailiffs handled it."

Madison had begun edging away. Suddenly, she turned and hurried down the hall.

Ashley rolled her eyes. "Forgive Maddy."

Linking her arm with mine, she pulled me close, her voice lowering to a conspiratorial whisper. "Madison has *issues.* She's seeing a shrink."

A psychiatrist? Not good.

Having hooked my arm like a fish, Ashley tugged me down the corridor. Caught off guard, I let her. Courtney smiled sweetly, keeping pace.

It occurred to me that I'd been maneuvered into Madison's place.

An unpleasant thought.

I still couldn't process these vultures wanting to be friends. I had zero interest.

Behind me, Jason waved farewell. Hi and Shelton trailed our procession by a few paces, bemused looks on their faces.

Shut it, you two. I've been taken hostage.

"You should join us for lunch today," Ashley said casually. "The boys' soccer team baked us cookies, or something. Can you believe it?"

"Jason might be there," Courtney chirped. "He likes you."

"Oh." Not a brilliant response. "Yeah, maybe. I might have a thing, though."

Wonderful. Good job, good effort, Tory.

Behind me, I heard Hi fake coughing to cover his snickers.

The bell rang again, saving me from further awkward conversation.

"Bye, Tory." Ashley released me with a parting squeeze. "Talk later, promise?"

"You bet." *Dear God.*

The boys and I watched them saunter down the hall, classmates scurrying from their path.

"I can't tell if they're *actually* being friendly, or just messing with me," I whispered. "Ashley gives me the creeps. And Courtney is terminally stupid."

"I think that *is* Ashley being nice." Shelton pushed his glasses up the bridge of his nose. "She's just not very good at it. Lack of practice, and all that."

"She's using you to get to me," Hi said confidently. "Both of them. They've caught Hiram fever."

I nodded. "Of course. It all makes sense now."

We entered the classroom and took our seats. I was digging in my bookbag when a hand touched my shoulder, causing me to jump.

"Oh!" Giggles. "Maybe less caffeine tomorrow, Brennan?"

My heart rate slowed as I identified the offender.

"Sorry, Ella. I just survived another Tripod drive-by. I'm still a little spooked."

"Bleh." Ella Francis slid into the chair beside mine. "I have Purell if you need it."

Ella was a recent addition to my playlist. We'd met by chance. After catching Shelton and I chatting during one of his lectures, Mr. Terenzoni had switched his seat with hers. The "punishment" had resulted in my making a wonderful new friend.

Ella was beautiful in a textbook, Gap-model way, with gray-green eyes, pale skin, and a thick braid of sheeny black hair that fell to her waist. What surprised me most was her biting sense of humor. Ella was mercilessly sarcastic. I couldn't get enough of her.

"When can you come back to practice?" Ella asked. "The defense is suffering."

"Hopefully soon," I said. "This trial has to end sometime, right?"

Ella patted my hand. "I heard you did great. That bastard is going to rot in jail."

"Thanks." Slumping down in my seat. "I just want the whole thing finished."

I'd learned quickly that Ella could be persuasive. So much so, in fact, that she'd accomplished the impossible—after weeks of prodding, I'd actually tried out for the soccer team.

I still don't quite know how it happened, but yours truly was now the Bolton Prep Lady Griffins' newest fullback.

Ella was our midfield maestro. She could run all day, attack and defend, and generally own the ball for ninety solid minutes. Last season she'd been selected first team all-conference. Everything we did ran through her nimble feet.

Me? I barely understood the rules.

That said—and loudly tooting my own horn—I'm pretty damn good. I've always been well coordinated, and in decent shape. From the first scrimmage the game came fairly easily to me. Most parts, anyway.

I tend to stay in the back—the intricacies of both midfield and forward still elude me, and I prefer facing the other team's goal at all times. Nonetheless, Coach Lynch told me privately that I've got the skill set to become a striker. Not too shabby for a novice.

Of course, that was before the trial began.

I hadn't made a single practice in two weeks.

A thump sounded behind me.

Ella and I turned to see Shelton, red-faced, scooping books off the floor. "Sorry. They must've waxed these desktops."

"Look," Ella whispered as she pointed to the back row. "The Gable twins are out again. How many days is that?"

"I haven't seen Lucy or Peter all week," I said. "That's not like them."

The Gables were both honor students, and math freaks to boot.

"Vacation?" I guessed.

"In April?" Ella shrugged. "Nice timing."

The third bell rang. We spun to face the front, where Mr. Terenzoni was already scribbling on his dry-erase board. A prickly man, he liked to publicly embarrass anyone who wasn't paying attention. I locked in on his lesson.

Ten minutes later, the classroom door swung open. Mr. Terenzoni's head whipped toward the disturbance, his mouth opening to complain. Spotting the visitor, he snapped it shut.

Headmaster Declan Paugh entered, leaving the door ajar behind him. Fit and trim for a man nearing sixty, he had a tuft of thick white hair encircling an otherwise bald dome. Paugh wore a natty tweed jacket, white shirt, and tan slacks. A purple bow tie completed the ensemble.

Known as a strict disciplinarian, the headmaster was obsessed with upholding the lofty standards of Bolton Prep. He'd been a quiet opponent of allowing LIRI to provide scholarships for Morris Island kids, but he'd never mistreated us once the decision was made.

Nonetheless, I'd spent my entire career at Bolton carefully avoiding his attention.

Paugh scanned the room with watery gray-blue eyes. Settled on me.

Perfect.

"Miss Victoria Brennan, please come with me." His nasally tenor oozed pretentiousness. "You as well, Misters Stolowitski and Devers. Quick now."

My heart sank.

Two things I knew for certain.

One: Headmaster Paugh *hated* the publicity of the Gamemaster's trial.

Two: The man was known to hold a grudge.

Stomach knotted, I gathered my things, threw a last mournful glance at Ella, and headed for the door.

CHAPTER 5

"I don't mind telling you, this is a *decided* inconvenience."

Headmaster Paugh drilled me with his bird-like glare, then swung it to pierce Hi and Shelton. We stood in the hall, just outside the classroom. I had no idea what we were doing there.

Paugh continued before any of us could respond.

"The district attorney has requested your presence at her office." He folded skinny arms across his chest. "She had the temerity to *insist* I interrupt your lesson immediately."

"Did she say why she wants us?" I asked, as politely as possible.

"No. And I inquired."

Ouch. No wonder he was peeved.

"Must be the trial." Hi. Stating the obvious. "Things got real in there, yesterday."

The headmaster's eyes came to rest on Hiram's reversed uniform jacket. Narrowed.

Shelton edged sideways, straining for invisibility.

"You three might think you're some sort of heroes," Paugh said abruptly. "And I suppose you must do your civic duty, as required by law. But know this—this whole business is beneath the dignity of Bolton Preparatory Academy. It's unseemly."

I kept my mouth shut. The boys did likewise. Safest course.

"One bad seed has already been removed from our rolls." The headmaster paused for effect. "There is no guarantee he'll be the last. I will not tolerate children carrying on like tabloid celebrities."

My temperature rose. It's not like we'd *asked* to be sucked into a lunatic's web. We hated the attention more than anyone.

But I kept my anger in check. Sometimes, the deck is stacked against you.

No one spoke.

The awkward moment stretched as I examined my shoelaces.

"Go." Paugh jabbed a thumb at the front entrance. "I expect you back by lunchtime. If not, I'll be forced to consider this a full-day absence."

He turned and strode down the corridor, heels clicking every step of the way.

"What a douche," Hi whispered. "I bet that bow tie is a clip-on."

"Shush!" Shelton pushed him toward the door. "That fossil hears like a bat."

We hurried outside and through the gates, turning left on Broad Street. The city's main court complex was just a few blocks east across the peninsula.

"Whaddya think Harris wants?" Shelton was already tugging an ear. "I thought the prosecution rested after your testimony."

"It did." My shoulders rose and fell. "I don't have a clue. I hope to God it's not a mistrial."

We walked along one of the city's oldest thoroughfares. Antebellum mansions alternated with historic churches and tree-lined parks. Spring had come early, and window flower boxes overflowed with jessamine, lilacs, and other Lowcountry blooms. Dogwoods and azaleas mingled with towering magnolias and weeping willows, giving the neighborhood a sleepy, placid feel. Few cities could rival Charleston's aesthetic beauty.

To our right was the exclusive district known as South of Broad. The most expensive quarter of the city, it stank of privilege, tradition, and old money. Brazen wealth. Prestige.

Ella's family lived there. Chance, too, of course.

That morning I was in no mood to gawk. The DA's unexpected summons had me rattled. What could Harris want? What more was expected of me?

For the first time, I acknowledged how frightening the previous day had been.

I didn't want a repeat showing. I'd had enough.

We turned left at Meeting Street. As we paused for the traffic light, I glanced in the opposite direction, looking south toward The Battery and White Point Gardens at the end of the peninsula.

Claybourne Manor was a mere three blocks away.

Even in that swanky zip code, Chance's ancestral home stood out.

I wonder what he's doing in that giant house. Right now.

"Yo, Tor?" Shelton had paused in the crosswalk. "You coming or what?"

"Quit daydreaming, Brennan." Hi nudged me into the street. "Chance is probably out fox hunting. Or fencing. Something rich and super lame."

"I was *not* daydreaming." I fired ahead before either could say more.

Okay, fine.

I'd had a thing for Charleston's biggest catch. Once.

But it wasn't my fault—Chance was more than just good-looking, he was absurdly hot. Smart. Funny. Charming. *Every* Bolton girl had crushed on him at some point.

But that was before Chance lied to me. Before he manipulated me. Before he used my feelings as a tool to get what he wanted.

I'd recovered from my infatuation. Had learned a valuable lesson about naïveté.

My eyes were wide-open now.

The DA's office was housed in a dour brick building beside the courthouse. We climbed to the third floor, then followed a long corridor to Harris's corner office, which overlooked Meeting Street.

The door was wedged. As we approached, voices spilled out into the corridor.

Inside were Harris, her legal assistant, three members of the Charleston Police Department, and a few other men I didn't recognize. All told, perhaps a dozen people were crammed into the narrow office.

Several animated conversations were taking place at once. No one noticed our arrival.

I knocked on the doorframe. "Hello?"

"Tory!" Harris swept over, face flushed, blue eyes twinkling. She wore a smart gray suit and square-toe pumps. "Have you heard?"

"Heard what?"

The DA herded us inside. "About the plea deal. It's over!"

My brow furrowed. "What's over?"

"The trial," said a familiar voice.

I turned. Ben was sitting in a chair against the wall.

"How can the trial be over?" Hi asked Harris, while extending a quick fist bump to Ben. "The defense hasn't presented its case. Not that they have one."

"Defense counsel called this morning." A satisfied smile spread across Harris's face. "Mr. Parrish was despondent, said his client was finally ready to plead guilty. Like they had much choice, after that outburst. Lazarus Parrish may be a horse's ass, but he isn't stupid."

"You gave the Gamemaster a deal?" I was incredulous. The man was a monster.

"Not much of one," Harris said smugly. "Life sentence, no parole. My *only* offer. They took it quickly, too. I guess they're convinced the jury was heading toward the single punishment worse."

Thinking it over, I nodded slowly. "And our case wasn't airtight."

"No, it was *not.*" Crossing her arms, Harris leaned a shoulder against the bookshelf lining her office wall. "It's a very good result, Tory. That bastard is going to prison, and never getting out. And don't forget, there are charges pending in a half-a-dozen other jurisdictions."

"It's a *great* result," a voice boomed.

Three overweight men joined our circle. Exchanging glances, Hi and Shelton retreated to a pair of open chairs beside Ben, leaving me alone. There the boys huddled together, whispering.

I stayed put. Didn't want to talk to Ben.

Harris stood a little straighter, adopting her courtroom voice. "Miss Brennan, this is Deputy Mayor Richard Skeen, Police Commissioner Antony Riggins, and Detective Fergus Hawfield of the Major Crimes Division. Gentlemen, meet my star witness."

"So you're the little lady who made that felon go berserk." Skeen was a pear-shaped man with a pug nose and close-set eyes. "Never seen anything like it. Lordy day!"

"Thanks." I had nothing else. *Little lady?*

Commissioner Riggins was a wide-framed bear of a man, with wire-rimmed glasses that sank deep into his sallow, puffy features. He extended a meaty paw, which I reluctantly shook.

Sweaty palms. *Blech.*

"You did well on cross-examination," Riggins said. "I've known career police who've faired much worse."

"Ain't that the truth," said Detective Hawfield.

Hawfield was also condo-sized, with the thick neck of an ox. Red-faced, sporting a bristly salt-and-pepper mustache, he looked more construction foreman than police investigator.

"You did good, kid." Unlike the other two, Hawfield didn't sound condescending. "Kept your head, even bested that rat lawyer a few times. The city owes you one."

My pride swelled just a little. "I only did as Ms. Harris instructed. She prepared me well."

Harris puffed beside me. Gave me a grateful nod.

Whatever. I wanted *out* of the spotlight.

"Well, I, for one, am glad this circus is *over,*" Commissioner Riggins said. "Now we can get back to regular, boring police work. Won't that be nice?"

Detective Hawfield snorted. "Like chasing down matching teenagers?"

Riggins shot Hawfield a sharp look. The detective blanched. Harris glanced at me, then quickly away.

Something clicked. *Matching teenagers?*

"Do you mean the Gable twins?" I asked. "Lucy and Peter?"

Hawfield winced. The adults' eyes found one another's, before settling on me.

"Well . . . *er* . . . yes." Riggins glared at Hawfield. "Lucy and Peter Gable are technically missing persons at this point. But that's not something the public has been made aware of yet."

Hawfield was frowning at his shoes.

"Missing?" My mind leaped to the empty desks in calculus. "For how long? I know they haven't been in class for a couple of days."

"There's no need to get worked up." Hawfield raised both palms. "Most likely, those two just ran off for a little mischief. But the family has made it a police matter, so we're looking into it."

"Run off?" I glanced at the boys. Their faces were as dubious as mine.

The Gable twins were honor students. Both played violin in Bolton's student orchestra. Peter was president of Key Club, and Lucy had founded an organization for students learning Mandarin Chinese.

Not the type of kids to jet out for few days without telling anyone.

"Is there suspicion of foul play?" I watched Hawfield carefully.

"Not at all," the detective answered firmly. "This is purely a worried-parent situation. I'm sure we'll have them found in no time."

Skeen grunted. "Except for that card, of course."

Both police officers frowned at Skeen. Harris squeezed the bridge of her nose.

The deputy mayor didn't seem to notice, dabbing a handkerchief to his sweaty forehead. "You have to admit, that was a *peculiar* thing to find on the girl's pillow." Skeen stretched the word to four syllables.

"What do you mean?" I asked. "There was something on Lucy's bed?"

"It's nothing." Riggins made a chopping gesture with one hand. "We found a playing card of some sort in Lucy Gable's room. Antique, with a picture painted on its face. Her parents didn't recognize it, so we're checking it out."

"That information isn't to be shared with anyone." Hawfield caught Skeen's eye, who shrugged. "Miss Brennan, I'll need you to keep this conversation confidential."

"Of course." I couldn't resist. "May I see the card?"

"No." Hawfield and Riggins spoke at once.

"Until the twins turn up, we're treating the object as evidence," Hawfield said. "We have to follow protocol."

Shelton abruptly butted in beside me. "Makes perfect sense." He spoke in an overloud voice, a sheen of sweat suddenly glistening his forehead. "But here's the thing. Let me ask you guys a question."

Shelton paused. Coughed into his fist. Held up a finger.

The four adults waited expectantly.

"Do ya'll think that, like, uh, maybe . . ." Shelton extended his arms awkwardly. "Like, maybe the school should . . ."

He trailed off. Forcibly cleared his throat a second time.

I stared. What in the world was he talking about?

Confused, I glanced over at Ben and Hi.

Ben hadn't moved, was sitting stone still in his chair.

Hiram, however, had crossed the room and was gazing out a window.

Harris, looking confused, opened her mouth to reply to Shelton.

"Check their lockers!" Shelton blurted, hands fluttered up wildly. "Shouldn't the police investigate those?"

Then he sighed. Shoulders slumping, Shelton wiped his brow, muttering under his breath. I don't think he even heard the response.

"In due time, and if necessary," Hawfield said. "But right now, we're not too worried. Nor should you be."

But something in his eyes betrayed him.

The detective, at least, suspected something more sinister.

"Don't fret over this." Commissioner Riggins flashed what I'm sure was supposed to be a reassuring smile. "And please, don't share this information with any of your classmates."

"Okay." Me and Shelton. *Jinx.*

Riggins turned to Ben and Hi, who'd slipped back into his chair. Both nodded.

"That's settled, then." Riggins clasped his hands before him. "And I think it's past time you four returned to school. The department thanks you for your service in this ugly business."

Handshakes were exchanged, then the four of us stepped out into the hall. Harris closed the door behind us, no doubt so we wouldn't see her victory dance. I knew this conviction would boost her career.

"Tory!" Shelton waved for me to hurry. "Let's go! Double time."

Hi and Shelton sped-walked to the elevator. Shelton punched the down button repeatedly, his foot tapping mile a minute.

"What's the rush?" I said after catching up. "Is there a lunch special I don't know about?"

Ben strolled up at his usual, leisurely pace, but a smile quirked his lips.

Shelton gestured for quiet, then hustled everyone into the elevator. Hi was grinning from ear to ear. Ben's face was unreadable. I took a spot on the opposite side of the car.

We descended in silence. When the doors parted, Shelton and Hi beelined for the exit.

What's with them?

Ben didn't hurry. We found ourselves walking side by side.

No eye contact. Neither of us spoke.

Ben held the door as we exited the building. I mumbled a thank-you.

Outside in the warm sunshine, I hurried down the marble steps. Chasing Shelton and Hi. Leaving Ben behind.

My thoughts returned to the Gable twins.

Something in Hawfield's body language. The way Riggins had emphasized the need for secrecy. There'd been tension in the room, carefully masked. I was certain there was more to this disappearance than those two were letting on.

The police were worried.

Which made *me* worried.

I wasn't tight with Lucy or Peter, but I knew them okay. We had three classes together every single day. Peter was the quiet type. Lucy was more vocal, but never antagonistic. They'd never been part of the crowd that mocked us. All in all, they seemed like smart, decent kids.

Hi and Shelton were already at the corner, turning onto Broad Street.

What are those morons up to?

A glance over my shoulder. Ben was a few yards back, and following.

I was more willing to chase after the doofus brothers than deal with Ben.

At damn near a run, I fired down the sidewalk.

CHAPTER 6

Hi and Shelton waited two blocks ahead.

"Why are we running?" I shouted. "Hi, did you lose a bet?"

"Just come on." Shelton was moving again. "You'll understand in a minute."

We hustled another block. At the next intersection, both boys stopped and peered at something behind me.

I turned. Ben was ambling down the sidewalk, in no particular rush.

Though of average height, Ben is muscular, with a deep, coppery tan earned by spending most of his time outdoors. Black shoulder-length hair, usually tucked behind his ears. Dark brown eyes. Darker moods.

Ben claims to have descended from the long-lost Sewee tribe, a Native American group that disappeared three hundred years ago. No proof, but it's not something we contest—Ben takes his heritage seriously. He'd even named his boat *Sewee.* A nature freak, Ben would rather spend the day cruising salt marshes, or fishing for red drum, than just about anything else.

The other thing about Ben is his temper.

It's a loaded shotgun, set to pop at any time.

Don't get me wrong, Ben isn't a constant storm cloud. He's wicked smart, and could be surprisingly sensitive and thoughtful. Perceptive, too. And loyal as bloodhound.

Before The Game, anyway. Before he betrayed us.

"Why is Ben following?" I whispered. "Wando is the other direction."

"Be cool," Shelton replied. "He'll want to see this, too."

My eyes narrowed. "See what?"

"Hold your horses." Hi was still grinning like an ape. It made me nervous.

Ben finally reached the group. He'd slipped on dark Ray-Ban sunglasses, hiding his eyes. Freed from the Bolton Prep dress code, he wore his typical black tee and jeans.

"Well?" Ben demanded.

"Well what?" I said defensively.

"Not you." Ben was looking at Hiram. "What'd you snag?"

Hi dug a folded sheet of paper from his pocket.

"I should be a secret agent." Hi blew on his fingernails, then buffed them on his lapel. "Or a magician. Maybe both. Someone write that down."

"Give me some warning next time!" Shelton snatched the page from Hi's fingers. "You know I'm terrible at improvising."

"*Check their lockers!*" Ben mocked. "You sounded crazy."

"*Somebody* had to distract the *police officers,*" Shelton griped. "Stolowitski's not as smooth as he thinks. I could hear him rifling Harris's desk clear across the room."

I spun to face Hi. "You *stole* something? Seriously?"

The scene replayed in my head. Shelton awkwardly drawing attention to himself. Hi puttering around the office. Things suddenly made sense.

Except, of course, why Hi had risked swiping something in the first place.

"Just look." Hi tapped the sheet Shelton had unfolded. "You're welcome."

The page was a color photocopy of a single object.

"Ah."

I flashed Hi a thumbs-up. He winked.

The image was some kind of old-fashioned playing card. An odd figure adorned its face: an elderly bearded man, dressed in what appeared to be a toga, wrestling a giant snake that coiled around his body. Above the figure was a lone symbol: Φ

"This *must* be the clue from Lucy's room!" I squawked. "Hi, you're a genius."

"Of course I am," Hi replied. "I spotted the pic while you were talking, and knew you'd obsess over it. Now we don't have to break in at three a.m. to get a look."

"How about we don't steal or rob at all?" Shelton suggested, eyes scanning the cross streets for hidden eavesdroppers. "I was looking forward to a felony-free semester. Been a while. And won't Harris know you stole this? That cop said it's the only evidence they have."

"The folder had four copies," Hi said. "If we're lucky, she won't even notice."

I tapped the symbol above the figure's head. "This is Greek. The letter phi."

"Duh," said Hi. "But who is Captain Snake Wrangler?"

"No idea." My voice firmed. "But we're going to find out."

"See what you did?" Shelton glanced heavenward. "Now Tory won't *ever* let this go."

"Wise up, kid." Hi tapped his temple. "She wasn't letting this go, period. Not after hearing there's a freaking clue."

All three looked at me.

I shrugged. "Hi's right. I'm hooked."

There was something unnerving about the image. The man with the snake gave off a cold, sinister vibe. Dead eyes. Unsmiling lips. His stern visage sent a chill along my spine.

The card itself looked old, maybe even ancient. Though hard to be sure from a copy, the figure appeared hand-painted. My gut said the card was rare, and probably valuable. I hadn't the faintest idea where you'd find something like it.

I didn't know Lucy well, but this didn't strike me as something she'd purchase.

My sixth sense shivered in warning.

"The twins might need our help," I said. "Maybe we should dig a little."

"Need us how?" Shelton took off his glasses and wiped them on his tie. "The police are already on the case. What can we offer that they can't?"

"You really have to ask?" Ben scoffed.

Shelton looked at him blankly.

"We have superpowers, dummy." Ben smirked as he scuffed a shoe against the sidewalk. "I doubt those CPD clowns can match that."

Ben's flippant attitude infuriated me. "Shouldn't you be heading the other direction?"

"I'm taking a personal day." Ben stretched his arms, locked his hands behind his head. "Wando can get by without me until tomorrow. Plus, I parked around the next corner."

After moving to Mount Pleasant, Ben had taken his share of our stash and purchased a beat-up blue Ford Explorer. The mid-nineties clunker looked ready to die at any moment, but Ben now had wheels to complement his Boston Whaler runabout.

The rest of us didn't have so much as a motorized scooter.

"I'm not suggesting we put ourselves at risk." I spoke carefully, addressing all three boys rather than just Ben. "Or go on some wild flaring binge. In case you've forgotten, we have plenty of abilities besides the ones we inherited from Coop."

Ben snorted. I could sense his eyes rolling behind his shades.

"In fact," I continued, disturbed by his dismissive manner, "I think we should be more careful about our powers in general. At least until we access Karsten's flash drive."

"How are we gonna do that?" Hi nodded toward Shelton. "Hack-Master General here says he can't crack the code."

"That's *commercial*-grade encryption we're talking about," Shelton replied testily. "Top-of-the-line security software. I'm good, but not *that* good."

"Then we need an expert," I mused. "Someone who'll do the job, but also keep their mouth shut."

"Good luck," Shelton grumbled. "I doubt Anonymous could hack that drive."

Ben crossed his arms. "What do you expect to learn, anyway?"

He'd addressed me directly. I was forced to respond.

"We need to know *exactly* what Karsten was doing with Parvovirus XPB-19." I ticked off fingers. "How he constructed the supervirus, what happened during testing, and how the microbe might mutate in the future."

"The future?" Shelton reached for an earlobe. "Why so concerned? Is this because of that . . . feeling . . . you get?"

"Partly." I took a deep breath. "I won't lie. I'm worried about the stability of our flare powers in general. Things have gotten weird lately. We need to be careful."

Shelton's eyes dropped. Hi shuffled his feet.

They didn't like talking about it. Wanted to avoid the issue altogether.

But I wouldn't budge. "We need to know if our condition will continue to evolve. And, if so, whether there's a possible vaccine. Some kind of cure."

"A cure?" Ben hooted. "Insane. Why in the world would we *want* a cure?"

I opened my mouth, hot words at the ready. Then closed it.

Was Ben right?

We had a unique gift—special abilities unknown to the rest of our species. Was that something we should consider giving up? Something we *could* give up?

I shrugged off the question. Ben was being a jerk.

Watching him now, he didn't seem like the same friend I'd known for so long. I couldn't put my finger on it, exactly. The arrogant set to his shoulders? The bitter sarcasm dripping from every word?

Ben had always had a temper, but this seemed worse.

I worried the media coverage had affected him. As the centerpiece of the prosecution's case against the Gamemaster, Ben had been alternatively cast as victim and villain, depending on the source. Either way, he'd been at the eye of the storm.

At first Ben had seemed spooked, almost paralyzed by the spotlight. Though I'd kept my distance, Hi and Shelton had reported his skulking, disappearing aboard *Sewee* for hours, always trying to avoid being seen.

Then, abruptly, he'd seemed to accept the notoriety. Maybe even relish it a little. According to Hi and Shelton, in the last few weeks Ben had been out and about, wearing his dark designer shades, apparently unfazed by the gossip and the stares.

The sudden change concerned me. It felt like a front.

I was sure something was wrong. That Ben was bottling his issues deep inside.

But I wasn't ready to talk. Still couldn't bring myself to forgive.

As we lingered on the sidewalk, I examined Ben from the corner of my eye. He seemed relaxed, almost languid. Carefree. An unnatural response to the morning's events.

Then Ben yawned like a jungle cat uncurling from a nap. His movements snared my attention. Scratching his nose, Ben's fingers moved just a little too fast.

Pieces suddenly clicked together.

Dark shades. Quick hands.

Alarm bells began clanging in my head.

Ben!

My hand shot for the Ray-Bans, but Ben caught my fingers mid-flight.

"It's not nice to grab," he said calmly.

"You're *flaring,*" I hissed. "Right now!"

Ben chuckled. "So? No one can tell."

"Oh, man!" Shelton whirled to scan the block. "Bad idea, Blue. *Spectacularly* bad."

"Why are you flaring in public?" I whisper-shouted. "For no reason!"

"You have some kinda death wish?" Hi snapped. "You wanna end up dancing for quarters in a government zoo? Because that's what you're risking, and you have terrible rhythm."

"Relax." Ben's voice had an edge. "I'm wearing sunglasses. Being careful."

"You are burning our secret superpowers, in broad daylight, in the middle of downtown Charleston!" My eyes flicked to a couple rounding a nearby corner, and heading our way. "Here come some tourists, Benjamin. Wanna show them your special skills?"

"I should," Ben snickered, waggling his shades. "It'd make their visit memorable."

I was about to straight flip the frick out when Ben's shoulders quivered, sweat beading at his temples. Then he sighed, sucked in two deep breaths.

Ben slipped off his shades to reveal normal brown irises. "Happy, grandma?"

He tossed a mocking wave at the tourists as they strolled past.

"No," I said, once the couple was out of earshot. "I'm pretty damn far from happy." Then, with a monumental effort, I moderated my tone. "You're playing with fire, Ben. And if you screw up, we *all* get burned."

"I'm not a child, Victoria." Replacing his Ray-Bans, Ben strode away up the block.

"Well, *that* wasn't great," Hi said dryly. "But at least you two are talking now, right?"

"I can't handle all this tension," Shelton moaned. "Too much fighting."

Hi nodded, watching as Ben disappeared down a side street. "We need to work on our conflict management. Maybe attend a seminar."

"Ben's going all flare crazy," Shelton muttered. "Hi's burglarizing the DA's office. Nobody's *talking* about anything. Things are getting out of hand."

My palms came up. "What can we do? Ben's impossible."

Shelton surprised me by jabbing a finger in my face. "You do nothing but look daggers at him, when you bother to acknowledge his presence at all. How's he supposed to act? When are you gonna get over this, so we can move on?"

"When Ben creates a time machine," I shot back. "And undoes what he did!"

Dumb words, but I didn't care. I was seething.

"Ben's been flaring a lot lately," Hi said quietly. "Every day, I think. I wonder if he's just chasing the rush."

Those alarm bells became blaring sirens.

Ben seemed totally different. I'd assumed it was stress from the trial, but now I worried it was something else. A more disturbing possibility.

I knew our powers were becoming unsteady. I'd felt the tremors myself.

But had they also become addictive? Or destructive?

Ben was flaring often, even in public. Could *that* be changing his personality?

Or could Ben's overindulgence be causing the problems in the first place?

What have we gotten ourselves into?

Shelton checked his watch. "We'd better move. The headmaster wants us back by lunch, and we're cutting it close."

"Fine." What more was there to say?

I walked the last few blocks in a fog, my mind sifting unpleasant possibilities. Considering dire scenarios. The chronic problem of our viral transformation suddenly seemed urgent. We'd put off seeking answers for too long.

We *had* to learn more about the experiment that changed us.

Which meant, we *had* to get into Karsten's flash drive. But how?

Thoughts wandering, it took me several moments to notice a feeling I'd been ignoring.

The odd sensation had returned. That itch I couldn't scratch.

Two days in a row. It's happening more often.

As soon as I recognized the vibe, it began to dissipate.

Concentrating, I struggled to capture its essence. Felt a *closeness* I'd not noticed before. As though my mind were trying to connect with something outside my body.

But how? I'm not flaring.

Then, like a sigh escaping, the moment passed. I nearly ground my teeth in frustration. Another opportunity to learn something—*anything*—had slipped through my fingers.

With my mind a thousand miles away, I didn't see the land mine right in front of me.

Hi grabbed my arm. I glanced up, startled to see Bolton's wrought-iron gates.

And more surprised to see Chance Claybourne standing between them.

My stomach backflipped.

Some reactions are purely involuntary.

Chance was exiting the grounds, a dog-eared folder tucked under one arm. He wore a hand-tailored black suit, crisp white shirt, silver tie, red argyle socks, and black patent-leather shoes. The outfit oozed casual expense.

He paused mid-stride, chiseled face unreadable.

Chance seemed carved from shadows, with dusky skin and deep, dark eyes. He had a swimmer's build—tall and slender, yet wiry strong, with lustrous black hair framing a perfect chin. His every move was graceful.

Chance was, hands down, the best-looking person I'd ever met in real life.

"What are you doing here?" I blurted.

"Manners, Victoria." Chance *tut-tutt*ed. "And here I thought we were old friends."

I cleared my throat, buying time to pull my thoughts together. Finally, "I didn't expect to see you at Bolton. After you graduated, I mean."

"I didn't expect to be here again," he replied airily. "But apparently my employer needs a transcript for my file."

An eyebrow rose. "Your employer?"

"Candela Pharmaceuticals. I've been named to the board." Chance casually plucked a fallen leaf from his sleeve. "Not all that surprising, since I *do* own most of the company."

I stiffened. Candela triggered bad memories.

"They put *you* in charge?" Hi snorted. "Remind me to sell my stock."

"Thanks for the vote of confidence, Hiram."

"How can an eighteen-year-old run a major corporation?" Shelton said. "You were still in high school, like, five minutes ago."

"It's not a one-man show," Chance said dryly. "I've been tasked with running a small division focusing on special projects. The rest of Candela's leadership stays the same."

"Special projects," I repeated. Felt a chill.

"Research and development, mainly." Chance stepped onto the tree-lined sidewalk. "I'll get to play around a little. Crack a few eggs, so to speak."

My voice raised an octave. "What does that mean?"

Chance's face was unreadable. "It *means,* I'll be able to work on whatever I want. Get some answers I've been seeking."

"How dramatic." Hi tapped his head. "You wanna make a difference? Create a deodorant that doesn't suck. The brand I use leaves pit stains on all my undershirts."

"I'll pass." Chance's hair dancing rakishly in the light ocean breeze. "My interests are a touch more exotic."

His eyes found mine. I looked away.

Chance's past accusations flashed through my mind.

"I have to go," he said abruptly. "Maybe I'll see you soon."

He walked past without another word.

I watched his form recede down the block. Chance never glanced back.

"That guy ain't right," Shelton whispered. "But at least he's out of our hair now."

"Yeah."

But I had a sinking feeling.

Special projects.

Cracking eggs.

Answers.

For some reason, I felt like Chance had threatened me.

CHAPTER 7

Chance dropped the battered file on his desk.

He'd studied its contents a hundred times. The hundred-and-first reading had revealed nothing new.

Bong. Bong.

A grandfather clock chimed 2:00 p.m. Chance could barely make out the stately timepiece, tucked as it was in the far corner of his father's private study.

My study, rather.

He still hadn't gotten use to that.

Long shadows crisscrossed the wood-paneled walls and expensive Persian rugs. He meant to install more lights, but never got around to it.

Chance spun his chair to face giant floor-to-ceiling windows overlooking the estate's inner yard. Below, a landscaper was carefully sculpting a wall of the hedge maze. Chance didn't know the man's name. Claybourne Manor had dozens of gardeners.

Once more, Tory Brennan crashed his thoughts.

Maddening.

He was no closer now than on the day he'd first discovered the information.

No closer, but out of ideas.

And time, perhaps.

Frustrated, Chance swiveled back to his desk. Lifted the folder once more. Eyed the red block lettering stamped on its face:

CANDELA PHARMACEUTICALS
DR. MARCUS KARSTEN—RESEARCH NOTES
TOP SECRET. PROPRIETARY R&D

He'd found five more folders identical to this one. A hidden cache, locked away in his father's private cabinet. Another secret among the many Hollis Claybourne had kept.

His father never mentioned this project. Not once.

Chance grinned sourly.

The Old Man hadn't shared much before getting hauled off to prison.

Chance opened a desk drawer. Placed the file inside with the others.

He was obsessed. And knew it. But recognition made no difference. He could more easily hold back the tides than abandon this endeavor.

Tory Brennan.

So many emotions, derived from a single name.

The girl was nothing. A transplant science geek from the barrier-island sticks. Still a sophomore in high school. She didn't come from wealth, or have an influential family name. It was borderline miraculous that he was aware of her existence at all.

But he was. In fact, he noticed *everything* about her.

Chance leaned back and closed his eyes.

Inevitably, his mind began picking at the memories he'd been counseled not to trust.

Tory and her Morris Island friends, in the darkness of his basement. Moving way too fast, eyes glowing unnaturally bright.

Those same four, darting like arrows across a pitch-black beach. Same unnatural speed. Same blazing irises.

He'd thought himself crazy. His doctors had agreed. Together they'd painstakingly constructed a new reality—a *rational* one—where Chance hadn't seen those things at all.

Then it happened *again.*

The debutante ball.

He hadn't witnessed the last event firsthand—Tory had seen to that—but those outcasts had accomplished the unthinkable. A feat of strength beyond anything remotely reasonable.

It. Was. Not. Possible.

Third time's a charm.

His tortured laugh echoed in the cavernous chamber.

Chance's gaze dropped to the drawer. He tapped the handle with an index finger.

These folders hold the key.

He didn't know how. Didn't understand why. But Chance was certain.

Karsten's records would solve the riddle of Tory Brennan and her sidekicks. The answers he sought lurked somewhere inside those reports.

Chance yanked the drawer open again. Slapped a new file onto his desk.

He paused a moment, shaking his head at the part of the story he knew.

A hidden lab. Secret tests. Corporate espionage. Payoffs and payouts.

His father had ordered an illegal medical experiment, off the books, bankrolled by an untraceable shell corporation using Candela funds. The harebrained scheme violated dozens of laws and regulations. It was both a criminal and fireable offense.

The arrogance of it boggled Chance's mind.

Thankfully, his father had been careful. Chance had checked for records thoroughly, spending hours sifting through boxes at Candela's file storage warehouse, and even more time combing the database. He was satisfied no other documents existed.

No one would learn of Karsten's work.

No one but me.

It'd taken Chance months just to comprehend what he was reading.

At first, the connections were hidden. Even with a mole at LIRI feeding him intel, Chance had learned little of use. Dr. Mike Iglehart was a major disappointment. The secret link to Loggerhead Island hadn't borne much fruit.

But then he'd found it.

Chance flipped to back of the file. Selected a computer printout.

The bridge had been there all along. He just hadn't seen it.

Page sixty-four. Third paragraph. Second line. Twenty-five words.

Subject A for Parvovirus XPB-19 is a wild canine hybrid captured on Loggerhead Island, the offspring of a female gray wolf and male German shepherd.

In other words, a wolfdog.

So simple. Yet he'd missed it repeatedly.

"Cooper," Chance whispered. Tory's too-smart mongrel was the key.

Though, admittedly, Chance *still* hadn't put it together at that point.

Karsten had used Coop as a parvovirus test subject. So what? The dog had clearly recovered and survived. Perhaps Tory had adopted him afterward. What difference did it make?

But Chance had held tenaciously to his theory. And his diligence paid off.

He'd simply needed to find the other pieces.

Chance removed a third file from the drawer and placed it beside the other.

Paging to the middle, he found the crucial line. He'd only apprehended its significance that morning.

Bottom margin. Handwritten. So easily overlooked.

The highest caution must be employed. Due to its radical structure, Parvovirus strain XPB-19 may be infectious to humans.

There.

There there there.

A connection. One that might explain *everything*.

What he'd seen. What he'd experienced with those Morris Island weirdoes.

What, exactly, had Cooper carried?

What happened after Tory took him home?

Chance didn't know. But he was going to find out.

At that moment, a startling thought occurred to him. Something that, shockingly, he'd never considered before. The implications shot ice through his veins.

Chance quickly dug out and opened his MacBook. Fingers flying, he accessed his secure database and scanned the research protocols for Brimstone, the first project he'd commissioned at Candela. His anxiety level rose.

Dear God.

He'd green-lit the secret venture immediately upon discovering Karsten's files, content to improvise, learning as he went. Hoping hard science would give him answers, even without knowing the exact questions.

But had he taken the proper precautions?

Switching to an outside server, Chance reviewed several encrypted files with an entirely new set of concerns. What he discovered sent his heart hammering.

Chance's hands found his forehead.

Was it dangerous?

I don't know.

Popping from his seat, Chance strode for the door. He hurried down two flights of stairs and into the grand entrance hall.

At the massive front doors, he paused.

Squeezed his eyes shut.

Drawing a deep breath, Chance straightened his tie and smoothed his hair.

Then he stepped outside and called for his driver, desperately hoping he hadn't made a colossal mistake.

CHAPTER 8

"All hail MegaDock!"

Hi led us across the marina parking lot, heading for the southernmost section known as Pier Group Z. There we'd meet *Hugo* for our trip home.

The afternoon sun had ramped up the heat. I stopped a moment to shed my jacket. Shelton shuffled along beside Hi, loosening his navy-blue-striped Bolton tie.

The Charleston City Marina is a behemoth, with over nineteen thousand feet of dock space covering forty acres of water. Located in a sheltered zone where the Ashley River flows into the harbor, the sprawling facility is packed with amenities, including restaurants, stores, bars, and a floating boathouse.

And MegaDock, of course.

At a whopping 1,530 feet, MegaDock is the longest freestanding, floating fuel dock in the Southeast. Equipped with state-of-the-art power uplinks, boat-side assistance, and twenty-four-hour security, plus every other nautical perk you can imagine, its length is always crammed with massive yachts and expensive pleasure boats.

We trooped through the marina twice every school day. I barely noticed the opulent crafts any more, though at first I'd gawked like a tourist.

I trailed the boys, stuck in a funk.

Chance was in my head. I couldn't shake a feeling of impending doom.

Was it coincidence we'd run into each other? Or had Chance been waiting? And what was up with his new job?

I'd assumed that, after graduation, Chance would relax into a life of playboy luxury. Work on his polo game. Collect oil paintings, or Italian sports cars. Date Victoria's Secret models. After all, he didn't have to work. Didn't *have* to do anything but spend his money.

So why take on a dreary job at Candela? It made no sense.

We passed a small outbuilding crammed with yacht sales offices, then swept by the Variety Store Restaurant. As we approached the pier walkways, I heard a TV newscast floating from inside Salty Mike's Deck Bar.

The faint audio caught my attention.

"Hi! Shelton!" I pointed, then ducked through the open door.

Salty Mike's interior was rough but clean, with neon beer signs adorning a large central tiki bar. A pair of gnarly dartboards flanked a flat-screen TV on the right-hand wall.

I raced over, tried to figure out the volume. Heard feet behind me.

"What is it?" Hi asked. "I thought you were anti-booze. Plus, it's three o'clock."

"Shh!" I jabbed a button, then hissed in frustration as snow filled the screen. The bartender shot me an irritated look.

"Here, let me." Shelton somehow corrected the feed and jacked up the sound.

A tinny voice filled the room. "Repeating our top story this morning, police sources have told Channel Five News that two Charleston teens have officially been designated missing persons . . ."

Smiling pictures of Lucy and Peter Gable flashed onscreen. Each wore a Bolton uniform.

"Holy crap," Shelton breathed. "Guess the cat's out of the bag."

Hi snorted. "Color me *shocked* that those ace cops couldn't maintain radio silence."

"Quiet!" I barked. "There's more."

The image shifted to a live shot of Bolton's front gates, where a breathless female reporter took up the story. "The Gable siblings are both juniors at Bolton Preparatory Academy, the same prestigious private high school that recently made headlines for its connection to the sensational Gamemaster trial."

The three of us groaned in unison.

"Headmaster Declan Paugh declined to be interviewed for our broadcast—" they cut to a clip of Paugh, red-faced, waving the camera away, "—but stated that the school will cooperate fully with the police investigation. Currently, there are no leads regarding the twins' disappearance."

Shelton covered his mouth. "Oh, man, he looks upset."

The program jumped to a noticeably annoyed Commissioner Riggins, standing on the steps outside police headquarters. "At this time we have no evidence of foul play, or even that a crime has been committed. We ask the media to refrain from creating undo panic and let us do our jobs."

The scene shifted to a large waterfront house with several police cruisers parked outside. A deep male voice began narrating. "Rex Gable, father of the missing teens, is a prominent local businessman who serves on the Charleston University Board of Trustees, and is an alderman at Saint Michael's Church. Channel Five has learned that police investigators searched the family's Daniel Island home early this morning."

The coverage shifted to a flashy news studio, where a silver-foxed anchorman addressed the camera. "The Gable family has temporarily relocated to assist with the investigation."

"Maybe we'll get lucky," Hi offered. "This should bump the Gamemaster's trial from page one."

Shelton slapped Hi's shoulder. "C'mon, man. Not cool. We know those guys."

The anchor continued. "If you know the whereabouts of Lucy or Peter Gable, please contact the Charleston Police Department. A reward is being offered for information leading to their safe return."

The broadcast switched to an empty-headed weatherman predicting partly cloudy skies. Shelton turned the volume back down and we stepped outside.

Absently, I began walking toward our slip, where *Hugo* would arrive any minute. The boys followed. But my feet slowed as we approached the long wooden walkway to Pier Group Z. Halfway across, I stopped altogether.

The boys halted behind me, uncertain, matching puzzled expressions on their faces.

For a long moment, I stared out over the harbor in silence.

A feeling was hardening inside me. A resolve.

"We *have* to do something," I said finally. Forcefully. "We *have* to get involved."

Shelton scratched the back of his head. "Okay. Fine. But what?"

"We've got that voodoo card," Hi suggested. "Let's find out what it means."

"More," I urged. "We need to fully investigate the twins' disappearance."

"I distinctly remember being told this was a police matter," Shelton grumbled. "More than once, yo."

"But we can help." I spun to face them. "What *are* we doing these days, anyway?"

Hi's face scrunched. "What do you mean?"

"I mean, what's our purpose? We have these—" I stepped closer and lowered my voice, "—*abilities*, but no direction. No goal. We should be doing more."

"We're keeping our heads down," Shelton countered. "Avoiding the spotlight while we figure out what happened to us. Jeez, Tor. Isn't that enough? I thought that's what you wanted?"

"No. Not anymore. I was wrong."

Both boys gave me confused looks. I couldn't blame them.

I tried to express what I was feeling. "We need to *do* things. Accomplish something. Make a difference with . . . whatever it is these powers are."

Hi spread his arms wide. "With great power comes great responsibility. Ask Spider-Man."

"So now you two wanna fight crime?" Shelton shook his head, incredulous. "Where is this coming from? Should we make costumes?"

Hi's face lit up. "I've *definitely* got some ideas in that area, if—"

"Of course we don't need costumes!" I paused, took a breath. "Look, I'm not even sure what I want. And, yes, I realize this is coming straight out of nowhere. I was the one who said we shouldn't be flaring at all."

I glanced at the door to Salty Mike's. "Maybe it was seeing Lucy's and Peter's pictures onscreen. Like mug shots. It just hit me—we *have* these powers, why not *apply* them to something worthwhile? Solve problems normal people can't."

Shelton's eyes narrowed. "You sound like a guidance counselor."

I ignored him. The more I thought about it, the more I believed in what I was saying.

We *did* need a purpose. Could this be it?

"Hey, why not?" Hi shrugged. "We know the twins, and they seem all right. And it's only a missing persons' case anyway. What are you afraid of, Devers?"

"The unknown," Shelton snapped. "Jail. Being dissected by Navy Seals."

He petulantly kicked a rock. I crossed my arms, waiting.

Shelton removed his glasses and ran a hand across his face. Finally, he sighed. "I guess we could help out a little. Can't see the harm in that."

"So what's the plan?" Hi cracked his knuckles. "Head into North Charleston and shake down some perps? Buy hand grenades? I've mapped out the first couple verses of a Virals theme song, so—"

"The Gable house," I said. "The report said the family relocated, probably so the cops can tear it part. No one should be there. Let's snoop around a little."

"*Arrgh.*" Shelton pressed both fists to his skull. "More midnight black ops. We've done so much B and E this last year, we should apply for college credit. I think my black sweat pants are dirty, and I don't—"

"No, doofus. Let's go right now. If the Gable family isn't staying there, the house should be deserted. Hi, can you—"

"On it." Hi began tapping his iPhone. A moment, then, "Daniel Island. Nice digs, too, not that I'm surprised. The lot borders the Wando River."

"Waterfront," Shelton said quietly. "They probably have a dock."

"Easiest way to avoid detection," Hi added in a singsong voice.

Both boys looked at me.

There was no way around it. We needed Ben. He had the damn boat.

"Fine." I practically growled. "Text him."

Shelton punched in the message. His iPhone buzzed back in moments.

"Ben's in." Shelton rolled his eyes. "Snarky as hell, but he'll pick us up at the Morris dock."

"Getting the band back together!" Hi tossed Shelton a high five, then aimed one my way. "Look out, world!"

I raised my palm in reluctant acceptance.

Look on the bright side. We'll do this at full pack strength.

If only I knew how to feel about that.

CHAPTER 9

Sewee's nose kissed the Gables' private dock.

Ben killed the engine and running lights. Shouldering my pack, I vaulted the port rail and tied off the bowline while Shelton and Hi tightened the stern ropes. Vessel secured, Ben and Coop leaped to join us and we hurried down the planks.

The sun was setting in a fiery tangerine ball, giving a hint of cover. I prayed the neighbors wouldn't notice our boat, but it was a risk we had to take. Thankfully, the Gable property was tucked into a tree-lined cove that blocked an easy view by passing watercraft.

An hour earlier I'd managed to beg off dinner. Kit and Whitney had accepted my study group explanation without too much fuss. After all, I'd promised to be home by eight. What trouble could I possibly get into?

Daniel Island is all the way across Charleston Harbor from Morris. An affluent four-thousand-acre planned community situated between the Cooper and Wando Rivers, the pricey real estate had only recently been developed. In addition to residential neighborhoods, the islet boasts a swanky golf club, its own schools, churches, and parks, and a vibrant little downtown featuring boutiques, restaurants, and high-end office space.

Fresh, conspicuously green, and close to downtown, Daniel Island had quickly become a coveted address. It's where I'd live, if given the choice. With my friends close by, of course.

We halted in the shadow of a boat shed at the end of the dock.

"You guys ready?" I whispered.

A round of nods. Coop sat back on his hind legs with an expectant look.

"We shouldn't have brought the freaking wolfdog," Shelton griped. "We can't take him inside the house. What if he barks? Decides to chase rabbits?"

"Coop will stand guard," I assured him. "Plus, he amplifies our flare powers. That might come in handy, don't cha think?"

Assuming they work properly. Or at all.

I brushed the unpleasant thought aside. To pull off this home invasion, we *had* to use our powers. There was no way around it. Lucy and Peter needed our help.

We'd just have to be vigilant to any . . . irregularities.

"Enough talk." Ben's eyes already gleamed. "We need to be quick. If anyone spots *Sewee* before we get back, we're cooked."

I ignored Ben. My current strategy was to pretend he wasn't there.

Closing my eyes, I tripped the mental breaker.

SNAP.

Fire. Ice. The opposing forces sent waves thrumming through my body.

Raw energy balled within my chest, compressing and compounding until I felt ready to explode. The power *raged.* Primal. Bestial. Something ancient, yet newborn at the same time. The intensity was unlike anything I'd felt before.

Shelton dropped to a knee, bathed in sweat. "What . . . what . . ."

Hiram shook, his lips moving soundlessly.

"Amazing." Ben staggered sideways, steadying himself against the shed.

I didn't move. Couldn't. Every muscle in my body had seized.

The maelstrom peaked, then shattered like a dropped vase. Darts of adrenaline circumnavigated my nervous system.

My canine DNA rose from its hiding place. Stretched it paws.

Every sense hummed. The world around me sharpened to a laser-like precision unlike anything my species was built to experience.

My eyes cut like diamonds. I scanned the cove, searching for signs of movement. Detected none. My ears picked out a ticking clock inside a neighboring house, fifty yards away. Distant car horns blared inside my head.

I flexed my fingers, reveling in their sudden dexterity. My arms and legs throbbed with energy. Lifting my nose, I sniffed, read the panic sweat dripping from the other Virals.

Except Ben.

He reeked of something else entirely. A sweet, musky scent. My mind made connections, though I didn't understand how, or why.

Was it . . . hunger? Joy? Triumph? I couldn't be sure.

"That was . . . intense." Hi's voice cracked on the last word.

"We haven't flared all together in a while." Shelton pocketed his spectacles. "Tory's right. The powers are getting . . . wilder. Almost rabid."

Sister-Friend.

I glanced down. Coop was at my side, tail wagging. I rubbed his snout.

Hello, Coop.

The boys jumped. Six golden eyes shot to me.

I grinned. Shut my eyes once more.

Stilling my thoughts, I delved deep into my subconscious. Visualized the hidden connections between our minds.

I *knew* they were there. Had learned that much about our powers.

Wherever we went, whatever we did, telepathic bonds linked us. Viral to Viral. Those bonds were the essence of what made us a pack.

A web sprang to life—flaming cords, stretching between us in a fiery grid, dancing and humming with vitality.

So much easier than before.

Guided by instinct, I . . . *reached* somehow, gripping the gleaming ropes with my consciousness, overlaying my thoughts in a manner I can't fully explain. My spirit soared as I imbedded myself into our shared thought matrix.

I sent a message.

Hello to you guys, too.

"Oh, man." Shelton grabbed his head. "I'm *never* going to get used to that."

"Is it like before?" Hi asked, wide-eyed. "Can you see through our eyes? Read our thoughts?"

"She better not." Ben took a step back down the dock.

"Relax." Cradled inside this magnificent *oneness,* I felt totally at ease.

Just like before.

I tried to untether my mind from my body. At the same time, I willed the flaming cords to grow and expand. Transform into conduits through which my thoughts could pass.

No good. Something blocked the flow.

I couldn't create the tunnels. My mind wouldn't travel.

I don't understand.

The links were discernible. My pack was assembled. Everything felt in place.

But I couldn't force the union. The pack refused to coalesce.

The bonds connecting us thrummed wildly, like guitar strings wound too tight.

Frustrated, I concentrated on the wolfdog, knowing he focused our power.

Coop's ears perked. His gaze locked on to mine.

One last time, I tried to *force* the mind-meld, picturing the Virals as an extension of Coop. The effort failed. I couldn't untie the pack.

"Tory?"

My lids opened. Hi was waving a hand in front of my face.

"I can't connect our thoughts. I don't understand it. I can't even hear yours."

"Sounds perfect." Ben jabbed a thumb at the house. "Can we get on with it?"

I nodded. He was right. We had a task to complete.

But this isn't over.

Kneeling beside Coop, I ruffled his fur. A surge of love flowed along our bond.

"Stay here, boy." Holding my palm before his nose. "Keep watch for anyone approaching the house."

I felt a flash of annoyance from Coop. He snorted, then pawed the wooden planks.

"No back talk."

Taking his head in my hands, I forced the wolfdog to meet my gaze.

Stay. Watch. Please.

I released him. Coop whined softly, but circled three times and sat.

Watch. Guard.

Impressions more than words.

"Good boy. See you in a few."

A small backyard stretched to the rear of the Gables' white stucco house. We crossed it quickly, then waited for Shelton to pick the back-door lock.

"Come on, maestro." Hi was bouncing on the balls of his feet. "Work your magic."

Click.

"Gotcha." Shelton took a breath. "Here goes. Be ready to haul ass if an alarm goes off."

Cringing, he turned the knob, then slowly eased the door open.

Nothing. No wailing sirens. No flashing lights. The system was deactivated.

"Move!" I hurried everyone inside, leaving the door cracked for a quick getaway.

Unleashing my flare senses, I searched for any sign of occupancy.

Just because a house is *supposed* to be empty, doesn't mean it is.

Flaring, I heard a ticking clock. Purring AC. Tiny feet scritch-scratching inside the stucco walls. Sand mice. They're everywhere on the islands.

The Gables need an exterminator.

"Nobody's here," Shelton said at last. "At least, nobody that's breathing."

I exhaled. If Shelton's ears gave the all-clear, then I was satisfied.

We stood inside a large kitchen with a central island. A breakfast nook hooked off to the right. Beyond it, a narrow back staircase rose to the second floor. To the left of the island, a pair of doorways accessed the rest of the ground floor.

"Let's split up," Ben suggested. "Shelton and I will look down here."

"Hiram and I will check upstairs." I spoke as though the two-pronged approach was my idea. Technically, I still wasn't speaking to Ben.

I led Hi up to the second level. A long hallway ran the length of the house, ending at a closed door. Two additional doors spaced each side. In the center of the corridor, a wide staircase descended to the foyer and front door.

"I'll take this side." Pointing left. "You sweep the other."

Hi nodded. I moved to the first room and slipped inside.

The square chamber was small, with a single window. Desk. Computer. Bookshelf. File Cabinet. Clearly a home office. The room's most notable feature was how immaculate it was. Clear desktop. Empty trash can. Not a displaced pen or paper clip. The carpet still had vacuum lines. I wondered if anyone ever went in there.

Forgoing the lights in case of any watchful neighbors, I prowled in the growing gloom, trusting my flare vision to pierce the shadows. Senses on high alert, I poked around—opening drawers, jiggling handles, checking the closet—but quickly moved on. I'd seen nothing relating to either twin.

Back in the hallway, I bumped into Hi.

"Office," I said.

"Guest bedroom," he replied. "These people sure like Pottery Barn."

My next door accessed a much larger chamber, with bay windows overlooking the water. A king-sized bed occupied stage center, heaped with lacy throw pillows. A Katy Perry CD was resting on the bedside table.

Sensing I'd found Lucy's domain, I closed the drapes and flipped a wall switch.

The card had been found in there. Her room required a thorough examination.

The first thing I noticed was pink. Everywhere. Walls, sheets, bedspread, even a lighter shade for the plush wall-to-wall carpeting. *Blech.*

The furniture was elegant and tasteful. Simple wooden pieces, painted white—bed, side tables, dresser, bureau, bookcase, desk. A private bathroom split the far wall, next to a large walk-in closet. Framed prints adorned the walls. Monet. Dalí. Van Gogh. Classics, all, but highly impersonal. An easel and violin stood in the corner. A day bench curved beneath each window.

I crossed to the dresser, where a handful of framed pictures were aligned in a row. Lucy and Peter playing violin. Lucy smiling as she received an award. A Gable family portrait. Lucy's yearbook photograph.

As I looked around, two things bothered me.

First, Lucy's room was as spotless as the office. Either these people were neat freaks, or they had one hell of a maid.

Second, The room lacked . . . character. It was cold, and impersonal, like a hotel suite. Beyond the violin, I saw nothing that made me think of Lucy Gable, the person.

Get to work, I chided myself. *Not everyone is Hiram.*

Harnessing my flare senses, I inspected the bedroom from top to bottom. I rifled the dresser, checked inside the desk and bureau, crawled under the bed, and even snooped behind the bookcase and headboard. Everywhere a personal item could be stashed.

But what I was hunting?

More weird cards? A note? Signs of foul play?

I didn't know, and so far my probe had turned up diddly-squat.

Opening the closet, I received my first surprise—a giant Ryan Gosling poster taped to the back of the door.

"That's more like it." I took a moment to admire the artwork.

Finally, a little spark. Some evidence that Lucy had a normal human personality.

But why was it hidden in there?

World's Sexiest Man aside, the remainder of the closet disappointed—nothing but pricey clothes, Bolton Prep unis, and more shoes than four girls could wear. No box full of love letters, no trashed Google Maps printouts, no secret diary filled with shocking revelations, stashed inside a winter coat pocket.

My spirits sank. I began to worry I'd forced us here for no reason.

A quick search of Lucy's bathroom drew a similar blank. Sighing, I slapped off the light and stepped back into the hall. Hi was exiting the door at the end of the corridor.

"Media room." His golden eyes gleamed in the darkness. "A total snoozer. Although somebody bought *The Last Airbender* on Blu-ray, which might be the worst purchase ever."

"Is that the last door?"

Hi nodded. "I already checked Peter's room. Other than being the lamest sleeping chamber ever conceived, there's nothing suspicious. Not that I know what I'm doing. Because I don't, FYI."

I suppressed a sigh. "I trust your instincts. I got the same vibe from Lucy's room. It's a little weird. Other than a few framed pictures, the place felt like a high-end corporate rental or something."

"We may need to face the fact that the Gable twins are the two most boring people on earth." Hi paused. "Though Peter did have a pretty killer CD collection. White Stripes. Nine Inch Nails. Death Cab. He keeps it under his bed, though, which is kinda bizarre."

"Huh."

Under his bed? And Lucy hung her poster in the closet. What was that all about?

"Did you find anything like Señor Snake Scarf?" Hi asked.

I shook my head. "Based on her room, I can't believe that card belongs to Lucy."

"Let's check with Shelton and Ben," Hi suggested. "Maybe they found something downstairs." But he didn't sound optimistic.

I'd taken one step down the main staircase when an image arrowed into my head.

Cooper. *Inside.* Scratching at a thick wooden door.

I stumbled, nearly fell. Hi grabbed my arm to prevent a header down the stairs.

"Tory?"

"I'm . . . okay." The image faded, but I knew what it meant. "Hurry. Coop's inside the house. He wants to show me something."

"Your dog just spoke to you, inside your head?" Hi shivered. "Crazy sauce."

"Just come on!"

I felt an electric charge in my nerves.

Coop *had* sent me a message. The image was only part of it.

The wolfdog's nose had caught something we'd missed.

A harsh, coppery scent.

One I had no trouble identifying.

Cooper was on the trail of blood.

CHAPTER 10

Shelton and Ben were waiting at the foot of the stairs.

"We found zilch," Shelton grumbled. "What are we even doing here?"

Ben jabbed a thumb over his shoulder. "That way is the living room, den, and dining room. Everything's completely normal. We were about to recheck the kitchen, since we don't know what else to do."

"There's a second passage off the kitchen," I said. "Coop's there."

"Coop?" Shelton's hands flew up. "What's he doing in the house?"

Ben frowned, golden light smoldering from his dark brown eyes. "How do you know he's there?"

"He told me. I think he found something."

Shelton's arms dropped. "Told you?"

"Yes. Now follow me."

We hurried back to the kitchen. I spotted Coop standing, legs splayed, halfway down the back corridor.

Coop looked at me, a low growl rolling from his throat.

"What do you mean, Coop told you?" Shelton was tugging his ear-lobe double time. "You mean, like . . . like, he spoke to you? Mind to mind? I didn't hear anything. How come you and the mutt can connect, but we can't?"

"No idea." I reached down to scratch Coop's ears. His body was rigid, head to tail. He pawed the oak door in front of his snout.

"It was more like an impression, and it only lasted for a second." I said. "Coop caught an odor. In here."

With my flare still burning, I felt the tiniest of tickles along my skin.

I placed my hand near the crack, where the wood met the jamb.

Air flow. This wasn't a broom closet—there was open space behind the door.

The knob turned easily in my hand. The door swung open, revealing a narrow set of carpeted stairs descending into darkness.

Coop fired down the steps.

"Cooper! Stop." But the wolfdog was gone.

"A lower level?" Hi's brow furrowed. "The Zillow listing for this address didn't mention a finished basement. Those are pretty rare for Charleston. The Gables must've completed this recently. They're *supposed* to update their total heated square footage, but I bet they're trying to avoid a higher property tax assessment."

We stared at Hi.

He shrugged. "What?"

"Total heated square footage?" Shelton asked.

"Property tax assessment?" Ben added.

"My uncle's a real estate agent," Hi said defensively.

"Enough." I flipped a switch, illuminating both the staircase and the room below. Waving for the others to follow, I started down after Coop.

The area below was spacious, spanning half the house. The single room was divided into nooks, with a small bathroom to one side. The black-and-white tile floor held a pool table, an elliptical machine, a wet bar, and a small movie theater with four recliners. On the far wall, two skinny rectangular windows flanked a thick steel door, which allowed access to a courtyard beside the house. Two more windows dotted the near wall, allowing a ground-level view of the Gables' backyard and dock.

"Being rich seems nice," Hi commented. "Remind me to get on that."

I was already moving to where Coop was snuffling beside the steel door.

"Heel, boy." I didn't want him destroying evidence.

The wolfdog trotted a few steps away, turned, then crouched on his paws, watching me.

"How'd he get inside?" Ben scratched his cheek in annoyance.

"We left the door cracked, and he smelled something." I pointed to the floor space that had drawn Coop's attention. "Over there, I assume."

"That's our big lead?" Shelton gave the wolfdog a hard look. "This mutt could be tracking a bologna sandwich."

I shook my head. "Coop sent me his perception—it wasn't lunch meat. Coop thinks he smelled blood."

"Do what now?" Shelton took a step backward. "Did you say *blood*?"

"Yikes." Hi ran a hand through his hair. "This just got serious."

"Agreed." I slipped my pack from my shoulders, thankful I'd thought to bring my evidence kit. "First, we turn this room upside down."

As I knelt to lay out supplies, Ben began a careful circuit of the basement, golden irises blazing. After a moment's hesitation, Shelton joined him.

I tried to hide my nerves, but was scared of what we might find.

Cooper's nose had been sure.

Still nothing to worry about, Detective Hawfield?

"Whatcha thinking?" Hi squatted down beside me, wearing an eager look. He loved experiments more than anyone, and had guessed my intentions.

"I'm gonna spray this area with Luminol."

"Luminol? How'd you get that? Sounds expensive."

"Not if you make your own."

"Make your own?" Hi shifted to get a look at my face. "Victoria Grace, have you been holding out on me?"

"Sorry." I shoved aside my fingerprint kit, sticky tape, digital camera, and box of plastic baggies. The brown cylinder of homemade Luminol was nestled in the bottom of my bag.

"Well, at least tell me how you did it," Hi insisted.

"You cut up vinyl gloves and boil the pieces with rubbing alcohol." I pulled out an empty spray bottle and poured in the cylinder's contents. "That process extracts a compound called diethylhexyl phthalate. Filter that solution, then boil it again with water and some drain cleaner. After a few more filtration hoops, you have pure phthalic anhydride."

Hi seemed to be memorizing my words. "And that's Luminol?"

I shook my head. "After that it gets . . . complicated. I'll forward you the link from ChemHacker. Promise."

"Yes, you will. I can't believe you did this without me."

"Sorry." I tested the spray bottle. "The chemical process has some dangerous byproducts, and the whole thing was pretty hard to pull off, even working at LIRI. My first attempt bombed."

"Kit lets you synthesize chemicals in his labs?"

"What my father doesn't know won't kill him."

Hi snorted, but let the matter drop. "So we spray this science project on the floor to detect . . . what, exactly?"

I cleared my throat. "Blood."

"Ugh." Hi paled. "That's what I thought."

"You think there's blood on the floor?" Shelton had spoken close to my ear, causing me to jump. "I don't see any."

Ben stood beside him. "Circuit complete. Nothing unusual." Pointing to the base of the doorframe. "That's where Coop was poking around. Did he find something?"

"I don't know yet." Curt. "I'm going to spray and see."

"See what?" Ben appeared unfazed by my frosty tone.

"Luminol exhibits chemiluminescence." *Grrr. I'm not talking to you!*

Shelton frowned. "Chemi-what-now?"

"Chemiluminescence." I inched closer to the door. "In other words, it glows when mixed with an oxidizing agent. Blood contains hemoglobin, which, in turn, contains trace amounts of iron. That's what causes the Luminol to react."

"Just watch where Tory sprays." Hi popped up and slapped the wall switch. The only remaining light beamed from ten glowing eyes. "If you see a blue glow, that's means blood."

"Thanks, Hi." Adjusting my weight, I leaned forward. "I'm going to saturate this whole area evenly. Any blood, and the glow should last about thirty seconds. Shelton, can you snap a few pics with my Nikon? Use a long-exposure setting."

"One sec." Shelton lifted the camera and popped off the lens cap. A few more fidgets, then, "All set."

Deep breath. "Here goes nothing."

I pumped the nozzle, applying the chemical evenly as I moved my arm in a slow arc.

The reaction stunned even me.

A strong glow sprang immediately to life—a thick blue patch that covered the door's bottom quarter and a three-foot semicircle on tiles beneath it.

I moved robotically, expanding the circle by pumping more spray. The only sound was the rapid-fire click of the Nikon. Shelton, frozen in place, simply held down the button.

So much blood.

Cool radiance oozed from the floor. As I continued spraying the perimeter, tiny arrows of illumination fired outward from the solid disk centered on the doorway.

When I'd finished, I stared at a glimmering blue sun, edged by broken streaks.

My mind practically gibbered in horror.

No one moved. The glow crested, then slowly faded from existence.

"So much blood," Hi whispered. The golden light vanished from his eyes.

Inside my head, a string abruptly severed.

SNUP.

Waves of dizziness crashed over me. I braced myself on the floor with both hands, waiting for the world to stop spinning. Slowly, it did.

Shelton began coughing so hard, I feared he'd vomit. Ben wrapped an arm around his shoulder and pounded Shelton's back. Both of their flares were gone.

"My flare shut down on its own again." Hi shivered as if spiders were crawling his back. "*Poof.* Gone." Shelton looked up, but could only nod. Ben glanced away.

"Same here." I pounded my leg in frustration. "What in the hell is going on?"

"Hit the lights," Ben ordered.

Hi scampered over and turned them on.

"My God," Shelton wheezed, eyes glued to the doorframe. "Nobody can lose that much blood and live!"

It was true. The blue circle had been massive, and dense throughout.

I tried not to imagine that much blood spilling across the floor. Could think of nothing else.

Lucy. Peter.

Sweet Jesus, what happened down here?

The analytical portion of my brain rebooted, came back on line. Made a connection.

Of course.

"Wait!" I hissed. "That's not blood!"

"Oh please plcase *please* tell me that's true!" Shelton was maniacally shirt-cleaning his glasses. "'Cause otherwise . . ."

"It *can't* be." I shoved my nose within an inch of the tiles. "There's no visible bloodstain here. That's impossible for such a huge reaction to Luminol."

"True." Hi cupped his chin. "And the edge of that circle seemed pretty regular, now that I think about."

I rifled through every fact I knew about Luminol.

An answer popped out at me.

"Bleach."

Hi looked at me sideways. "Huh?"

"Bleach reacts to Luminol just like blood." The pieces started falling into place. "Someone scrubbed this area with a bleach solution."

"So someone was cleaning up," Ben said. "But why bleach? And why use so much?"

"What were they cleaning?" Hi asked grimly.

I remembered the streaks at the perimeter of the glowing circle.

My eyes found Coop. I recalled the tangy, metallic odor he'd sent my way.

He'd been certain. Now I was, too.

My heart sank.

"I think something terrible *did* happen down here."

Ben grunted. "Explain."

"Remember the spatter along the rim of the circle? Those streaks reacted to the Luminol, too. And based on their form and shape, I doubt they were part of the cleaning process. I think the Luminol picked up two different substances."

"So there *was* blood," Hi said. "And bleach was used to clean it up?"

I nodded. "Someone spent a *lot* of time and energy cleaning that area. My guess is, they were concealing evidence."

"Of a violent crime," Shelton finished. "Oh Lord."

Hi gulped. “The Gable twins didn’t run off, did they?”

I shook my head. “I think somebody snatched them. Or . . . worse.”

I didn’t want to finish that thought.

“What should we do?” Ben asked.

I considered our options. “We already took pictures. Now we treat this entire room like a crime scene. I’ll dust the door for prints, while—”

A loud bang broke the stillness.

My head whipped to the windows facing the backyard.

I saw a dark form kneeling in the grass outside.

Watching.

“Whaaaa!” Shelton wailed.

Cooper lunged across the room, baying at the apparition.

Hi dove behind a couch. Ben pulled Shelton under the pool table.

I froze, staring at the shadowy figure.

The basement lights reflected off the glass, blurring the scene outside. Our observer was kneeling, stone still, ignoring Coop as he growled below the sill.

As I watched, the figure rose and vanished, a moment before Ben slapped off the lights.

Hiram’s head popped from behind the couch. “Tory, what should we do?”

“That wasn’t a cop!” Shelton shrieked. “Believe that!”

“Relax!” Ben moved to the bottom of the staircase and peered up. “It’s probably a neighbor. They likely saw *Sewee* and came to—”

An ear-shattered wail sounded from upstairs. All five of us jumped.

“The alarm!” I shouted.

“Someone must’ve set it off!” Ben yelled. “From inside the kitchen, too!”

My eyes shot to the door so recently cleaned with meticulous care. “Out this way!”

I jammed everything into my bag and bolted for the door. Frazzled moments passed as I scrambled to throw the deadbolt. Finally, the way swung open.

Cool air flowed around me as I paused on the threshold, scanning the darkness for any sign we weren't alone. The blaring alarm rattled my concentration.

"Go left." Hi was crouching beside. "We have to get to the boat."

"Through the backyard?" Shelton hissed. "That's where the dude was!"

"Move!" Ben ordered from behind us. "I think someone's coming down the stairs!"

That clinched it. Time for a sprint.

But, turning to go, I noticed Coop stalking back toward the steps. Ears flat. Tail rigid.

I felt a rush of panic. "Coop, no! Here!"

Coop growled, his entire posture expressing reluctance.

I slapped my side. "Heel, boy! Now!"

With a last snarl at the staircase, Coop spun and bounded to my side.

"Go, go, go!" I pushed the boys ahead of me, one by one, then grabbed Coop's collar just to be safe. Together we raced into the night.

A dozen strides brought me to the corner of the house. The boys were halfway across the yard, sprinting toward the dock.

Porch lights flicked at houses adjoining the Gable property. Neighbors. Alerted by the commotion.

Coop needed no further prodding. Side by side, we pounded after the other Virals, shooting across the yard, down the dock, and aboard *Sewee.*

Hi and Shelton frantically untied the lines, then piled aboard.

Ben gunned the engine and threw it into reverse.

Sewee lurched from the pier, spun a tight 180, and then fired into the river, leaving behind nothing but choppy wake and a lightly rocking dock.

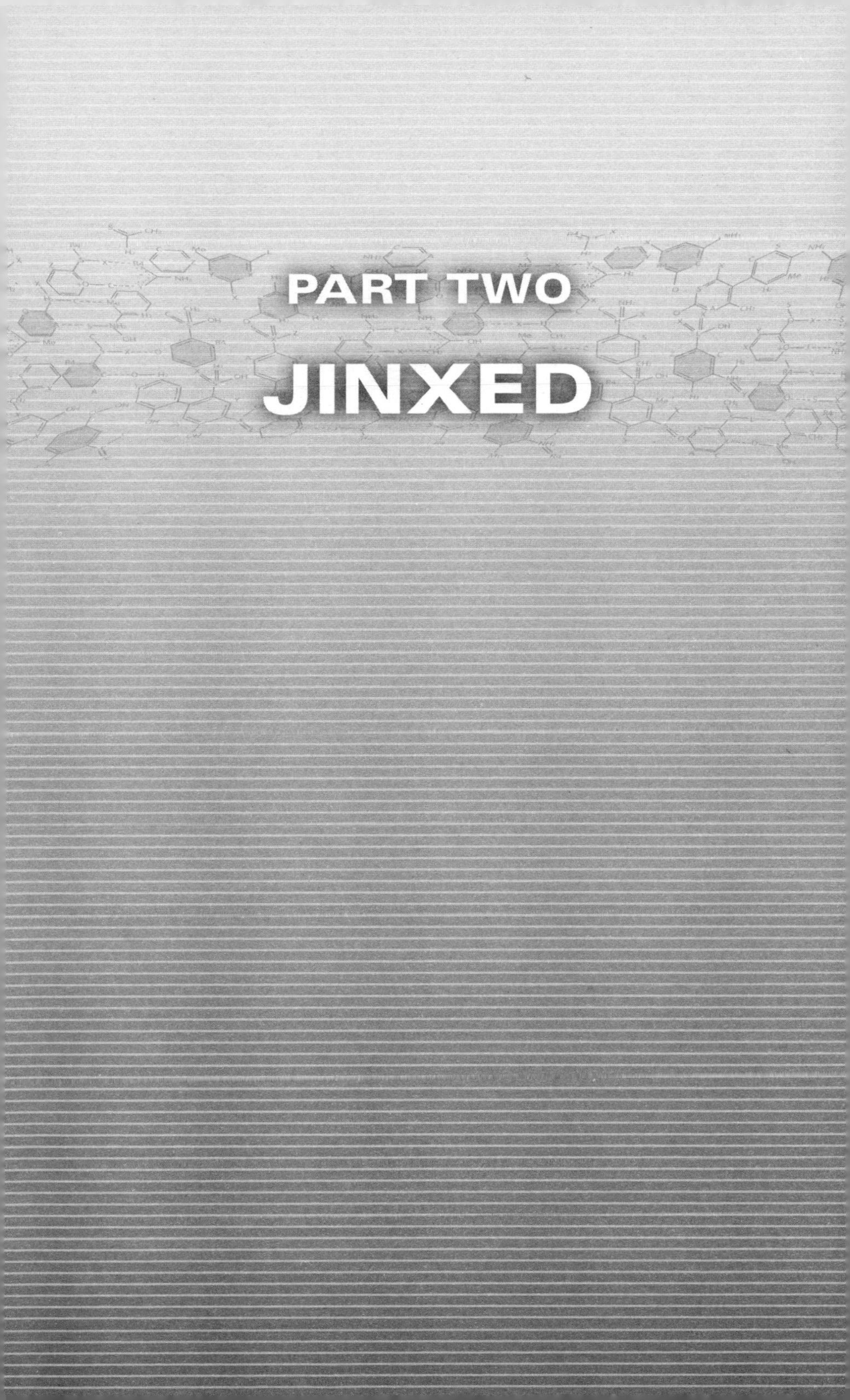

PART TWO

JINXED

CHAPTER 11

Wednesday

I rose early the next morning.

The moment my eyelids opened, there was no going back.

Last night's scare had soured my dreams.

So I sat on my bed, half asleep, examining the photocopied Man with Snake. I turned the page this way and that, hoping a change in orientation might trigger some insight. *Nada.*

On a whim I grabbed my laptop and tried a few Googles, but quickly gave it up.

Searching "Old Man + Snake + Toga" is not an exercise I recommend.

A glance at my clock. 6:07 a.m.

Gonna be a looong day.

My mind began to wander. For the umpteenth time, I wondered who'd seen us inside the Gable home. A concerned neighbor? A cop? For some reason, I didn't think it was either.

Why had the person crouched outside the basement window? Why set off the alarm?

The more I thought about it, the more uneasy I became.

How long had that stranger crouched there, in the dark, spying on us? I broke out in goose bumps, remembering the feel of those hidden eyes.

Once spotted, our watcher hadn't run. Hadn't immediately charged inside. Hadn't raised a shout. The figure had remained frozen in place, observing us for a few moments more. As if committing our faces to memory. I shivered at *that* thought.

We'd high-tailed it back to Morris Island, watching *Sewee*'s wake for any sign of pursuit. None had appeared. Back home, Coop and I had scurried into the townhouse. I'd spent the rest of evening pretending nothing was amiss.

But I couldn't stop thinking about the Gables' basement. The glowing circle of blue.

Blood on steel and tile, carefully and methodically cleaned.

We have *to do something.*

Lost in thought, I glanced at the page in my hands. Was startled by its clarity.

I could make out tiny wrinkles on the paper's surface. Microscopic creases, creating subtle variations in color and grain. The black ink practically leaped off the page, refining into a hundred variations of gray and assuming almost three-dimensional properties. Its acrid smell infested my nostrils.

A loud clicking made me jump. My eyes darted to the clock, where every shift of the second hand now reverberated like a snare drum.

I became aware of a raft of scents surrounding me. Shampoos and soaps wafting from my bathroom. Frying bacon drifting from downstairs. A half-gnawed bone Coop had deposited underneath my bed.

I sprang to my feet, unsure what was happening.

Too quick—I toppled over backward in a heap. Lay there panting.

"What the hell!?!"

Moving more carefully, I hurried to my bathroom. Knew what I'd find.

The mirror revealed a frazzled-looking redhead in light blue pajamas, a distressed expression crimping her face. Impossibly, her eyes glowed with golden fire.

"Whoa whoa whoa!" I backed away, stunned.

I was flaring. But I hadn't reached for my powers. Hadn't invited the wolf to come out.

There'd been no *snap.* No grueling transition. No spikes of pleasure or pain.

My powers had simply switched themselves on.

I sat back down on my bed, mind racing. What did this mean? Had I lost control? The thought of my powers randomly coming and going, without warning, was beyond terrifying. I wouldn't avoid detection for a single day!

The flare came so easily this time.

The realization stopped me cold.

Usually, the transition all but floored me, testing my strength and endurance. And lately, that struggle had become more pronounced. I'd begun to worry my powers were getting too wild to trust. That removing the leash was growing too dangerous to justify the benefits.

Yet *this* flare had bloomed without the slightest ripple of difficulty, unfolding so gently I'd fail to notice anything was happening. I had no idea what to make of that.

Was there a better way to flare? Had my unconscious mind found a solution?

Have I been doing it wrong, all along?

A prickling sensation crashed my train of thought.

I wasn't alone.

Close by, someone *else* was flaring, too.

I squeezed my eyes shut.

The flaming cords sprang to life—fiery ropes that connected my mind to those of my packmates. The lines thrummed wildly, illuminating then fading as they skittered across the black field of my unconscious mind. I could barely follow their frenetic movements. Had never seen them react like this.

One line in particular danced and twirled, glimmering with twice the radiance.

I sensed Coop, snoozing in his doggie bed downstairs. Calm. Unperturbed. But the wolfdog always seemed linked to our pack's shared head space. His presence was never fleeting, like that of a flaring Viral. Coop wasn't who I'd detected.

Concentrating, I *shifted* my perspective, attempting to impose my will on the links in the manner I'd tried the night before.

This time, the cords became tunnels with ease.

I didn't hesitate, firing my consciousness down the gleaming conduit.

A shock of cold. A blast of heat.

Suddenly, I was in another bedroom, staring at a computer through thick-lensed glasses. Dark-skinned fingers pounded a keyboard faster than I could follow.

Shelton?

My vision lurched as the typist shot to his feet, head swinging wildly.

"Who's there? Tory? Is that you? This ain't funny!"

I felt an unpleasant tearing sensation as my awareness slammed backward. *Outward.* Like a pilot's ejector seat. Untethered, my thoughts tumbled in a black haze.

I could hear Shelton shouting. Then, oddly, I sensed Hi's presence. Both boys seemed to be trying to communicate something, but my mind was wrapped in cobwebs. I floated farther and farther away.

An image appeared, small at first, but rapidly growing in size.

Cooper.

My pet. Charging toward me. Teeth bared. Tail low.

Not rest. Bad place.

Hey, Coop. Good boy.

The wolfdog drew close.

Drifting, listless, I reached out a hand.

Coop's teeth sank into my flesh.

An electric shock sizzled through my brain. My mind recoiled like a rubber band.

SNUP.

I awoke from the trance. Heard Coop whining and scratching at my bedroom door. I stumbled over and unlocked it. Coop bowled me to the floor, then planted his front paws on my chest and licked my face.

"Thanks, boy."

⬡ ⬡ ⬡

Sixty seconds later, I was bounding up Shelton's front steps.

He opened the door before I could knock, eyes wide behind his clunky black specs. Shelton slipped outside and followed me down to the common.

We huddled on the dew-covered grass, me in girly pastel PJs, him in yellow basketball shorts and a Green Lantern tee. The sun was just breaking the horizon, sending out tentacles of soft yellow-orange light.

"What's going on, Brennan?" Shelton grimaced like he'd eaten something rotten. "I just emptied my stomach into the porcelain god. Do I have you to thank?"

"I don't know. Probably." In a rush, I told him how my flare had sprung to life on its own, and about the harrowing out-of-body experience that followed. "I think something is seriously wrong with our powers," I finished.

Shelton looked everywhere but at me.

"The transition came easily." I tilted my head, trying to catch his eye. "I could reach you with no trouble. Which means *you* must've been flaring, too. Right?"

Shelton bobbed a guilty nod. "I was feeling run-down this morning. Tired. Bad headache. But lately, if I flare for a few minutes, whatever's bothering me seems to fade away."

I was about to scold him—couldn't Shelton understand how *dangerous* that sounded?—but managed to hold my tongue. At that moment, I was in no position to criticize.

But using our powers as some kind of magical cure-all? A way to sidestep the daily grind? My instincts screamed in warning. Nothing is ever free.

Every shortcut has a price. Every action, a consequence.

I was about to say as much when a door opened a few units down from where we stood.

Hi emerged, spotted us, and hurried over. He also wore sleeping attire—black pajamas adorned with the crest of House Stark. *Where does he get this stuff?*

"Where'd you get those?" Shelton asked, but in a reverent tone.

"The Internet." Hi popped his shirt, then made hand explosions. "Serious business, Devers. They've got House Lannister, too, if you prefer reppin' the baddies."

"Why are *you* up?" I asked.

"Good morning to you, too," Hi answered primly. "I saw you guys from my window, thought I'd mosey on out, and inquire into what just happened to my brain."

"What do you mean?" Though I knew the answer.

"Well, I was minding my own business, enjoying some pre-breakfast toilet time, when I felt eyes on my back." Hi frowned. "No, not my back. More like, *inside my skull.* Not a great feeling while manning the throne, I assure you. Then you and that mutt hijacked my thoughts and started dancing Gangnam Style on my cerebral cortex. Next thing I know, Shelton's inside my head, yelling, Coop's howling like a rabid monkey, and then something red-hot came and scrambled my brain completely. When I snapped out of it, I was lying facedown on my bathroom floor, which isn't nearly as cool as Taylor Swift would have you believe. Oh, and I was suddenly flaring, FYI."

"Oh, man." Shelton reached for his earlobe. "That's not good."

Hi snorted. "No, Shelton, it isn't. So, would either of you mentalists care to shed some light on these events?"

Glumly, Shelton and I filled Hi in.

Color drained from Hi's face. "If we can't control when our powers come and go, we're screwed with a capital *S*. Hell, in *all* caps."

My eyes strayed to the last unit in the row. It occurred to me that I hadn't felt anything from Ben during the flare incident.

"Is Ben here?" I asked quietly.

"No," Shelton answered. "I texted him last night. He's at his mom's this week."

"We need to know if he felt what happened." My tone made it clear that *I* wasn't going to ask. "Are his flares getting screwy at all? Have any sparked uncalled? Find out."

"Yeah." Hi's gaze flicked to Shelton.

"Um." Shelton looked at his shoes. "About that."

"What?" I knew I wouldn't like what was coming.

Hi cleared his throat, then looked me square in the eye. "We told you Ben's been flaring a lot, but it's worse than that. He's like a bonfire, all the livelong day."

"Almost every time I see him," Shelton confirmed.

Worse than I thought.

"Tell me everything."

"You're not gonna be happy," Hi warned. "Don't kill the messenger."

"Or his good-looking buddy," Shelton added.

I motioned impatiently for Hi to continue.

"Last week, Ben and I went to Captain's Comics over in West Ashley. So there I am, browsing back issues of *The Walking Dead,* having a grand old time. I look up, and *boom.* Ben's rockin' his stupid shades inside the store, burning like a Roman candle. My skin got tingly ten feet away. When I discreetly flipped out on him, he just chuckled, and kept strolling around. There must've been a dozen other people there."

Stunned, I turned to Shelton.

"Pretty much the same." He took a deep breath. "On Saturday Ben and I drove to Johns Island to see *Skyfall.*"

"You did?" Hi said sharply. "Thanks for the invite, jerks."

Shelton raised his palms. "You were at temple. We're supposed to just wait around? Plus, you've seen that movie like five times."

"You still could've *asked,*" Hi grumbled. "I don't—"

"Guys!" I clapped my hands once. "The story, please."

"An hour in, I go for a popcorn refill." Shelton shuddered. "When I get back, Ben's sitting in the dark, flaring away, and he's not even wearing his sunglasses! I almost wet myself. He said he wanted to watch the movie in Viral HD. Man, I don't remember a single minute from the rest of the film."

"In a theater!?" My temper exploded. "That stupid mother—"

"Hiram!"

Our heads whipped. Ruth Stolowitski was standing on her front stoop.

"Get back in here this instant! You're not dressed."

Ruth wore a fuzzy pink bathrobe, her free hand vising the garment closed. Her eyes darted, as if worried that cagey perverts were surveilling our remote island, waiting for just this opportunity to get an eyeful.

Hi covered his face. "Kill me now."

"We'll talk more later," I whispered. "But no flaring until we figure things out."

Hi nodded, already hurrying back to his stoop.

Shelton hesitated, watching me nervously. "What are you going to do?"

I inhaled deeply. Exhaled. Tried to keep my anger in check.

"Our top priority is hacking Karsten's flash drive," I said. "We have to access those files somehow. But we can't forget about the Gable twins either. Not after what we found. Seems like our only move *there* is to identify the playing card. Let's give that a shot before going to the police."

Shelton looked at me funny. "I meant, what are you going to do about *Ben.*"

My mouth formed a hard line. "I plan on having a chat with him. Soon."

Shelton massaged his forehead. "That oughta go well."

I nodded, ignoring his sarcasm. For an instant, I let my fury boil.

I'm gonna rip you a new one, Blue. Count on that.

CHAPTER 12

Five hours later, the bell rang for lunch.

"Thank God." Shoving textbooks into my bag, I trudged for the classroom door.

Shelton and Hi waited in the hallway.

"Need to hit your locker?" Hi asked, straightening his inside-out blazer.

I peered down the hall. Saw Jason Taylor lingering.

Pivoting, I herded the boys in the opposite direction. "I think I'll buy my lunch today."

Running on fumes, I was too brain-dead for banter. Couldn't handle a flirty chat to nowhere. *No offense, Jase.*

"*O-kay.*" Shelton hitched his pack onto his shoulders. "The long way it is."

"So many gentleman admirers," Hi mused. "Must be tough, being a heartbreaker."

"Zip it. Unless you wanna see a leg-breaker, too."

Hi shook his head. "And such violent thoughts. I blame Bravo."

We worked our way around the building, eventually reached the cafeteria's side entrance. Lunch-less, I grabbed a tray and joined the line. Sloppy joe day. Hooray.

Someone poked me between the shoulder blades.

"Sellout!"

I spun, slightly panicked. Ella was standing behind me, a sly grin on her face.

"I thought you were above common cafeteria grub." Twirling, Ella flashed a dimpled smile at the two boys in line behind me. "Okay if I cut? I need to catch up with my friend."

Both stammered their permission. Ella nodded thanks, snagging a tray.

I wish I could do that. Wait, do I?

"So?" Ella asked. "Was it a sloppy joe that called to you, or the microwave pizza?"

"My delicious chicken caesar wrap is currently trapped inside my locker." A slight hesitation, then I leaned closer. "Jason was practically standing guard, and I didn't want to deal."

Ella's mouth puckered. "You're dumb, Brennan. Jason Taylor is hot, cool, and totes into you. Stop being a diva."

I gave a very un-diva-like snort. "Yeah, that's me. A Real Housewife of Charleston."

"I'm serious, missy. Ask me, you could use a little Taylor-touching time." Ella winked one gorgeous green eye. "Might ease the tension in your shoulders."

My ears burned, but I forced a laugh. Ella was only teasing.

And the truth was, I *loved* gabbing like this. Ella was the first real girlfriend I'd had in . . . ages? Ever? I hadn't realized how much I wanted one until she came along.

Don't get me wrong, the Virals were great. Nothing meant more to me than my pack.

But the boys were always . . . well . . . *boys.* There were only so many *Battlestar Galactica* episode debates one girl could take. I'd seen *Varsity Blues* like twelve times.

Reaching the buffet, I surveyed a grim array of greasy offerings. Elected for an all-vegetable plate. The meaty-armed cafeteria lady who served me seemed to take personal offense at my choice. Oh well.

"See you in class!" Ella called as I headed for the register line.

I took another step, then stopped. "Come eat with me."

Ella adopted a mock-serious tone. "Will your bodyguards consent?"

I giggled. "If Shelton and Hi are my muscle, I don't like my chances. And yes."

Ella received her bacon cheeseburger—because, of course, she could eat anything—and the two of us paid. Then we crossed to the Virals table in the back corner of the cafeteria.

Shelton's eyes widened as we approached.

"So I'm not using anything but two-ply from now on," Hi was saying. "Otherwise, the stuff just shreds—"

Noting Shelton's expression, he abruptly cut off. Turned. Went beet red.

"Hey." Sitting down as if nothing was unusual. "You know Ella. Okay if she joins us?"

"Okay if she joins us?" Shelton repeated. "I mean, yes. Join us. Okay."

"I was talking about art supplies," Hi blurted. "I'm into papier-mâché."

"Thanks, guys," Ella said as she sat. "I be *starving.*" She dove into her cheeseburger.

Shelton stared, as if he'd never seen someone eat before. Hi nervously fixed his tie.

I suppressed a snicker, but filed away several choice quips for the next time we were alone. I didn't want to embarrass them now. I understood Ella's effect on the opposite gender.

But later. Whoa boy, there'll be some fun later.

"When are you coming back to practice?" Ella asked between massive bites of her burger. "Coach Lynch understands, but he's getting frustrated at not having his starters together."

"Hopefully next week," I replied, munching a baby carrot.

Honestly, I had no idea. Recent events had pushed my burgeoning athletic career from the back burner to somewhere off the stove completely. But I didn't want to tell Ella that.

"Sports are good," Hi said. "To play, I mean."

Ella paused, mid-bite.

"How's the season going for you?" Hi followed up quickly. "Winning things?"

I winced. *Stop talking, Hi.*

"We haven't started playing games yet," Ella answered patiently. "I think we have enough talent to make the playoffs, if no one gets hurt." She aimed a finger at me. "And if our best players show up."

"I see." Hi nodded sagely. "Make the playoffs. Is that, like, a process?"

Ella eyed him strangely. "Yes, Hiram. Whether we make the playoffs is determined by our number of wins and losses."

"Ah." Another nod. "That seems fair. Good stuff." Hi abruptly busied himself with his sandwich.

Ella flashed me a confused look. Rolling my eyes, I waved off her question.

I'd long since given up trying to explain Hiram Stolowitski.

"You plan on avoiding Jason forever?" Ella spoke through another mouthful of burger. "That doesn't seem like a workable solution."

"No." Idly twirling my fork. "But I don't know how to let him down easy. This isn't an area of personal expertise."

"Direct is always better," Ella said confidently. "Like pulling a Band-Aid. Otherwise feelings get hurt. Then, suddenly, you're not even friends."

"I know you're right. I'm just a wuss. I'm not used to being pursued."

"Please. You could have your pick of these silly little boys. Heck, take two."

Shelton coughed into his fist, eyes glued to his hoagie. I didn't have to be psychic to sense how uncomfortable the girl-talk made him.

Get over it. I listened to you two doofuses handicap a wresting match between Kate Upton and Maria Sharapova. For once, lunch conversation will be my choice.

Ella and I chatted for the next few minutes. I cleaned my plate, surprised by the tastiness of the veggies. Score one for Mrs. Meaty Arms.

The boys ate in silence, though I knew they were listening to every word.

Ella finished her burger and dug into a side of fries. Hi watched, enraptured.

She couldn't help but notice. "Would you like one?"

"What? Sure." Hi smiled, made no move.

After a moment, Ella nudged the bowl his way. "Careful, they're still hot."

"Oh, no problem." Hi fumbled for a fry. "I like food that's hot."

I caught Shelton slowly shaking his head.

"Oh, shoot!" Ella winced. "I forgot to stop by the office. My mother had to drop off my shin guards." She slid her fries over to Hi. "Enjoy. They're hot, which you apparently like."

"Got that right. Hot hot hot!" Hi awkwardly shoved another fry into his mouth.

"Okay, wow." Ella gathered her things, then brushed my cheek with a kiss. "Later, Tor." Shouldering her bag, she hurried from the cafeteria.

A loud thunk drew my attention back to the table.

Hi's forehead was resting on his tray. "Tell me that wasn't as bad as I think."

"Worse," Shelton said. "So, so much worse."

The head rose, then thunked back down. "I don't remember parts. I think I lost time."

I patted his shoulder. "That's probably for the best."

"Such." *Thunk.* "A." *Thunk.* "Dumbass." *Thunk.*

Shelton laughed nervously. "See? That's why I don't talk."

Hi's face shot up. "Tell her I have brain seizures. A serious medical condition. Or that I have an evil twin who sometimes takes my place, but can't talk for crap."

"Got it," I promised. His head dropped once more.

Shelton changed the subject. "So what's our next move?"

I thought a moment. *So many balls in the air.*

Chance. Karsten. Ben. But I had no ideas for any of them.

Those people aren't in danger. The twins surely are.

"We check out Old Man Serpent," I said. "Let's find out who he is, and why his card was on Lucy Gable's bed."

Hi lifted his head halfway. Squinted at me. Nodded.

"Okay." Shelton stroked his chin in thought. "How?"

"A quick fact-finding trip." I downed the last of my Diet Coke. "And I *think* I know just the place."

CHAPTER 13

I skidded to a stop beside a weathered purple rowhouse.

The boys were a few seconds behind, Hi on his skinny Schwinn ten-speed and Shelton pedaling a mud-covered black BMX. Dismounting, I walked my Trek across the gravel lot to a rusty rack at the side of the building.

Bike secured, I checked the rainbow-colored sign hanging out over Center Street.

Fairy Dust Bookstore and Gifts. This was the place.

Folly Beach is the closest population center to Morris Island. The only community on Folly Island, the sleepy little hamlet has a two-street downtown made up of surf shops, boutiques, restaurants, and bars. Monopoly-like houses line the remainder of the island, a haven for laid-back vacationers seeking cheap vacation rentals and peace and quiet. The atmosphere is very chill—nobody moves too fast in Folly Beach.

The Morris bridge connects to Folly, whose police department has nominal jurisdiction over our remote neighborhood. Not that those bozos ever cross to our side. They prefer we look after ourselves.

But we Morris Islanders venture over quite a bit. Folly Beach has the closest grocery store, post office, and takeout pizza. But in all my trips, I'd never stepped inside Fairy Dust.

I'd persuaded Shelton and Hi that a visit there might do some good. Truthfully, I didn't really know. Returning home, we'd ditched our uniforms and biked over, the ride taking less than twenty minutes.

The store's front door was painted red and had a tarnished brass knob. The posted hours were Monday–Thursday, from noon to four, which gave me an idea about the owner. Not exactly a breakneck schedule.

Hi scanned white lettering stenciled on the shop window. "Tarot readings? Belly dancing instruction? Why Tory, it's not even my birthday!"

"Paganism 101." Shelton was frowning at a list of classes taped to the door. "Chakra Balancing. Reiki. Spiritual Counseling. What the hell kinda bookstore is this?"

"New Age." I pulled out my iPhone and read the store's online description. "Fairy Dust is a metaphysical ritual supply store for both pagans and non-pagans alike."

"Pagans?" Shelton tugged his earlobe. "You're talking about witchcraft. Do not like."

"Relax," Hi said. "These are the granola kind of witches. The ones that make herbal tea, and smoke clove cigarettes. I bet we find some killer crystals in there."

"It's a Wicca store," I said, "but the website claims they also have an astrology section. Those are my best guesses for ID-ing our toga-wearing pal. You got a better idea?"

Shelton shook his head. "Spells, though? Dancing in the woods at midnight? Creepy."

"Quit whining, wuss." Hi pointed. "This place *can't* be dangerous. They take Visa."

"Only one way to find out." I pulled open the door and stepped inside.

The tinkle of wind chimes announced our entry. The shop was long and narrow, with wooden shelves lining both walls. Every inch was packed with mysterious items. Books filled the left side of the store, grouped by subject matter—moon phases, dream studies, botany and horticulture, Druidism, the Sacred Wheel. Some designations, like Gaelic Polytheistic Tribalism, I couldn't even follow.

The opposite wall was like a hippie version of Bath and Body Works. Candles. Oils. Incense. Spiritual washes and cleansing waters. Even bags of feathers. Deeper into the store was an eclectic selection of items. An assortment of small cauldrons. Mortar-and-pestle sets. Hundreds of different crystals. Dried herbs. Crushed minerals. Tarot cards. Ouija boards. Rune stones. Hundreds of other things I couldn't peg. The place was certainly interesting.

Astrological items were in back, beside a circular wooden table covered in red felt and flanked by matching chairs. Beyond, a black curtain blocked off the rear of the building.

"This place is a tourist trap," Hi said. "You can get most of this stuff at an Indian casino."

"It still gives me the willies." Shelton tapped a cloth package hanging from an iron hook. "I've never heard of Bat's Heart Root, but I don't want it near me."

I was admiring a crushed-velvet star chart when the curtain parted. A young, brown-haired woman emerged. She had gray eyes, a small mouth, and wore an old-fashioned green dress that fell past her knees. She considered us a moment before approaching.

"You three looking for something specific?" Her voice was surprisingly melodious.

"Any sacrificial knives?" Hi raised an index finger. "Nothing too fancy, and I'll need a solid, no-slip grip. Me and the coven have some goats lined up for Saturday's bonfire."

I could've kicked him. I think I tried. Fortunately, the woman laughed.

"A comedian, eh?" she said dryly. "I *do* have some new knife-ware, actually, but for chopping herbs, not blood sacrifice. That's one of the many myths about witches that simply isn't truth. Wiccans respect the sanctity of *all* life. Animals are part of the same natural cycle as humans. I won't even eat one. My name is Clara. How about telling me what it is you're looking for?"

I slipped the photocopy from my pocket and handed it over. "We'd like to learn about this symbol."

Clara glanced at the page. Her eyes widened slightly. Then she looked up, subjecting the three of us to an entirely new level of scrutiny.

"You recognize the figure." I didn't phrase it as a question.

"Of course." Clara's free hand rose, fluttered aimlessly, as if she was unsure what to say next. For some reason, I thought she might ask us to leave.

I broke out my "earnest" face. "Any guidance you could provide would be greatly appreciated."

"Yes. Certainly." Clara gave her head a slight shake. "Please, sit. I'll grab more chairs."

She slipped behind the curtain and was gone.

"She got weird," Hi whispered. "But looking at this shop, that's not much of a shocker."

I nodded. Something about Snake Man had set Clara on edge.

"Of course she's being crazy—she's a witch, man!" Shelton face was pinched. "We need to get *gone,* before she comes back with her broom."

Fabric swished. Clara emerged carrying a pair of folding chairs.

"May I ask your names?"

We each took a seat as Clara placed the photocopy on the felt.

"Tory Brennan. These two are Hi and Shelton."

Clara nodded with each name. "This isn't a tarot reading, or a fortune-telling session, but I think that, under the circumstances, the same rates will apply. Forty dollars, please."

"*Forty doll—*"

I kicked Hi under the table. "No problem."

I nodded to Shelton. Grumbling, he dug out his wallet and forked over two twenties. Virals funds. We let Shelton be the bank.

"Excellent." The bills disappeared into the folds of Clara's dress. "So. What would you like to know?"

My finger tapped the paper. "Who is this guy?"

"That is Ophiuchus, thirteenth symbol of the zodiac."

"Hold up, lady." Hi gave her a sideways look. "As a proud Aries, I know there are only twelve zodiac signs."

"Incorrect," Clara replied, with some amusement. "And, FYI, you're likely *not* an Aries, though it's understandable how you've gotten it wrong your whole life. Most people have."

Hi sat up straight. "Excuse me?"

Clara adopted a lecturing tone. "Ophiuchus is one of thirteen constellations that cross the ecliptic at the celestial equator and, therefore, has been called the thirteenth sign of the zodiac." She cocked her head slightly. "That's not *quite* right, as it confuses signs with constellations, but it's basically accurate."

I scratched the back of my head. "I'm not following."

"Let's start with the basics," Clara said. "The *ecliptic* is an imaginary line that marks the path of our sun through the sky. It's mathematically predictable, in relation to the earth's orbit."

"Okay." I understood that.

"Now, imagine every star in the heavens as part of a great dome surrounding our planet. That's known as the celestial sphere. As the sun travels through our sky, astrologers pay attention to where it is in relation to the sphere. Specifically, they mark which constellations the sun passes directly through."

"You lost me," Shelton admitted.

Clara thought a moment. "Close your eyes. All of you."

After a few skeptical looks, we complied.

"Imagine you're riding a carousel. On horses, you swing in circles around the ride's central pillar. Watch the pillar a moment, then look *past* it, focusing on what appears behind it as you spin. A roller coaster. A ticket booth. A cotton candy stand. As you rotate, the scene changes until you complete the circuit and begin again. Now, replace the horses with planet Earth, the pillar with our sun, and the amusement park with the stars."

"I *think* I get it." Hi opened his eyes. "Because our planet is always spinning around the sun, the stars we see behind it change, depending on where we are in the Earth's orbit."

"Perfectly said." Clara spread her hands. "And that's how the zodiac constellations were determined."

"How did they pick?" Shelton asked. "Aren't there lots of constellations?"

"But only a handful through which the sun *directly* passes," she explained. "Twelve were selected as the tropical zodiac, which is the version most people are familiar with."

"You said people confuse signs with constellations," I stated. "What did you mean?"

"The current zodiac *signs* are a mathematically equal, twelve-way division of the ecliptic, aligned with the seasons. The dates for each have been set in stone. The *constellations,* however, are unequal in size, and based on the actual positions of the stars. They generally don't coincide with their signs anymore. For example, the constellation of Aquarius now largely corresponds to the sign of Pisces. This is because the time of year when the sun passes through Aquarius has slowly changed over the centuries, from when the ancient Greeks and Babylonians originally developed the zodiac. But the *sign* Aquarius has remained fixed to certain dates."

Shelton glanced at me askance. I didn't get it either.

Clara smiled. "Simply put, the dates for zodiac signs are no longer properly aligned with their constellations. The *whole* system is off-kilter."

Hi was wide-eyed. "Lady, you just blew my mind. You're saying I might *not* be an Aries? What? My birthday is this weekend! I've got all this ram crap at my house. My planet is Mars. My element is fire. It all fits!"

"Sorry, kid." Her eyes flicked to a giant star chart on the wall. "Next week, you said? Turns out you're really a Pisces."

"Pisces!?" Hiram's hands flew up. "A damn fish? No freaking way!"

"Tell me about the snake man." I wanted to get the meeting back on track.

"Ophiuchus is a sad story," Clara replied. "He was omitted from the tropical zodiac centuries ago, but remains in the heavens, and continues to hold sway. He occupies most of the days currently assigned to Sagittarius."

"Hold up." Shelton stared at Clara over the rim of his glasses. "*I'm* a Sagittarius."

"Birthdate?"

"November thirtieth."

Clara chuckled. "My dear boy, *you* are an Ophiuchan!"

"Am *not*," Shelton shot back, hugging his sides. "I *hate* snakes. Ask anyone."

"Sorry, dear. But the sun rises in Ophiuchus from November twenty-ninth to December seventeenth."

"That's one opinion." Shelton snatched off his glasses and wiped them on his shirt. "I'm gonna need a discount double-check on this stuff."

I waved for Clara's attention. "Ophiuchus?"

She turned to me. "The classical form of Ophiuchus is described by Manilius in his poem *Astronomica*: 'He holds apart the serpent, which with its mighty spirals and twisted body encircles his own, so that he may untie its knots and back that winds in loops. But, bending its supple neck, the serpent looks back and returns: and the other's hands slide over the loosened coils.' Their struggle will last forever, since man and serpent have equal power."

"Wait." Hi finger-jabbed the table. "Just stop. Before I accept that my entire life has been a lie, explain to me *exactly* how I'm not a freaking Aries."

Clara folded her hands on the table. "Slight changes in the Earth's wobbly orbit, over millennia, mean that our planet is no longer aligned to the stars in the same position as when the zodiac table was first conceived. In some cases the dates are nearly a month off, and that's not including those poor souls like Shelton, whose sign is rightly Ophiuchus, the thirteen symbol."

"Allegedly," Shelton snapped.

"Does Obama know about this?" Hi demanded, hands gripping his head. "How could this be true and *everyone* not know it? Am I speaking with a crazy woman?"

"This isn't groundbreaking," Clara replied. "It's two-thousand-year-old information to astronomers, and one of the reasons they mock astrology. But the ancient tropical zodiac has never been changed. People have grown attached to their incorrect signs."

"Not incorrect!" Hi insisted. "I'm an Aries. Everything about me *screams* Aries. I like diamonds. I live for the thrill of the moment. I'm adventurous, active, and outgoing. *It all fits.*"

"No need to get worked up." Clara reached under the table, retrieved a handout, and slid it over to Hi. "Take this, if you'd like to learn more. The zodiac's configuration has always been *somewhat* arbitrary. Constellations have shifted many times over the centuries, as has the sun's path through them, allowing for a wider range of signs than just twelve, or even thirteen. Ophiuchus was only excluded to begin with because the ancient Babylonians liked the symmetry of twelve astrological signs."

Hi looked to me, then Shelton. "I do *not* like this. My sign is *my sign.* It's not variable!"

"You're not the one stuck with the snake dude," Shelton groaned.

"Tell us more about Ophiuchus himself," I asked. "Specifically."

Clara glanced at the ceiling in thought. "The 'Serpent Bearer' appears in forms of sidereal astrology, which calculates the zodiac by using fixed stars instead of the celestial equator, showing the sun's true position against the constellations. This is very popular in Japan, where Ophiuchus is known as Hebitsukai-Za."

"Oh, snap!" Shelton sat forward. "I've heard of this dude. He's in Final Fantasy Legend!"

Blank stares from me and Clara.

"A video game series," Shelton explained. "From Japan. Hi knows. It's big."

Hi waved away Shelton's comment. "This whole meeting is under protest."

"However," Clara continued, "even mainstream sidereal astrology—which includes Hindu and sun-sign astrology—still use the traditional twelve-sign zodiac. Correctly realigned, of course, but dividing the heavens into twelve equal parts, rather than using constellational boundaries. Therefore, even those systems do not regard Ophiuchus as a true sign. But the sun rises in him every winter. That's a fact."

"If Ophiuchus *was* a thirteenth sign," I asked, "what would the associated characteristics be? What would it mean to have him as your zodiac symbol?"

Shelton huffed loudly, but I could tell he was paying attention.

"That's harder to answer. The Serpent Bearer has been excluded for millennia, and isn't regularly interpreted." She tapped her lip in thought. "Also known as Serpentarius, Ophiuchus has an affinity with snakes, obviously, and is said to offer protection from poisons. He's been associated with doctors and healers, likely because of the similarity between poison and medicine."

"Don't like snakes," Shelton grumbled. "Though Serpentarius sounds kind of awesome."

Clara flared a brow. "An Ophiuchan seeks wisdom and knowledge, has a flamboyant fashion sense, and usually doesn't reject authority. Twelve is the lucky number. They make great architects, have large families, and leave home at an early age. That's about all I can tell you."

I thought about everything Clara had said.

Interesting, all of it, but not helpful.

The info told me nothing about the Gables' disappearance.

"What type of person would be drawn to Ophiuchus?" I asked. "Who would the Serpent Bearer appeal to?"

"A poisoner, obviously." Clara stood, face troubled. "Beyond that, I can't say. And your time is now up. Please excuse me."

And like that, she spun and dipped through the black curtain.

"Um, bye." I was stunned by the woman's hasty retreat. "Thank you!"

"Stranger and stranger." Shelton popped from his seat. "That's all for me, folks. I'm out."

"I don't wanna be a stupid fish," Hi whined, trudging to the door behind Shelton.

I followed the boys outside, trying to digest what we'd learned.

A lost astrological sign? Snakes? A poisoner? How did any of it fit?

Maybe the zodiac has nothing to do with the twins at all.

But why had Clara reacted so strangely? Twice. I felt sure there were pieces missing here.

My thoughts were interrupted by the screech of tires on gravel.

I whirled. Ben's beat-up Explorer was idling ten feet behind me.

He leaned out the window. "You clowns need a lift?"

"No." I turned furious eyes on Shelton and Hi.

Shelton cracked first. "I told him. He's still a part of this, too, right?"

Before I could answer, Ben cut me off.

"Don't flip out, Victoria." He wore a satisfied smile. "I have news."

My hands found my hips. "Well?"

"Still wanna hack into Karsten's flash drive?" Ben asked innocently.

"Of course."

"Good. Because I can make it happen."

CHAPTER 14

Clara Gordon watched the kids load bicycles into an SUV.

They drove off. She exhaled, stepping away from the window.

Who'd have thought? *Exactly* as described. And so soon!

Clara rubbed her arms to quiet a rash of goose bumps. The whole business had her on edge.

A reading. Before I do anything.

Clara strode to a mahogany cabinet. Closing her eyes, she mumbled an incantation under her breath. Then she unlocked the door, removed a cloth-wrapped bundle, and returned to the table where she'd spoken to her vistors.

I shouldn't have done that. I may have said too much.

Clara unwound the sky-blue velvet, revealing a worn set of tarot cards. Hand-painted. French. Seventeenth century. A gift from her mentor only days before passing, Clara considered them her most precious possession in the world.

Clara shuffled the cards slowly, emptying her mind of distraction.

It'd been weeks since she'd done a personal reading.

Why? She carefully cut the deck, then placed the stacked cards on the red felt surface. *Am I hiding something from myself?*

Deep breath. Deep breath. Give thanks.

She allowed a question to crystalize in her mind. Clear. Concise. Simple.

Then, grounded and centered, she fanned out the cards. Flipped one at random.

The Tower.

Clara felt a chill travel her spine. A card of the Major Arcana, the Tower meant disaster. Upheaval. The destruction of peace and harmony.

Easy, now. Not always.

The symbol could also represent sudden change. Or revelation. The Tower energy was both a destructive *and* creative force.

Old attitudes and beliefs, perhaps? Something that must be let go, liked or not?

Troubled, Clara flipped a second card.

Justice. Reversed.

Clara's alarm grew. A second card of the Major Arcana. A rare occurrence.

This reading spoke of more than a mere day-to-day experience. That much was clear.

The cards foretold a life-changing event, with long-term influences.

Focus. The lesson here is important.

The inversion altered the card's meaning. Upside down, Justice stood for unfairness. Dishonesty. Lack of accountability. *To myself, or others?*

Clara thought furiously. Had she'd failed to scrutinize her own actions? Was she trying to dodge a bullet, or blame another for her mistake?

The key is to take responsibility. But how?

She thought of the two cards in conjunction. The Tower. Justice, reversed.

Disaster and Dishonesty. Upheaval and Unfairness.

The answer she'd sought abruptly smacked her in the face.

Those kids. The charge. Of course.

Clara nearly ended the reading right there, but some instinct compelled her to continue. Hands shaking, she flipped the last card in the deck.

And flinched. The chill on her spine morphed to an electric shock.

A *third* card of the Major Arcana. In ten years of readings, that had never happened.

The image grinned up at her. An armored skeleton, mounted on a white horse.

Death.

Clara moaned softly, though she knew the card wasn't literal. Death merely indicated that a significant transformation awaited. Change. Transition.

The end of something. But what will replace it?

Clara stared at the three cards. Tower. Justice. Death. She'd not flip a fourth.

Something profound was happening. Something that could go terribly wrong.

Disaster. Deceit. Change.

The message is clear. Do as instructed.

Clara gathered the cards and returned them to the cabinet. Grabbing her keys, she locked the shop and hurried to her car.

Do as instructed.

Three cards. All Major Arcana. Each fraught with danger.

She fired the engine, then spun from the parking lot, heading north.

Clara Gordon raced downtown like a bat out of hell.

CHAPTER 15

"Tory, you're a Capricorn now, so you'll have to accept an affinity for goats."

"Thanks, Hi. I think I'll be fine."

In the rearview, I saw Hi shake his head. "You're just being stubborn, like the Aquarius you *used* to be. But your days as a water bearer are over. It's time to accept and move on."

"I can't believe you follow that garbage." Ben turned onto the James Island Expressway. From there we'd link up with 17 North, cross the peninsula, and then traverse the massive Arthur Ravenel Jr. Bridge to Mount Pleasant.

"This affects you, too, pal." Hi snapped his fingers. "Like that, you've jumped from Capricorn to Sagittarius. Which suits you well, since you're both cocky *and* reckless. Plus, you look like a centaur."

"See this?" Ben glanced at the mirror and pointed to his chin. "This is my 'couldn't care less' face."

"Philistine." Hi turned to Shelton, with whom he shared the back-seat. "Tell me you've debunked this outrage by now."

"Unfortunately, the witch is right." Shelton glowered at his iPhone.

"About all of it, even Sir Snake Sleeves. But nobody seems to care. The first article I found is from 2010."

"No one cares because it's *astrology*." Ben rolled his eyes. "The whole concept is dumb, so who cares if it's accurate?"

"All *we* should care about," I cut in, "is whether Ophiuchus has anything to do with the Gable twins' disappearance. Whether that card is a clue, or not."

Shelton scratched his cheek. "I'm not saying I know her well, but radical astrology? Doesn't seem like something Lucy Gable would be into. Or Peter."

"Agreed." Still shunning Ben, I aimed my words at Hi and Shelton. "So the question becomes, did someone intentionally leave that card in Lucy's room? And if so, why?"

No one had an answer. We drove the next few miles in silence.

Hi broke it as we entered Mount Pleasant. "What's this guy's name again?"

"Eddie Chang," Ben replied. "I heard about him at Wando. He used to go there, and apparently he now makes fake IDs, rips movies and music, that kind of stuff. This dude I know says Chang is a serious hacker, too. Maybe even a member of Anonymous."

"So we don't really know anything about him," I said. To the windshield.

Ben's expression hardened. "You said we needed to hack the drive. I found a hacker."

I didn't respond, but mentally conceded the point. It's not like I had a better plan.

Ben turned into the parking lot of a run-down apartment building, one of a handful in the otherwise wealthy community. The brick-and-concrete box rose ten depressing stories, bristling with rusty metal balconies.

I knew Ben's mother rented an apartment somewhere close by. Was it like this building? Suddenly, I couldn't believe I'd never seen the place where Ben spent half the life.

"This is it." Ben killed the engine.

"You been here before?" Shelton asked, nervously eyeing the complex.

Ben shook his head. "My friend Ronnie has. He bought a killer fake from Chang."

He got out and slammed his door. Without other options, we hurried after him, across the cracked and crumbling blacktop to a glass-enclosed entry a dozen yards away.

We slipped through a pair of blurry glass doors into a small foyer. A second Plexiglas-and-steel barrier barred further access. A dingy call box was bolted to the wall beside it. Above the box, a metal-encased security camera glared down at us.

"Jeez," Hi muttered. "This feels like a gas station in Compton."

Ben pulled a scrap of paper from his pocket, read, then punched a four-digit code into the call box. It began to ring. At the same time, a red light appeared on the side of the camera.

A click. Static.

"Yeah?"

Ben cleared his throat. "I'm here to see Eddie Chang."

"Wrong number." There was a second click as the line disconnected.

Shelton shifted his weight. "Um, okay."

Ben glanced at the paper, then winced. "Damn. Hold on."

He jabbed the keys again. This time, no one picked up for several rings.

CLICK.

"Yes?" Irritated.

"I'm here to see . . . Variance. About a model airplane."

Dead air.

Buzz. The interior door swung open.

Ben waved us into a gloomy lobby. Spotting a decrepit-looking elevator, he mashed the up button.

I had a thousand questions, but held my tongue.

I will not *speak to you, Ben Blue.*

We rode to the ninth floor, where Ben led us down a drab floral-papered hallway to the last unit on the right.

The reinforced door had steel plates screwed into the wood. A newer, more expensive-looking video camera was mounted above its frame. It swiveled as we approached, tracking our progress down the corridor.

"Who is this guy?" Shelton whispered. "Are we in the Matrix?"

"I'm not taking any blue pills," Hi warned. "Zion sucked."

"Just be cool." Ben was about to knock when static poured from a speaker on the camera.

"Who are you?" a voice demanded.

"My name is Ben. My friend Ronnie said you can . . . provide certain services."

The lens panned left, then right, scanning the group. "Who are they? Why'd you bring them here?"

Ben shrugged. "Our project involves all of us. We have money."

The camera froze for a moment, then swung back toward the elevator bank.

A full minute passed.

"*Welp.*" Hi stretched. "This was fun. Anyone want to hit that Arby's on the—"

A series of bangs. The jangle of a large chain. Then the armored door swung inward.

I peered into the apartment. Saw no one.

"This is buggin' me out," Shelton whispered. "Let's bail."

"C'mon." Ben strode inside, forcing the rest of us to follow.

The unit was small. Beside the front door was a phone-booth-sized bathroom. Ahead was a modest living room crammed with computer equipment.

And I mean *crammed.* Racks of hardware lined the walls and covered every square inch of the baseboards. The sheer quantity of it put our modest bunker setup to shame. In the far corner, a narrow hallway led to the rear of the apartment, which presumably contained a kitchen and bedroom.

The living room's only furniture was a sprawling circular workstation, the kind used by fancy corporate receptionists. It held an array of monitors, laptops, modems, and drives, along with other devices and gizmos I couldn't identify.

Sitting in the center was an Asian man with spiky black hair and blue eyes. I guessed his age at maybe twenty. Chang wore a gray sweatshirt, cargo shorts, and diamond studs in both ears. Mandarin characters tattooed both his forearms.

"You're Ben?" Chang's voice was soft.

"I am. You're Eddie Chang?"

Chang smiled. "For this request, I'm known as Variance. Did you bring the flash drive?"

Ben nodded, then snapped his fingers in my direction.

"You told him?" I hissed, furious. The snap hadn't helped. "Just like that?"

Ben gave me an exasperated look. "How else was I supposed to explain the job?"

"Relax," Chang said smoothly. "You're Tory, I presume?"

He knows my name. Damn it, Ben.

"I am." Icy. "I take it Ben has already explained what we want?"

"Yes. And don't worry, I'm a pro. Cracking files is what I do, and I know how to keep my mouth shut." Chang leaned forward. "A trait I expect *your* party to emulate. Clear?"

"Clear," I said.

"No problem at all." Hi stared at our host with something close to awe. "And if you need, like, an assistant on weekends, or something, I'm your man. I know how to brew coffee."

"True that." Shelton was eyeballing Chang's equipment, his prior reservations forgotten. "This is the coolest place I've ever seen in my life."

Chang winked. "Thanks, guys, but I work alone. It's a hacker thing. Now let's get down to business, shall we?"

Ben nodded my direction. "She has the drive."

"We'll get to that. You said you have the money?"

"Five hundred," Ben replied. "As agreed."

"Excellent. Now would be a perfect time to hand it over."

Ben looked to Shelton, who scrambled for his wallet. He handed Chang a thick wad of twenties we'd withdrawn before leaving Folly Beach.

"Cash is going fast these days," Shelton muttered. "Better be worth it."

"Thank you, sir." Then Chang gave me an expectant look.

I hesitated. The contents of Karsten's flash drive could potentially devastate our lives.

"We have to show it to someone," Ben said quietly.

Ben was right. Sighing, I dug the drive from my pocket and extended it to the hacker.

Pulled it back just as his fingers drew near.

"One condition."

Chang smiled wryly. "Of course."

"You don't read the decrypted files. Ever. If you *can* access them, that is."

"Fine." He shrugged. "Honestly, I'm not all that interested."

I dropped the drive into his open palm.

"Much obliged." Chang popped the data stick into a USB drive and began tapping keys.

"The files are encrypted," Shelton said. "Commercial grade."

"I imagine so," Chang quipped, "or you wouldn't need me. First step is to determine how tightly the windows are nailed shut."

Minutes passed as Chang typed, studied the screen, typed, then studied more. Then he swiveled his chair, his fingers hammering a second keyboard. A stream of characters filled the monitor to his right.

Finally, Chang rubbed his chin. "Well, this isn't the kiddie stuff I expected."

"Can you explain what you're doing?" I asked.

Chang spun back to face us. "What do you know about file encryption?"

"Almost nothing," I admitted. "That's Shelton's department."

I felt Shelton swell beside me, but he didn't speak. A trainee does not interrupt a master explaining his craft.

"Encryption is the process of encoding information so that only a person with the proper key can read it." Chang tapped the monitor filled with letters and numbers. "Computer encryption is based on traditional cryptology, which has been around forever. Microchips just give it more juice."

"So it's just fancy codes," I said. "And the ciphers needed to unlock them."

We had some experience on those counts.

"Exactly. Online, ciphers are called algorithms. They allow a user to craft a message and give a certain range of possible combinations. A key, on the other hand, helps the user figure out the one correct answer on any given occasion."

I followed so far. "So what's on this flash drive?"

Chang pointed to a monitor on the opposite side of the workstation. "These files are protected by a simple symmetric-key encryption. To open them, we have to match the key used by the originating system."

"So you need to crack the code."

"Of course. But there's a problem."

Chang leaned back in his chair. "The strength of any key is determined by the length of its code, which is measured in bits. I can crack any 56-bit DES system with brute force, and that's working through seventy quadrillion possible combinations."

Hi whistled. "I take it you don't type them in, one at a time."

"Not on your life. But that's not what we're facing here. These files are protected by an AES key system. A real nasty one, too, with 128-bit keys. That's more combinations. A *lot* more."

"How many?" Shelton asked.

Chang grinned. "A brute force attack—trying all possible combinations one at a time—would have to cycle through 3.4 × 10 to the 38th power number of keys. The human mind can't grasp a number that big."

I blinked. "That sounds impossible."

"It *is* impossible. That's the point. Even with a supercomputer, it'd take a billion billion years to run all those combinations. Exponentially longer than the universe has existed."

I gave him a flat look. "So how are you going to beat the encryption?"

Chang thumb-tapped the desktop. "I could look for a cheat algorithm, to give me some portion of the key, but even that wouldn't help much against 128-bit encryption. I'll have to use a backdoor instead."

My arms crossed. "Backdoor?"

"Some encryption programs have a weakness," Chang explained. "A way around the system-key construct. A shortcut, if you will, that bypasses the need for matching keys altogether. Programmers use these backdoors to get into and out of their programs during coding. Many leave one of those secret ways intact, even after they're finished, in case they want to poke around in the future."

"Seriously?" I scoffed. "That's pretty dishonest."

Chang laughed. "Most programmers grew up as hackers. It's in the blood, so to speak."

"That's *awesome,*" Hi said. "So does this system have a backdoor?"

Chang smiled wide, exposing a row of pearly whites. "It does. I recognize this encryption system, and, more importantly, I know who wrote it. He's a weird guy, lives in a Soho loft filled with goldfish tanks."

My pulse began to race. "And you have this backdoor?"

"Yes. For a price."

"We agreed to five hundred," Ben growled.

"That was before. Now you're asking for the crown jewels."

"How much?" I demanded.

Chang met my eye. "Five thousand. Cash. Non-negotiable."

Damn it.

"Fine."

What choice did we have?

⬡ ⬡ ⬡

"They're back." Chang reached beneath his super-desk and pressed a button.

The door buzzed, then swung open. Shelton and Ben entered.

"Any problems at the bank?" I asked.

Shelton shook his head, handed me two bound stacks of hundred-dollar bills. "We're getting close to tapped out, though. I hope this is worth it."

Me too.

I slapped the cash onto the desktop. "Here. Now get to work."

"Already done."

Chang handed me an unlabeled CD in a clear plastic case. "All files, decrypted and ready for viewing. Unread, as agreed."

"The flash drive?"

His blue eyes danced with amusement. "Almost forgot."

Chang was about to remove the drive when something caught his attention.

"Hold up." He scooted to the closest monitor, hands searching for a keyboard.

"Yes?" I asked.

"There's something . . . else on this drive. It's odd. Here."

An image flashed onscreen—a scrambled list of folders and subfiles.

I leaned over the desktop for a better view. "Did you miss those?"

Chang shook his head. "This is a shadow file tree. Those files aren't physically contained on this data stick, but they can be accessed by it."

Shelton joined me by the monitor. "I don't understand."

"This drive *can* access those files," he explained, "but not remotely. The documents listed here are actually stored on a server located somewhere else. To read them, you'd have to insert this drive into that specific server."

Chang eyed me curiously. "This is *extremely* sophisticated. Military grade, or something else that's ultra-secure like medical records, or corporate R and D. *256-bit encryption.* What kind of files are these?"

"That's not part of our deal," I replied frostily.

Chang nodded, but the speculative looked didn't fade.

"So you can't open them?" Ben said.

"No. No one else can, either. What you see are similar to links, but they won't work online. To open those files, you'd have to physically connect to their home network. And I'd bet my PlayStation it's a closed system, which means you'd have to actually be in the server room."

"Can you tell us anything else?" I pressed.

Chang was silent for several heartbeats. "Maybe. Hold on a minute."

More like ten.

Chang typed. Grunted. Rotated among his stations. Even consulted a three-ring binder.

“Here’s what I got,” he said finally. “It’s not much. These shadow files were created within the last three months, by a different user from the batch I just decoded for you. But I can’t identify either one. Your drive appears to be a legacy key to another system, in another network. Theoretically, it can still access the servers.”

I straightened. “Three months old? From a different user?”

That made no sense. Karsten obviously didn’t open new files.

Then who did?

And how would *new* files be linked to Karsten’s mothballed parvovirus experiment?

“That’s right.” Chang shrugged. “But I can’t open them. As I said, you’d have to find the server to match the encryption key. What’s strange is that, when I got past the encryption, this file tree downloaded *itself* onto your flash drive. That’s high-tech synchronization, even though you can’t access the content.”

“And there’s no explanation of what the files are, or where they’re from?”

“No. Just a group heading. B-Series.”

B-Series? Why did that send a jolt to my nerves?

“If you let me keep the stick,” Chang said, “I might be able to find the server.”

“No,” I said instantly. Then, “No, thank you. We’ll take it from here. Can I have the drive back please?”

An odd look twisted Chang’s features. Annoyance? Frustration?

Before I could say more, he spun and tapped a few keys. Data streamed across all four monitors, then they all went blank.

Chang removed Karsten’s drive and handed it to me.

“Good luck. Change your mind, and you know where to find me.”

With a series of waves and mumbled thanks, we made our way out.

All the way down to Ben’s car, my thoughts raced.

We had Karsten’s files! Finally.

But what was this B-Series? Who was running active files, ones that magically appeared on Karsten's old data stick? Who else even *knew* about Karsten's secret work?

"Success." Ben clicked on his seat belt. "You're welcome, by the way."

I nodded, distracted. Not quite sharing his enthusiasm.

We had what we came for. The mission was a success.

So why did I have a sinking feeling?

CHAPTER 16

Dinnertime snuck up on me.

Whitney pounced as soon as I opened the front door, foreclosing any notion of examining Karsten's files right away.

"You ready to eat, dear?" She wore a pink taffeta dress with matching flats. To dinner. On a Wednesday. At home.

Suppressing a groan, I allowed myself to be ushered to the table.

Kit was sitting on the couch watching *Jeopardy*, drinking a glass of red wine. Whitney continued to putter about, setting out dishes and straightening the place settings. The whole scene felt *very* domestic, like a glimpse into my future.

That thought nearly sent me screaming down the beach.

Coop trotted over and brushed against my leg.

"Hey, dog face." I knelt and rubbed his cold, wet nose.

Cooper yipped. Pawed at my shoulder.

"I know. I left you behind today. Sorry about that."

Whitney was smoothing her dress, a stink-eye on the wolfdog. "The table is set, sweetie."

"One sec."

I scurried upstairs, unzipped my bag, and shoved the CD and flash drive into a desk drawer. Then I trudged back down, bracing for an hour of forced smiles and stilted conversation.

That evening's spread was pork chops with country ham gravy, green beans, and Gouda mac and cheese. We don't eat healthy, but we damn sure eat well.

"Anything interesting going on, kiddo?" Kit dug into his meal. "We missed you at dinner yesterday." He left the question unspoken.

Oh, sure, Kit, lots! The gang and I broke into Lucy and Peter Gable's house last night and discovered a bloodstain the size of Texas, but were chased off by a stalker before we could be 100 percent sure. This afternoon, we took a clue Hi swiped from the district attorney's office—the only piece of evidence in the twins' disappearance—and had a witch look it over. After that we stopped by a hacker's apartment to break in to your old boss's research files. You know, the ones from his secret medical experiment, which accidentally gave me superpowers. How was your day at LIRI?

"No. Same old."

Kit nodded as if he'd expected my response. "I'm just glad the trial is over. Things can finally get back to normal."

"Here, here!" Whitney, hand to chest. Then she folded her napkin and placed it on the table. "Now, Tory, please don't get upset."

"Upset?" Not a good opener.

"You've been distracted lately, so I took it upon myself to help you along with the Magnolia League. I filled out all the paperwork for you, so it wouldn't be a bother."

My eyes closed. Snapped open.

I didn't scream. Didn't stomp my foot. Didn't storm from the table.

At this point, we were past all that.

Instead, I met Whitney's gaze directly. "You anticipated this would upset me."

"Whit's just trying to be helpful." Kit's hazel eyes were pleading.

"Thank you for explaining her actions," I said coolly. "Again."

Whitney's lips parted, but I raised a hand for silence.

Awkward pause. Then I slowly shook my head.

In the end, I *always* lost these battles. Why bother fighting them?

Sighing, I speared a green bean on my plate. "What *exactly* is this going to entail?"

Whitney goggled at my unexpected surrender, but quickly recovered. "Being a Magnolia isn't hardly work at all. You'll *love* it! First-year girls attend two chapter meetings a month, then perhaps join a committee, or help organize a charitable event."

"The deadline is approaching fast, and those ladies are sticklers for rules." Her shoulders tensed, as if expecting a blow. "I went ahead and submitted your application yesterday."

I couldn't help but laugh. "Of course you did."

Whitney nervously giggled with me, but her eyes betrayed her anxiety.

Screw it. Done is done.

"I assume you'll let me know their response?"

Whitney covered her mouth with both hands, as if she couldn't believe her luck. A child who'd gotten a coveted Christmas present. "Tory, you're *assured* of acceptance. Trust me."

Whitney unleashed a torrent of words about all the "rewarding" activities the Magnolia League had to offer. As she droned on and on, something nudged my foot under the table.

Kit's loafer.

I glanced at my dad. He mouthed a thank-you.

My eyes nearly rolled through the ceiling, but I nodded. We both knew this would make life easier.

"And we can go shopping for hats!" Whitney prattled. "I know a *great* boutique on King Street that will have just the thing, plus—"

"You owe me," I whispered from the side of mouth.

Kit nodded ruefully. "I know it."

"What's that?" Whitney, just now discovering she'd been talking to herself. "Tory, you'll still help with the neighborhood party, won't you?"

Ugh. I'd forgotten that gem. Though, admittedly, it wasn't her worst idea.

"Yes, Whitney. Just let me know what you need."

"Wonderful! We should've hosted an event like this *ages* ago." She tapped her bottom lip with a manicured fingernail. "I think invitations would be fitting, even though everyone lives close. We can hand deliver them."

As Whitney ramped back up, something in the living room caught my eye.

Breaking News was interrupting Alex Trebek.

"*Ssh Ssh Ssh!*" I pointed to the television.

"Good evening," intoned the same oily anchorman, with all the grave solemnity he could muster. "There's been a shocking development in the disappearance of Lucy and Peter Gable. In a *Channel Five News* exclusive, we've obtained footage from a *ransom video*, received by police officials mere hours ago, confirming that the Bolton Academy twins have been forcibly abducted."

"Oh my God!" I shot from my seat and ran to the screen.

"A warning to our sensitive viewers." If possible, the anchorman's face grew even more somber. "The following images are disturbing. You may wish to look away."

A grainy image appeared. I watched in horror.

It was a boy and a girl, trapped behind rusty metal bars in a stone chamber. The five-second clip contained a single shot of their dirty, haggard faces.

I recognized both.

We were right.

The enormity of the video sank in.

This was no game we were playing. No lark to kill time, or soothe my frustrated psyche. The Gable twins' lives were hanging by a thread. Two kids I saw nearly every day.

The anchorman's face filled the screen. "Channel Five News has confirmed that a ransom demand of five million dollars accompanied the video."

The program cut to an apoplectic Commissioner Riggins, barking into a half-dozen microphones shoved before his face.

"This tape is part of an *ongoing police investigation*," he snapped. "Releasing it publicly was *highly* irresponsible. I ask the media to *please* respect the gravity of the situation, and make no unauthorized disclosures that could further jeopardize the safety of these children. I will personally investigate these leaks. And when I find who's responsible, they'll be prosecuted!"

Beside Riggins stood Detective Hawfield, arms crossed and visibly seething.

Big week for Channel Five. They must have a solid source at police HQ.

The anchorman resumed, without the slightest twinge of guilt. "Tune in this evening for up-to-the-minute details of the astonishing Gable twins' kidnapping. Good evening."

Final Jeopardy blipped back onscreen. I sat down, stunned.

Kit was by my side immediately. "You okay, Tor? Do you know those kids?"

"I'm fine." Trying to pull myself together. "We have a few classes together."

"How dreadful!" I was surprised to see tears leaking from Whitney's eyes. "Those poor babies!"

Kit seemed about to say more, but I needed to process.

"I'm going to my room." I bolted upstairs before they could say more.

My door closed with a bang. I heard Kit climb halfway up in pursuit, then stop. A few beats passed, then he slowly descended back to the main floor.

I sat in my chair, mind-blown. Everything was suddenly real, and I didn't like it.

Then do *something about it.*

But what?

Then I knew.

Before, there'd only been one piece of evidence.

Now there were two.

And the Virals needed both if we hoped to help Lucy and Peter.

A plan began to form. The boys weren't going to like it.

But a simple truth was inescapable: we needed a look at that videotape.

And there's no time like the present, right?

CHAPTER 17

The Explorer's dashboard clock read 1:00 a.m.

"Now or never," Ben murmured.

I didn't move. Watched the building across from where we'd parked.

This was unquestionably the riskiest stunt we'd ever considered pulling.

Charleston Police Headquarters is tucked away on the northwestern edge of the downtown peninsula, overlooking the Ashley River. The compound consists of several structures of various size, shape, and level of security.

Some were dark. Others were lit up like Christmas trees.

The boys in blue never fully close for business.

We were casing a two-story compound outside the main cluster. An ugly, dreary pile of bricks, surrounded by a ten-foot chain-link fence topped with razor wire. Though flickering floodlights illuminated the enclosed yard, none burned within the building. A sign at the gate proclaimed it "Annex A."

"We're really doing it this time," Shelton muttered. "We're gonna break into a freaking *police station*. And not some backwoods precinct. Ho, no! That wouldn't be *stupid* enough. This team of geniuses is about to invade the damn HQ."

"We need the ransom tape," I replied. "It's in there."

"Why not hit NASA next?" Shelton squawked. "Or CIA headquarters?"

"We *could* visit Channel Five first," Hi suggested. "They have a copy."

I shook my head. "We don't know if they have the whole recording, or just a clip."

"Tory's right." Ben's fingers drummed the steering wheel. "Plus, our plan is solid."

I watched Ben from the corner of my eye. Worried. While I appreciated his enthusiasm, Ben seemed unnaturally excited to undertake something this dangerous.

An hour ago, he'd picked us up on Morris. I'd barely made it out—slipping past Whitney was significantly more difficult than eluding Kit alone. While Kit slept like a hibernating polar bear, Whitney woke at the slightest floorboard creak. And lately, she'd begun setting our security system every night.

That actually worked in my favor. Whitney's not a tech-savvy person—she thought the alarm couldn't be deactivated without beeping. Not true. A quick read of the instruction manual had introduced me to silent mode.

That night I'd snuck downstairs, killed the alarm, slipped outside, and then reengaged the system from my iPhone. If the bimbo woke up she'd see a steady red light, and wouldn't suspect a thing.

The trickiest moment had been getting by Coop. Even bribed with two Greenie bones, the wolfdog hadn't been pleased to be left behind. Thankfully, he hadn't blown my cover.

"You're sure about this tunnel?" Shelton asked for the fifth time.

"Absolutely." Hi wiped orange Doritos crumbs on his black sweatshirt. We all wore dark, athletic clothing. Our ninja garb, Hi called it.

"Explain it one more time." Sitting there, on the brink, I wanted to visualize our strategy step by step.

Hi sighed theatrically, but repeated the story. "Last fall, my dad had to come down here to reclaim the LIRI hardware stolen from Lab Three. He brought me along to help lug the gear. That afternoon there was a baseball game up the street, snarling traffic around headquarters, so the detective took us on a shortcut."

He pointed to the building across the street. "We went in there. Annex A. That ugly shack has a tunnel to the main building. Even better, the passage connects to the basement, right where evidence storage is located."

"So we enter here, sneak along the tunnel, find and copy the tape, then retreat."

I sounded much more confident than I felt.

"Exactly." Ben was actually smiling. "It's perfect."

"Perfect?" Shelton began ticking points on his fingers. "We don't know how to get inside this building, if the tunnel will be manned, or if the video is actually *in* the evidence room, which is almost certainly guarded, alarmed, and recorded twenty-four/seven."

I tried not to cringe. Shelton was right. Our plan was borderline suicidal.

But it didn't matter. I couldn't get the twins' faces out of my head.

"We'll improvise," was all I said.

"Nope." Shelton wagged his head fatalistically. "We're getting caught, and going to jail. At least they won't have far to take us."

"Enough wasting time." Ben killed the engine. "Light 'em up."

"Do we have to?" Shelton glanced at me with troubled eyes. "Flaring is starting to feel a little like playing Russian roulette. How do we know the powers won't suddenly go sideways on us while we're sneaking past the po-pos?"

"Honestly, we don't," I answered grimly. "But there's no other way to do this. We'll just have to be careful. Keep it simple."

“Which means,” Ben said sharply, “you staying out of our heads. No mind scrambles.”

Though bristling at his tone, I nodded. “I won’t try to merge our thoughts.”

“Good. Now let’s get moving.” Golden light exploded behind Ben’s irises. He gasped, then shook like a wet dog.

“See you guys in lockdown.” Hi closed his eyes.

“Not funny.” Shelton took a deep breath, then shuddered as his power burst to life.

I rolled my neck, then whispered to myself. “Go time.”

SNAP.

My flare opened easily. The usual jolt of fire and ice, but nothing like the last time. Waves of pure energy flooded my limbs, powerful and addictive. I almost cooed with the pleasure of it.

Senses boosted to hyperdrive, I stepped from the SUV and scanned our target with preternatural precision. The boys huddled by the rear bumper, waiting for my signal.

Not yet. I wanted to test something first.

Take it slow.

Eyes shut, I visualized the flaming cords in my mind. They danced and spun, seemed almost eager. I harnessed them easily. The cords became tunnels.

I felt an odd sensation, like plunging into freezing water.

Thoughts poured into my head.

So easy this time.

As one, the boys winced.

“Are you reading my thoughts?” Ben demanded, hands clenching into fists. “You *just* said—”

“No.” I concentrated on the fiery tunnel leading to Ben. Our connection held, but the mind-meld remained tantalizingly out of reach.

I resisted the urge to try to force it. My flare felt surprisingly stable. I didn't want to risk a meltdown.

The telepathy is imperfect, I sent. *I can't harness your senses, but we can communicate.*

This is plenty weird enough. Shelton nearly ripped an ear from his head.

Coop isn't here. Hi overlaid the thought with an image of my wolfdog chasing his own tail. *Maybe that dilutes the effect?*

I nodded. *This will have to be enough. Let's go.*

Ben stepped into the street. *Follow me.* For some reason, his sending was faintest.

Moving single file, we hurried across and cut left, moving along the fence. An alley ran between the wire-capped chain link and the next building over. We bolted down its length to the rear of the property, which faced the river.

Tucked in the shadows, we peered into the Annex A enclosure, at a parking lot crowded with slumbering snow vehicles. Those don't get a ton of work in Charleston, South Carolina. Ten feet from where we hid, a second gate split the fence. Chained and locked.

Shelton hurried to it without prompting. We crouched, waiting as he picked the lock.

Click.

Got it. Shelton swung the gate wide. We slipped through and darted toward the building.

Look for a door that—

My thought was interrupted by the scrape of claws on asphalt. My flaring nose caught a whiff of wet, musky fur.

We whirled in unison. Two German shepherds were pounding toward us.

Panic flooded my brain as the boys scrambled for hiding places. I froze, unable to move.

Growling, both dogs barreled toward me.

Instinct took over. I flung my thoughts at the charging animals.

HOLD.

Both shepherds stopped short. The larger one—perhaps a grizzly bear in disguise—shook his head, black fur rising along his spine. The other beast cocked his head and yapped, eyeing me with icy brown eyes.

I could sense their thoughts—a jumble of confusion, and thwarted aggression.

The larger dog tensed, preparing to charge again.

Focus on the alpha.

I sent a mixture of impressions and images, trying to communicate as I did with Coop.

No harm. No threat. Leaving your territory.

Grizzly Bear sat back on his hindquarters. Regarded me. Then, slowly, he settled down on his haunches. Brown Eyes whined at his companion, but followed suit.

Pass.

I thought it was Grizzly Bear, but couldn't be sure.

Thank you.

I waved the boys toward the building. Hoped Shelton could get us inside. Quickly.

The guard dogs watched as Shelton reached a set of steel doors, began frantically fiddling with a knob.

Brown Eyes abruptly stood. Drilled me with a look.

Pass. Once.

I felt an emphasis on the second word.

Understood.

After long seconds, the lock yielded. We piled inside and slammed the door shut.

Phase One was complete.

But we were going to need a different way out.

⬡ ⬡ ⬡

What now? Ben asked, his smile gone.

We'd just completed Phase Two—the tunnel had been easy to locate, and blessedly abandoned at that late hour. It'd taken less than five minutes to reach the basement of the main headquarters building.

Where the weak point in our plan reared its ugly head.

Let me think. I peered through a tiny window in a hallway door.

Not only was the evidence room locked up tight, but so was the corridor approaching it. Halfway down its length sat a duty officer, drowsily reading a Dan Brown novel. A security camera perched above him completed the disaster.

"I told you!" Shelton hissed, forgetting to send his thoughts. "And we can't even go back now, unless you wanna be dog chow."

We huddled in the dim hallway, trying not to panic. My mind raced, searching for a miracle solution. At this point, just getting away sounded wonderful.

Then an idea occurred to me.

Hi, where is Hawfield's office?

Hi whipped out his iPhone. Tense moments passed as he surfed the web.

Finally, he looked up. *Major Crimes is on the fifth floor.*

Are you nuts! Shelton's hands shot skyward. *Hawfield knows who we are!*

No, she's right! Hi bounced on his toes. *And nobody that matters will be here this late.*

Ben pointed back the way we'd come. *Elevators.*

With my enhanced vision, I easily spotted the bank of doors twenty yards away.

We go up, I insisted. *But first, snuff the flares.*

Ben reared back. *That's nuts! We can't give up our edge.*

I gave him a hard look. *We might run into someone. We can't risk an officer spotting our glowing eyes, even if it means getting caught.*

Ben crossed his arms. *I'll take my chances.*

I nearly slapped him. *No! It's too dangerous. Stop being stupid.*

A pulse of anger radiated from Ben. He turned and stormed toward the elevators.

I slapped my sides in frustration. Didn't know what to do.

Would Ben really gamble everything? Risk exposure?

Feeling a hand on my shoulder, I turned. Hi gave me "calm down" hands as the golden light faded from his eyes. I glanced at Shelton. He'd also powered down.

Deep breath.

SNUP.

I shivered as the shock waves dissipated. Losing my flare made me feel small and weak. A terrible hollow feeling, that seemed worse each time.

"Let me." Hi hustled up the corridor.

Shelton and I waited, unable to pierce the gloom, not speaking for fear of discovery.

I counted seconds in my head.

"Come on," a voice finally whispered.

Shelton and I jogged to the elevators. Ben stood at the doors, his eyes their normal dark brown. Wordlessly, he punched the up button.

We waited, pulses pounding. A door beeped, then opened. The car was empty.

The four of us piled inside. Hi pressed five. The doors slid shut.

"Hope nobody else needs a lift," Shelton whispered.

"We can make something up," Hi hissed. "Say we lost our pony."

I snorted. "And came to report it at one a.m.?"

"Better than breaking in to steal evidence," Hi countered. "Maybe we loved that pony."

My heart rose in my throat as we passed each floor. One. Two. Three.

The elevator slowed. I was close to losing my dinner.

I imagined the doors opening to an office full of detectives working overtime. Heads turning. Confused eyes gradually growing suspicious. Hawfield, outraged, dialing Kit's number.

Four. Five. The doors hissed open.

Before us was an open space filled with interlocking cubicles, surrounded by glass-enclosed offices lining the walls. Every light was off. No one was there.

I gasped in relief. Shelton actually fell to his knees, while Hi rubbed a hand across his face. Ben chuckled nervously, wiping sweat from his brow.

"Hurry." I moved along the row of offices. The one I sought was third from the end.

Hawfield, Fergus.

Rounding the standard issue gray metal desk, I considered where to start. I woke his computer by tapping the space bar. No good—the system was password protected.

Then I noticed an iPad on the desktop. I flipped the cover and pressed the home button. The display winked to life. A collection of icons covered the screen.

The right one was obvious: GableRansomVideo.

"That's it!" Hi squealed. "But how do we get it?"

I thought furiously. Had no idea.

"Give it here," Shelton demanded.

He opened the iPad's web browser and navigated to Gmail.

"Brilliant," I breathed.

"Won't be so brilliant if they trace what I do," Shelton said. "But I have a blank Gmail account for joining websites, so I don't get spam. I'll use that."

He typed quickly.

"Tony Domo?" Hi scoffed. "Great name, genius."

"Can it. I was in a hurry."

Shelton logged in, attached the file, and mailed it to himself. Then he logged out, closed Safari, and opened Utilities to erase the iPad's browser history.

"Best I can do," he said nervously. "As long as no one suspects, no one will check the hard drive and notice what I did."

A squeaking noise in the hallway.

"Someone's coming!" Ben shoved everyone deeper into Hawfield's office.

We dove behind the desk in a ragged dog pile. Froze. The sound grew closer.

I stared at the tiny slice of doorway I could see. A yellow bucket wheeled into view. Passed, followed closely by a worn pair of Nikes. The squeaks sounded for another few seconds before fading completely.

We let out a collective breath.

"Let's get the frick out of here!" Shelton moaned.

"Deal."

Sticking my head through the door, I scanned the hallway. All clear. We bolted for the elevator. Painful moments passed as we waited for the car to arrive.

Adrenaline jolted me as the door opened.

Empty again. All the gods were smiling on us.

"What now?" Hi asked, once inside. "We can't go back through the tunnel."

"Now we go for broke." I pressed *L*.

The boys flinched, but didn't argue. They understood.

I pulled out my cell, tapping keys until I found what I needed. Then I cupped the iPhone tightly in my left hand.

We rode in silence.

The car stopped. The doors slid open.

Squaring my shoulders, I strode into the lobby.

Several officers lounged behind a counter running the length of the room. Opposite them, a man in handcuffs was slumped on a wooden bench, a huge welt forming on his forehead. Beside the suspect, an officer was calmly filling out paperwork.

On the next bench over, a pair of elderly ladies were seated, waiting, with matching scowls on their faces. Farther down the line, a trio of disheveled college students were scrolling their cell phones.

I spied a row of glass doors at the opposite end of the room.

Hesitate and you're finished, Brennan.

Straight from the elevator.

Across the lobby.

Through the doors.

The boys at my back like white on rice.

We walked swiftly, but not unduly so. Everyone stared straight ahead.

Behind the counter, an officer glanced up as we passed. His mouth opened, a confused expression on his face.

The phone beside him rang.

With a last look our way, the man shrugged, then reached to answer.

We exited the building, skipped down the steps, and then hurried around the corner.

I hit disconnect, ending my call to the CPD intake desk.

Together, we sprinted down the sidewalk.

CHAPTER 18

We scrambled into the bunker an hour later.

Ben had driven almost all the way there, something we *never* do. But I couldn't wait.

We had Karsten's files. We had the ransom video. Sleep wasn't coming anyway.

Shelton dropped into the workstation chair. "What first?"

I weighed options. The danger to the twins was more immediate.

"The ransom video."

We gathered behind Shelton as he logged into his fake Gmail account. "It's an MP-four file. Twenty seconds long. Probably shot by a handheld digital video camera. HD mode. Nothing embedded in the recording. No private streams."

I nodded, clueless as to what Shelton was talking about. But I trusted his expertise.

"Play it," Ben said.

Shelton double-clicked the file, then expanded to whole screen mode.

We watched in silence.

The shot was eye level. A dirty stone chamber, bisected by a line of rusty metal bars. Harsh light poured from somewhere off camera. Beyond the bars, a boy and a girl were huddled together on the floor, squinting in the radiance. The room didn't appear to have a ceiling. Water dripped from unseen heights above.

"It's them," Hi breathed. "They're looking right at the camera."

Shelton shivered, rubbed his arms. I understood.

It appeared the twins were looking right at their captor. I couldn't imagine the feeling.

"Turn up the audio," Ben said.

Shelton adjusted the QuickTime player settings, then fiddled with the desktop speakers. "No can do. There isn't any."

As we watched, the camera moved left to right across the chamber, as if being carried. The focus remained on the two miserable teens in the center of the cell.

Lucy and Peter didn't twitch a muscle, but their eyes tracked the camera.

After twenty seconds, the screen went black.

"Again," I breathed.

Shelton clicked play a second time. The clip repeated.

When it ended, I began chewing a thumbnail. Unfortunately, nothing about the video jumped out at me. The scene was horrifying, no question, and confirmed that the twins had been abducted. But from an investigative standpoint, the tape seemed like a dead end.

"There's nothing useful," Hi said. "The kidnapper knew what he was doing."

"Roll it again. And watch for details," I instructed. "Everyone take a quadrant. Look for any kind of hint where this was filmed, or by whom."

After agreeing on who was eyeballing what, Shelton replayed the recording. I watched the northwest quarter of the screen. Came up empty.

"I got nothing," Ben said.

"Same." Shelton and Hi. Jinx.

"Rotate sectors clockwise," I said. "We'll watch this a million times if we have to. There has to be *something.*"

"Won't the police already be doing this?" Shelton asked. "With, like, professional editing equipment, and a video expert?"

"You ready to give up on these two?" I touched the image frozen on the monitor.

"No." Shelton shoved his glasses into place. "No, I'm not."

We watched again. Rotated once more, and repeated the process.

I was scanning the southwest section of the screen when a thought struck me.

"Those bars look old," I said. "Like they've been there forever."

Hi nodded. "Good point. This . . . cage likely wasn't built for this kidnapping."

"Run it again," Ben said. "Everyone examine the bars."

The scene replayed.

"Holy crap!" Hi yelped.

"What?" I said immediately.

"Shadow!" Hi jabbed a finger at the center of the screen.

Shelton turned to face Hi. "Say what?"

"Run it half speed. Watch as the cameraman crosses the room. There!"

Hi was right. As the shot moved, a shadow briefly appeared on the floor, lengthened, then shrank back and disappeared.

"That's the kidnapper!" Then my spirits sank. "But how does a shadow help?"

"If we can isolate it," Hi said excitedly, "we could conceivably estimate the person's height and weight, maybe even gender. It's a place to start, at least."

I clapped my hands. "LIRI has amazing AV equipment—half the visiting researchers film documentaries of their work."

"What's that?" Ben pointed to a bar at the edge of the shot. With the tape paused, the chamber's background light was striking the steel at an oblique angle. Squiggly lines ran a foot of its length.

My pulse thumped. "Is that *writing*?"

Shelton boxed and enlarged the image. "It is! But I still can't read it."

We strained our eyes. Manipulated the image this way and that. Even considered flaring. But the grainy squiggles wouldn't form anything legible.

I pounded the desktop in frustration. "We need to see those words."

"We'll have better luck at LIRI," Hi promised. "We can play around with their equipment and really enhance the shot."

"Tomorrow," I said firmly. "Right after school."

"If we're gonna do that," Shelton said, "then let's check Karsten's files now."

"Good idea." I handed over the CD from Chang.

Shelton inserted the disk and opened the drive. A directory listed hundreds of files.

"Wow," Hi said.

"This might take a while," Shelton agreed.

My arms crossed. I'd waited too long for this moment.

"Then we'd better get started."

⬡ ⬡ ⬡

"This is pointless," Ben complained.

5:30 AM. We'd been skimming files for three straight hours.

I could barely keep my eyes open, but snapped at Ben nonetheless. "This is what we've been searching for—the entire record of Karsten's parvovirus experiments!"

"Which we can't make any sense of," Ben fired back.

Hi rubbed his face. "I mean, it's all interesting. Lab cultures. Data sets. Karsten's research protocols and stated objectives. But most of this material is way beyond me."

Shelton nodded wearily. "It's great to understand the *mechanics* of what Karsten did, but I can't see how it helps us. Our infection was unanticipated. Totally unplanned. There won't be a record of *that,* which is what we really need."

"This stuff helps, though." I stole the mouse and double-clicked a file. "Here. Karsten emphasizes that XPB-19 is contagious to humans. He knew!"

"*How* does that help?" Ben demanded. "How do we *use* any of this information? Without Karsten to explain his work, these files might as well be written in Chinese. They're useless."

"We don't know that." Voice stubborn. "There are *hundreds* of pages here, and we've barely skimmed half of them."

"These aren't the records we need! You want *answers,* Victoria?" Ben made air quotes with his fingers. "Well, here's some real talk: In order for this data to be *any* use, we'd have to have a basis for comparison. We'd need records of *our current condition,* right now. That means submitting *ourselves* to medical testing, by someone who knows what they're looking for. That sound good to you?"

I bit my tongue, suddenly discouraged.

Ben continued, relentless, biting off his words. "Unless you're ready to throw on a white gown and become a full-time lab rat, these files are totally useless. End of story."

I stared daggers at Ben, who glared back.

My God. Is he right? Have I been fooling myself all along?

Hi raised both palms. "It's almost dawn, guys. Let's call it a day before we kill each other. We can get back to this tomorrow."

I tore my gaze away. Nodded sharply.

This had been one of the longest days of my life. I was exhausted.

We crawled outside and piled into the Explorer. Ben drove in silence.

Nearing the complex, he switched off his headlights. Dropped us off fifty yards away. Then he sped down the blacktop, heading off the island.

Shelton, Hi, and I crept to the rear of the building. Mouthing goodbyes, we split up and slunk toward our respective units.

At the back door, I dug out my phone and deactivated the house alarm. Slipped inside.

Coop was standing in his doggie bed when I reached the main floor.

Maybe I was tired. I missed the signal.

Turning the corner, I ran smack into Whitney at the bottom of the stairs.

"Tory!" Her eyes widened. Then, taking in my clothes, narrowed.

Whitney's arms crossed over her white satin robe. "Sneaking out again? Your father is going to explode!"

My sluggish mind groped for an excuse. Struck out.

I stood there, gaping like an idiot.

Whitney was right—Kit was going to murder me.

Panicking, I blurted the first thing that came to mind.

"Please don't tell! I was meeting a boy."

Why did I say that!?!

Whitney's eyes nearly popped from her skull.

"A boy?" she hissed. "At this hour?! Who on earth—"

"Jason Taylor."

It felt like someone else was speaking. My mind was a melted slushy, suggesting ideas it thought Whitney might enjoy.

Whitney paused. Frowned. Finally, "Very well. I won't tell your daddy, but this does *not* happen again, young lady. Do you hear me?"

I nodded, too tired to process what was happening. "Yes, ma'am. Thank you."

Then I gave her a quick hug. Whitney, tensed, then returned it.

For some reason, I felt bad.

You're manipulating her to get out of trouble.

"Now up with you!" Whitney shook her head. "It's nearly dawn already, and you won't be missing school tomorrow."

I nodded. Climbed to my room.

My reserves were gone.

I was asleep before my head hit the pillow.

CHAPTER 19

Thursday

Morning came way too soon.

"Ghaaah." I slapped my alarm clock, hoping it would break.

Head pounding. Nasty taste in mouth. Eyes glued shut.

I'd never felt more drained.

My door swung open. Whitney stuck her head inside.

"Rise and shine," she said coolly. "I'll expect you downstairs for breakfast in twenty minutes. No exceptions." She withdrew with a knowing glance.

Our encounter an hour before came crashing back. Nightmare.

Why in the world had I mentioned Jason? How long would she hold her tongue?

From this moment forward, I'm at her mercy.

The thought made me want to crawl under my covers and never resurface. I imagined the day ahead, and the long hours before I could sleep.

"Blargh."

⬡ ⬡ ⬡

Sixty minutes later I was in uniform, aboard *Hugo*, and motoring toward downtown.

I sprawled on a bench in the stern, staring at our trail of wake.

Face slack. Mind numb. Body exhausted.

Shelton sat beside me, head in his hands. We hadn't exchanged two words. Hi was inside the passenger cabin, flat on his back and dozing.

My thoughts wandered. I replayed the horrifying ransom tape in my head. Composed a silent prayer for Lucy and Peter.

We'd put the Gamemaster behind bars, but a new evil had taken his place. I felt swamped with hopelessness. The world was dark, and full of monsters.

My focus drifted to Karsten's secret files. Ben's angry words.

Was he right? Was the information on the flash drive useless? I was forced to admit he'd made a compelling argument. Karsten wouldn't have any notes specifically pertaining to our condition.

Don't give up hope. Work the problem, and good things will come.

But I was zonked. Just wanted to sleep. To shut the world off. Check out.

An idea bloomed. Drained as I was, I didn't immediately dismiss it.

I straightened in my seat. *Why not?*

Because it might be hazardous, my rational mind shot back. *Because it's exactly what you were blasting Ben about, which makes you a total hypocrite.*

But both logic and pride were sorely overmatched.

I was dog-tired. Miserable. If my canine DNA could provide some relief, I wanted it.

Stupid stupid stupid.

Deep breath. Eyes shut.

SNAP.

The power scorched through me. I tried to hide the transformation from Shelton, fighting to keep still as my body thundered and raged.

As the flare unleashed, my weariness fled. The headache disappeared. Energy infused my muscles. My mind sharpened along with my senses. It felt wonderful.

This is bad. Dangerous.

At that moment, I didn't care. Just sighed with pleasure.

"Tory! Are you crazy?!"

Shelton shoved his sunglasses onto my face.

I started, suddenly aware of how careless I'd been. My eyes scanned the boat. Thankfully, no other passengers were on deck.

Shelton's gaze bored into me. "Has *everyone* lost their minds lately?"

"Sorry, you're right. But, Shelton, my fatigue just . . . melted away. I feel *great.*"

"Really?" His expression grew hopeful. "Okay, watch my back."

I slipped on my shades and handed his back. Shelton swapped them with his eyeglasses.

"This feels wrong."

"I know." But I held my flare anyway.

Shelton's thin frame shuddered. He gasped, grabbed his head.

Slowly, his breathing eased. Shelton's head came up, a smile spreading his lips.

"I take it back. This feels fantastic."

"Which worries me. Flaring is becoming addictive."

The cabin door opened and Hi stepped out. He stared as though we'd grown horns.

"I knew it." He joined us on the bench. "Explain yourselves."

"Light one up," I said ruefully. "You'll understand."

His eyebrows rose, but Hi dug out his shades. Seconds later, he gasped as the inferno erupted inside him.

"*Ahhhh.*" Hi linked his hands behind his head. "That's nice. Does this mean we don't need to sleep anymore?"

"Of course not." Exactly the thinking I feared. "I'm no flare expert—who is?—but I know *everything* comes with a price. When you burn energy, it's gone. Freeing the wolf probably taps a hidden reserve. Useful, obviously, but we can't cheat the laws of physics just by using our powers."

"I don't know, Tor." Hi tapped his feet. "I feel pretty damn super right now."

"This is what Ben was talking about," Shelton added.

My head whipped. "Huh?"

Shelton's fingers found his ear. "Nothing. Just something he mentioned."

I glanced at Hi, who looked away.

"Boys?" I stood and faced them. "Something to share?"

"It *was* a secret." Hi aimed a kick a Shelton, who dodged easily. "Ben made us swear not to tell you."

I crossed my arms. Waited.

"Ben flares first thing every morning," Shelton said. "He says it centers him. Makes him strong. He said *we* should do it, too."

Hi shrugged. "Maybe he's right. Right now, tell me you don't feel great. I might go beat someone up."

"No." I felt certain. "Ben is being incredibly reckless."

Hi spread his hands. "Right now, who are we to judge?"

Ouch. Hi had a point.

"Snuff 'em," I ordered. "Now."

SNUP.

The power vanished. I nearly groaned at the loss.

Still, I felt better than before. Some lethargy crept back, but not much. I couldn't deny that flaring had chased away most of my exhaustion.

But I didn't trust it.

Nothing is that easy. Every action has consequences.

Hi and Shelton removed their sunglasses.

"I feel fresher," Hi said. "Fact is fact. Maybe Ben's not as crazy as you think."

"Ben's gambling blindfolded," I said firmly. "He's gone way too far. Flaring in public. Flaring for pleasure. Flaring just to face the day! He's totally out of control, taking risks we *all* might suffer for. It has to stop."

Shelton slid his prescription specs onto his nose. "So what are you going to do?"

"Talk some sense into him. Right now."

⬡ ⬡ ⬡

I took a city bus from the marina to Mount Pleasant, then connected to a local line. A few more stops, and I was standing outside Wando High.

Which was crazy.

Hi and Shelton would cover for me at Bolton, but I didn't have a clue where to find Ben. This was not the greatest plan ever concocted.

I have to talk to him. Things have gotten out of hand.

I was testing various excuses to summon Ben from class when I spotted him.

Ben was loitering in the parking lot, chatting with two other guys. He wore his standard black tee and jeans. His taller companion sported a purple ski cap despite the eighty-degree weather, while the other boy had an inch-thick wallet chain hanging from his cargo shorts.

"Cutting class," I muttered. "That idiot."

Ben did a double-take when he spotted me, then slowly shook his head. As I drew near, he whispered something under his breath. His moron buddies exploded in laughter.

I'll kill him. Then murder him afterward.

"What the hell are you doing?" Not the most diplomatic of greetings, but my temper was long gone. "Is your first class Parking Lot Maintenance?"

Ben waved a hand at me. "You see what I mean?"

Wallet Chain chuckled as he toked a cigarette. "That's not very nice, sweetheart."

"You'll never land a man like that," added Ski Cap. "This ain't Beantown."

"Ben?" Seething. "May I speak to you privately?"

Ben rolled his eyes. "Give me a sec, guys. I've been naughty."

I waited until the stoners were out of earshot.

"Great crew you've assembled." Dripping with sarcasm.

"Leave them out of this," Ben warned. "What, I can't even *have* friends, now that I've been kicked from the Ivory Tower?"

"Maybe go to class. You might find a better peer group in there."

Ben snorted. "I'm pretty sure *you* have class right now, too."

Touché.

"What are you doing here?" he demanded. "We're packmates and all, but you're not my mother. I've already got one of those, thanks."

I took a calming breath. Yelling at Ben would get me nowhere.

"Hi and Shelton told me you've been flaring every morning. To feel good." Hiding my guilt at having just done the same.

It was . . . an experiment. I won't do it again. I won't!

Ben snorted, tucking his long black hair behind his ears. "Remind me to compliment their secret-keeping skills."

"Ben!" I forced him to meet my eyes. "That *can't* be a good idea."

"Why not? For all we know, flaring might be the healthiest thing ever. We don't know." He pointed a finger. "*You* don't know."

Valid point. But my instincts were clear.

I chose a different tack. "Every time you flare in public, you put our lives in danger. Not just your own. Mine. Hi's. Shelton's. The whole pack, Ben."

"I'm careful." Dismissive. "You might not believe this, Victoria, but I'm not an idiot."

"Then don't *act* like one! Show some restraint. Show some *character.*"

I regretted the last word even as I spoke it.

"Oh, I see." Ben looked away. "This is still about what I did."

"No, it isn't." *Was it?*

"I've apologized." Ben scuffed the pavement with a shoe. I could feel him shutting down. "A hundred times. I can't make you accept it."

My lips froze. No words came.

I didn't know what to say. Honestly didn't know if I'd forgiven him.

Ben looked me square in the eye. "I can't undo my mistakes," he said quietly. "No one can. If you can't get past it, there's nothing more to say."

He turned and headed for the building.

"Ben. Wait."

He didn't stop. In seconds I was alone in the parking lot.

"Damn it."

Walking back to the bus stop, I was more upset than ever. This trip had accomplished nothing. I might've screwed things up even worse.

I couldn't get through to Ben. He wouldn't listen.

What'd you expect? Technically, you're not even talking to him.

My steps slowed.

When was the last time Ben and I had spoken alone?

The hurricane. The hospital.

When he admitted his feelings for me.

The realization jarred me to a standstill.

That morning's fight had been our first private conversation in *five* months.

I never said anything back. About any *of it.*

Because I don't know what to say.

Suddenly, the hairs on my arm stood at attention. With a slap of awareness, I realized *it* was happening again. The ephemeral feeling had returned, lodging at the edge of my conscious thoughts. I could barely detect its presence.

I stopped dead, extending my arms like wings, as if achieving outward balance might create the same within me.

No good. The sensation abruptly winked out, leaving no trace.

"This is getting *really* annoying," I muttered.

My mind raced, struggling to record some data about the mysterious feeling. Make even the slightest link to something I could recognize. Once more, I failed.

Wrapped in such thoughts, I nearly missed the BMW idling across the street.

Tinted windows blocked any view inside the vehicle. Its jet-black hood gleamed in the early morning sunshine.

Something about it felt . . . off.

The car was blocking a fire lane, close to nothing in particular. No stores. No restaurants. No businesses of any kind. There was no reason for anyone to park there.

Unless you're watching the school.

Two dots connected in my mind. I'd seen that car before.

Yes. Switching buses by the library.

An identical BMW had circled the bus stop, then pulled into a McDonald's across the highway. The shiny ride had caught my eye. I'd wondered, in passing, why no one had gotten out to make an order.

I halted with a sudden disturbing thought.

Was I being followed?

Before I could consider more, the BMW swerved into traffic and sped away.

CHAPTER 20

I shoved my lunch away.

No appetite. The visit to Wando High had been a disaster.

Hi glanced at my sandwich, one eyebrow raised.

I waved permission. He slid my tray before him with a grin.

"I *told* you it was a bad idea," Shelton said between bites. "You can't push Blue like that. He just doubles down on whatever he's being stubborn about."

Hi made a gagging noise. "Aw, what is this? Alfalfa sprouts. *Blech.* Pass."

The tray came back my way. "Keep your horse food."

"It was worse than that," I admitted. "I hurt Ben's feelings, too. He thinks I don't trust him because of the Gamemaster."

Hi swished his mouth with Diet Coke. "Well, do you?"

"Do what?" I asked, raising my voice to be heard over the cafeteria din.

"Trust him. Because last I checked, he was headlining your no-fly list."

"I don't know." Rubbing my forehead "I mean, yes, I trust Ben. It's not like I think he'd betray us again. Or that he'd known what his lies would lead to."

I paused, trying to sort out my feelings. "It's not a trust thing. It's more about . . . forgiveness. I *want* to let it go, believe me. I just can't seem to." I blew out a breath. "Every time I think about what Ben did, the anger bubbles back up."

Shelton nodded, but didn't speak.

I leaned back in my chair. "How'd you guys get over it so fast?"

Hi shrugged. "It's Ben. I've only got three real friends. I can't afford to lose one over some Greek tragedy."

My eyes narrowed. "Greek what?"

Hi slapped both hands on the table, fixed me with an intense stare. "Ben did it for love of a woman, Victoria. One he can never possess."

My face burned. This topic we *never* discussed.

Shelton chuckled. "You're such a dope, Stolowitski."

Hi balled up his lunch bag and took aim at a nearby trash can. "It's true, though."

Throw. He missed by a good six feet.

"Foul!" Hi turned back to me, his face serious. "You wanna know why I forgave Ben so quickly? Because I felt sorry for him. Can you imagine being in his shoes?" Hi held up an index finger. "He took one little shortcut, to impress a girl he liked, *and it almost got his friends killed.* Almost got the *girl* killed. That's you, by the way."

Hi sat back in his chair. "I can't imagine the guilt he must carry around."

"It eats at him," Shelton agreed. "All the time. Though he'd never let you see."

I didn't respond.

To be honest, I hadn't thought about how Ben's betrayal affected *Ben.*

Something new to consider.

Hi leaned forward. "Our pack is only five strong. We *have* to forgive one another, even when it's bad. How else are we gonna survive whatever comes next?"

Shelton nodded like a bobblehead. "Ben's not just some guy, he's family. *Pack*. You don't throw that away."

"I know!" My hands rose ineffectually. "I wish it were that easy. There's more to—"

I cut my words short as Hiram's gaze flicked to something over my shoulder.

"Hey, guys." Jason's voice was right behind me. "Hi, I rebounded your miss. Give it more arc next time. Follow through with the wrist."

He set his tray down beside mine.

My fingers found the bridge of my nose. I didn't have time for our usual dance.

"Jason!" I snapped. "Private conversation! Do you mind?"

"Not at all," he said smoothly, smiling, but unable to hide the hurt in his eyes. "I was on my way out anyway. Later." Jason strode toward the exit, a pace too quickly.

Shelton and Hi both gave me a look.

"What?" Then I covered my face with both hands. "Argh! I can't stop screwing up today."

"He'll be fine," Shelton offered. "I think."

"Don't sweat it," Hi said. "Jason always bounces back. That guy's like a puppy dog, he can't stay mad at you. Let's get back to that beemer. You really think it was following you?"

"I don't know anymore." I slumped in my seat. "You shouldn't trust anything I say this morning. I'm cursed."

"The Fairy Dust witch!" Hi whispered, waggling his eyebrows. "She got you."

"Blargh."

"I'm keeping an eye out anyway," Shelton stuffed his lunch bag into his backpack. "If I see a black BMW on my six, I'm running first, asking questions later."

"We're still going to Loggerhead this afternoon, right?" Hi glanced around, then dropped his voice. "For the . . . home movie thing?"

I nodded. "We might as well deal with what we can. Let's take the afternoon shuttle. I'll think of an excuse for Kit, though I'm open to suggestions."

"Ben?" Shelton asked.

"Not today. I think the two of us need a little distance."

The bell rang. We gathered our things and headed for the door.

"Tell Kit we're cutting a music video," Hi suggested as we walked. "Something real gangster, so we need to smash-cut our dance routines. Lay down some visuals. We could offer to let him freestyle rap over the second verse."

I gave him a thumbs-up. "Foolproof. Anyone need a locker stop?"

Two head shakes, so we proceeded directly to class.

Fourth period. AP English Language and Composition. We had Mr. Edde again for second semester, which wasn't bad. He knew his stuff, and wasn't nearly as uptight as some of the other faculty. He'd shaved his Afro, however, which was a crime.

Ella was in this class, too. There were no assigned seats, so we'd taken to sharing a table by a large bay window looking out over the soccer field. Hi and Shelton manned the one directly behind us.

Jason was also on the roster. Spotting him enter, I waved enthusiastically, beaming from ear to ear. He stopped and raised a hand—a confused smile on his face—before taking his seat by the door.

Hi's right. Jason never stews on anything. So different from Ben.

The next group to enter was less pleasant.

The Tripod, in formation.

Ashley, Courtney, and Madison glided to the very back of the room, which they considered theirs. All three sat together, though the tables were designed for two. Mr. Edde had given up trying to separate them.

At first, the Tripod's appearance in an AP class had stunned me.

Not so much Ashley—I knew she was whip smart, as all deadly predators must be. But Madison seemed indifferent to education, even before her . . . funk. And Courtney was downright idiotic.

Not for the first time, I wondered at their marks. Mr. Edde was not an easy grader.

"Scouting the enemy?"

I jumped as Ella's bag thumped onto our table. How did she always sneak up on me?

"Just wondering what they're doing here."

"Their parents must be humored, I'm sure." Ella dropped into her chair, her stormy gray eyes twinkling with amusement. "At least until they rope a husband who'll let them lounge by the pool all day."

I snorted. "If that's the case, they'd love my Annoyance-in-House."

"Why?" Ella tossed her braid over her shoulder. "What'd Whitney do now?"

I ducked too late, took Ella's glossy black rope right across the nose.

"Be careful with that!" But I giggled at her favorite trick. I'd toyed with the idea of growing my hair out just as long, then repaying the favor.

I'd look like a carrot-colored homeless person. Not gorgeous like she does.

I shoved hair envy aside. "Whitney signed me up for the Mag League. I've been reading about the organization, and it sounds like a never-ending cotillion. *Not* pleased."

"You're not alone." Ella's eyes rolled. "Mommy dearest thought it best as well."

"Really?" I perked up immediately. "Oh thank God!"

Ella smiled sarcastically. "I'm glad our mutual imprisonment cheers you so."

"Oh, it does."

I couldn't chase the smile away. At least Ella would be there with me. Who knows? Maybe it'd be fun. We could turn this thing into an all-out snark fest.

Once again, I thanked my lucky stars for having met her.

It was *so* nice having a girl to talk to.

Grinning like a fool, I accidentally let my gaze meet Ashley's. She smiled sweetly. Without another option, I nodded as though I'd sought her out. Then I quickly glanced down, pretending to search for a page in my book.

"Do *not* be afraid of that girl," Ella whispered, without looking up.

"Can't help it." Eyes on my text. "She's terrifying."

"She's nothing. A spoiled little princess who thinks terrorizing a high school actually means something. I wish she'd pull that crap on me."

"Not likely."

I risked another peek at the Tripod. Ashley was scolding Madison, who nodded meekly. Courtney was staring out the window, toying with her long blond hair.

"They *do* give you a wide berth," I said. "Why is that?"

Ella scowled as she dug in her bag for a pen. "It wasn't always like this. Freshman year, I dodged them every time I walked the halls."

She slapped a Uniball on the table, then squeezed my hand. "Soccer did the trick. It gave me confidence. I realized I was *letting* those bitches get inside my head. The whole thing was stupid. So I stopped avoiding them. Quit ducking every time they snapped their fingers. Pretty soon, they stopped testing me. Sound familiar?"

It did. The Tripod had quit harassing me only after I'd shown some backbone.

Well, a bit more than that.

Not for the first time, I wished I'd met Ella sooner.

Chance told me. He gave the same advice.

Suddenly, I wanted to tell Ella about the Gable twins. Ophiuchus. The ransom video. The black BMW. For a single deranged instant, I wanted to tell her about my powers.

But I didn't. Couldn't. Ella was a true friend. Maybe even a "best" one.

The *last* thing I wanted was for her to see the crazy part of my life. To drive her away.

"Something wrong?" she asked. "You've gone totally pale."

"Blame my Irish roots." Trying to play it off. "I'm just tired."

The second bell rang. Mr. Edde rose and walked to his whiteboard.

Wiping the troubling thoughts from my head, I tried to concentrate on *Paradise Lost.*

At least *it* was something I could control.

CHAPTER 21

We marched single file through LIRI's front gate.

A blazing sun hung in the western sky, without a single cloud to keep it company. Temperatures in the mid-eighties kept the tropical air muggy and hot. Forest sounds surrounded us as we headed for Building One.

Hugo had taken us directly to Loggerhead Island, so we hadn't changed from our school uniforms. Trooping through the woods, my sweat glands began a formal protest under my heavy wool blazer. I wasn't the only casualty—Hi lumbered beside me, red-faced, panting like a dog. The hike from the dock had him close to combusting.

Outside the perimeter fence, a troop of rhesus monkeys prowled the treetops, hooting challenges from the heights. The isle itself is a wildlife preserve, home to dozens of animal species, including a large population of our simian observers.

Inside the chain-link barrier, white-coated scientists filled the courtyard, moving purposefully between buildings, or relaxing on stone benches. On a weekday in spring, the institute bustled like a beehive. Guest researchers arrived daily from around the globe.

The LIRI compound consists of a dozen glass-and-steel buildings, arranged in two rows facing each other across a manicured central common. The larger edifices contain offices, conference rooms, administrative centers, and, most importantly, six state-of-the-art veterinary research labs. The smaller ones are storage facilities, vehicle depots, and equipment sheds.

My father, Kit, managed the whole thing. Still getting used to that.

We passed through sliding glass doors into Building One. Four floors high, it was easily the largest structure on Loggerhead. The Flagship, as Kit called it, contained the most offices and workspace, including the director's suite, security headquarters, and three of the labs.

Upon assuming the directorship, Kit had massively increased security. Along with expensive equipment and systems upgrades—state-of-the-art video cameras now covered every inch of the grounds—LIRI also employed three full-time guards. At least one was on duty 24/7, manning a kiosk in the lobby.

I crossed my fingers as we entered, hoping we could avoid one in particular.

Thank God for small favors—Sam was on duty. Blessedly, Hudson was somewhere else.

Security Chief David Hudson ran his department like a Shogun warlord. An ex-military, by-the-book ball-breaker, the prickly man wasn't a fan of unsupervised teenagers on Loggerhead.

Kit had overruled him on that point, granting us permission to visit the island.

So long as we respected Hudson's rules. Of which there were *hundreds.*

And we did. Grudgingly. Usually.

Hudson's two underlings couldn't have been more different.

Carl Szuberla was a short, enormously fat bowling ball of a man. Though a bit moody—and definitely not the sharpest knife in the drawer—overall he wasn't so bad.

Sam Schneider was older than Carl, somewhere in his sixties. Rail thin, and bald as a cue ball, he was much sharper than his portly coworker. Sam had a sarcastic tongue that rivaled even Hi's. I rarely saw him without a hunting magazine in his claw-like fingers.

As we approached the desk, I kept an eye out for Hudson. The man could materialize out of thin air, and I was hoping to avoid him altogether.

Sam, I could usually handle. While not as easy to fool as Carl, he preferred doing as little as possible. A clever mind can exploit that fact.

Sam spied us approaching.

"Hello, Tory." Setting down his copy of *Field & Stream*. "Come to complicate my day, maybe get me fired?"

"Hi, Sam." I flashed my cheeriest smile. "Don't be silly. I'm here to see Kit."

"Director Howard won't be expecting you, of course." Sam sat back and crossed his arms. "Because that'd be too easy."

I shrugged. "Everyone likes surprises, right?"

Sam snorted. "It's been *my* experience that absolutely no one likes surprises. I'll call up."

He lifted the receiver and dialed an extension. Spoke to someone on the other end. Hung up. "Your father isn't free at the moment, he's with the accountants. They're probably cutting my salary."

I'd known that. Kit had complained about the meeting over breakfast.

"Okay. We'll just head up to his office and wait."

Sam's expression soured. "I'm not supposed to permit that. Which you know."

"Come on, Sambo!" Hi winked. "Live a little. What are we going to do, rob the place?"

The guard crossed his arms. "Wink at me again, Hiram, and I'll throw you to the wolfpack." But he was already reaching for a clipboard. "Sign in. And let's not get lost, hey?"

I scribbled my name. "Thanks, Sam. You're the best."

"Clearly not, since I'm letting you in anyway. Now scram before Hudson gets back."

Needing no more prompting, we hurried to the elevator. Once inside I pressed two, thankful that the car's location wasn't displayed in the lobby.

The director's suite is on the fourth floor. We were headed for the photo lab.

Our luck wasn't perfect, however.

When the doors opened, Mike Iglehart was waiting impatiently.

I suppressed a groan. For some reason, this bozo always gave me a hard time.

That day was no different.

"Miss Brennan." Curse or greeting, hard to tell.

Iglehart had thinning black hair, combed horizontally across his scalp. He examined us critically, tiny, close-set eyes staring down a long nose.

"Hello, Dr. Iglehart." Unsure what else to say, I moved past him into the corridor.

"Wait."

I paused. Turned. The boys bunched at my back.

"Yes?"

I could tell Iglehart was itching to interrogate me.

Behind him, the elevator doors began sliding shut. Iglehart stuck out a hand to keep them from closing.

An awkward moment stretched.

"Nothing. Never mind." Iglehart stepped into the elevator as the doors began closing a second time. We watched to make sure he didn't suddenly reemerge.

Shelton grunted. "That guy is so weird."

"Keep moving," Hi warned. "By now, half the building knows we're here."

At the end of the hall was a tinted glass door. Audio/Video Editing and Production.

I looked left. Right. The coast was clear.

We slipped inside and locked the door.

The small room had a horseshoe-shaped counter running along three walls. Expensive-looking equipment lined every inch. Boom microphones. HD monitors. DVD players and burners. A massive soundboard. Behind the high-tech workspace, a table and chair arrangement hugged the rear wall.

"You guys know how to use this stuff?" I asked doubtfully.

"Yep." Shelton was rubbing his hands together.

"Of course I do." Hi sounded offended. "How else would I record *my debut album*?"

"Prove it." I swept a hand toward the mountain of hardware. "Get to work."

"Why don't you just have a seat?" Shelton pointed to the rear table. "Back there, for now. We'll call you when ready."

I thought of some choice words, but held my tongue.

"Fine. Your show."

With nothing to do, I opened Words With Friends on my iPhone.

I usually crushed Ella, but this time she had the upper hand.

Shelton and Hi chatted excitedly, examining components and hashing out a game plan. Shelton inserted his flash drive into the closest USB port.

Unable to contribute, I concentrated on my letters. V V Q O C A L. Ugh.

I tried to get comfortable. It might be a *long* afternoon.

⬡ ⬡ ⬡

"Tory?" Shelton called.

My head jerked.

"Whaa?" More yawn than speech.

Not surprisingly, I'd drifted off. Lack of sleep was definitely taking a toll.

Hi pointed to one of the monitors. "We might have something."

Groggily, I pulled my chair next to theirs. "Show me."

"Using PhotoSpy, we were able to isolate the shadow on the ransom tape." Hi maximized a window, revealing a grainy white outline on a black field. "We calculated its dimensions by using what we know of Lucy and Peter—since the twins appear in the same image, we can use their measurements to create a scale for quantifying the shadow."

"That's great, guys."

"Not really," Shelton said. "Unfortunately, we don't know the distance between the cameraman and the light source. Without it, our scale is imperfect. What we *can* determine doesn't tell us much—the cameraman is between five foot six and six foot eight and weighs one hundred to three hundred pounds."

I gave him a flat look. "That's practically useless."

Shelton nodded. "We know. That's not why I called you over."

Hi pressed more keys. The steel bar with squiggly lines appeared onscreen.

"We had more luck with this," Shelton said. "Check it out."

He signaled Hi, who tapped a sequence of buttons. The image passed through a sequence of filters. Some made the scrawling loops sharper. Others made them impossible to see.

"The program ran hundreds of these," Hi said. "We think this one's a winner."

Another keystroke. The image snapped into tight focus, the once-fuzzy lines resolved into letters. Something was definitely printed on the bar.

"So close," I hissed, squinting and angling my head. "But still too small to read."

Shelton nodded again. "We were about to zoom in, but I called you over first."

"Do it."

Hi pushed an arrow key. The image doubled in size, but lost clarity.

"Enhancing," Hi intoned.

The image rippled, then snapped into focus. The lettering was clearer, but still illegible.

"Damn it," I muttered. "Can we do that again?"

"Enhancing," Hi repeated in a robotic cadence.

I glanced at him. "You're really enjoying this, aren't you?"

"Yes." Same voice.

The process repeated. This time, we had something.

Four words ran vertically along the bar. I tipped my head sideways for a better look.

"Hold on." Hi rotated the image so the letters ran left to right.

"Try reversing the ambient light," Shelton suggested. "And tint the image a bit. Maybe take the background out altogether."

More typing. Suddenly, the words leaped out at us, clear as day.

Ironwork of Philip Simmons.

Hi sat back. "Well, that sucks. Now we know who made the freaking bars."

"No!" I spun excitedly. "This could be useful. The twins' dungeon looks ancient, right? Certainly not built recently. We can research this—" eyes to the screen, "—Philip Simmons, and find out where he did business."

"Which could lead to the cell's location," Shelton finished. "Or at least point to an area where the twins might be imprisoned. Tory, that's brilliant."

"Like I said," Hi interrupted, "this is *huge.*"

I was about to say more when something on another screen caught my eye.

"What's over there?" I pointed.

Shelton swiveled. "Oh, that's nothing. We got an idea to watch the twins' faces up close, and see if they mouthed anything to the camera. That's what *I'd* do. But they didn't."

The screen was frozen on an extreme close-up of Peter Gable's face.

Something about the picture disturbed me.

"Can you play it for me?" I asked.

"Sure."

Shelton shut down the equipment we were using and moved to the other bank. Seconds later the video began rolling.

I watched Peter intently, unsure what was bugging me.

The clip ended. "Again, please."

Shelton gave me a quizzical look, but reran the tape.

Halfway through the second showing, I had it.

"Peter's eyes." I circled a finger, signaling for another viewing. "They track the camera across the cell. But watch his *face*. Don't you think that's a weird expression?"

We watched a third time.

"Huh." Hi stroked his cheek. "There *is* something strange. In his eyes."

"Can you blame him?" Shelton said. "He's staring at his kidnapper. I'm not sure there's a standard-issue look for that scenario."

"No." I tapped a fist to my chin. "It's *more* than that."

Hi shifted in his seat. "What do you think—"

"Hold on. Shelton, one more time."

As the clip rolled, my gaze bore into Peter, deconstructing him. The itch persisted.

Then, in a flash, I had it. My instincts screamed in unison.

"He knows the cameraman."

"What?" Hi leaned closer to the screen. "How can you tell?"

"I just can." Spoken with quiet certainty. "It's in his eyes. Whoever Peter sees, he knows. I'd bet my life on it."

Shelton reached for an earlobe. “So what does *that* mean?”

“It means we’d better learn more about the Gable family. Everything we can.”

I was about to say more when the doorknob rattled.

“Crap!” Hi scrambled for the keyboard. “Close out everything! Don’t save the files, or leave anything onscreen!”

Shelton and Hi raced about the room, frantically shutting down programs and equipment.

There was a jingle of keys.

“Tory!” Hi pointed to the main CPU. “Flash drive.”

I dove for the data stick, pocketing it a heartbeat before the door swung inward.

Hudson’s head popped into the booth.

“In here.” He wore a deep frown.

Hudson stepped inside, followed by Iglehart. Followed by Kit.

Oh fudge.

⬡ ⬡ ⬡

I tried to scramble, but Kit wasn’t buying what I was selling.

“We’ll discuss this when I get home,” was all he said.

Kit marched us down to the lobby, then had Hudson escort us to the dock.

LIRI privileges revoked, until further notice.

Hudson watched us depart, remaining on the dock until *Hugo* motored from sight.

“Well, that could’ve gone better,” Hi said. “Methinks your dad is a bit pissed off.”

“At least he didn’t tell *our* parents,” Shelton said. “That’s something, right?”

Hi dropped heavily onto the stern bench. “What’s our next move?”

I rubbed my forehead. The day had been a debacle.

In one solar rotation, I'd managed to upset Ben, Jason, *and* Kit.

Make way for Tory, gents!

"Next, I take a freaking nap." I sighed. "I'll use my brain again tomorrow. Maybe."

We rode the rest of the way home in silence.

CHAPTER 22

My nap was not to be.

Once again, Whitney blitzed me as I stepped into the house.

She had a plan. In fact, she was already squeezed into a skintight cocktail dress.

"It's going to be wonderful!" she gushed. "I've already spoken to your father, and he'll be home in thirty minutes. Go get ready!"

"You talked to Kit?" I asked cautiously. "Just now?"

"Yes, sugar. He agreed that our family *desperately* needs an evening on the town together. And this opening is at the Gibbes!"

I questioned the accuracy of Whitney's reporting, but didn't press the issue. Kit must've agreed to her proposal. Which meant I'd gotten a reprieve.

Reprieve? I'm going to a freaking art show with Whitney and Angry Kit. No es bueno.

A thought occurred to me. *Why not?*

"Is it okay if I invite someone to join us?"

Whitney's mouth thinned. "Tory, dear, I don't think any of those boys would enjoy—"

"I don't mean the guys. I was thinking of my friend Ella. From school. She's joining the Mag League, too."

Whitney's eyes widened. Then her face exploded with joy.

"Of *course* you may, sweetie. In fact, you simply must!"

⬡ ⬡ ⬡

Kit arrived home as I was dabbing on blush. My pulse spiked as he trooped upstairs.

Knock knock.

"Yes?"

Kit stuck his head in my room. "Art show."

I nodded. "Ella's coming. We play soccer together."

Kit's brow furrowed, but he shook it off. "Downstairs in ten. Tonight seems important to Whitney, so we'll talk about this afternoon another time."

He withdrew and closed the door.

"Wonderful."

So Kit was keeping my LIRI excursion from Whitney.

And Whitney wasn't telling Kit about my sneak-out the night before.

Blargh.

What a mess. Things were getting complicated. I felt a noose tightening around my neck.

Abruptly, I wondered what secrets *they* were keeping from *me*?

My mind arrowed back to Whitney's casual statement a half hour ago.

That *our family* needed a night out. I shivered at the implications.

She *was* moving out again, right? As soon as her house was fixed?

Kit's voice boomed up the stairwell. "Tory! Chop chop!"

I checked myself in the mirror. Black dress, strapless. Tasteful flats. Hair up. Light makeup. Was this how you dressed for an art show? I hadn't the faintest, and using Whitney as a template could result in disaster. If there was a line, she usually pushed it.

"Come on, honey!" I could hear the bounce in Whitney's voice.

With one last primp, I headed downstairs.

⬡ ⬡ ⬡

Ella met us on the front steps of the Gibbes Museum of Art.

She wore a hunter-green Christian Dior number that set off her eyes, and made her stand out from the black-clad crowd. But in a good way, like a centerpiece.

I felt gangly and awkward—a little girl playing dress-up—but Ella seemed totally at ease. Which helped *me* relax.

Ella aced introductions, charming Kit and positively delighting Whitney. When it came to schmooze, she was light-years ahead of me. Whitney nearly teared up, so happy to see me with a friend from the "approved" list. And a *girl* to boot.

The Gibbes Museum is a domed, white-columned monolith on Meeting Street, tucked away in the heart of Charleston's historic district. Designed in a Beaux Arts style that was popular at the beginning of the twentieth century, the gallery first opened in 1905, and has been a fixture of the art world ever since.

The evening's festivities were in the Alice Smith Gallery, the largest room on the museum's first floor. A local sculptor had rented the space to display, and hopefully sell, his recent works.

Perhaps a hundred guests mingled among the dozen or so sculptures arrayed around the chamber. Tuxedoed waitstaff circled the room, silver trays balanced on white-gloved hands, offering an array of hors d'oeuvres. A string quartet played in one corner, beside a cash bar that was getting a lot of attention.

Ella elbowed my side. "Check out *that* guy."

I followed her sightline to a man in the center of the room. He wore black skinny jeans and a ribbed white turtleneck.

And a beret. A *raspberry* beret.

"Oh my," I whispered.

"If he's not being ironic, I'll pee myself."

I snorted, then we both broke out in giggles. I was *so* thankful she'd agreed to come.

Thankfully, Whitney missed the exchange.

"Jean-Paul!" she squealed, waving for the man's attention. "Everything looks lovely!"

Jean-Paul smiled smugly, every inch the stereotype of a self-important artist. He crossed to our group. "Welcome. So glad you could attend my moment."

Introductions were made. I could sense Kit struggling for something to talk about.

Time to make my exit.

"We're gonna do a lap," I said quickly. "Bye."

"Are you kidding me?" Ella said, once we'd scurried away from Kit, Whit, and The Moment. "Look at all these pretentious blowhards, sipping champagne and munching duck tartar. They'll all pretend to know about art, but none actually do. This is going to be great!"

We worked our way around the room, scarfing the various offerings and critiquing both artwork and aficionados. Several of the pieces simply made no sense.

"What's this one called?" Ella asked, chomping a crab cake.

I read the placard. "*Man's Inhumanity to Man.*"

Ella smirked. "It's a half-inflated balloon."

"Attached to a six-foot fire hydrant," I pointed out. "Painted gold."

"I see. He shouldn't let this go for less than five billion."

"Cash."

My giggle cut off with a jolt. Ice traveled my spine.

The sensation had returned, stronger than ever. For a fleeting moment, I felt a web of loose connections spin away from my mind, casting about as searching for a light switch. Then just as quickly, the feeling passed.

"Tory?" Ella eyed me with concern. "You've gone pale. See a ghost?"

"It's nothing." I seized a glass of water from a nearby buffet table. Downed it in one go. "Thirsty," I wheezed when finished.

"Well, it *is* important to hydrate," Ella said wryly. "Come on. This one looks like a inflatable pitchfork."

I nodded, gathering myself. A quick mental probe confirmed the sensation was gone.

So frustrating.

Pushing the disturbance aside, I followed on Ella's heels.

We were circling toward the next piece when I saw him. "Oh, crap."

"*Way* worse than that," Ella said. "Jean-Paul isn't going to make his deposit back."

"No." I pointed behind my palm. "Headmaster Paugh. Naturally, *he's* here."

Paugh wore a tweed jacket and brown pants, and looked like a college professor who'd stumbled into the building. He spotted us before we could turn away.

"Miss Brennan," he said, cutting through the crowd. "And Miss Francis. I didn't know you were fans of Mr. Delacourt's work."

"This is my first time. It's all very . . . nice."

"Modernist garbage," Paugh scoffed. "He'd be lucky to sell that silly hat he's wearing. But I believe in supporting our local arts community, even when they foolishly abandon the classical forms."

Paugh nodded to a sculpture on his right. "I mean, this *thing*. What is it? A giant rake? A TV antenna? My grandson made something similar in his preschool class."

"I, uh . . . yes." The best reply I could formulate.

"Well, enjoy." Paugh swept on, pausing to shake his head at the next exhibit.

"I can't believe that!" Ella whispered. "He usually just glowers."

"I know, right?" I couldn't help but chuckle. "Does our headmaster secretly have a sense of humor?"

I spotted more familiar faces ahead. Nell Harris was clutching a wine flute, chatting with Lazarus Parrish. The defense attorney saw me first.

"Tory Brennan!" His gravelly voice carried across the gallery.

I had no choice but to join them. Ella followed.

"Congratulations on your testimony the other day." Parrish extended a hand, which I reluctantly shook. "You were an excellent witness. The district attorney had you well prepared."

Harris dipped her glass in acknowledgment.

"Thank you, sir."

I wasn't quite sure how to take the compliment. This man was the enemy.

"I'm not your enemy, Tory." Parrish read my mind. "The Gamemaster was my client—and it was my duty to defend him to the utmost—but I won't be losing sleep over his conviction. His last check failed to clear."

Harris chuckled, blue eyes rolling. "You don't change, do you, Lazarus?"

"God, I hope not. Who is your lovely friend?"

I introduced Ella, but the conversation faltered. After a few banal pleasantries we excused ourselves and moved along.

"Remind me not to go to law school," Ella whispered.

"Let's make that a blood oath."

We'd completed a circuit. I searched for Kit, saw him trapped in a corner with Whitney, Delacourt, and a half-dozen ruffled hipsters. I wished him luck, but no chance was I approaching that nightmare.

Then I felt Ella stiffen at my side. "Tor!"

I turned. Chance Claybourne was weaving toward us.

Is everyone in Charleston at this stupid gala?

"Ack." My eyes darted. "Nowhere to hide."

"For you, maybe." Ella backed away with a wink. "Get him to take you home!"

"Traitor!" I hissed, but she'd already melted into the crowd.

Chance wore his now-customary black suit. I was growing used to seeing him dressed like a playboy rather than a Bolton student. No sane girl would complain.

Stop it. He's dangerous to you.

Chance finally wound a path to my side. "Can't say I expected to see you here."

"Likewise." Playing it cool. "Does Claybourne Manor need more artwork?"

"Always. But this stuff is nonsense. I just bought the one that looks like a plastic hubcap. That twit Jean-Paul is a friend of my cousin."

I couldn't help but laugh. "Nice. Picked out a spot?"

"Bathroom. Gardener's shed."

Needing a distraction, I snagged an appetizer off a passing tray and stuck it in my mouth. Salmon mousse. Gross. I tried not to make a face.

"Should I expect you at these events now?" Chance asked. "I thought you and the others were in hiding on that island."

His tone put me on edge. Chance was watching me closely. There was a tightness to his jaw, and around his eyes. It could've been a trick of the lighting, but Chance's face seemed paler than usual, his hair a little more ruffled.

"Why would I be hiding?" I scanned the room to avoid eye contact.

"*Everyone* has secrets." Matter-of-factly. "Ones we work very hard to protect."

My blood froze. I couldn't meet his gaze.

What did *that* mean? What did Chance know? What *could* he know?

"Is that so?" As calmly as I could muster. "And what dark secrets am I hiding?"

"I wish I knew." Chance drew near, and this time, I couldn't dodge his stare. "I'm getting closer, though. I've been doing some *very* interesting reading lately. Groundbreaking stuff."

With no line of retreat, I squared my shoulders. Gave him a hard look. "You have something to say to me, Chance?"

Our eyes locked. My fingers curled into fists so my hands wouldn't shake.

Several beats passed. Then several more.

Chance broke first. "Just that you look stunning, as always. Enjoy the party. And for God's sake, don't buy any of this lawn furniture."

Chance strolled away. I began breathing again. Willed my heart to resume beating.

He'd been close to saying something, but at the last instance, chose not to.

Then my pulse began racing.

Chance had so many pieces. Had seen more than he should have.

And now, the cryptic comments. The piercing looks. That knowing smile.

It felt like Chance was ramping up the pressure on me. Forcing things to a head.

What has he learned?

Ella appeared at my side. "That looked intense. Are you two in love?"

I started, having nearly forgotten where I was. "Hardly. I don't think we're in *like*."

"BS." Ella pinched my arm. "I caught him looking at you before he came over. I know a man with a crush when I see one."

"What?" Startled. "That's ridiculous."

"Whatever." Ella's tone implied her opinion.

But she was wrong.

Dead wrong, I was sure of it. At this point, Chance and I were practically enemies.

Ella was confusing affection with ferocity.

Chance had feelings toward me, no doubt. But they didn't involve moonlit strolls on the beach. They involved revenge.

I suppressed a yawn. One hour of sleep in the last forty-eight was taking its toll.

"I'm ready when you are," Ella said. "Is your dad still trapped by Beret Boy?"

"I'll grab him. And Whitney, if I must. Can you snag our jackets?"

Ella nodded, heading for the coat check.

On my tiptoes, I spotted Kit stuck in the same corner. Poor guy.

I was halfway across the gallery when something caught my ear. The room was buzzing with dozens of conversations, but I'd distinctly heard a name.

Gable.

I moved left, causally joining a group admiring the show's centerpiece. To me, it looked like an old windmill covered in silly string. But several patrons *ohh*ed and *ahh*ed like the Michelangelo's David had been flown in.

Across from me, on the opposite side of sculpture, stood a group of older men. The Gable name had floated from that bunch.

I sidled clockwise for a better view. Noted a large, bearish man in a charcoal-gray suit.

Rex Gable. His face had been on TV all week.

What's he doing here?

His children had been abducted. A gruesome tape of their imprisonment was airing nonstop. The *last* place he should be is at Jean-Paul Delacourt's Awful Sculpture Extravaganza.

As I watched, Rex Gable broke out in laughter. He elbowed a shorter man at his side.

"Come off it, Miles." Gable drained a highball glass, then slapped a beefy hand on his companion's shoulder. "Two weeks in Argentina is just the thing. I'll book my private plane."

My head snapped back.

Argentina? *Vacation* plans? What was this guy's problem?

I was trying to slip closer when Ella tugged my elbow.

"Less than stellar progress," she quipped, handing me my coat. "Should we just ditch our chaperones and go clubbing?"

I whispered in her ear. "See that big guy in the dark suit?"

Ella glanced surreptitiously. Nodded.

"That's Rex Gable. Lucy and Peter's father. What's he doing here?"

Ella shrugged. "Maybe he likes terrible art."

"If *my* kids had been snatched, I wouldn't go whooping it up with my buddies. What if the police get a second ransom demand, right now? What kind of father does that?"

"Stepfather," Ella corrected.

That stopped me short. "What?"

"He's their *step*father. Lucy and Peter's biological dad left when they were little. I think he moved to Italy, and married a baker. I remember because my mom was friends with their mother a million years ago."

"Stepfather." Implications danced in my head.

Peter Gable's image flashed in my brain. His eyes. His posture. The set of his teeth.

He knew the person.

I watched Rex Gable wave a dismissive hand at Jean-Paul's not-a-windmill centerpiece, then lead his group over to the bar. Made a decision.

I'll be checking into you, sir. Count on that.

"Here they come." Ella grabbed my hand and pulled me toward the exit.

Kit and Whitney appeared, one bored to death, the other raving about the wonderful art. You can guess which was which.

We made our way outside. Kit handed his ticket to the valet attendant. We'd drop Ella at home, then proceed back to Morris.

As I stood curbside, trying to process my scattered thoughts, I noticed a black BMW idling twenty yards down the block.

What the what?

Before I could react, the car pulled from the curb and disappeared down the street.

I rubbed my face, then my eyes. Tried to make sense of things.

A black luxury car at a Gibbes Museum event? Not exactly a rarity.

But I don't believe in coincidence.

My body was tired, and my mind completely shot, but my instincts were wide-awake.

And they were in total agreement.

I'm being followed.

CHAPTER 23

All I wanted was sleep.

My head weighed a thousand pounds. Every bone ached. Something was throbbing behind my eyes.

Every fiber of my being yearned for the sweet oblivion of unconsciousness.

But too many questions needed answers.

Once inside my bedroom, I lurched to my desk chair, stifling a series of groans that might never have ended. I shot a text to the other Virals, then booted my Mac and waited.

And waited.

I was close to nodding off when Hi joined the chat.

"You've gotta be kidding," he mumbled, hair matted to the side of his face. "Sleep deprivation is how we break the minds of terrorists, Tory."

I was spared the need to reply by Shelton's appearance. He waved at the webcam, too tired to speak.

A minute ticked by. Two. Finally, I gave up.

"I guess Ben isn't coming."

"Can you blame him?" Shelton yawned. "I know it's only eleven, but I'm way behind on my beauty rest. This couldn't wait?"

"No." I sighed. "I don't know. Maybe. Did you tell Ben what we found at LIRI?"

"Yeah. He wasn't thrilled about being left out."

"He'll be fine. But I need him to—"

Just then, Ben's face appeared onscreen. He didn't look tired at all.

"Yeah?" He still wore his black tee and jeans.

"Oh, good." Hiding my surprise. "Here's what happened."

I told them about my encounters with Rex Gable and the black BMW. At the last instant, I decided not to mention my face-off with Chance.

When I'd finished, support for my theory was less than resounding.

"Black luxury cars aren't all that rare," Shelton pointed out. "You didn't get the plate?"

I shook my head. "I know it isn't much to go on, but my gut says it was the same one."

He nodded. The boys trusted my instincts. Usually.

"Maybe Rex Gable is just a prick," Ben said. "If he's not the twins' biological father, that might explain everything."

"You could be right," I said diplomatically. "But the whole scene was just . . . off. I can't explain it better than that. Even Ella agreed."

Hi perked up. "Ella was there?"

"Did I not mention that?" My brain truly was deep fried. "We went together."

"Oh." Hi and Shelton at once. Ben looked away.

"Hey, wait." I leaned closer to the screen. "You guys wouldn't have wanted to go. I took Ella so I wouldn't be paraded around like Whitney's toy poodle."

No one spoke. Nonplussed, I decided to change the subject.

"Anyway, on the way home I got an idea. Which is why I called this meeting."

I paused. We needed Ben for this, and I wasn't sure how he'd react.

"I want to investigate Rex Gable," I said. "Something isn't right. I thought the best place to start might be his phone records. That's what the cops would do."

"You want to hack Rex Gable's cell phone?" Shelton pinched his nose. "Based on a hypothetical trip to South America?"

"If that was all, I'd agree this is rash. But I'm convinced Peter recognized his kidnapper in that ransom video. Put those facts together, and—"

"You think Rex Gable videotaped his stepkids locked in a dungeon?" Ben scoffed. "That seems plausible to you?"

"No!" I wasn't explaining my thoughts well. "But what if the kidnapper Peter saw is *connected* to his stepfather somehow? A coworker. A drinking buddy. Someone close to the family that Peter recognized."

"It's a shot in the dark," Hi said gently. "If that."

"Okay," said Ben.

I sat back, stunned. "Okay?"

"Sure." Ben shrugged. "I assume you want Chang to do it, since we wouldn't have a clue where to start."

"Yes." Thrown off. "That's exactly what I was thinking."

"I'll call him. Back in five." Ben's face blipped from the screen.

"Are we sure that was Ben?" Hi joked. "He's never that agreeable."

"Did you guys patch things up?" Shelton asked me.

"No. We haven't spoken since our catfight in the Wando parking lot. I'm as stunned as you are."

Ben reappeared. "He'll do it for another five hundred. I have a PayPal address."

"E-mail it." Shelton pulled a notepad from his desk. "But we're short on cash, people."

A minute passed as Shelton executed the transaction. Once complete, Ben logged off again to confirm with Chang. The rest of us waited, fighting off sleep, unsure how long this process might take.

Less than five minutes later, a message appeared in my inbox. The sender was Variance.

Call logs and text messages for the last six months. Enjoy! V

Attached was an eighty-page PDF.

Ben returned to the chat. "You guys get the email?"

"Yep." Shelton was skimming on his monitor. "This might take a while."

"True," Hi said, "but check out last weekend. Gable made thirty calls to a private number."

"Thirty?" I skipped ahead to the dates in question.

Something occurred to me. I quickly scanned the rest of the call logs.

"Rex Gable never called that number on any other day," I said. "Before or since. At least, not in the last six months."

"Suspicious," Shelton agreed, "but *not* proof. Maybe his car broke down somewhere, and he was talking to a mechanic. There are lots of reason why a cluster of calls might appear."

"You're right." I rubbed my eyes, unsure what to do next.

Then a fifth box opened on my monitor.

Eddie Chang smiled at me from his mega-desk.

"Greetings, friends!" Chang was munching on a Twizzler. "Mind if I cut in?"

"How the frick!?!" Shelton sputtered.

"This chat group is totally private," Hi fumed. "You can't join without an invite!"

Even Ben looked startled.

"Guys," Chang said breezily, "I just delivered a stranger's phone records in less than ten minutes. You think hijacking a dinky little video chat was much trouble?"

Okay. Fair point.

"What can we help you with, Variance?" I asked, as politely as possible. Acquiring a computer-hacker enemy was not on my bucket list.

"Actually, I'm here to help *you*. I did some more digging into that file tree we found."

"How?" Shelton squawked. "We took the flash drive home with us."

"Yeah, I copied your data stick. Sorry, it's what hackers do. Don't stress, though, I found the decoded files super-boring—I couldn't care less about veterinary medicine. But that ghost tree is cutting edge. I *had* to see if I could crack those B-Series files."

My blood ran cold. Chang had read Karsten's files. Could we trust him?

Stay calm. Nothing in those records ties back to us.

"Well?" Voice level. "Did you?"

"Not even close. There's no way around it—in order to read *those* files, you'll have to physically connect to their home server. I'm bummed, too."

"Well, thanks for trying," Hi said. "Even though you lied to us, and we asked you not to."

"No problem. I *did* manage to locate the server, however."

I sat straighter in my chair. "And you'll tell us where?"

"Take this freebee as my apology." Chang drum-rolled his fingers. "The B-Series files . . . are physically housed . . . on a server *at* . . . the South Carolina Aquarium!"

An actual rimshot played on my speakers.

"The aquarium?" Ben looked as confused as I felt.

Chang shrugged. "I'm a hundred percent certain, hombres. The server in question is leased to the freaking aquarium. But get this, the hardware is *licensed* to another entity. A Big Pharma outfit. Who knew drug manufacturers are bankrolling all the little fishies?"

My heart dropped. "You have a name?"

Chang tapped a button. A logo appeared on my screen.

"Candela Pharmaceuticals. Sounds incredibly boring. Peace out!"

Chang's grinning visage blinked from my screen.

CHAPTER 24

Friday

That night, I slept like the dead.

But when my alarm sounded early the next morning, I staggered to my feet, showered and dressed quickly, and hurried downstairs. I wanted to avoid Kit.

I needn't have bothered.

"Your daddy already left for work." Whitney was wrapped in a floral bathrobe, blending a smoothie. "He said your attendance at dinner is *required.*"

"Thanks." Execution deferred.

"We can talk then about tomorrow's block party. I'm going to need your help setting up, and getting the food all squared away."

"Sure." Grabbing a banana. "Just let me know."

Twenty minutes later, I was down at the dock.

Hi and Shelton were waiting, Bolton jackets slung over their shoulders. The temperature was already eighty degrees, with the humidity on full blast, putting my deodorant to the test.

"You still wanna go this morning?" Hi asked.

I nodded. "The aquarium opens at nine. If we get there early, we can avoid the tourist rush."

"There won't be any *tourists* in the off-limits areas," Shelton grumbled. "Just security guards, killer fish, and a maze of rooms we don't know how to navigate."

"We'll manage," I said simply. "We always do."

"You missed two classes yesterday, chasing Ben." Hi waggled a finger. "Another absence might catch Headmaster Paugh's attention."

My mood soured. "I know. And Kit's on my case about our stunt at LIRI." *Not to mention Whitney. Or Chance.* "But Chang has me spooked about those B-Series files. Candela being involved really freaks me out. I don't think we can risk waiting."

Tom Blue appeared from inside *Hugo*'s cabin and waived us aboard.

"Actually, I agree." Hi led us toward seats in the bow. "We're gonna go eventually, so why *not* today? The crowd should be small. No one visits the aquarium on a Friday morning in April."

"Ben's picking us up at eight forty-five," I reminded unnecessarily. "A block from school, on Gadsden. We go to first period, then ditch second. Hopeful we're back by lunch. Maybe sooner."

Hugo rounded Morris Island and slipped into Charleston Harbor. The downtown peninsula appeared, grew larger as we chugged for the city marina. Seabirds filled the air, calling and circling the stern. The breeze carried the twin perfumes of salt and seafoam.

Another beautiful morning in the Lowcountry.

I rose. Stretched. Tried to shake away my lethargy.

Get ready. Today is make or break.

⬡ ⬡ ⬡

"That's just stupid, Tory! Quit being so damn stubborn!"

"Not a chance! You've got some kind of death wish! We can't even *trust* our powers lately. They're too erratic for a public heist."

Ben thumped the steering wheel in frustration. "Maybe for *you*."

I glowered at Ben from the backseat. I'd given Hi shotgun, having sensed this argument was inevitable. I didn't want to be close. The urge to slap might become overpowering.

"Why don't we all use our friendly words?" Hi suggested. "Let's take five, and everyone can say something we *like* about each other. I'll start. Shelton, you're super at—"

"Shut up, Hi!" Ben and I shouted, the first thing we'd agreed upon all morning.

"*In any case,*" I continued, "we're not flaring downtown, in broad daylight, inside a packed aquarium," I repeated. "The risk is *way* too high. I can't believe we're even *discussing* this!"

"You want us to find the server room," Ben shot back. "That means sneaking around where we're not supposed to be, dodging guards, and generally trying to be invisible. You don't think that our particular set of skills might come in handy?"

"Like Liam Neeson," Hi offered to no one in particular. "He *did* find his daughter."

"Tory's right," Shelton said from the seat beside me. "I love the edge that flaring give us, but it's not something we can use *everywhere.* Never has been. What happens if we run smack into somebody, eyes glowing like a pack of werewolves?"

"We won't run into anyone if we use our powers," Ben insisted. "That's the *point.*"

"No." I crossed my arms. "Either we agree on this, or I'm walking back to Bolton Prep."

Ben tensed. I could practically feel his exasperation. Then he took a deep breath. When he spoke again, the heat was gone from his voice.

"Fine. No flares. Happy?"

"Thank you." I exited the vehicle before the argument could rekindle.

The South Carolina Aquarium is on the opposite side of downtown from police HQ, on the peninsula's eastern edge. Opened in 2000, the building has approximately ninety thousand square feet of floor space, and is home to over ten thousand animals.

Not just tropical fish, either—the aquarium houses a vast array of aquatic-based wildlife. Alligators. Pythons. Hawks. All told, sixty exhibits are organized into five groups, each representing a region of the Appalachian watershed—Mountains, Piedmont, Coastal Plain, Coast, and Ocean.

The main draw is the Great Ocean tank, a 385,000-gallon, two-story behemoth that holds nearly a thousand sharks, sting rays, sea turtles, and other saltwater creatures. I'd seen it twice, and was amazed both times.

"Can we check out the dolphins before breaking and entering?" Hi asked as we crossed the nearly empty parking lot.

"None inside." Shelton consulted a handout he'd printed. "It's illegal to keep a dolphin or whale in captivity in this state. But there's a viewing deck that overlooks the harbor. You can see a ton of dolphins from there."

"Does that have a map?" I asked. The entrance was a few yards ahead.

Shelton nodded. "There are two floors, and a trail you're supposed to follow."

"I guess it makes sense to just go with the flow. Until we see a likely entry point."

"Sounds like a plan." Hi unbuttoned his collar and rolled up his sleeves.

We'd ditched jackets and ties in the SUV, but our matching outfits marked us as truants to anyone paying attention. Nothing to be done. If hassled, we'd make something up—I was confident Hi had an outlandish cover story prepped and waiting.

We bought four student tickets and stepped into the main lobby.

"According to this flyer, you start upstairs," Shelton said. "Then you snake through the exhibits, working your way around the second floor and then back down."

"Lead on," I said.

We ascended a level, found ourselves in the Mountain Forest. A family of river otters welcomed us to their domain. Moving as quickly as possible without drawing notice, we passed through the Piedmont with no more than a few glances. At the Coastal Plain, however, we were forced to stop a full ten minutes while Hi ogled the albino alligator.

"You're the coolest thing alive," Hi breathed, as close to the bone-white reptile as he dared. "Don't let anyone tell you different."

Crossing the building, we buzzed past the Salt Marsh's birds and the Coast's sea turtles. At each exhibit we searched for service doors and non-public areas, but found nothing promising.

"Let's go back downstairs," I suggested.

"Head for the Great Ocean tank." Shelton pointed to the center of the building. "There's a staircase beside it that spans both levels."

The massive enclosure rose from the ground floor up through the second level—the aquarium's central spoke—with viewing nooks at intervals around the glass.

"That's one huge honking fishbowl," Hi said as we descended. "Must be hell keeping the pH balance correct. I know how it is. I owned a goldfish once."

"Once?" Shelton asked.

"It died. Almost immediately."

"Nice work."

"Guys." Ben had reached the lower landing. He nodded to a black door in the corner. "First one I've seen."

Shelton's head whipped this way and that. "Coast's clear."

"The Coast is upstairs," Hi quipped. "Where the octopus was."

Ben smacked the back of his head. "Stop being funny."

"You'll regret that," Hi hissed. "A Stolowitski always pays his debts."

We scurried to the door, and, with a last scan for observers, barged through.

Thankfully, nothing began flashing or gonging. This portal wasn't alarmed.

We found ourselves in a chilly hallway lined with doors on both sides. The walls were white cinder block, the concrete floor a dull hospital gray. Fifty feet ahead, the corridor ended with a flight of steps going upward.

"What now?" Shelton asked.

"Start trying doors," Ben suggested.

Hiram and I took the left side, Shelton and Ben the right. Our first two rooms were locked. The third was a bathroom supply closet. I glanced at Shelton, who shook his head. They'd had no luck either.

Suddenly, footsteps echoed down the hallway.

Two pairs of shoes were descending the stairs at the end of the corridor.

"Hide!" I whispered.

"Where?" Shelton whined.

Without a better option, I flung open the supply closet and pointed inside. We jammed in like sardines, closing the door as voices drew near.

I held my breath. We'd barely made it twenty feet. So far, our mission was a joke.

"I don't see the point," one said irritably.

The footsteps halted right outside the supply closet door.

Come on. Keep moving, you two.

"I'm not paying you to think. I'm paying you to spy."

"Of course," the first speaker stammered. "I meant no disrespect. It's just . . . the girl and her friends are hard to track. They came by yesterday, but apparently spent the whole time in the video editing suite. I have no idea—"

"Yesterday?" the second voice interrupted. "You're certain?"

"Absolutely. I saw them myself."

A bomb went off in my head.

Girl? Video editing? Were these strangers discussing *me*?

"What game is she playing?" the second speaker mused.

The bomb became a supernova. *I know that voice.*

"I'll keep watching." The first voice became ingratiating. "Anything you need."

"Just do as you're told and you'll get paid. But don't get cute, or make a move without my permission. Are we clear?"

"Yessir. Very clear."

The footsteps resumed, heading for the aquarium floor.

Before the boys could stop me, I cracked the door and stuck my head out.

I had to see if my ears were correct.

Twenty feet away, Chance Claybourne was striding down the corridor.

Mike Iglehart was hurrying at his side.

Someone tugged my shirt, pulling me back into the closet. The door snapped shut.

"Are you crazy?" Shelton had an earlobe in each hand.

"That was Chance!"

"Say what?" Hi carefully eased the door open a second time. "There's no one out here."

Shelton eyed me strangely. "Chance is working at the aquarium?"

"Of course not!" Then my eyes widened. "But he *is* working for Candela."

Hi pushed the door wide and we stumbled out. As one, the boys scrutinized me.

"It *was* Chance!" I insisted. "And not alone, either. That creep Iglehart was with him. He must be Chance's mole at LIRI."

Things started falling into place. How Chance always knew things he shouldn't. How Candela was connected to the institute. I wondered how long their slimy arrangement had been in place. I worried what Iglehart had been able to share.

"Chance has been suspicious of us for months," Hi said. "Hiring a spy at LIRI *is* somewhat logical. If you're a paranoid, whacked-out trust-fund baby with too much time on your hands."

"He knows about Karsten." I was suddenly sure. "The lab. The parvovirus experiment. The whole deal. Chance might even have access to Karsten's records."

"What? How would he know any of those things?" Ben demanded.

"Remember. Candela was bankrolling Karsten in the first place. The whole experiment was a pet project of Hollis Claybourne, Chance's father. It stands to reason that Chance might've found out about it."

"He's on our trail then," Shelton worried. "Chance could expose us!"

"Nothing in Karsten's files leads to us." I spoke for my own benefit as much as theirs. "At worst, Chance learns about Parvovirus XPB-19. But that won't tell him squat about us."

That was true, right?

Yet something nagged at me.

Karsten never wrote a word about the Virals—he never planned for us to exist. Therefore, logically, nothing in his records could connect to us. Our genetic transformation occurred completely off the grid.

So why did I feel so anxious?

"Hey, people! We're still in the process of committing a crime," Hi reminded everyone. "Maybe this isn't the best place to debrief?"

"Right." Ben pointed toward the staircase. "Keep moving."

We tried the remaining doors, with no luck. So, hearts in our throats, we snuck up the steps Chance and Iglehart had descended.

At the top was another hallway. This time, the left-hand doors were labeled. Nutrition. Medical. Surgical. Chemical. The doors on the right had vertical window slits. Mounds of hoses, ropes, pipes, and clear plastic tubing were visible through each one.

"This must be a veterinary area," I said. "And exhibit maintenance. Not what we want."

Hi spotted a set of steel double doors. "That way, maybe?"

I nodded, gesturing for him to lead.

The hallway beyond was carpeted and wallpapered, with large square windows allowing view inside several offices, a conference center, and a copy room. Rounding a corner, the next door down contained what we sought.

"Jackpot," Shelton whispered. "I see a dozen blade systems. This must be the place."

The door was unlocked. Once inside we paused, uncertain what to do next.

"We're looking for a Candela server, right?" I shrugged. "Start hunting for the logo."

We fanned out to scan the rows of equipment. I found our target nestled in a corner.

"Bingo." I tapped the trademarked cursive letter on the unit's side. "*C* marks the spot."

Fired up, I started barking orders. "Hi and Ben—guard the door. Shelton, find an access panel and get to work."

Spotting a mobile interface, Shelton flipped down its keyboard to reveal a small monitor. "I *love* technology." He inserted Karsten's flash drive.

An icon appeared onscreen. Shelton double-clicked.

"I'm not sure how to . . ." Shelton trailed off as the file tree flashed onscreen. "Excellent. The program works automatically."

Shelton cracked his knuckles. Then his fingers danced across the keys.

"I'll try copying everything back to the data stick," he said. "Hopefully, the files won't disappear when we disconnect, but we can't sit here and read them."

"Sounds good." In this realm, I had no advice to give.

"B-Series files," Shelton mumbled. "Gotcha. And if I disable *this* setting . . . we should be able to actually store them on the drive . . ."

There was a series of whirrs and clicks.

"Damn," Shelton murmured. "Come on, now."

"What is it?"

"I got the B-Series files downloaded, but they're *encrypted,* too. We'll need Chang again."

I shook my head. "I don't trust that guy. We'll figure something else out. Are you connected to the Internet?"

"Yeah. Got a strong wireless signal."

"Mail everything to your dummy account, just to be safe. Then close up shop."

"Roger that." Shelton mashed a few more keys, then removed the drive from the server. He was folding up the keyboard when Hi pounded over.

"Someone's at the door." Eyes wide. "There's no other way out."

Ben looked my way, his expression a thunderhead. "Two security guards. They snuck up on us, because *you* didn't think sonic hearing would be useful."

I was about to respond when the door opened.

Bright halogens flashed to life.

My eyes darted left, then right. Then squeezed shut.

Cornered like rats.

There was no place to run.

CHAPTER 25

"Don't move!"

I didn't. There was no point.

A twitchy senior edged into the room, one hand clamped to his utility belt, a tan security uniform hanging loosely on his skinny frame.

Hi raised both hands in the air. "Don't taze me, bro."

The rest of us followed suit. The elderly guard was joined by a second, a muscular black man with a wispy mustache.

The younger guard barked into a shoulder radio. "HQ, this is Hines. Spencer and I have located the intruders. Just some punk kids. Over."

Beside me, Ben seethed, furious we'd allowed ourselves to be trapped. I ignored him.

Flaring *might've* made a difference, but we'd never know.

And if we'd been caught with glowing irises? Yikes. No thanks.

"Anyone else in on this prank?" the guard named Hines demanded. His partner watched in silence, equal parts terrified and elated. No doubt this was usually a slow gig.

"No, sir." I replied. "We got lost. Which way is the Madagascar Journey?"

Hines snorted. "About four plausible wrong turns back. Let's go. And nobody even *think* about making a break for it. I *live* for the idea of running someone down."

"Let me flare and try your chances," Ben snapped.

"What was that?" Hines got right in Ben's face. "We got a problem, Bono?"

Ben looked away. "No, sir."

"All right, then." Hines pointed to the door. "Single file down the hall. Follow my man, Spence. Don't get cute, neither."

We did as instructed. Spencer led us deeper into the bowels of the aquarium, passing three more sets of doors before arriving at some sort of holding area.

"In there." Hines pointed to a small room with a table and four chairs.

We entered and sat. Hines locked the door from the outside.

"Well, we're finally busted." Shelton sighed. "Gonna look great on my college apps. Think they'll knock it down to probation for first-time offenders?"

"Relax," Hi said, but a tapping foot contradicted his own advice. "We know the district attorney. Harris owes us at least one get-out-of-jail-free card. Right?"

"We shouldn't even *be* here." Ben's fist slammed the table. "Those clowns wouldn't have gotten the drop on us if we'd been flaring. Not in this lifetime."

"Done is done." I took a deep breath. "Maybe Hi and Shelton are right. We might be able to duck any serious charges. After all, we didn't actually *do* anything. No theft. No damage. Just some light trespassing."

And computer fraud. But, hey, they didn't know that.

"Tell that to my mother." Hi laid his head on the table. "She's gonna roast me alive. Then shoot me. Then kick me in the man parts."

I patted his shoulder. "Whatever happens to you, I'll get worse."

Kit was *already* mad. I shuddered, thinking about how to explain this one.

The door swung open.

"Everybody up," Hines barked. "Seems you've got a fan."

A fan? What could that mean?

Hines marched us to a nearby elevator. When the car arrived, we ascended two floors. This section was nicer, with high ceilings and plush red carpeting. Spacious offices lined the hall, each with a window overlooking the harbor.

For some reason, I got a bad feeling.

And I *trust* those feelings.

"Move along," Hines said. "Last room down."

I spotted a fish tank halfway down the aisle. Dug into my pocket.

"Hi," I whispered. "Distraction in five. Four. Three . . ."

I broke off as we neared the tank.

Hi spun. "Yo, warden. When do we eat around here? I'm hypoglycemic, plus I've got a hernia. And rabies simplex D. Basically, I need a ton of pills or my arms will fall off."

"Boy, you're on my last nerve."

As Hines glared at Hiram, I palmed the flash drive and dumped it into the fish tank. The yellow-and-black rectangle tumbled to the bottom.

So long, friend. Let's hope Shelton's email went through.

"It's a cultural thing," Hi was saying. "I think you're being very insensitive."

Hines snorted. "Do you want me to cuff you?"

"Kinda."

"Hi." I nodded.

He turned from Hines without another word.

At the end of the hall, the guard knocked on the door of a corner office.

"Come in." A voice I knew well.

Score another one for my gut.

Chance was sitting behind a desk, typing on a laptop. Behind him, a huge window looked out over the dolphin-viewing platform.

“Thank you—” Chance glanced up, “—Mr. Hines. I’ll take it from here.”

The guard withdrew without a word.

“You have an office here?” Shelton blurted. “This makes no sense.”

Chance’s eyes had returned to his monitor. “I’m allowed to use this space as needed. And it makes *perfect* sense, since my family’s foundation helps keep these lights on.”

He finally looked at me. There was no humor in his eyes.

“You stole something. Give it back.”

“Sorry, Chance.” I took a seat, crossed one leg over the other. “It’s a big place, and we got lost. Hiram wanted a smoothie.”

“Mango strawberry,” Hi confirmed. “Heard the break room had a blender.”

Chance spun the laptop on his desk. A clip was playing onscreen—the four of us, poking around in the server room.

“For some reason, this surveillance system doesn’t have sound. Foolish, but there it is. I can’t see what you’re doing in the corner, but it’s obvious you’re hacking the system. Why?”

His last word carried true bafflement.

He doesn’t know why we’re here.

“I’m sure you’ve had the server room inspected,” I said. “You know nothing is missing.”

“Indeed. That’s the only reason they gave you to me.”

I shrugged. “Like I said, we got lost. It happens.”

Chance leaned back in his chair. Seemed to consider for a moment.

“You understand that I can have you arrested for trespassing?” he said coldly. “Or that, alternatively, I could arrange for you to walk right out the front door, scot-free?”

He’s trying to bully me.

"Do what you have to, Chance. We. Got. Lost."

His eyes flicked to Hi, then Shelton. Finally to Ben. Whatever he saw there didn't improve his mood.

"I'll let you go."

Sighs escaped from both Shelton and Hi. I felt a similar relief.

I might talk a big game, but I was desperate to avoid Kit finding out about this.

Chance held up a finger. "One condition."

"Name it."

"A minute alone, Tory. I'd like a quick chat."

Ben shot forward. "You can stick that *chat* right up—"

"Ben!" I stared daggers at him. "It's fine. Please wait in the hall."

With a simmering glare, Ben turned and stormed out. Shelton and Hi followed on his heels, calling after Ben as he stomped down the hallway. The door swung closed.

I turned back to Chance. Was surprised by the naked anger in his eyes.

"You think you're so smart, don't you, Tory?"

"*That's* what you wanted to say?" I rose. "If so, I'll pass on your chat."

"SIT. DOWN." For a moment, his cool slipped completely. "Or you can spend the rest of your morning arranging bail."

I retook my seat, trying to hide my shock.

Something was very wrong. Chance might be callow, but he was never cruel. There was a tension in his posture I didn't like. His fingers drummed the desktop, as if unable to remain still. Both feet bounced on the floor.

"I know about Karsten," he said simply.

"Who?" Knee-jerk. My mind slipped into panic mood.

"Come off it, Tory. I know all about the good doctor, his parvovirus experiments, and XPB-19. I have his research files. They're stored on a Candela blade server, downstairs." Chance tapped the laptop on his desk. "The same server you spent five minutes huddled beside in this surveillance video."

I didn't reply. When you're nailed to the wall, it's best to say nothing.

"I've had Karsten's files for months," Chance went on. "Couldn't make heads or tails of them. But then I saw something *very* interesting."

No response. I schooled my face to stillness.

Let him tell you what he knows. Give nothing back.

"Do you know the subject Karsten used to test XPB-19?" Chance winked. "I bet you do."

Oh no.

"It was a wolfdog. One he'd capture on Loggerhead Island. How extraordinary!"

No no no.

Chance leaned forward. "I find that *exceedingly* interesting, in light of Karsten's research notes. This one in particular."

He reached into a drawer and pulled out a single sheet.

Slid it across the desk toward me.

No no no no no.

Unable to resist, I craned my neck to read it. Knew what I'd see.

It was the page I'd suspected, with the handwritten note at the bottom.

I sat stone still, breathless, unable to formulate a response.

Chance read the notation aloud. "The highest caution must be employed. Due to its radical structure, Parvovirus strain XPB-19 may be infectious to *humans.*"

My mind gibbered.

Impossibly, he'd made a connection. Recognized a link no one else would've noticed.

Chance laid the truth bare. "Karsten used Coop as his subject. Coop was patient zero for Parvovirus XPB-19. Parvovirus XPB-19 is contagious to humans. *You* own Coop."

"This means nothing." Even I didn't buy my words.

He had hard evidence tying us to Karsten's experiment.

Suddenly, to the Virals, Chance Claybourne was the most dangerous man alive.

"Enough dancing around!" Chance thundered. "Tell me the *truth.* Tell me what I don't know. *Tell me what I saw!*"

"No." I tried to rise, but my legs were jelly.

"Why did you steal Coop from the institute? Did you catch the virus? What happened when you did?"

A manic intensity filled Chance's eyes. One I'd seen months before.

"I've seen things I can't explain," Chance hissed. "*You* will explain. Now!"

"Be careful, Chance."

"Excuse me?" He seemed momentarily taken aback.

"I said, be careful."

Chance's face hardened. "Are you threatening me, Tory?"

I steeled my nerve. Was tired of being pushed around.

Chance wanted to play hardball? Thought he could bully me into revealing my secrets?

Not a chance, Chance.

You have no idea who you're dealing with. What *you're dealing with.*

Chance rose, planting his hands on the desktop. "Your secret won't stay hidden forever."

I placed my own palms on the desk. Stuck my nose inches from his.

"You'd better hope it does, Chance." Barely a whisper. "Otherwise, you might not like what you find. Not one . . . little . . . bit."

Our eyes locked.

An electric charge filled the room.

What are you doing? Did you just threaten him?

Hiding my misgivings, I met him stare for stare. Felt his hot breath on my cheek.

For the second time that morning, Chance broke first. He flopped backward into his chair, sweat glistening his brow.

He swiveled to face the window. "Get out of here. Now."

I didn't wait for a second invitation.

CHAPTER 26

"You okay, Tor?"

Hi set his roast beef sandwich aside. He and Shelton were watching with troubled eyes.

"I'm fine. It's nothing."

We sat at our usual table in Bolton's cafeteria. Ben had dropped us off right as the lunch bell sounded. We'd all missed second and third periods, which looked suspicious, but so far no one had made a fuss.

I hadn't spoken since fleeing Chance's office. Not as we exited the aquarium, on the drive back to school, or upon sneaking into the lunch crowd.

I hoped they thought my silence a result of my argument with Ben.

I had zero intention of telling them what Chance had said. Not yet.

Is that my call? Who am I to keep that kind of information from the pack?

I pushed the doubts aside. There was no reason to create panic. Not without some notion of how to deal with the situation.

Honestly, I worried what Ben might do. If he thought Chance was threatening him . . .

Ben? That's a laugh. I just threatened Chance to his face.

I shivered at the memory. What had I been thinking?

Self-preservation. It's a powerful motivator.

"You don't wanna talk about what Chance said?" The third time Hi brought it up.

"It was nothing. Chance wanted to know what we were doing in the server room. He tried to bully me, but I convinced him to let us walk."

Hi nodded slowly, but I could tell he still had questions.

"Chance keeps popping up in weird places," Shelton said. "He's got connections to LIRI, to Candela, *and* to the aquarium. That can't be coincidence."

"I'll deal with Chance."

But could I? Which rabbit up my sleeve would make him walk away?

None of them. Chance had questioned his own sanity over our secret.

I made him think he was crazy. He won't let this go until he learns the truth.

"Okay." Hi tapped his thumbs together. "So what's next? Lotta balls in the air."

I was happy to change the subject. "Should we tell the police about Rex Gable?"

"Get directly involved?" Shelton looked at me askance. "Seems a bit messy, don't it?"

"We could make an anonymous tip," Hi suggested. "Call from a pay phone, like in one of those prehistoric movies. There still *are* pay phones, right? Like, where old people hang out?"

"When was the last time you saw one?" Shelton countered.

"Whatever. We could buy a burner. Call from a rooftop, then dump it."

Shelton snorted. "You've been watching *The Wire* too much."

Static cackled from the cafeteria speaker. A bored female voice came on. "Victoria Brennan, please report to the headmaster's office. Victoria Brennan to the headmaster's office."

Classmates glanced our way. Whispers sprang up around me.

"Not good." Shelton was reaching for his earlobe.

"Tell them you have amnesia," Hi said. "Or dementia. Pretend you're Joan of Arc."

"Thanks for the support, guys. If I'm not back for class, look for my body in the harbor."

Hiram's hand flew up. "I call her iTunes collection. Shelton can have the mutt."

"Nice."

I took a deep breath. Tried to count the tightropes I currently walked.

Kit. Whitney. Ben. Chance.

Now the headmaster? What's one more in the mix?

With a groan, I hurried to meet my fate.

⬡ ⬡ ⬡

"That's *four days* this week," Headmaster Paugh scolded.

"I know." Head down, face meek. He hadn't invited me to sit. "I'm very sorry, sir."

"That's quite a lot to excuse." Paugh watched from across a delicate antique desk that must've cost a fortune. "Even from one of our best students."

"It's been a crazy week, sir. But that's over with now. I'll make up all the work."

Paugh steepled his fingers. "I accept that on Monday you were called to testify in an important matter. And on Wednesday, you were summoned by the district attorney herself." He sat back in his overstuffed leather chair. "But yesterday, without warning, you missed two more classes. And this morning, you did so *again*."

"We were wrapping up court business," I said quickly. "There were papers to sign, and a conference with the DA. You can call Ms. Harris's office to confirm, if you'd like."

Please God, don't.

Paugh pressed his fingers to the desktop. "You missed Spanish *four times out of five* this week. That cannot continue. I won't allow it."

"No, sir." Serious nodding. "Understood. The court doesn't need me anymore, not even for sentencing. It's all worked out so that I won't miss any more school."

"See that you don't." Paugh's scowl deepened. "First this Gamemaster debacle, and now two of our students *kidnapped.* I don't know what's happening to this city."

Then he glared, as if I might be the cause of all the trouble.

I remained silent. Eyed the door.

"Have you been following the Gable case?" Paugh asked.

"What?" The question caught me off guard. "Oh! Yessir, of course. I have several classes with the twins." A pause. "Terrible thing."

"The worst I can remember." Paugh removed and wiped his glasses, his eyes taking on a faraway look. For an instant I saw real pain.

Why not tell him about Rex Gable?

Paugh was the headmaster. He could tip the police without revealing a source. In a way, he was perfect.

I opened my mouth to speak.

Paugh fixed me with his bird-like stare.

Something in his demeanor. A coldness to his glance. The set of his shoulders.

I didn't like it. Didn't trust it.

I closed my mouth, abandoning the idea until I'd given it more thought.

"Did you have something to say, Miss Brennan?"

"No, sir. Just that I hope the police find Lucy and Peter. And that they're well."

“Yes, of course.” Paugh replaced his glasses. “Your island friends missed class this morning as well. Same reason?”

“Yessir.” Hoping my eyes didn’t betray me.

“Ella Francis also? She missed a presentation she’ll have difficulty making up.”

I stiffened. “Ella missed psych today?”

“Yes.” Paugh’s eyes narrowed. “She wasn’t with you?”

“No,” I said, unable to hide my surprise.

The headmaster was right—Ella had a major group project due that morning, one that counted for a third of her semester grade. She’d been whining about it for weeks. Missing the presentation was going to cause her all kinds of headaches.

Paugh waved a hand. “Very well, please return to class.”

I beelined for the door.

“And, Miss Brennan?”

I turned, doorknob in hand. “Yes?”

“No more of this. I’ll be paying attention.”

I nodded, then scurried into the hallway.

How many offices will I run from today?

⬡ ⬡ ⬡

I was grabbing my econ book when I remembered Ella.

She must be sick as a dog, or she’d have been there.

Slipping into the ladies room, I checked to be sure I was alone. Then I dialed Ella’s cell.

Four rings. No answer. Voicemail.

I called again, thinking she might be asleep. Same result.

“Ugh.”

I disconnected and sent a text: U OK? U missed psych!

After waiting a full minute, I gave up and stepped back into the hall.

I had my own problems.

The B-Series files we'd downloaded from Candela's server. What could they be? Why the encryption? How did they fit with Karsten's old project?

I hadn't the slightest doubt Chance was involved.

But why the freaking aquarium? What was Chance doing there?

Find out. Crack the files.

Hurrying to class, a single question dominated my thoughts.

How?

CHAPTER 27

Headmaster Declan Paugh peered through his office blinds.

Making a space with his finger, he watched Tory Brennan disappear down the hall.

Trouble from the start.

Paugh released the slats and returned to his desk. It was Edwardian, a rare example of late-reign oak treatments that fell out of the court's favor.

Paugh adored it.

Like so little else in a world filled with disposable plastic abominations—cheap, soulless replications—this desk had *character.* A testament to the class and refinement of a better time.

Paugh's mission in life was to preserve Bolton Preparatory Academy in the same manner.

To hold back the creeping poison of modernity that was destroying polite society.

And I'm failing. One concession at a time.

Allowing the Loggerhead Trust to send students on scholarships had been a mistake. That much was obvious now. But at the time, money had been vital.

Paugh's predecessor had possessed no head for business. He might even have been a crook. It'd taken years to right the books, all while hiding the academy's dire fiscal picture under the rug.

But he'd done it. Bolton was back on firm footing.

If the parents only knew what Herculean measures he'd taken to make it so, they'd give him a service medal. A parade.

Not to be. Burying all signs of distress had been Rule Number One.

Without its sterling reputation, the academy was nothing.

But those kids are still here. Three of them, anyway.

That cursed trial! What a nightmare. Publicity was anathema to everything Bolton Prep stood for. Paugh didn't care about putting some petty thug away. He wanted the *media* away.

And now they were back. Prowling his gates. Disturbing his sanctuary. If those cretins kept poking around, who knows what they might find?

Those blasted Gable twins. A problem without an answer.

Things were spiraling out of control. Paugh had begun to feel very, very nervous.

Just do as you were told. No more, no less.

That wasn't the headmaster's style, but in this matter his hands were tied.

Sighing, Declan Paugh picked up his cell phone and dialed.

CHAPTER 28

I checked my iPhone after last period.

Nothing. No calls. No texts. Ella had been absent all day.

I swung by Coach Lynch's office, but he hadn't heard from her either. After begging my way out of practice—promising to rejoin the squad ASAP—I headed for the gate.

Shelton and Hi were waiting.

"Change of plans," I said. "I'm gonna run by Ella's place before going home."

Shelton scratched his nose. "Why? Looking to collect another virus?"

"She missed a big thing in psych today, and didn't return any of my texts. That's not like her. I wanna make sure she's okay. See if she needs anything."

"You want us to walk with you?" Hi asked casually. "I've got nothing else to do."

I smirked. "You can come, Romeo."

"You sure?" Hi licked his palm, then used it to slick his hair. "With me around, she might not even notice you're there."

"I'll risk it. I'm just popping my head in, anyway. Shelton?"

He shrugged. "Why not? Mr. Blue will want to ferry us together anyway."

"Good point. Can you text him we'll be late?"

Shelton nodded, digging out his iPhone as we headed down the street.

The Francis family lived in South of Broad, the ultra-exclusive neighborhood at the tip of the peninsula. While not as imposing as Claybourne Manor—located just a few blocks away—Ella's home was still a registered historical landmark.

After a few short blocks, we turned right onto Logan Street. Ella lived directly across from Saint Peter's Cemetery, which she claimed gave her the creeps.

As we strolled down the row of pristine mansions, it occurred to me how improbable our friendship was. If I hadn't been lucky enough to attend Bolton on scholarship, it's unlikely Ella and I would've ever met. The thought made me sad.

Which is why I didn't see the flashing lights.

"Tory?" Shelton pointed to a knot of houses ahead. Several squad cars were parked on the street before the. "Is one of those Ella's?"

"Yes." I was running before the word left my mouth.

As I streaked down the block, an evidence recovery van began backing into a narrow driveway. I nearly moaned. That was Ella's property.

The Francis home was constructed in traditional Charleston style: long and narrow, with the side of the house parallel to the street. Cops were milling by the front door, which opened onto a sweeping piazza that ran the length of the house.

The bright yellow structure rose three stories, with balconies on each level overlooking an interior courtyard garden. A round metal plaque bolted to the gate detailed the building's three-hundred-year history.

I burst through a gaggle of cops and onto the porch, then raced to the door leading inside. Shouts chased after me, but I ignored them, panic bubbling in my chest.

Ella's parents were seated on a narrow couch in the parlor, hands tightly clenched.

Mr. Francis's eyes were bloodshot. Tears streaked his wife's cheeks. Opposite them, a visibly uncomfortable Detective Hawfield was perched on a slender divan, taking a statement.

I shot to their side. "What's happened? Where's Ella?"

"They've taken her!" Mrs. Francis wailed, collapsing into her husband's arms. "My precious little girl!"

"Tory!" Detective Hawfield juggled his clipboard, struggling to stand. "What are you doing here? This is a crime scene."

I don't think I heard. My mind had jumped the tracks.

Taken. Ella.

Oh please, please, no.

"Officer Kirkham! Please remove this child from the premises! How did she get by—"

A hand reached for me. I spun, kicked the man in the shin. I leaped back from the muttered curses and fired up the stairs.

One flight. Two. Three. Ella's bedroom was on the top floor.

"Grab her!" Hawfield bellowed. "Don't let her taint the crime scene!"

Boots thundered on the steps behind me. Then a crash, followed by angry shouts.

"Leave her alone!" Hi's voice.

Reaching the top floor, I ran to Ella's room. Found three CSI techs inside, snapping pics.

"You can't be in here," a woman said. "This room is sealed."

I ignored her, eyes scanning the room. I didn't know what I was looking for. Didn't have a plan. But I *had* to help. Had to find a clue. A lead. Some evidence to solve the case.

Anything to save my friend.

Then I saw it.

An old, hand-painted playing card was sitting on Ella's bed.

I flew over and picked it up, drawing shouts from the CSI crew.

My eyes drank in the design.

A serpentine fish, painted gold, bristling with claws, teeth, and scales.

The image struck terror into my heart. I lost control.

"What is this?" I shrieked at the card. "What have you done with Ella!?!"

Hands on my shoulders. An arm around my waist.

I was dragged backward from the room. Someone snatched the card from my fingers.

Everything came crashing down.

I screamed at the top of my lungs. Kept screaming, over and over.

Then the world went black and I remembered nothing more.

PART THREE

JIGSAW

CHAPTER 29

Kit's footsteps receded down the hall.

With an ear pressed to my bedroom door, I heard him mumble something to Whitney. Her response was inaudible. Seconds later the TV clicked on.

Beside me, Coop nuzzled my hand. I absently scratched his back.

I knew Kit was worried. Who wouldn't be? His teenage daughter just had a nervous breakdown at a crime scene.

Retreating onto my bed, I grabbed my iPhone. Checked email. Voicemail. Text messages. Chat. Nothing from the other Virals. I hadn't heard from anyone since this afternoon.

Clock check—8:00 p.m.

Coop settled down beside the bed, his eyes never leaving me.

The holes in my memory were slowly filling.

I recalled flashing lights. The mass of police officers. Mr. and Mrs. Francis, red-eyed on their silly little couch. My mad dash up the stairs. A rush of blood to the head.

Ella had been taken. Ella was missing.

I felt panic bubble up inside me once more.

Calm. Breathe.

I glanced at the light blue pill resting in my trash can. Maybe I should've swallowed it.

No. I need a clear mind to be of any use.

I knew I was barely keeping it together. Could feel the shrieking desperation, just below the surface, that threatened to engulf me. To blind me. To turn out the lights a second time.

Ella has been taken. *Ella* was missing.

I grabbed my phone. Still nothing.

On the Francises' porch—as three EMTs were guiding me from the property—Shelton had whispered he would gather the pack. Hi had waved from across the front yard, where he was sitting between two officers, waiting for his mother to arrive. Apparently he'd body-blocked the first cops to chase me through the house. The police were none too pleased.

I owe you one, Hi. You bought enough time.

That strange, unnerving playing card. Its ghastly image was seared into my retinas.

A golden sea monster. Some horrid snake-fish hybrid, all sharp teeth and vicious claws. Hi's intervention had given me precious seconds to examine the clue.

The *link,* I should say. There was no doubting that whoever kidnapped Lucy and Peter Gable had also abducted Ella. The snake-fish card was a smoking gun.

No one could compare it to Ophiuchus and *not* see a connection. The items were clearly of common origin.

A madman's signature.

The twisted calling cards of a psychopath who steals children from their homes.

On its own volition, my mind leaped to Rex Gable. The man seriously gave me the creeps.

But would he really imprison his own children? Did he grab Ella, too? Why?

I was forced to admit it didn't make sense.

What would Rex Gable have to do with Ella Francis?

Yet . . . Rex Gable *was* at the art show. He'd have seen Ella there with me, radiant in her rebellious green cocktail dress.

And the black BMW. The type of car Rex Gable might own. *It* was at the opening, too.

My hands found my face. Rubbed slowly, up and down.

I didn't know what to think. My brain felt like scrambled eggs.

Against my will, I pictured Ella, locked in that awful dungeon with the Gable twins.

Or worse, all alone.

Cracks in my calm resurfaced. Anxiety threatened to overwhelm me.

Coop popped onto the bed and curled up beside me. He rested his giant head on my knee. I dove forward and hugged his body close.

Knew that someone was looking out for me, always.

The tide of dread receded, but didn't fully disappear. Disturbing thoughts about Ella kept exploding inside me, like popcorn on a hot stove. But Coop's warm, solid presence helped keep the demons at bay.

I hadn't felt like this since losing Mom.

Stop it. Ella's missing, not . . .

I shook my head to dispel the terrible thought.

Do something. Work the problem.

Go to the police? With *what*, exactly? My suspicions? A few wild theories?

We had next to nothing concrete. Not really.

A bleach-stained area in an otherwise spotless house. No help there.

The authorities had surely identified the Ophiuchus card by now. No sense revealing Hi's sticky fingers just to pass along stale info.

And how could I possibly convey the feeling I got from watching Peter Gable's eyes?

The writing on the steel bar. That's definitely *intel the police could use.*

Moving to my desk, I powered my MacBook and googled "Philip Simmons Ironworks."

Dozens of hits. The links momentarily distracted me from my grief.

Philip Simmons was a renowned African-American blacksmith and ironworker. Scrolling Wikipedia, I discovered he'd recently passed away at age ninety-seven. He began his career at a small shop on Calhoun Street, before moving into the specialized field of ornamental wrought iron in the 1930s. All told, Simmons fashioned over five hundred decorative pieces—gates, fences, balconies, and window grills—many of which still grace the area's richest mansions and estates.

I clicked a few more sites, impressed. In 1982, the National Endowment for the Arts awarded Simmons its National Heritage Fellowship, the highest honor the United States can bestow upon a traditional artist. The South Carolina legislature gave him a "lifetime achievement" award, and commissioned several public sculptures for museums and the city of Charleston. Simmons was inducted into the SC Hall of Fame in 1994, and received the Order of the Palmetto—South Carolina's highest award—in 1998. Some of his pieces are displayed in the Smithsonian.

I leaned back in my chair. "Not bad."

This man was no common grunt. Though Simmons began his career making penny nails and horseshoes, he became a world-famous artist. A *real* one—not like that fop Jean-Paul Delacourt and his horrible interpretations. Philip Simmons was a true master at shaping metal.

So how did steel bars bearing his name end up forming a dank prison?

I surfed a bit more. Late in life, Simmons had been in extremely high demand. His works literally blanket the Lowcountry. Without more to go on, his mark was useless for locating the twins' dungeon.

Still, I knew the CPD had more resources than Google. This was a tip they could use.

But how would I explain having a copy of the ransom tape? Impossible. Commissioner Riggins would have a stroke.

In all honesty, I doubted they'd even let me through the door. Who was going to trust a high schooler's video analysis? The silly girl who'd fainted while contaminating a crime scene.

I'd get handed a second blue pill. And this time, they'd check under my tongue.

Fine. No police. Then *what*?

The card from Ella's room. Find out what it is.

I reached for my iPhone. Ran a search. Placed a call.

"Yes?" The same melodious voice.

"Miss Gordon?"

"Speaking." A tad hesitant. "May I help you?"

"This is Tory Brennan. We met the other day in your shop. You told me and my friends about Ophiuchus, and the zodiac?"

Silence.

I forged ahead. "I have another question, about a different symbol. Would it be possible to pay for a session over the phone?"

No response. But I heard breathing on the line.

"Miss Gordon? Hello?"

"Now's not a good time."

I felt the brushback pitch sail by my chin. Ignored it.

"I know it's after business hours, but I'd appreciate if we could just talk. I'm willing to pay double, if that helps."

"It's not the money. Look, why don't you—"

"Clara?" My voice shook. I was suddenly on the brink of tears. "I'd really, *really* like to do this now, if you don't mind. I've had a horrible day. Can you please help me?"

There was another pause. Then, "What would you like to know?"

"Thank you. How should I send payment?"

"Never mind that." Brusque. "Ask your question."

"I've encountered another symbol, similar to the first one we showed you."

I described the card from Ella's room in exacting detail.

"That is Cetus," Clara said. "Known as the Sea Monster in Greek mythology, he was slain by Perseus while saving Andromeda from Poseidon's wrath. He's commonly referred to as The Whale today. Cetus is in the same boat as Ophiuchus—omitted from the zodiac."

"There's *another* missing sign?"

"Yes. Cetus is located in a celestial region known as the Sea, because of the many water-associated constellations nearby. Pisces. Aquarius. Capricornus. Others as well."

"Is Cetus a sign, though?"

"He has claim to be. The constellation passes *very* close to the ecliptic. Once a year—at the boundary between Cetus and Pisces—a sliver of our home star strays into Cetus for not quite a full day. March fourteenth. The planets also appear in Cetus on rare occasions. Thus, his inclusion in the zodiac is arguable, though not as clear-cut as Ophiuchus."

I thought a moment. "What does Cetus mean to people?"

There was a sigh on the other end. "It's hard to say. What you describe is a seventeenth-century depiction of Cetus, that of a dragon fish. In other times, Cetus has been portrayed as simply a large fish, or whale, or shark."

"But who would care about him now?" Frustration tinged my voice. "Who would follow Cetus *today*? Who would carry his symbol around in their pocket?"

"I'm not sure, Tory." Gordon sounded disappointed that she couldn't answer. "Sailors, maybe. Cetus is often a ship's name, chosen to express a lack of fear of the sea. But he's usually viewed as a bad omen, or a bringer of misfortune. Superstitious mariners associate him with bad weather, pirates, lost cargo, pretty much anything negative. On some ships, merely saying his name can trigger reprisals."

Sailors? What?

"Is there anything else you can tell me?" I pressed.

Another pause. I could almost see Gordon debating whether to say more.

"Clara, please."

"Just this." She spoke quickly, as if wishing to dispel a bad taste. "In most legends and myths of the ancient world, Cetus is associated with wickedness and ferocity. Some believe his sign represents pure evil. Unrelenting depravity and corruption."

Her words jarred me. What kind of monster were we dealing with?

Click.

"Hello?"

The line was dead. Surprised, I hit redial. The call went straight to voicemail.

She hung up. Without getting paid.

Why would Gordon do that?

Flopping back against my pillows, I replayed the conversation in my mind.

She'd been hesitant to speak. So unlike her friendly demeanor when we'd first entered Fairy Dust. Upon reflection, Gordon's reticence seemed more than annoyance at the late hour.

Why did I get the sense she'd been frightened?

A gong sounded on my computer.

"Finally!"

I leaped for my desk, startling Cooper from the bed.

Entering the Virals chat room, I found all three boys present.

Uh-oh.

They'd met there ahead of time, before alerting me. To *discuss* me.

"I'm fine." Wanting to nip any sympathy in the bud. "What I'd like is to focus on this case. No emotion. No distraction. We need to help Ella, *now*, in any way we can. And the Gable twins. Will you help me?"

For a moment, none of them spoke. Prepared speeches seemed poised on their tongues.

"Okay," Hi said simply.

"I can do that," Shelton promised.

"Anything you need." Ben's voice crackled with anger. "Let's get this bastard."

"Then listen up." I gave a quick summary of what I'd learned.

When I'd finished, Hi piped up. "I also learned something that might help."

"Please." Nodding encouragingly. "Anything."

"I know where Ella was snatched from." Hi rubbed his left shoulder. "After I *accidentally* tripped those officers inside the Francis house—"

"Thank you for that."

"No problem. Anyway, the police took me out on the lawn. They were probably all so terrified of me, they couldn't concentrate. Who can blame them?"

I made get-on-with-it gestures into my webcam.

Hi's voice grew serious. "The cop assigned to babysit me was a talker, said that Ella was last seen at her job the night before. She took a break, went outside, and didn't come back. Never got home."

A surge of adrenaline. This was useful information. Ella waitressed two evenings a week at a pizza joint called the Flying Tomato.

"Great job, Hi. That's our next move. We'll turn that place upside down."

"Tonight?" Shelton asked. Though this time, his voice carried no reservations.

I considered it. Wanted to agree. But police would be swarming that restaurant right now. Plus, there was no way I'd get past Kit and Whitney in the next few hours.

"No. But let's go early tomorrow morning, before they open. Agreed?"

Shelton nodded.

"You got it," said Hi.

"In." Ben jiggled his keys. "I'll be there first thing."

I logged off and lay down on my bed. Coop jumped up beside me. As I tussled his scratchy chin, some of the weight lifted from my shoulders.

For the first time since waking, I felt a measure of control.

Lying there in the dark, the panic began to recede. Transform. Become something else.

Anger.

A slow-boiling rage filled me inside, head to toe.

I captured the feeling. Harnessed it. Enslaved it to my purpose.

Someone out there had attacked my friend. Stolen her. Put her life in danger.

That person is going to pay.

Coop's head rose from his paws.

He regarded me with lidded eyes, then gave a low, dangerous growl.

"That's right, boy." Stroking his head. "That's damn right."

CHAPTER 30

Saturday

The Flying Tomato was closed and shuttered.

No police tape. No squad cars keeping watch. Whatever the police might've discovered the night before, they hadn't sealed the premises.

The restaurant was on Tradd Street, two short blocks from the Francis home. Ben pulled into a public lot around the corner on King. We walked the last fifty yards, not wanting to advertise our presence.

The sign was garish—a giant ripe tomato, wearing white sunglasses and sneakers, flying off a half pike. A funky, hipster hangout. I knew Ella loved working there.

She'd taken the job against her parents' advice. Getting out of the house, meeting new people, and making a little money had appealed to Ella's sense of independence.

She made minimum wage, plus tips. Ella got *plenty* of those.

Ella thought a girl should work, even in high school. I totally agreed, and had harbored secret hopes of joining the Flying Tomato staff once old enough to drive.

That dream was out the window now.

The pizza parlor was a white one-story structure with red shutters. A long front porch ran its length, set with tables for eating outside. We entered a gravel lot adjacent to the building. At eight o'clock on a Saturday morning, there were no cars present.

"Ready?" Ben fought to keep the eagerness from his voice.

I nodded. "Light 'em up."

For once, I didn't argue the point. We'd flare, and leave no stone unturned.

When it came to Ella's safety, I wasn't holding back.

SNAP.

A crackling sensation, followed by a blast of scorching heat.

Sweat erupted from my pores. I held my face in my hands, trying not to scream as every hair on my body stood at attention.

"Too much!" Shelton moaned, rubbing his temples.

Beside me I saw Hi wobble, then collapse. Yellow light strobed from his eyes.

Something is wrong.

The inferno inside me continued to build. My arms shook. I couldn't feel my legs. Staggering like a drunk, I fought to control my breathing.

I saw Ben wheel and swing his fists, as if fighting an invisible foe. His eyes flickered between golden and brown.

He stumbled. Then, hand on his knees, Ben vomited on the ground.

Pressure built inside my skull. I felt like a balloon inflated well past the point of safety.

Desperate, I squeezed my eyes shut, willing the flare to level. Instead, the pain amplified.

In my subconscious, the flaming cords that connected us thrummed out of control. Their forms were disjointed, indistinct. Unbound, they flailed and twanged wildly.

An atonal warble filled my ears. I could barely track the lines, much less control them.

This isn't right. We have to let go!

I don't know if I sent the message, or if the boys simply arrived at the same conclusion.

"Screw this," Hi gasped. "I'm shutting down."

"True that!" Shelton howled.

Both stiffened. Convulsions racked their bodies, but, moments later, they released twin sighs of relief.

SNUP.

My own flare died.

I sagged, nearly crumpling in relief. The agony receded.

When my head cleared, I heard Shelton screaming at Ben. "Release it, Blue!"

"*No.*" Ben spoke through gritted teeth. "*I'm* in charge . . . not some . . . dog DNA . . ."

He shuddered, falling against the side of building.

I ran to his side. "Ben, stop it! You have to let go!"

Ben's face swung to me, eyes slitted. His jaw and back were rigid. A vein pulsed in his neck as he grimaced, panting, on the verge of passing out.

"Ben, please." I took his hand, voice suddenly calm. "You need to stop. We'll figure this out together. I promise."

Ben looked away. For several heartbeats he continued to fight. Then his hand squeezed mine as his body went slack.

He staggered, nearly dropped. Shelton and I caught him, then eased him to the gravel.

For a full minute we sat in a clump, catching our breath, no one speaking.

Finally, "I don't know *what* that was."

"That's never happened before," Hi wheezed. "It's like my flare was attacking me."

"Oh, man." Shelton was shirt-cleaning his glasses with jerky motions. "We got problems, ya'll. I knew our powers were getting wilder, but that was a whole 'nother level."

Ben rose, brushed dirt from his jeans. "Let's try again."

"Are you crazy?" Hi struggled to his feet. "No thanks, pal. One barbequing was enough for me."

"Ben, be reasonable." I tried not to scold. "Whatever just happened, it was serious. Maybe even deadly. We have to consider this carefully."

Ben seemed about to argue, but turned away. His shoulders rose and fell.

"Fine." His back to us. "For now."

We dusted ourselves off. A quick scan of the neighborhood confirmed we were still alone. Which was fortunate—our group seizure would've been tough to explain.

"We'll do this old-school," Hi said. "Using only the power of our massive brains."

Shelton chuckled. "A throwback."

I smiled, trying to mask my anxiety.

What the hell just happened?

Every fear I'd harbored about the nature of our mutations came roaring to the surface.

Was our short circuit merely an aberration? Some odd quirk, never to return?

Or was it the beginning of the end? Was my body rejecting the canine DNA?

Or worse, was the new genetic material . . . taking over?

We don't have time for this now.

My mind returned to the task. Ella was *missing.* Our flare problems would have to wait.

"Shelton, please open this restaurant." Striding for the door. "There's no time to waste."

○ ○ ○

"I'm out of ideas." Hi was leaning against a red-brick oven. "And no leftover pizza *anywhere* in here? Unreal."

We stood inside the cramped kitchen. For the last thirty minutes we'd turned the place upside down, examining every square foot of the restaurant. Dining room. Kitchen. Pantry. Storeroom. Office. Even the two bathrooms. Nothing was out of the ordinary.

"We should bounce," Shelton urged. "Somebody might show up to make spaghetti sauce any minute."

Both boys glanced at me.

I punched my leg in frustration. I hated quitting, but they were right. This was serving no purpose.

"We didn't check the Dumpster," Ben said from across a counter. "Or anything out back."

"The cop said Ella went outside," Hi added. "Maybe she was snatched behind the building?"

I snapped a nod. "Shelton, lock up behind us."

Slipping out the back door, we found ourselves in an alcove paved with concrete. A large Dumpster was hard against the building. Beyond it were three rolling recycling bins and a pair of rusty folding chairs. A wooden fence enclosed three sides. The fourth was open to the gravel lot where we'd had our flare meltdown.

Hi pointed to the chairs. "Cigarette station. I don't suppose Ella is a smoker?"

"The Lady Griffins soccer captain?" I scoffed. "Not likely."

Hi began lifting bin lids while Ben rooted in the Dumpster. Without a better plan, I began a slow circuit of the enclosure. Looking for what, I had no idea. A tightness was building in my chest—that crushing feeling of helplessness, creeping back in.

"Hey, Tor." Shelton was kneeling beside the chairs. "What's this look like to you?"

I was hurrying to his side when we heard the screech of tires on loose stone.

Hi dropped into his battle crouch. "Oh crap!"

Ben stepped away from the Dumpster. Shelton and I moved to his side.

All eyes watched the corner of the building.

Nowhere to run. If someone came back here, we'd have some explaining to do.

Footsteps on pebbles. Approaching.

A familiar face rounded the corner. The last person I expected to see.

"What?" The only words I could manage.

"You're in a position to question?"

Chance wore tan shorts and a gray polo. I couldn't recall seeing him so casual before.

"You shouldn't be here, Claybourne." Ben's voice was menacing. "Leave."

Chance barely glanced at him. "I don't take orders from you. I assume *you've* stopped by for a breakfast calzone?"

I stepped in front of Ben. "Why are you here, Chance? Did you follow us?"

For a moment, Chance's gaze roved the group. Finally, "Yes."

My breath caught. "Why?"

"I heard about Ella on the news." His tone softened a degree. "I'm sorry, Tory. I know you two had become friends."

Tears threatened. I fought them back, surprised at how close to the surface my emotions lurked.

"We thought maybe we could help." I left it at that.

"Help how?" Chance pressed. "What can *you* offer that the police can't?"

"Mind your own business," Ben said darkly. "For once."

"No." Chance gave a quick headshake. "No, I think we're past that."

I could feel the tension rising. Shelton hid behind my shoulder. Hi was acting nonchalant, but his tapping foot gave him away. And Ben . . .

"I know what you were doing at the aquarium." Chance either didn't sense the danger, or didn't care. "You were snooping in Marcus Karsten's old files."

Ben tensed. The charge in the air became palpable.

Then, like a lightning strike, the odd sensation returned. For one blinding instant, I felt lines of connection blasting from my mind and looping around the others. Ben. Hi. Shelton. Even Chance. Then my mind twitched and the feeling completely evaporated.

What was that!?

"I don't know how you tracked them down," Chance continued, oblivious. "Or what led you to the aquarium. Questions for another day." His voice hardened. "But there were *other* files on that server you had no business viewing."

I struggled to regain my bearings. "I don't know what—"

"Save it, Tory." Chance's pupils dilated. "You copied my B-Series files. *You* know it, and *I* know it. I want them back. Every last megabyte."

Suddenly, I saw it. Beneath the cool exterior, Chance was furious.

And scared. Maybe even terrified.

No more lies.

"No." I was pleased my voice didn't quaver. "Those files involve Karsten's secret work. We have an interest in that."

His cheek twitched. "The files are encrypted. You'll never get in."

"We'll see about that."

Chance's gaze bored into me. I met him, stare for stare. As best I could.

"I could go to the police," he said softly. "Breaking and entering. Wire fraud. Tampering with Candela property. I have you *on tape,* red-handed. One phone call and you're done."

Bluff.

"You won't do that." Spoken just as calmly. "You don't want the cops to know about the B-Series, either. Those files are *your* dirty little secret, aren't they? Like father, like son."

I saw the punch land.

Chance's eyes betrayed him. My guess was dead-on.

"I can destroy you." The heat rose in Chance's voice. "You're *nothing* in this city. I'm rich. Powerful. *Respected.* Cross me, and you'll pay dearly. Your parents, too."

That was the line. Chance crossed it.

Ben charged forward and shoved him to the ground.

Chance tumbled backward, taken totally by surprise. Ben stood over him, chest heaving. Lifting Chance by his shirt, Ben cocked his other fist.

I raced forward and grabbed Ben's elbow. His head whipped to me, nostrils flaring.

"No." Holding his gaze. "That's not what we do."

Ben snorted. "Whatever." But he dropped Chance and walked away.

Chance roared to his feet. "Try that again, boy!"

Ben spun, a smile splitting his face. "Gladly."

"Stop it!" I placed myself between them, one arm outstretched toward each.

Ben had surprised Chance, but he was the smaller of the two. This could get ugly, fast.

Shelton and Hi moved to Ben's flanks, began whispering in his ears.

My hand touched Chance's chest. "Be the bigger man," I said softly.

Livid eyes met mine. Then rolled.

"Once." Swatting my hand from his chest. "This *one* time, Tory. For old time's sake."

"You're lucky, Benjamin." Chance nodded toward me. "You have a guardian angel."

"Another time," Ben promised. "We'll see who's lucky."

Chance turned my way. "You're upset about Ella, and not thinking clearly. We'll revisit this issue later. But those files are mine, and I want them back. That isn't a request."

Without another word, he strode from the alcove. I trailed him around the building—to make sure he actually left—and watched Chance climb into a car.

"Well, well."

The other Virals approached behind me.

"Well what?" Hi asked. "Did you want to sock him, too?"

I pointed. "Chance has nice wheels."

The boys followed my finger.

We watched a gleaming black BMW tear from the parking lot.

CHAPTER 31

"Him!" Hi shouted dramatically.

"It adds up." I shook my head, sliding facts into place. "Chance has plenty of spare time, and has been suspicious of us for months. Given everything he knows, following me isn't the craziest thing in the world. Plus, he was at the art gala that night."

"So the mystery car isn't connected to the kidnappings?" Shelton asked.

I hesitated.

Surely Chance wouldn't have anything to do with . . .

"No." I dismissed the notion. "Looks like Chance was simply keeping tabs on me."

"Because he knows too much." Ben aimed a finger at me. "And you don't seem very surprised, Brennan."

I flinched. "Chance *may* have mentioned a few of those things at the aquarium."

A bit guiltily, I told the boys about our showdown in the corner office. When I'd finished, they gaped at me, equal parts anxious and angry.

"How could you keep that from us?" Hi sputtered. "Chance knows about Karsten!? About Cooper!? He knows about the virus we caught!?"

"This is so, *so* bad," Shelton moaned. "That punk could expose us at any time!"

"He's a threat." Ben had a look in his eyes that left me cold. "If Chance suspects we were infected, combined with what he's seen this last year—"

"Calm down." Trying to do so myself. "Chance doesn't have all the pieces yet. He knows Coop was infected with XPB-19, and he knows we have the wolfdog. But that's it."

"You said *yet,*" Hi pointed out. "That implies he'll put it together eventually."

Deep breath. "Chance suspects we caught the supervirus. And given what he's witnessed over the last year, I think he believes it affected us somehow. But he has no idea *how,*" I added quickly. "He doesn't know the whole truth. And, most importantly, he can't *prove* anything, or tell anyone. Not without exposing Candela's involvement with illegal experiments. Which he obviously won't do."

"We're supposed to trust *Chance freaking Claybourne* with our deepest, darkest secret?" Ben growled. "That's the plan?"

"Give me some time to think it over," I pleaded. "Come up with a solution."

Ben fixed me with a dangerous stare. "Okay, Tory. But don't take too long. I won't have Chance running around, endangering my freedom. My *life*. He needs to be dealt with."

I suppressed a shiver. Didn't want to understand what Ben was implying.

"It's time to jet," Hi said. "People might start showing up here soon."

I nodded, took a step toward the street.

For a brief moment, my thoughts returned to the spike of interconnectedness my mind had experienced. The frequency was increasing, the intensity escalating. Yet the attack—that's what I was forced to call them at this point—came and went without warning. The onset seemed completely random. I couldn't even *guess* at a pattern.

There has to be a trigger. Something that sets off the effect.

"Wait!" Shelton pointed to the rear of the Flying Tomato. "Almost forgot."

"You found something?" My concern for Ella shifted back to the forefront. A deeper contemplation of Viral side effects would have to wait.

"Maybe." Shelton led us back to the alcove. "I'm just trying to figure out what *that* is."

On the ground between the folding chairs was a fist-sized chunk of red-orange rock. Pockmarked, misshapen, with a rough, bubbly exterior, the lumpy stone seemed oddly out of place.

Shelton knelt to scoop it up.

"Wait."

I moved closer and dropped to one knee. Hi and Shelton snagged the chairs and set them aside, exposing the multi-hued rock to the morning sun.

I stuck my nose inches from the rock. It had an odd, sulfurous scent.

Something was stuck to the stone's surface. A shiny filament, rising on the breeze.

Gently, my fingers extended, capturing the slender line. I held the wisp before my eyes.

A single hair. Black and glossy.

I carefully stretched the strand between my fingers. It was over a foot long.

Ella.

"We've got something." My voice was steady, but my heart raced as I removed a plastic vial from my pocket. "Hiram, please grab a large plastic baggie from my evidence kit. It's in the car."

As Hi hurried off, I carefully inserted hair into vial. Then, dropping to my elbows, I examined every centimeter of rock I could see without touching it.

A tiny rust-colored oval marked the left side, with a thin streak descending from the center of the discoloration, as though made by a dripping liquid.

I didn't need Coop's nose.

"I found a hair. And maybe blood."

Shadows fell across the stone. I glanced up to see Shelton holding latex gloves. Hi had the ziplocks. Ben handed me a cotton swab and stopper. "Anything else?"

Despite the circumstances, I smiled. "Just one thing. The green packet in my kit."

I pulled on the gloves. When Ben returned, I opened the packet and laid out several items. After moistening the tip of the swab with a squirt of filtered water, I gently rubbed it against the stain. Then I removed a thin plastic strip from a white pill bottle.

"This is called a Hemastix strip," I explained, "which contains the chemical tetramethylbenzidine. TMB for short. It's like a dipstick test for human blood, and works better than Luminol on trace samples. Bottom line—if this strip changes color, it's a presumptive positive for blood."

"Presumptive?" Shelton asked.

"Best we can do. But with the hair attached, and this stain appearing on an out-of-place rock at a possible crime scene, I think that paints a pretty clear picture."

"Any more toys you're holding out on?" Hi grumbled. "I don't know you anymore."

"Thank Aunt Tempe for this one," I replied. "She stocked my evidence kit. But an entire bottle of Hemastix strips only costs like thirty bucks."

As precisely as possible, I rubbed the dampened swab against the yellow material at the end of the strip. In seconds the patch turned blue-green.

"Bingo." I placed the used strip into a second vial. Then, nodding to

Hi, I lifted the rock in my gloved hands and placed in the plastic bag. Sealed it tight.

Hi shook his head. “Man, Charleston has the worst cops in the world. How could they miss this?”

“It’s just an ugly rock,” Shelton countered. “I’m not sure why *I* noticed it.”

“So we take this stuff downtown?” Ben asked.

I was about agree, then stopped myself. “Why?”

This seemed to take the boys aback.

“What are *we* supposed to do with it?” Shelton countered. “The cops can run DNA tests, and figure out whether that’s Ella’s hair. And . . . blood.”

His voice faltered as the implications hit home.

“I know it’s hers already.” I had zero doubt. “And those tests won’t help us *find* her.”

Hi scratched his head. “Then . . . what?”

“The rock.” Ben’s eyes found mine. “We should track the rock, not the DNA.”

“What? That could be from anywhere,” Shelton whined. “The rock may not even be a clue. The kidnapper could’ve scooped it from a roadside ditch.”

“It’s all we have.” I stared at the bagged hunk of stone. “The police already know Ella was abducted. They don’t need DNA to confirm it. An investigation is already going full swing.”

Hi nodded slowly. “But if the rock can be traced to somewhere specific . . .”

“What about prints?” Shelton said. “If the kidnapper hit Ella with that, then—”

I shook my head. “Such a basic mistake? I don’t see it.”

“We can examine the rock ourselves first, *then* give it to the police,” Hi suggested. “No harm, no foul. Everybody wins.”

“Examine it how?” Ben cocked his head. “You mean LIRI?”

"With Kit and Hudson already on our case?" I snorted, packing up my kit. "Not a chance. Not after the video debacle. Plus, to learn anything that way we'd need the mass spectrometer, or the gas chromatograph. But you can't even power those machines without a dozen permissions. We wouldn't last five minutes."

"Then let's find an expert," Hi said. "Some weirdo rock junkie who can eyeball this bad boy, and tell us what it is."

I tapped my nose. "My thoughts exactly."

Shelton's face lit up. "CU has a geology department. We're close to the campus, too. Maybe somebody's working on a Saturday?"

"It's worth a shot." Zipping up my bag. "Let's get moving. Today, there's no time to lose."

CHAPTER 32

Charleston University's Department of Geology and Environmental Sciences was eight blocks away, on Coming Street.

We drove past Ella's house on the way. It was all I could do not to cry.

Ben found a spot out front. We entered a three-story brick building and took the elevator up one floor. Stepping into a small lobby, we asked a passing student for the office of Professor Wiley Marzec.

Marzec was younger than I'd expected—no more than forty. A bit thick around the middle, with a round, friendly face and a mullet of brown hair. He wore lime-green shorts and a brown T-shirt that said "Rocktastic." When he spoke, his voice filled the room.

"Come in, come in!" Half rising, Marzec waved to a pair of wicker chairs facing his desk. His office was small, but cozy, lined with wooden bookshelves holding an assortment of stones, fossils, and thick textbooks. Something called the International Stratigraphic Chart was taped to one wall. A fantastic geode rode his desk as a paperweight.

"Cool!" Hi zoomed to the sparkling rock.

"I know, right?" Marzec waved permission for Hi to touch it. "It's amethyst, which is the purple version of quartz. And check out that red streak circling the core. That's pure hematite under the crystalline surface. Found it at Thunder Bay, up in Canada. All the other rock-jocks are jealous."

"Dope." Wisely, Hi didn't attempt to pick it up. "Five bucks?"

"Not on your life." Marzec smiled as he turned to me. "Tory, I presume?"

"Yessir." Slipping into a seat. "And thank you so much for seeing us on short notice."

"My father's name was Sir." Wiley leaned back in his creaky office chair. "I'm Wiley. Or Professor Marzec, if you must. Now, what can I do you for?"

"We found a rock that seemed out of place." I snapped for Shelton, who was standing behind me. Hi had filled the other seat, with Ben looming over his shoulder. "We were hoping you could tell us what it is."

Shelton handed me the ziplock. Hesitating only slightly, I passed it to Marzec.

"Ah!" Marzec smiled wide. "A phosphate nodule. Were you guys down by the river?" His fingers found the bag's seal. "May I?"

"I'd prefer you didn't," I said quickly.

Marzec's brows quirked, but he set the bag on the desk and peered through the plastic.

"You said something about a river?" Hi prompted. "Which one?"

Marzec's whole focus was on the stone. "Copper. Wando. Edisto. Any of them. But I was mainly thinking of the Ashley." He sat back. "What do you know about phosphate mining in the Lowcountry?"

Our blank faces gave him his answer.

Marzec glanced at the ceiling in thought. "Where to start?"

"How about the Cliff Notes version?" I suggested.

"Sounds good." Marzec tapped the plastic bag. "What you have is called a phosphate nodule. A real beauty, too, must weight five pounds. Can't you smell that odor? These rocks are found throughout the

Charleston Basin, and along the banks of the tributary rivers. Their ages range from the Oligocene to the Pleistocene epochs. In South Carolina, phosphate deposits run parallel to the coast for about seventy miles, extending south from the Wando to the Broad River, and then inland for approximately thirty miles."

My heart sank. That sounded like a *lot* of real estate.

"What exactly *is* phosphate?" Shelton asked.

"Let's start with phosphorus." Marzec's voice became professorial. "One of the seventeen nutrients required by all living plants and animals, it's absolutely *crucial* for growing food. If the dirt you're farming lacks phosphorus, that deficiency will severely limit production. To compensate, farmers use various fertilizers to correct any shortfall and increase crop yields."

"Soil needs phosphorous to grow crops," I summarized. "Got it."

"Exactly. Phosphorus is *essential* to life—there's no substitute for it in agriculture. The element readily combines in nature, forming crucial organic compounds. For example, it's a vital component of nucleic acids—DNA and RNA molecules—from which all life springs. It's also a key component of phospholipids, plasma membranes, and solid structures like bones and teeth."

"Need phosphorus to live," Hi said. "Roger that."

Marzec winked, perhaps acknowledging his long-winded style. "I'll cut to the chase—phosphorus itself is highly reactive, and doesn't appear naturally in its elemental form. Instead, it occurs in phosphates—charged groups of atoms. Basically, a phosphorus atom hooked to four oxygen atoms."

"Okay." This was getting more technical than I'd expected.

"You can't mine pure phosphorus," Marzec simplified. "It doesn't exist anywhere. Instead, you have to look for phosphate rocks—like this one—dig them up, then break the stones down."

"Okay." I shifted, not totally sure I understood. "Phosphate rocks contain phosphorus, which is essential for making good fertilizer. So people dig them up for sale."

"Perfectly stated." Marzec spread his hands. "This was a *major* industry in the late 1800s. The amount of available farmland was limited, which meant the same tired plots had to be replanted over and over. Overuse was leaching essential nutrients from the soil. Farmers were desperate for a way to get those minerals back. Enter phosphate mining."

"They needed prehistoric rocks to make fertilizer?" Hi asked. "Nothing else worked?"

"Before the mining boom, farmers were dependent on guano for fertilizer. But that had to be imported, and was very pricey. Finding high-quality fertilizer buried right beneath their feet was a godsend for local sharecroppers."

"Wait. Guano?" Hiram's eyes narrowed. "You're saying—"

"Yes." Marzec grinned. "Farmers were buying the droppings of seabirds and bats, which are high in both phosphorus and nitrogen."

Shelton crinkled his nose. "Man, farming is just nasty. For *real.*"

"Are phosphate rocks widespread?" I asked.

"Actually, no." Marzec jabbed a thumb at a multicolored map behind his desk. "There are large deposits in central Florida, certain regions of Idaho, and along the North Carolina coast. Smaller ones in Montana, Tennessee, and, of course, here in the Lowcountry. Phosphate rock was so prevalent along the Ashley River that many landmarks in that area still bear its name."

"Ashley Phosphate Road," Ben said. "I've driven there."

"Correct." Marzec stroked his chin. "The banks of the Ashley River were *riddled* with phosphates. Once their utility was discovered, mining companies sprang up along the waterfront. For the next fifty years, strip mining for phosphate rock was *the* major industry in that area. By

1885, South Carolina was producing *half* the world's supply. Some folks got rich, although Mother Nature won't be sending them any thank-you cards. Entire sedimentary layers were dug up, ripped out, and then barged downstream."

There was a pause as Marzec seemed to run out of steam.

"Is phosphate mining still a big business today?" I prompted.

"Oh no." Marzec took a long pull on a Diet Coke. "Most of the local deposits quickly tapped out. By the 1900s, the vast majority of operations had shuttered. Fertilizer production had all but ceased in these parts by the 1930s."

I shifted again, thinking hard. "So are these phosphate sediments still prevalent near the riverbanks?"

"I wouldn't say prevalent." He tapped the bag once more. "Honestly, I'm surprised you found a pure nodule of this size just lying around." Marzec eyed me curiously. "Where *did* you pick this up?"

"Wake-boarding off Folly Beach," Hi inserted. "I was attempting a heel-side five-forty when I wiped out. Found this little guy bouncing in the surf."

"I see." I could tell Marzec was skeptical, but he let it pass. "Well, any other questions?"

"No, Dr. Marzec." I flashed my very-grateful smile. "Thanks so much for your time."

"Delighted." Marzec scratched behind his ear with a snort. "I've been working here five years, and you're the first non-students to ever ask me a thing. Come back anytime."

We gathered our things, Hi gently scooping the rock from Marzec's desk, then exited with another round of thanks. I waited until we were safely inside Ben's SUV before speaking.

"What do you guys think? Marzec kept mentioning the Ashley River."

"But these rocks were everywhere," Hi said. "He listed every other river in the area, too."

Shelton shook his head. "We could maybe narrow our search to locations near a riverbank. But that's still miles and miles. And for all we know, the kidnapper just picked up the stupid rock while out driving around. It might not lead to anything."

I looked at Ben. He glanced away.

No one wanted to say it straight out.

"So we're still nowhere." My voice trembled slightly.

Silence filled the car.

I could sense the boys wanted to comfort me. Had no idea how to.

"Let's go home," I said softly.

⬡ ⬡ ⬡

"Tory, where have you been?"

There was real concern in Kit's voice as he sprang up from the couch.

I elected for half truth. "The boys and I went to where Ella worked. I thought maybe we could spot something."

"Oh, honey." He wrapped an arm around my shoulder.

I felt tears welling behind my eyes. Forced them back.

Kit released me. Held me at arm's length so he could look into my eyes.

"If you want to cancel this barbeque, just say the word. Whitney will be fine."

The block party. I'd completely forgotten.

Of course we can't have a stupid cookout today. My friend was abducted!

"It's fine." A glance at the clock. "Tell Whitney I'll be ready to help in an hour. Where's Coop?"

"He's asleep on your bed." Kit ran nervous fingers through his curly brown hair. "Are you sure, kiddo? I don't know if this party is a good idea."

"It's okay. Better a dumb cookout than nothing. Maybe it'll keep my mind off . . . things."

Kit nodded slowly. "Only if you're certain. And we leave the minute you want to."

I forced a smile. "Thanks, Dad."

He tried to hide his surprise. I never called him that.

Then I saw today's *Post and Courier* sitting on our dining room table.

I started. "What is that!?"

Kit tracked my eyes, then winced. "There's a story. Maybe now's not the best—"

Ignoring him, I grabbed the newspaper. A giant picture dominated above the fold.

Two playing cards, side by side. Ophiuchus. Cetus.

A banner headline screamed: "Zodiac Kidnapper Baffles Police."

Eyes wide, I read the full-page story. Then I slammed the paper on the table.

"The police don't know *anything*!" Sides heaving. "But the press has it all the next day!"

Kit grabbed the newsprint and dumped it in the recycling bin. "Forget that nonsense. I'm sure the police have leads they aren't sharing."

I shook my head angrily. "Someone has leaked every major development in these cases so far. Yet the cops don't have a *damn* clue."

"Tory, I understand how upset you are, but we have to trust—"

"*I* know more than those bozos!"

Kit stopped short. "I'm sorry?"

Careful!

I buried my face in my hands. Worry for Ella was compromising my judgment.

Then I made a decision.

"Kit?"

"Yeah, kiddo?" Watching me closely.

"Please sit with me. I have some things to tell you."

We each pulled a chair from the dining table. Sat facing each other.

Deep breath.

It's the right thing to do.

"We need to visit police headquarters. Today. I have evidence they need to see."

CHAPTER 33

Kit led me inside the lobby of police headquarters.

My eyes shot to the intake counter—thankfully, a female officer was on duty.

I released a pent-up breath. At least I wouldn't be recognized from our late-night visit two days ago. This meeting was going to be bad enough.

Shelton, Hi, and Ben were a few steps behind me. I'd argued that we didn't all need to be there, but Detective Hawfield had seen things differently.

Ruth Stolowitski had Hiram by one elbow, a murderous look on her face. Shelton's father, Nelson, had accompanied his son. Ben came alone.

Kit spoke to the desk officer, then waved us toward the elevator bank.

"Fifth floor," I told him.

He raised an eyebrow.

"Lucky guess."

Arriving at the Major Crimes department, we were greeted by a junior detective who led us to a conference room with a circular table large enough for everyone to sit.

At least they didn't throw us in the box. That's something, right?

Moments later, Hawfield walked in. He wasn't alone.

"You've *got* to be kidding!" Hi blurted.

Carmine Corcoran's scowl was as deep as ever. He'd lost a few pounds, but was still a large man, with muttonchop sideburns and a bristly black moustache. His hair was graying at the temples, making him appear more distinguished than his forty-five years merited.

Ruth popped the back of her son's head. "Mind your manners, Hiram."

"Why does *everyone* do that?" Hi muttered. "And that was child abuse. In front of the police, I might add."

"Sergeant?" I tried to decipher Corcoran's insignia. "Or is it still Security Director?"

"It's *Captain* Corcoran now, Miss Brennan." Spoken with evident satisfaction. "I was asked to rejoin the force after foiling those felonies last summer. I've moved up in the world."

"You're welcome." Hi dodged another matronly swat.

Corcoran shot Hiram a hooded glance, but didn't rise to the bait. He'd been the officer in charge during our investigation of the skeleton on Loggerhead Island last spring, and had worked private security during our pursuit of Anne Bonny's lost fortune the following summer. Neither encounter had been overly pleasant.

Corcoran was on the short list of people I wouldn't mind avoiding forever.

But here we were. Our luck never seems to improve.

Detective Hawfield pulled out a chair and sat. "Let's get down to business, shall we? I thought it prudent that Captain Corcoran attend this interview, since he has some . . . experience with the witnesses."

I'll say.

Hawfield spread his hands. "This is your meeting. Please begin."

Kit glanced at me. Reaching into my pack, I removed the bagged phosphate nodule and placed it on the table. Then I set two vials beside it—one containing the long black hair, the other holding my Hemastix strip.

Hawfield frowned immediately. "What is that?"

"Evidence in the kidnapping of Ella Francis." I was surprised at how calm my voice sounded. "We discovered it behind the Flying Tomato this morning."

"Bubby, what *is* this?" Ruth squawked.

Hi held a finger to his lips. "Quiet, Ma! Just listen."

Hawfield's hand found his forehead. "You're telling me that you've handled evidence from a possible crime scene? That you removed it?"

I nodded. Corcoran made a noise in his throat I choose not to interpret.

"In our defense, the rock was just sitting there." Shelton looked to his father. "The cops missed it the night before. What if it rained? Or some dog got it? We couldn't just *leave* it."

Nelson put a comforting hand on his son's shoulder.

"You had no business there in the first place," Corcoran huffed. "Like moths to a flame, the four of you. Like it or not, your actions have tainted the crime scene."

"We didn't touch the stone," I said coolly. "It's been sealed in that evidence bag since we discovered it. Shelton's right—we couldn't just leave it lying outside."

Hawfield raised a hand for quiet. He seemed to have regained some of his equanimity. "Why do you believe this stone is evidence?" he asked.

I rotated the bag to expose the rust-red blemish. "The rock seemed out of place. Examining it, I noticed two things. This red stain on its side, and a twelve-inch black hair stuck to its surface, which I think might belong to Ella."

My voice broke on her name. Kit reached over and squeezed my hand.

Hawfield gave me an appraising look. "I assume the hair is in that test tube?"

"Yes. The other vial contains a Hemastix strip I used to assess for blood. It came back presumptively positive."

Hawfield reached over and collected the three items. "I can't condone what you've done. Proper procedure is for a citizen to alert the police—"

"It's a disgrace!" Corcoran spat, folding his beefy arms. "By handling these items, they're now useless in a court of law. Any lawyer worth a bag of Doritos could have them withheld."

"Maybe," I snapped. "But I'm more worried about *finding* Ella and the twins. Your people missed this completely. Without us, you wouldn't even have it."

"We do multiple sweeps! We'd have found it eventually."

"Done is done," Hawfield said calmly. "We'll need statements explaining what you found, where, when, who handled it, all the details."

I nodded.

"Good. Now, is there anything else?"

"We showed the rock to a geologist."

"More hands?" Corcoran lifted his palms to the ceiling. "Great Lord in the morning!"

Ignoring Corcoran's dramatics, I related our visit to Professor Marzec and the information he provided. Hawfield took careful notes, then rose and left the room. We waited in uncomfortable silence for his return.

"Okay." Hawfield sat heavily in his chair. "Is there anything else we need to discuss?"

I thought about the bloodstain at the Gable house. The labeled bar in the ransom video. Both pieces of information could be useful to the investigation.

But explaining *how* we obtained that evidence might land us in juvie.

I looked at Corcoran. He glared back. That made up my mind.

"Just one other thing. I think you should look into Rex Gable. The twins' stepfather."

"*Excuse* me?" Corcoran sat forward, red-faced. "What are you implying, young lady?"

"Some of his actions since the twins went missing seem . . . questionable." I couldn't mention his phone records, but was trying to push them in that direction. "I'm just saying that Rex Gable might merit additional consideration."

"Of course," Corcoran scoffed. "The evil stepfather is the culprit. Thank goodness we have Nancy Drew on the case."

Kit straightened. "Now wait just a min—"

"Dr. Howard, we've been down this road before." Corcoran shook his head. "These kids have gained a little notoriety recently. So now, suddenly, they think they're expert crime fighters. I think the celebrity status has gone to their heads."

My temper exploded. "And *I* think you're still the same stupid, brain-dead—"

"Everyone, please!" Hawfield looked like he'd rather be anywhere else on the planet. "Let's not lose our composure. Miss Brennan, we'll take your opinion under advisement."

I knew what that meant. But what else could I do?

"We done here?" Ben's first words.

Hawfield and Corcoran wheeled on him as one.

Abruptly, I got a bad feeling.

"Mr. Blue." Hawfield's voice became less cordial. "Are you able to give an account of your whereabouts on Thursday evening?"

Ben's eyes narrowed. "Why?"

"Please answer the question."

"I was in Mongolia. Surfing."

"Don't get cute, son." Shifting his bulk, Corcoran attempted to loom menacingly. "You might've wriggled off the last hook, but you've got no more get-out-of-jail-free cards."

My eyes widened. "Are you suggesting *Ben* had something to do with Ella's disappearance?"

"I'm not suggesting *anything*," Hawfield said curtly. "I simply asked a question."

Ben's face reddened, but he answered. "I was at home. Watching TV."

"Was anyone with you?"

Ben shook his head. "My mother works second shift this week."

Corcoran crossed his arms. "What about the morning of March twenty-eighth?"

"No idea."

Corcoran leaned on the table. "Think. Harder."

Ben's face went rigid. I could see him shutting down.

"That's enough." Kit put a hand on Ben's shoulder. "We came here voluntarily, to provide information regarding Ella's abduction. Not to be interrogated. If you want to ask Ben any more questions, you'll need to speak with his parents first."

Then my father steeled his voice. "And let me be frank—accusing this boy of having anything to do with the kidnappings is offensive and grotesque. I expect better from our police."

Captain Corcoran snorted, but said no more.

Hawfield rose quickly. "Thank you for coming down. If you'll follow me, we can knock out those statements . . ."

⬡ ⬡ ⬡

I walked outside and stretched. The paperwork had taken over an hour.

Ben sat on a bench nearby, staring at nothing.

"Hey."

"Hey." He slid over, making room for me to sit.

After a slight hesitation, I did.

For several moments, neither of us spoke. I sat very still, feeling awkward, watching a gaggle of children play hopscotch in the riverside park across the street.

"They think I know something," Ben said sourly. "That I might be working with someone again. 'Craving the spotlight,' Corcoran said."

"I wish you had an alibi."

His head spun. "Why? *You* don't think I had anything—"

"Ben, no! I just meant that it'd be easier. That they'd go away."

Ben held my gaze. His shell was crumbling. I saw raw emotion hiding behind his eyes.

"Because if you thought I was capable of something like . . . like *that*, I might . . ." His voice cracked. "I couldn't take it."

He looked away. The harbor breeze ruffled his silky black hair.

My hand found his, almost by its own volition. "Ben."

"What?" He didn't turn.

"I want you to know that I forgive you. It's past time I told you that."

He tensed. I squeezed his hand, letting him know I meant the words.

I did. I couldn't be mad at Ben anymore. It was like being mad at my left arm.

And right then, I needed my arm back.

Ben's head dropped. Then, shockingly, his shoulders began to shake.

"I never meant for . . . It wasn't supposed to . . ."

"*Shhh.*" I scootched close, wrapped an arm around him. "I know. I know."

I heard snivels, desperately masked. Ben's whole body trembled. Then he relaxed.

"I'm sorry about the flaring." Wiping his checks with his palms. "I can be such an idiot sometimes."

"Sometimes?" I joked, trying to lighten the mood. "I understand. Let's just tone things down for a while, until we figure out what's wrong."

"Okay." He sat back, too embarrassed to look at me.

Our hands parted. My arm slipped from his shoulder.

"I just wish we could *do* something." Ben punched his thigh. "For Ella, and Lucy and Peter. Some whacked-out monster has them, and we've got these incredible gifts. But right now, they don't mean anything. We're nowhere. I've never felt so . . . *useless.*"

"Helpless." I hugged myself close. "It's like I can see Ella drowning, but can't save her."

Unbidden, thoughts of my friend flooded my mind. Her mischievous smile as we whispered secrets in calculus. The two of us laughing at the terrible artwork. A quick give-and-go we'd executed on the practice field.

Ella Francis had become one of my closest friends. Maybe even a best one.

My own walls caved. Tears trickled from the corner of my eyes.

Then strong arms enveloped me.

"Don't cry." Ben's hot breath on my cheek. "We'll find her. And the twins. I promise."

"Don't make promises you can't keep," I hiccupped. "People *always* do that."

"I mean it." Firmly spoken. "I won't *let* us fail. Not at this."

The sobs broke free. I burrowed into Ben's chest, letting everything go. I cried and cried and cried, unthinking, releasing a week's worth of pent-up emotion in a few hot seconds.

Ben held me, silent, softly rubbing my back.

A thought floated from somewhere far away.

This isn't so bad.

I pushed away, gently breaking Ben's embrace. Looked into his eyes. His face was a whisper from mine.

I thought of Ben's confession during the hurricane. How he'd wanted to be more than just packmates. Emotions swirled in my chest, making me dizzy. Off balance.

"Ben . . . I . . ."

"Tory?"

My father's voice sent us flying apart as if electroshocked.

Kit was descending the steps, an odd look on his face.

"Yes?" Discreetly wiping away tears.

I saw a thousand questions fill Kit's eyes, but, thankfully, he kept them shelved.

"I hate to do this, kiddo, but Whitney's party starts in an hour. She's trying to be patient, but, frankly, that isn't her strong suit."

"No. Right." I stood, smoothing clothes and hair. "Mustn't keep the Duchess waiting."

Kit frowned. "Say the word, and we cancel right now. No question."

"No, sorry. I was just being flip. It's really fine." Forced smile. "Might be just the thing."

"All right, then. We need to get moving."

Kit glanced at Ben, still sitting on the bench, striving for invisible.

A smile quirked my father's lips. "And you, Mr. Blue? Ready for a good ol'-fashioned backyard barbeque? My daughter will be there."

Ben's uneasy smile was his only response.

CHAPTER 34

The party was surreal.

The weather that afternoon was perfect. Sunny, mid-seventies, with a light breeze sweeping in off the breakers. Everyone wore shorts, sandals, and shades, luxuriating like house cats in the warm April sun.

The food was top-notch. Whitney had chosen JB's Smokeshack for catering, and the local barbeque hotspot totally delivered. Spare ribs. Smoked chicken. Pulled pork. Cornbread. Okra casserole. Cabbage. Yellow potato salad. Apple cobbler. I'd shoveled down two plates, and was considering a third.

The whole neighborhood turned out. All twenty of us. Lorelei Devers spread a blanket on the grass, and in moments five more appeared beside hers. Ruth and Linus Stolowitski sat on their stoop, greeting everyone who passed by. Kit bounced here and there, tweaking the sound system, hauling bags of ice, and making sure food and drink flowed smoothly. Tom Blue brought out an old croquet set, and soon half the guests were playing.

Younger kids scampered about, invited by Morris Islanders with family in the area. They ran laughing across the common, or tossed

Frisbees and plastic horseshoes. All told, perhaps fifty people were milling about, smiling and stuffing their faces.

All but Coop—Kit made me lock the wolfdog away. Probably for the best.

Above it all lorded Whitney, a queen bee managing her hive. She seemed everywhere at once, greeting new arrivals, stocking the napkin dispensers, even organizing the parking lot. All while wearing a face-splitting smile, and giggling like a schoolgirl, totally in her element.

But even Whitney's effervescence couldn't shake the pall hanging over the festivities. Most conversations inevitably gravitated to the kidnappings. Heads shook in dismay. Theories were exchanged. And dozens of surreptitious glances were cast the Virals' way.

Everyone knew the missing kids were our classmates. Some had learned that Ella and I were close.

I tried to avoid notice.

Though I played the dutiful daughter—wearing a sundress, shaking hands, even helping little ones find a bathroom—inside, I cringed. The whole thing felt like a betrayal.

While I was sipping raspberry lemonade, Ella was imprisoned somewhere.

I couldn't shake the feeling that I should be doing more.

At least my emotions were in check.

After my crying jag with Ben, it felt like my feelings had simply shut down, or somehow switched off. The well had run empty. I'd gone numb.

In a way, that was good. I felt more capable of rational thought than I had in days.

After the party's first hectic hour, the boys and I had settled down at the edge of the lawn, where the grass gave way to sand, and eventually surf.

I finished scarfing a bowl of banana pudding and pushed it aside. "We need to discuss our options."

Hi rolled to a sitting position. He wore an orange Charlotte Bobcats tee and navy shorts.

"We're stuck," he said. "The rock is our best clue, but it doesn't lead anywhere."

Shelton set down his sweet tea. He wore white on white—polo shirt and cargo shorts. Hi had dubbed it Shelton's "Carlton" look. I didn't get it.

"I can't crack those B-Series files," he admitted. "The encryption is light-years out of my league. 256-bit keys. The universe will end before anyone forces through *that.*"

"Just do your best," I encouraged.

"My best won't get the job done. We need to call Chang."

"No." On this point I was certain. "We can't trust him. We don't know what's in those files, and Chang's already proven he's a loose cannon. We go it alone."

Shelton sighed. "I'll keep looking. Hope for divine intervention."

"I know you can do it." Trying to buck him up. "Eddie Chang's not half as smart as the great Shelton Devers."

"I don't know," Hi said. "That dude's pretty sharp."

"Thanks," Shelton grumbled.

"Now," Hi continued, "if she'd said *me,* I'd be on board. I'm super intelligent."

Ben reached up from where he was lying with his eyes closed. Smacked Hi's dome.

Hi rubbed his head. "I'm getting pretty tired of that move."

"Then quit being a dope." Ben's lids remained shut.

"Hey, sure. No problem. I just need to—"

Hi lunged for Ben, intending a flying body slam. Ben caught Hi in midair and tossed him downhill in one quick motion. Hi tumbled, rolled, and dropped over the berm onto the sand.

"That was dumb," Hi informed the blue sky.

"Yep," Ben agreed, settling back on his elbows.

Hi began dusting himself off. "I shouldn't have spoken before I pounced."

"Wouldn't have mattered." Ben rose and walked to the berm, then extended a hand to help Hi climb up. They sat back down as if it never happened.

Boys.

⬡ ⬡ ⬡

The party was winding down.

Caterers began loading their truck as Kit disassembled the tent. Mr. Blue packed up his croquet mallets and headed for the driveway.

Shelton and Hi had already gone inside, leaving Ben and me alone.

Somehow we found ourselves down on the dock.

We sat in companionable silence, tossing sunflower seeds into the surf. The sun dipped in the west. Seagulls rode late afternoon thermals, cawing into the wind.

Ben started talking about Wando High. I countered with news of Bolton. Before long, we'd exchanged our stories, catching up on the last five months in each other's lives.

I hadn't realized how much I missed Ben. How badly I wanted him back at Bolton.

"Think there's any chance they let you back in?" I asked hopefully.

"Headmaster Paugh?" Ben laughed. "Don't bet on it. That's okay anyway. For all I bitch, Wando's a pretty nice school. I'll be cool there. I really don't skip much, FYI. I'm not sure what I was thinking that morning. I barely know those guys."

"The Rhodes scholars I met in the parking lot? They aren't both Harvard bound?"

"Ease off, Brennan." Spoken with a smile. "Not everyone is born a genius. The world needs us ditchdiggers, too."

"You're not a ditchdigger."

"Hey, I *like* digging holes. Don't try to change me."

Several minutes passed quietly as the sun slowly dropped toward the horizon.

Ben broke the silence. "Why do you think our flares have gone crazy?"

"Wish I knew." I tossed an oyster shell into the water. "Maybe our powers are still evolving. We don't really understand the extent of our mutations."

"Maybe the wolf is tired of hiding," Ben said quietly. "Maybe he wants a permanent seat at the table."

My head shook on its own volition. "I feel like it has to do with *us,* though. Like, maybe our pack is screwing things up somehow. Not connecting right. It's hard to explain."

Ben nodded. "I've never understood what you do. Honestly, it freaks me out."

I snorted. "You don't say."

"Oh, come on. How would you like it if I read your thoughts? If you couldn't keep a single secret."

"I *don't* keep secrets from you."

"Everyone has secrets." Ben's voice was suddenly serious. "Even you."

My back stiffened. Ben had repeated Chance's words nearly verbatim, and it jarred me.

He was right, of course. I was keeping several secrets from Ben.

Like how comfortable it felt to be alone with him. How much I'd missed his reassuring presence. His quiet strength.

Why keep that a secret?

Ben changed the subject. "What should we do about Chance?"

“Another crap sandwich.” I made sure to catch his eye. “We’re *not* going to hurt him, or anything like that. That isn’t on the table.”

He waved my words away. “I know that. Heat of the moment. Forget it.”

“We’ve dealt with Chance before. Usually, he can be reasoned with. We just have to find out what he wants.”

We avoided talking about Ella. At this point, what more was there to say?

Ben removed his shoes, plunged both feet into the lapping saltwater. Then he leaned back against a post, sighing contentedly.

The little-boy maneuver brought a smile to my face.

I reflected on how often I misjudged Ben. How often he came through when it mattered.

My breath suddenly caught. Were my feelings toward him changing?

Did I just miss my good friend, or was this something more?

I didn’t know. Wasn’t sure I wanted to find out.

Ben and I were *pack*. Nothing could be closer than that. Could it?

That dangerous train of thought was broken by a buzzing in my pocket.

Incoming text. I unlocked my iPhone and read.

“Who’s that?” Ben asked absently. “Did Hi finally figure out how to take screen shots?”

“It’s Jason,” I answered without thinking. “There’s a party in Old Town, though he’s selling the thing like it’s some kind of prayer vigil.”

Water splashed.

I looked up.

Ben was retying his shoes, a closed-off look on his face.

“Have fun.” He rose quickly. “We can talk more tomorrow.”

“Ben, wait!” Popping up as he strode by me. “I’m not going!”

Ben waved without turning, heading for his father’s door. I watched him disappear inside.

Ugh. Never forget how moody that boy is. Always a live wire.

Then I laughed without humor.

My best girlfriend was missing. No ransom tape had appeared. I had no idea how to help.

Boy problems were less than meaningless.

Determined to accomplish *something* for Ella's sake, I hurried for my own home.

CHAPTER 35

I stared at online pictures of the zodiac cards.

The paper's website had posted full-color shots, much more detailed than the photocopy we'd stolen from the DA's office. Both Ophiuchus and Cetus were shown in vibrant clarity.

Not that it mattered—the images told me nothing about the kidnappings.

I slumped back in my desk chair, wondered again who was passing this stuff to the press. The leak obviously had access to the evidence.

Rex Gable might fit that bill.

But the pieces had yet to make sense.

Why antique zodiac cards? What did they mean to the criminal? What message were they intended to convey?

Clara Gordon's words ran through my mind.

Cetus often represented unrelenting evil. Is *that* what we were facing?

A chilling thought struck me. Ella had been snatched outside the Flying Tomato, not at home. Which meant this lunatic had broken into her bedroom and left the card there.

Why take the risk? Such brazen disregard for danger was unnerving.

Suddenly curious, I searched the Internet for the location where Lucy and Peter were kidnapped. Found nothing. Score *one* for police secrecy, at least.

I tapped my lip, thinking. Had the twins also been abducted away from home?

If so, the criminal had separately planted the Ophiuchus card as well.

I shivered, recalling the shadowy form that had watched us rifle the Gables' basement.

Had that been the kidnapper?

Another thought. How had the criminal taken *both* twins at once? The Gables weren't exactly athletes, but they were healthy teenagers. How could one individual overcome both kids at the same time? Or were they grabbed separately?

I need more details about the Gables.

Idly, I spun in my chair. Coop's head rose from his paws. Noting my attention was elsewhere, the wolfdog settled back down to nap.

Something else was bothering me.

Why was Ella abducted at all? It didn't seem to jibe with the first crime.

The twins were taken for money. That was crystal clear—there was a ransom tape and a demand for five million dollars. Uncharitably, I wondered if Rex Gable had made any effort to gather those funds.

Would he actually pay? My gut said no.

Of course, my gut also suspected him of committing the crime in the first place.

Which, admittedly, didn't make a ton of sense. At least, not if money was the motive.

But there's been no ransom tape for Ella.

No million-dollar demand, at least not yet. And, based on what

I'd seen of Ella's parents, they would *definitely* pay. Anything. Gladly. Whatever it took to get their daughter back safely.

So why nothing from Ella's captor?

If it wasn't for the zodiac cards, the kidnappings wouldn't seem connected at all.

The phosphate nodule was more important than I'd thought—it was tangible evidence of an assault, assuring that Ella's case was treated as a crime from the beginning.

Take away the cards, and I'm not sure the police would've linked the disappearances.

Three Bolton Prep kids missing, in the same week?

Okay. The cops would've investigated any possible connection. But that didn't change the fact that Ella's disappearance seemed entirely different from that of the twins.

There was still too much I didn't know.

Had the police responded to the ransom demand? Contacted the twins' kidnapper? Was there a way to do so?

When was the payoff required? Where? Who was supposed to make the drop?

I slapped my leg in frustration. I needed more on the Gable case.

That investigation was the only link to our adversary. Find the twins, and I'd find Ella.

I was considering options for stealing a police case file when a fanged unicorn appeared on my screen. Shelton. Requesting a meeting.

I was logging into our chat room when a second message popped up.

Shelton wanted to meet at the bunker. Said it was important.

Clock check—8:00 p.m.

Saturday night. I can pull that off.

Grabbing keys and iPhone, I tapped my thigh for Coop to follow.

"C'mon, dog brain. This time, you're more than welcome."

○ ○ ○

"I'm a genius," Shelton announced smugly.

A smile split my face. "You cracked the encryption."

"What? Oh, hell no." Shelton waved the idea away. "Keep dreaming. But I found something else you're not gonna believe."

The four of us were gathered around the bunker's circular table. Hi was munching on a sleeve of double-stuffed Oreos. Ben watched with distaste, his feet up and hands behind his head.

I sat next to Shelton, who'd brought his laptop from home.

Coop was gnawing a rawhide in the back chamber.

"Spill it," Ben commanded.

"I wasn't getting anywhere with those B-Series files." Shelton opened the computer and typed quickly. "So I decided to poke at something else for a while. Get my mind right. My first thought was of Rex Gable's phone records."

Shelton spun his laptop to face the group. "Check out this nugget in what Chang sent us."

His finger tapped a word at the top of Chang's email.

"Bellweather." I looked at Shelton in confusion. "What does that mean?"

Shelton smiled triumphantly. "It's the name of Rex Gable's favorite hunting dog. I found a random reference online."

Ben's feet hit the floor. "You dragged me out here to talk about a dog?"

"Kind of," Shelton said slyly, "since that dog's name is Gable's password for his cellular account."

"Hey, genius," Hi said, mouth encrusted with chocolate crumbs. "We already *have* those records. You're looking at them right now."

"Use your brain cells, Stolowitski. For how many different accounts do you use 'Westeros' as the password?"

"For everything!" Hi blurted. "And now you've ruined it, jerk!"

Suddenly, I understood.

"What'd you find?" I asked excitedly.

Shelton made a sweeping gesture toward his laptop. "Rex Gable has a Gmail account."

He pulled up an inbox. Dozens of emails, filed in separate folders.

"Shelton, that's awesome!" Trying to decide where to start. "We can divide—"

"Ahem."

I blinked. "You've already found something, haven't you?"

Shelton's face grew serious as he punched more keys. Then he spun the computer to face us once more.

Onscreen was a single email.

From: Rex Gable. To: Rex Gable. No subject. No message.

One attachment. An MP4 file.

Noting our attention, Shelton double-clicked.

The twins' ransom tape played in its entirety.

Hi scratched his head. "I don't get it. Of course Gable has the ransom tape. They're his own stepkids, for Pete's sake."

Shelton tapped the *date* of the email.

Monday, April 1.

I had it in a flash. "That's the day I testified! We ran into Detective Hawfield the next morning, in the DA's office. Commissioner Riggins, too. At that point, neither of them were treating the twins' disappearance as a crime."

Ben followed my drift. "Which means they hadn't seen the ransom tape yet."

"Which *means*," Shelton finished, "Rex Gable had a copy at least a full day before the police. Maybe even two!"

"He mailed the clip to himself," I said aloud. "Why do that?"

"Because *he* filmed the dang thing, like you said!" Shelton was so amped his voice cracked. "He's the kidnapper!"

My fingers drummed the table. "You could be right."

"*Could* be?" Shelton sounded incredulous. "That's a smoking gun, girl!"

"Not necessarily," Hi countered. "Maybe the kidnapper emailed the tape directly to Rex Gable first, and he panicked for a day, not knowing what to do. Or maybe the kidnapper told Gable he *couldn't* go to the police."

"But why did he email it to himself?" I repeated.

"I do that sometimes," Ben said, "when I don't wanna risk losing an important document, like a paper for school. Uploading it to Gmail is like a free backup in case my computer dies."

I nodded, thinking aloud. "Shelton still could be right. Gable uploads the file and sends it to himself, backing it up externally, like Ben said. Then he destroys every other copy. Now the tape is out there in the cloud, but *not* on his hard drive or camera. It creates a level of distance. So long as he's not a suspect, the police won't check his personal email."

"Still, not very smart," Hi said. "I mean, *we* found it. If we're right, Rex Gable's an idiot. Why not delete that email after sending it on to the police?"

"He *did* delete it," Shelton answered. "But the fool never emptied his trash. I found that message in his deleted items folder. I figured that would be the most interesting place to start."

"You're *killing* it tonight, Devers!" Hi tossed him a high five.

I shook my head in wonder. "Could Rex Gable really be that dumb?"

I didn't think so, but it was surprising what silly mistakes people could make.

Maybe the man was simply computer illiterate, and forgot to cover this one track.

And we found it. But what to do now?

Suddenly, I was furious.

That bastard. His own family! And then grabbing Ella for no reason . . .

"Wait."

I flattened my palms on the table. Thought hard.

The boys quieted.

"Rex Gable wouldn't hold his own stepkids for ransom," I said. "That makes no sense. There must be another motive."

"I can think of a few," Ben said quietly. "None of them good. Maybe Rex wanted Lucy and Peter out of his hair. Permanently."

Ben's statement was like a ten-foot icicle through my heart.

If Rex Gable was the kidnapper, and he didn't want his stepkids found, then Ella . . .

"But why take *her*?" Louder than I'd intended.

"That part, I can't even guess." Hi sat back, face ashen. "What does Ella Francis have to do with the Gable twins? If a stranger snatched Lucy and Peter, then grabbed Ella later to up the stakes, why haven't we seen a second ransom video?"

Hi was echoing my confusion from earlier. I was still just as puzzled.

"The police need to know," Shelton said. "This email will make Rex Gable a suspect."

"Screw those jokers." Ben moved to the window bench. "I'm done talking to them. About anything."

"Today's meeting didn't exactly go well," Hi conceded. "That douche-bag Corcoran would rather arrest *us* than anyone. If he finds out we're conducting an investigation, breaking into other people's emails . . ." He spread his hands. "I just don't see how to do it."

"Dealing with Corcoran is pointless," I said. "He clearly isn't interested in anything we have to say."

"I haven't even checked Gable's inbox yet," Shelton said. "If the dumbass left a copy of the ransom video in his trash folder, who knows what other mistakes he's made?"

"First order of business." I brought my hands together. "We review every single email."

"Tomorrow." Ben shrugged at my disappointed look. "Sorry, but my mother said I have to be home in an hour."

"Same here." Hi wadded up his cookie trash and stuffed it in the wastebasket. "With a kidnapper on the loose, I can't believe my mother even let me outside. I had to convince her it'd be pretty tough to grab all four of us at once. But she'll be waiting by the door already."

I looked at Shelton.

"I'm free bright and early," he offered.

"Okay." I exhaled slowly. "I'll do what I can tonight, then we'll finish in the morning."

"You're staying out here?" Shelton asked. "Alone?"

"No big deal. I don't want Kit seeing what I'm up to."

"I don't like it," Ben said. Behind him, Hi looked uneasy.

"No one knows this place exists." I pointed to the other room. "And there's an eighty-five-pound predator in there that loves me. I'll be fine."

They relaxed. Coop might be a big sloppy puppy to us, but to the world at large, my pet was a dangerous-looking beast. A better bodyguard didn't exist.

"You can leave my laptop here when you're done," Shelton said.

"Text me when you get home," Ben requested. "Please don't forget."

I hid a smile. "Will do. Bye, guys. And *please* sleep. We've got a ton to do tomorrow."

Hearing movement, Coop padded into the chamber. Watched the boys crawl outside. Satisfied that I had no intention of following, he curled into a ball at my feet, closed his eyes, and began snoring.

"My hero."

I cracked a Diet Coke. Opened the first email.

"Watch your back, Rex," I whispered. "You can run, but you can't hide."

CHAPTER 36

"Ugh. Enough!"

I closed the laptop and shoved it aside.

Coop rose, stretched, and shook his muscles loose, the tags on his collar jangling loudly. He yipped once, then slipped through the exit.

"Right behind you." I turned off the floor lamps and killed the power. Pulling on my windbreaker, I crawled from the bunker behind my canine escort.

Outside, the night air was heavy and wet, with traces of rain lingering on the ocean breeze. Heavy squalls had swept across the island during the two hours I'd worked alone, delving through Rex Gable's Gmail, message by message.

I was well into the previous year's emails, but had found nothing of interest. A few hundred remained, but I wasn't optimistic.

The moon was three-quarters, waxing, reflecting enough light to see without a flashlight. The tall grasses bordering the overland trail would be soaked, so I elected to walk along the shore instead. A slightly longer route, but not much, and watching the crabs skitter and dance as we approached would entertain the mutt.

With Cooper trotting beside me, I split a stand of prickly pears, then ran-walked down the dunes to the beach. I paused a moment to bang sand from my shoes. Coop was already scampering for the tidal pools, snuffling everything in sight.

I love the ocean.

An odd thing to discover, having grown up in central Massachusetts. But I knew it now—wherever life took me, whatever career I might choose, ultimately I'd settle by the sea.

I scooped up a stick as we strolled, in no particular hurry. Catching Coop's attention, I tossed it into the darkness ahead. He fetched it four consecutive times—a new record—before loping inland with the prize between his teeth.

Coop has the chasing part down cold. Bringing things back is always touch and go.

I took two more steps, then nearly stumbled.

The feeling had returned.

A now-familiar sensation swelled inside my brain, its accompanying sense of oneness arrowing outward in an expanding, spiraling circle. For a fleeting moment, I felt connected to all things around me.

My mind opened like a flower. Inviting. Welcoming. Searching?

Then the sensation vanished once again, leaving no trace.

I held my body still, hoping that, this time, maybe, some clue would reveal itself.

None did. After a few moments, I sighed, resumed my walk down the beach.

"Makes no sense," I whispered to myself. "None."

Shaking off the disorientation, I heard a rustling in the dunes directly to my right. Figured Coop had found a rabbit hole.

"Leave the bunnies alone!" I called.

But Cooper's head poked from the cattails fifty feet ahead.

His canine eyes found mine—two golden disks gleaming in the darkness.

My steps slowed. "How'd you get way up there, boy?"

Vines crunched. A rush of air beside me.

Something black and heavy swooped toward my head.

I barely had time to react, diving to my left as an object hummed past my forehead.

Hitting the ground, I tucked and rolled sideways as a hulking shadow crashed onto the space I'd just vacated.

A muffled curse. The dark shape rose, turning this way and that.

Instinct took over. As I scuttled away on my butt, the wolf *forced* its way out.

SNAP.

Fire exploded inside my chest.

The flare unfolded without being called.

Raw energy flooded my system, pooling and spreading, like a nuclear reaction spiraling out of control. The adrenal jolt was too powerful to withstand. I collapsed on the wet sand, my body convulsing, every muscle cramping at once.

I glimpsed the shadow streaking toward me—a sinuous figure in black, wielding some sort of club—before my eyes simply blanked.

The power was too much.

I lay there, helpless, my senses shutting down one by one.

A gust of wind. A throaty growl. Then a tearing sound, followed by a strangled scream.

"Coop!?!"

The thump of metal on flesh, followed by a yelp of canine pain.

Heavy breathing. Another terrified shout. Then footsteps pounding away.

I tried to rise, but the inferno inside left me paralyzed. Exposed.

SNUP.

The power fled as quickly as it came. I don't know if I consciously dispelled it, or if the flare simply withered and died.

Slowly, I came back to the world.

Legs standing over me. A rough tongue against my cheek.

As my vision refocused, I saw that Coop was straddling me, hackles raised, eyes fixed on the dunes.

"Good boy," I rasped.

Coop's gaze dropped for a moment. Another quick face lick.

Then he snapped back to attention, growling as he scanned for threats.

My brain slowly reassembled. I nudged the wolfdog aside and rose to my knees.

A deep breath as I worked the cobwebs out, then I stood.

Reality came crashing home.

Someone had attacked me. Here. On Morris Island.

Miles from anywhere a stranger should be.

Facts molded into conclusions.

I'd been targeted. There was no other reasonable explanation. Not for an attack on this deserted beach, at this late hour. Not out here in the middle of nowhere.

Coop nuzzled my side. I knelt, hugged him close.

"You saved me, dog face." Kissing his snout. "My hero, for real."

Coop took a step forward, then winced.

"You okay, pal?" I ran my hands along his sides, then down his legs. When I touched his left forepaw he yelped and stepped back.

I gripped his collar. "Let me see, boy."

Gently, I examined the paw. Two nails were smashed, and there was some mild swelling. A small gash ran along one side, cutting into the pad beneath.

Coop whined as I probed, but I held firm.

"Nothing broken, but it looks painful as hell." I glanced left, then right, assessing our position. It was another two hundred yards to the townhouses.

"We'll take it slow." Stroking Coop's head with my hands.

I thought about the assailant returning. Recalled the ripping sound, and cries of pain.

Coop gave worse than he got. That bastard is probably still running.

We covered the next hundred yards at a glacial pace. Coop was favoring his leg, and with each passing step I worried he'd need a trip to Dr. Abendroth.

Get home. Get inside. Get safe.

Then Coop froze.

His body tensed as his head swung toward the dunes.

Eyes wide. Ears erect and forward. Coop bared his teeth and growled.

I crouched beside him. My eyes darted to the lights of my complex just ahead.

Should I scream? Would anyone hear me?

In the gloom of the island's interior, six glowing circles appeared.

Red. Quarter-sized. Floating in close-set pairs.

As I watched two spheres vanished, then reappeared a dozen yards away.

I stood very still, spellbound.

The paired lights inched closer. I heard the slightest shifting of sand.

Abruptly it hit me.

Eyes.

Three pairs, spread out among the dunes.

The realization chilled my blood.

In all my life, I'd never seen red eyes like that. Not on any creature.

Coop lunged forward, barking wildly. Then he yelped as the injured paw took his weight.

The scarlet orbs stopped moving. Hovered in the blackness.

I stared. They stared back.

Coop went ballistic. On three legs, he began limping toward the dunes, howling and baying at the silent red circles. Ropes of saliva dripped from his jaws.

Floodlights flickered on at our complex. One. Then another. Then a third.

Each successive halogen dispelled more of the shadows.

As the illumination spread our way, the eyes vanished.

The beach felt suddenly empty. I counted to ten. Nothing reappeared.

Whatever had been watching was gone.

⬡ ⬡ ⬡

"Everything okay, honey?"

Kit was standing on our front stoop. "What's gotten into Cooper?"

"He hurt his paw."

My voice trembled. I hoped Kit would attribute its shakiness to concern for my pet.

"Poor guy."

Kit stepped down and took a quick look. "Yikes. How'd you manage that one, fella?"

He was clubbed, protecting me from a masked attacker.

"Coop stumbled by the rocks."

Kit eyed the stairs, then, squaring his shoulders, lifted the wolfdog and carried him up.

"*Oof.* What are we feeding you? Dinosaurs?"

Kit muscled Coop into the house and over to his doggie bed. Then he collapsed to the floor, wiping sweat from his forehead.

"Note to self," Kit panted. "This dog is too big for carrying."

Cooper licked his face.

I stood by the stairs, unsure what to do. A part of me knew I was still in shock.

I'd been attacked.

My powers had nearly killed me.

And then strange . . . *something* had stalked me in the darkness.

Unless I'm hallucinating. Oh, crap, am I hallucinating?

"Kiddo?" Kit was watching me. "You okay? I don't think his paw is broken. Rest and ice oughta do the trick."

I shook my head to clear it.

Kit couldn't know what just happened. Ella needed me. The last thing I could afford right then was my father restricting my movements.

"I'm just tired." Feigning a yawn. "I'm trying to think of how we'll get Cooper upstairs."

Kit's face fell. "Tory, I'm not sure I can manage that. I nearly died just now."

Sensing the issue, Coop rose. Limped to my side. Nipped at my palm.

Against all odds, it triggered a smile. I knelt and hugged my dog, ruffling his fur.

"We'll go slow. One step at a time."

No matter what, I wasn't leaving Coop downstairs, alone.

Not tonight. My protector deserved better.

Bu as we maneuvered my wolfdog up the stairs, riser by riser, the dark thoughts returned.

I'd been targeted. Someone had come for me in the night.

And there could only be one explanation.

I didn't know how or why. I couldn't fathom the connection.

But the truth was as plain as the smashed nails on Cooper's swollen paw.

The Zodiac kidnapper was now after *me.*

CHAPTER 37

Sunday

We reassembled in the bunker ten hours later.

I'd asked Ben to pick us up in *Sewee,* not wanting to walk across Morris that morning. I knew my attacker wouldn't still be hiding in the sand hills, but those glowing red eyes were fresh in my memory.

If they actually existed. If my brain hadn't gone fishing after the flare disaster.

But Coop had seen them, too. And gone ballistic.

Coop saw something, *but he was injured. It could've been the kidnapper considering a second pass.*

I'd left my canine protector at home that morning. His bum wheel needed bed rest.

Coop hadn't liked the idea, but I'd been firm.

"I'm on high alert," I'd assured him. "I'll be safe with the boys."

"Gift cards?" Hi's complaining brought me back to the present. "Why not just hand me a note that says: I don't care enough to make an effort."

April 7. Hiram Stolowitski's sixteenth birthday.

"When exactly were we supposed to shop?" Shelton was scrolling Rex Gable emails on his laptop. "It's been a hectic week, bro."

"I bought you *Assassin's Creed* six weeks before *your* birthday," Hi shot back. "Waited in line all afternoon. The guy behind me smelled like fish tacos, but *I* stuck it out."

Ben clapped Hi's shoulder. "If it helps, I didn't remember to get you any gift. Tory and Shelton picked that up. I signed the card though. See? Ben. Right there."

"These are the memories that scar," Hi huffed. "I'm gonna be so complicated when I grow up. I'll probably film documentaries."

I sat forward at the table. "Okay, so . . . like, don't freak out."

That got their attention.

"About?" Ben took the seat across from me, next to Hiram.

"There was an incident last night." Oh so calm. "I'm perfectly okay, but on the way home someone attacked me on the beach."

"What?!" Three stunned voices.

"*That's* why you didn't text," Ben muttered.

Keeping my emotions in check, I described the chain of events. All but the part about mysterious red eyes. I needed to gnaw on that one. Were they even real?

"That's the *last* time you walk home alone." Ben's voice simmered with anger. "Thank God for the mutt. He's okay?"

"Coop's paw took a hit, but otherwise he's unhurt." I held up my palms in surrender. "Hey, no more arguments here. You three can sleep on my bedroom floor if you want."

"You think the attack was random?" Shelton's gaze slid to the bunker's entrance, perhaps worried that storm troopers might barrel in at any moment. "I find that hard to believe."

"Not a chance." Hi shook his head. "The Gable twins, then Ella. Now you. All Bolton Prep students. But what's the connection?"

"Linking me and Ella is easy," I said, "but what ties either of us to Lucy and Peter?"

No one had a theory.

"And your flare actually took you out?" Shelton hugged his knees. "Not cool."

I nodded grimly. "Full-blown backfire. I collapsed like a fainting goat. My eyesight even cut out. If Coop hadn't been there to defend me . . ."

Ben's fist hit the table. "Worst possible timing."

I rubbed my eyes. "And that weird feeling keeps coming on out of nowhere. Like a ghost. It's happening more often, and the sensation is getting stronger."

"Great," Shelton huffed. "Another mental health issue to worry about. Still no idea what it is? Why the vibe comes when you're *not* flaring?"

I shook my head helplessly. "None."

"That's background noise." Hi tapped the table with his index finger. "We gotta catch the psycho kid-grabber. Like, right now. If the bastard came after Tory once, he might do it again."

"Let's go over every scrap of evidence." Shelton closed his computer. "These emails are going nowhere. If Rex Gable wrote anything else that's incriminating, he did a better job hiding it than the ransom tape."

"We should focus on locations," Hi insisted. "Find where the kidnapper is holed up."

"But *how*?" Ben rose and leaned against the bunker wall. "We don't have anything to go on. Should we just drive around, shouting Ella's name out the windows?"

"Wait." A thought was winging in my brain. "We know about the phosphate nodule, but never really investigated its source."

"I looked some yesterday." Hi moved to the computer workstation. "Check this out."

Hi pulled up an old map detailing the Charleston Basin and its tributary rivers. Labeled along the riverbanks were the locations of old phosphate mines.

"You thinking mineshaft?" Shelton watched from over Hi's shoulder. "Like, they're being held underground somewhere, near one of the rivers?"

"That's not how those operations worked." On the second monitor, Hi opened a magazine article. "I read this a few nights ago. The phosphates being mined weren't buried very deep. Maybe six to ten feet. The miners would dig trenches by hand alongside a deposit, then remove the topsoil in layers to expose the rock. Then they'd strip it all out and move to another spot."

"So they weren't underground mines." Shelton scratched his chin. "What then?"

A line in the article jumped out at me.

I pointed. "This says that a major drawback of strip mining was how badly it scarred the land." I read from the screen. "Dozens of beautiful plantations were destroyed to make way for the phosphate mining operations."

Ben glanced at me. "Yeah. So?"

"These mines were dug on old plantations along the riverbanks. Some of *those* probably had expensive manor houses. Ornate gates. Fancy kitchens. Sprawling barns."

Ben shrugged. "Still not following."

"Professor Marzec seemed surprised we'd found such a large nodule. That makes me think these rocks aren't that common. Maybe the kidnapper found it at a place where phosphates were actually brought to surface, and a few old samples were still kicking around."

"Okay." Shelton was fiddling with his glasses. "So the rock used to attack Ella likely came from near an old phosphate mine. I buy that. But this map shows *hundreds* of locations."

My voice grew excited. "But we have another piece of info as well."

Blank stares.

"The writing on the prison bar in the ransom video! We know who forged the steel."

"Philip Simmons!" Hi was already typing. "If we can find a map of his works, then cross-check *those* locations with old phosphate mining operations—"

"We can narrow the possible locations." Ben shook his head in wonderment. "Incredible. It's nice having a genius around."

"It's only genius if it works." But I flushed at the compliment.

"Got it." Hi had found exactly what we needed—a map of greater Charleston pinpointing the works of legendary ironworker Philip Simmons. "I love Internet more than pizza. Maybe."

Hi and Shelton exchanged places without a word.

We'd entered a Devers area of expertise.

"I'll superimpose the Simmons map over the mining chart." Shelton cracked his knuckles. "Won't take a minute."

Shelton opened GIMP and got to work. I watched impatiently as he merged the two images to create a unified picture.

When he finished, I stared at the screen, enthralled.

Only five places overlapped.

Hi was glancing from map to article. "The three locations on the Stono River are all out. Everything around there was demolished in 1943, to make way for the private airport on Johns Island."

"When did phosphate mining stop?" Ben asked suddenly.

It took a moment for Hi to find the answer.

"The 1930s," he said finally. "The industry peaked in the 1880s, then slowly ran out of steam over the next four decades. It was barely limping along by the turn of the century."

Ben looked at me. "Simmons wasn't born until 1912. And he must've spent a long time learning his trade, right? He wouldn't have run his own shop for at least twenty years, probably more. Which means the 1930s."

Hi frowned. "So?"

"Metal bars marked by Philip Simmons probably didn't even exist *during* the mining boom," Ben said. "I bet the bar in the ransom video was formed after all the phosphate mines had shut down."

"We should look for a plantation that survived the mining craze!" I blurted, then clapped my hands in excitement. "An estate that was still intact when its mine shut down, and wealthy enough to require expensive ironwork services sometime afterward."

"Of course!" Shelton nodded eagerly. "That would account for both a Simmons steel bar *and* phosphate rocks in the same location."

I squeezed Ben's shoulder. "Who's the genius now?"

He snorted, looked away.

Hi was now shoving Shelton aside. "Leave this part to the birthday boy."

Retaking the keyboard, Hi began running searches, pausing now and again to scan an article. Without a way to help, the rest of sat down at the table to wait.

An eternity later, Hi spun to face us. "Ladies and gentlemen!"

We rushed to his side.

A website was open, detailing the historic contributions of one Philip Simmons.

In the mid-1980s, Mr. Simmons repaired iron railings on the riverfront steps during a plantation-wide beatification project. But that was not his first encounter with the estate. As a young man, Simmons knew many of the African Americans living on the plantation, and would visit often and provide what services he could.

I checked Shelton's combined map.

The location was perfect—hard against the Ashley River, a phosphate mining operation had occupied the same grounds from the late 1800s until the early twentieth century.

I checked the website's header. Something about the name felt right.

"Drayton Hall," I whispered.

"There are two other possibilities," Hi pointed out. "A cotton plantation on the Edisto, and a horseback riding retreat a few miles farther inland."

Perhaps my head was still scrambled from the night before.

But I could practically hear Ella calling to me.

Trust your instincts. Trust yourself.

"No." My finger touched the screen. "This is the spot."

"And we're going there. Right now."

CHAPTER 38

A fancy tourist mansion?"

In the rearview mirror, I could see Hi shaking his head.

He'd said it before at the bunker, and I'd had the same response.

"However unlikely, that's where the evidence points." I twisted in my seat to catch his eye. "If this isn't the right spot, then we'll scout those other two locations."

He nodded unhappily. "All I'm saying is, how in the world would a kidnapper hold three high school kids hostage at a place you can buy a ticket for, six days a week?"

Hi did have a point. Frankly, a strong one.

"Drayton Hall is a huge plantation." Shelton was sitting beside Hi. "And some areas aren't open to the public. Maybe the kidnapper is using one of them?"

"Gimme facts." Ben was at the wheel. "I wanna know what we're getting into."

We'd crossed James Island and were driving northeast up Ashley River Road, about fifteen miles beyond downtown Charleston. Civilization slowly fell away—the Explorer cruised through a dense forest of magnolias and live oaks, which hugged the road on both sides, creating a tunnel effect.

No sound. Little movement outside the confines of our packed SUV.

The surrounding woods had a creepy, claustrophobic feel, as if the trees intended to keep all human life confined to the narrow two-lane blacktop knifing through their domain. Though the forest had a cold aesthetic beauty, the area didn't give off a friendly vibe. I couldn't imagine anyone living out here.

Shelton read from his iPhone. "Drayton Hall is a classic eighteenth-century Ashley River plantation in the heart of the Lowcountry. *Blah blah blah.*" He began skimming the description. "A marvelous example of Palladian architecture . . . survived both the Revolutionary and Civil Wars . . . National Historical Landmark. The seven-bay double-pile plantation house was built by John Drayton in the late 1730s . . . completed in 1742 . . . using both free and slave labor. *Ugh.* C'mon, man. Slaves?"

"Forget the house," Ben advised. "What about the grounds?"

"Don't rush me." Shelton scrolled his cell. "Six hundred and thirty acres. The plantation grew rice and indigo. The estate's been kept in pretty good shape, although some of the oldest buildings are gone. The phosphate mine was close to the river."

"That's our focus," I said. "Old phosphate nodules probably aren't scattered over all six hundred acres."

"There!" Hi pointed to a narrow road cutting into the forest.

An elegant wooden sign announced the entrance to Drayton Hall. Ben turned onto the long driveway—a slender black strip in a sea of brown and green. It looked like a path to the end of the world.

"Man! I thought *we* lived in the middle of nowhere." Hi's nose was pressed to his window. "I've changed my mind, Tory. This *is* the perfect place to hold someone prisoner. I'm keeping it on file."

Ben eased down the lane, keeping our speed low.

I didn't blame him. It felt like we were invading a foreign country.

"There's an administrative center, a library, and a gift shop. Not what we're looking for." Then Shelton's eyes lit up. "But there's a *bunch* of stuff near the water. A garden house. Barn. The old mining works."

"Perfect." Pulse racing.

Could we actually have solved this riddle?

It seemed like such a long shot, yet something inside me was certain.

This must *be the right place.*

"Can we wander around alone?" Hi asked. "Because I doubt any kidnapping cages will be on the official program."

Shelton nodded. "Eight bucks for grounds only."

Half a mile in, the woods ended. A trio of ponds slipped by as the road cut sharply left, then back to the right. Ahead, an expansive lawn ran a hundred yards to the foot of Drayton Hall itself.

The stylish manor house was three stories, brick, with twin front staircases leading up to a white-column-flanked front door. The roof was elegant red tile. A balcony opened on the second level, just above the main entrance.

A workers' platform was attached to the building's left side, with cans of paint stacked on each of its four tiers.

"Pretty," I said. "And whoever's in charge of maintenance is earning their keep."

The access road ended in a small parking lot beside the administration center. There were no other cars. We exited the vehicle, and Shelton hustled over to buy four tickets.

Seconds later his voice called out. "You're not gonna believe this!"

We hurried to where he stood by a pair of locked doors.

A sign was taped to the glass: "Closed for renovations. See you this summer!"

Ben turned on Hi and Shelton. "All that fancy googling, and you didn't catch that part?"

"No, guys!" My eyes widened. "How long has the plantation been shut down?"

They all took my meaning.

"Three weeks." Hi was squinting at his phone. "And it's out of commission for another two months."

Shelton stomped over. "Where'd you see that?"

"Home page. Clear your cache once in a while, dummy. Is this your first smartphone?"

"This *could* be the place." Ben was suddenly all business. "The timing works."

"The river." My intensity matched Ben's.

Ella might be here.

Trapped in a cage, somewhere on this sprawling estate.

The thought made me both anxious and determined.

I would *not* fail my friend.

The twins, too. If their stepfather is responsible, we might be their only hope.

Shelton's eyebrows rose above the level of his glasses. "Should we . . . you know . . . take the dog out for a walk?"

I shook my head, avoiding Ben's eye. "The last time I tried, I nearly lost consciousness. That makes two disasters in a row. We can't risk it today—this mission is too important."

Ben was first to respond. "I'm with Tory. We don't need superpowers to search the grounds. We can always revisit the issue, if necessary."

Hi and Shelton nodded, looking relieved.

At skipping the flares, or the lack of a fight?

Shelton scored a map from a nearby bin. "We should start at the house. A wide lane runs from its back door, dividing the property in half."

I waved him forward. "Lead the way."

We cut through a screen of magnolias, entering the football field of grass that served as the estate's front yard.

"Nice digs," Hi said. "But I'm not mowing this lawn. It'd take days."

We walked up to the manor, then circled the building to an arrow-straight path stretching from its rear.

"It leads to the Ashley." Shelton peered ahead, hand-shielding his eyes. "This road was how they moved materials and supplies up to the house. Back in the day, the river was the best way in and out of here."

We followed the sunken lane toward the water, moving in and out of shadows cast by azalea trees lining both sides.

I felt hemmed in. Constricted. As beautiful as it was, I didn't like it there.

But it's perfect for hiding something you don't want found.

"Eyes peeled," I warned. "If we're on target, what we're looking for will be up ahead."

In minutes we reached the riverfront. Beyond a few broken-down sheds and the remains of an ancient garden, we'd seen nothing along the trail.

Water gently lapped the high bank. Only the occasional birdsong broke the silence.

The stillness was unnerving. Even on Morris, it was never *this* quiet.

"Where is everybody?" Shelton's shoulders were tense. "This place feels like the dark side of the moon."

"There's not another house for miles." Hi kicked a pebble into the stream. "I guess that's what six hundred acres buys you—total isolation. And Sunday must be a day off for the workers."

Ben was surveying our surroundings. "You could hide *fifty* dungeons on this property."

I took a deep breath, trying to formulate a plan. "Shelton, you mentioned structures by the river?"

Repositioning his glasses, Shelton consulted the handout. "Barn and garden house to the left. Mining stuff and cemetery to the right."

"Let's split into pairs," I said. "Hi and I will check the mine and graveyard. You two take the garden house and barn. We'll meet back here in twenty."

Ben waved away my suggestion. "Shelton and I will check the mine."

"You heard her say 'graveyard,' too, right?" Shelton squawked. "Not my speciality, Blue."

I started to protest, but Ben cut me off. "You were *attacked* yesterday, Tory. And *your* flares seem wonkier than the rest of ours. We'll handle this one. You and Sweet Sixteen can sweep the gardens."

Hi tugged my elbow, whispering, "He's right. Let him have this."

I swallowed my pride. "Fine. But promise. If you see anything suspicious, you'll regroup with us before you act. No exceptions."

Ben nodded, looking relieved. "Deal. See you in twenty."

Snagging Shelton by the shoulder—who muttered "graveyard?" one more time before relenting—Ben headed west along the riverbank.

Sighing, I turned to Hi.

He smiled wide. "Heigh ho, heigh ho, off to the barn we go?"

"Blargh."

We moved eastward and reached the garden house in moments. What was left of it, anyway—three crumbling walls surrounded a few well-tended flowerbeds. A winding path led from it down to the waterfront, which was screened from view by a stand of weeping willows.

Fifty yards farther on was the barn, its wooden exterior cracked and weathered.

My jaw clenched. I was on a goose chase.

I spun to face him. "These structures aren't even maintained."

He looked away. "They, uh, don't look too . . . sturdy."

My eyes narrowed. Hi was in on it, too, eh?

Shelton must've been acting reluctant, so I wouldn't suspect their plan. I was being shielded from harm. Sent to investigate the unlikely spots. Kept away from the phosphate mine.

Snap decision. "You check this path. There might be caves by the waterline."

Irritably, I gestured to the barn. "I'll buzz that relic, then we head to the mining area."

"Search the river for prison caves. Got it." Hi gave me a thumbs-up. "By the way, worst birthday ever."

I hustled forward, making little effort to conceal my movements. I'd been tricked—sent from the danger zone by my macho companions—but I refused to waste all day on this sideshow.

The barn was surrounded by live oaks, its planks cut from the same wood. Drawing closer, I realized the building wasn't the owl-invested wreck I'd suspected.

An area before the entrance had been floored with wooden beams and bound by a low wall. Inside, a dozen sawhorse tables and benches were arranged in rows. Wood cuttings depicting wild animals had been nailed to nearby tree trunks. A large chalkboard hung beside the door into the structure itself.

It clicked.

An outdoor pavilion. The barn had been converted into a low-tech schoolhouse, perhaps for use by visiting school groups.

The barn door was new-looking and properly seated. A single window to its left was draped from the inside, blocking view of the interior.

I stood a dozen yards outside the pavilion, pondering whether I needed to approach.

Maybe there's a root cellar in there. Or a cold storage room.

Eyeing the damp foundation, I didn't think so. This close to the river was less than ideal for underground storage.

Then I saw it. Just beyond the pavilion were moldy piles of stones.

I hurried across and hefted the closest specimen.

Phosphate rock. I was certain. The smell alone convinced me.

Directly beside the pile was a stretch of muddy, beaten earth. Cutting through the slop were two lines of tire tracks.

My mind flashed to last night's rainstorm.

Someone drove here recently. The tracks were made today.

I rose, adrenaline pumping. My eyes flew to the barn window.

The drape's hem was flipped back in one corner, revealing a tiny patch of unobstructed glass. Enough to see inside?

Dropping the nodule, I crept forward. With each passing step, it became more clear.

A light was burning inside the barn.

Then I heard something.

Voices. Arguing?

I stopped dead. Strained to listen.

No good. The noise was too indistinct to make out.

Dropping to a crouch, I crab-stepped forward, vaulting the pavilion's low wall.

A board creaked beneath my feet. I froze, heart banging wildly.

The voices continued, undeterred.

One male. One female. Most *definitely* arguing.

Should I get Hiram? The others? What if the speakers moved?

Ignoring the condition I'd forced Ben to accept, I scurried to the base of the windowsill.

Oh so carefully, I rose on the balls of my feet.

Peered inside.

CHAPTER 39

The pane was filthy with pollen and grime.

Holding my breath, I stuck two fingers into my mouth, then gently rubbed a circle on the surface of the glass. Looked again. This time, I could see.

Inside was a medium-sized classroom, with a dozen wooden desks and chairs pushed against the left wall. In the rear was a tiny kitchenette. Dishes and pans were stacked haphazardly around a dirty sink. Beside the ancient refrigerator was a square table and a trash can overflowing with balled-up wrappers, food cartons, and empty soda cans. In the back corner was a door displaying a unisex bathroom sign.

My eyes were drawn to a blue-green assemblage in the room's center.

Is that a . . . tent?

The portable shelter had been erected atop two gymnastics mats shoved side by side.

I stared in consternation. What? Why?

Beside the tent were two folding beach chairs and a rolling AV cart, which supported a beat-up tube TV and what looked like a VCR. An extension cord ran from the back of the cart to an outlet ten feet away.

"What the hell?" I whispered to myself.

Was someone squatting in this barn? Homeless people? Hermits? Al Qaeda?

And what happened to the voices?

As I gaped, baffled by the peculiar scene, I heard the squeal of a zipper.

A dark line split the wall of the tent.

Someone was inside. And coming out.

A toilet flushed. I looked up to see a person exit the bathroom.

My jaw nearly hit the floor.

Shutting the door with a bang was Lucy Gable.

I almost collapsed in shock. The feeling doubled as Peter Gable crawled from the tent.

They're here! We found them!

Peter looked miserable—face pale and drawn, dark crescents beneath his eyes, blond hair matted to his scalp. Lucy was no better off. She wore a crumpled Bolton Prep sweatshirt that needed a heavy-soil cycle. Her yellow locks were yanked back into a greasy ponytail.

I dropped back below the windowsill. Frazzled. Uncertain what to do.

Then I spun a panicked 360, scanning for anyone else. I was lurking by the door, in the full view of anyone approaching the barn.

Should I gather the Virals? What if the kidnapper comes back while I'm gone?

Where's Ella?

The last question drove me back to my peep hole. Inside, Lucy sat heavily on one of the beach chairs. Her head fell to her hands. Peter had taken the other seat. Looking over at his sister, he seemed about to speak, but chose not to. He stared blankly at the ceiling instead.

I searched for any sign of a third person in the room. Was Ella inside that tent?

Impossible to tell. But my instincts told me she wasn't.

The only way to know is to get inside.

I dropped back to a crouch, eyeing the door. It was solid oak, with a sturdy new padlock affixed to its face.

I wasn't going through it. Not without a rhinoceros.

Swiveling, I checked the area where I'd spotted the tire track. Scanned the forest.

Nothing. No one around.

Yet I couldn't shake the feeling I was missing something.

But I couldn't wait. This might be the only chance to free the twins.

Ben would be furious, of course, but sometimes circumstances dictate. I had to seize this opportunity.

Maybe the twins know where Ella is being held. Maybe she's inside that tent after all.

But how to free them?

The answer came in a flash.

The window.

While the door might be impenetrable, the glass would shatter easily.

Why hadn't the twins done so already?

Decided on a plan, I raced across the pavilion and grabbed a bench. Then, using all my strength, began dragging it toward the window. The wooden seat moved grudgingly, kicking up a terrible racket along the way. After several frantic moments, I had it in position.

I stepped onto the bench, then nearly toppled off in shock.

Lucy and Peter were a foot away, staring wide-eyed through the glass.

"The door's padlocked!" I shouted. "I'm going to break the window and get you out!"

The twins glanced at each other in utter astonishment.

"Back up!"

I stripped off my windbreaker and wrapped it around my forearm. Then, without pausing to think, I punched the closest pane. I felt a terrific stab of pain—and a touch of embarrassment—when the glass held. I reared back a second time, ignoring the twins' frantic waves.

This time, I led with my elbow. The window exploded into shards.

My eyes reopened.

The twins were cowering inside, hands raised defensively to deflect the rain of broken glass. Ella didn't appear. I resigned myself to the fact she wasn't there.

"Tory Brennan?" Peter Gable looked like he was seeing a ghost. Or an alien.

"*Come on, come on, come on!*" I waved frantically. "There's no one out here but me. We can slip away if we hurry!"

The twins exchanged an unreadable look.

"How'd you get here?" Lucy asked in a shaky voice.

"I drove!" Were these two in shock? "We can escape. Have you seen Ella?"

Peter squinted in total confusion. "Ella? Ella Francis?"

Answer enough.

"Forget it. Let's go!" I reached inside to help them climb through the window. "The coast is clear, but it might not stay that way!"

I snuck a glance over my shoulder.

Felt someone take my hands.

Suddenly I was yanked forward, arms scraping across the window frame. I went airborne, tumbling through the window and landing inside the barn.

My head hit the floorboards.

Everything went dark.

CHAPTER 40

"What the hell?!"

I tried to rise, but my head was foggy. Peter Gable shoved me back to the ground.

"Cover the window!" he yelled at his sister.

"*You* were the last one over here!" But Lucy straightened the shade until it fully blocked the opening.

My thoughts swam. I noticed little things about the room around me. The scratchy wooden floorboards. A pair of rafter beams running the length of the barn. A giant American flag, on a pole by the door, capped with a bald-eagle headpiece.

Lucy spun, glaring at me like I'd kissed her boyfriend. "What are we gonna do with *her*?"

The truth hit me like a slap in the face.

A fake. The whole damn thing.

My eyes darted from twin to twin. "You weren't kidnapped at all, were you?"

Ignoring my question, Peter hauled me up and marched me to one of the ratty chairs.

"What *now*, Peter?" Lucy hadn't moved an inch. "What's next in your master plan?"

"Just let me think!" He ran a hand through his hair.

A clip played in my head—Peter's eyes, tracking the camera as it filmed his captivity.

The recognition I'd thought I'd seen. Peter *had* known his captor.

Because they'd orchestrated the whole thing.

"You *faked* your own kidnapping?" I couldn't fathom it. "Why would you do that?"

Lucy's hands rose to her mouth. They trembled badly.

Peter began pacing, his lips moving soundless. I could tell he was thinking furiously.

My surprise at the twins' duplicity was so complete—the shock so overwhelming—that for a few moments I'd forgotten about Ella.

But Ella *had* been taken. I knew my friend well—she'd never have staged such a thing.

Which means the twins are involved in Ella's disappearance.

The realization was like a bucket of freezing water.

I sat very still. Organized my thoughts.

Be careful. These two might be dangerous.

"Lucy?" At that moment, she seemed the less threatening of the two.

Her eyes met mine. Malice filled them, unlike anything I'd seen from Lucy before. The distant friendliness she'd exhibited at school was nowhere to be seen.

"Shut up!" As she worried her ponytail. "You stupid little busybody! What are you *doing* here? How did you find this place? You've ruined everything!"

Peter glanced at his sister, then me. Resumed pacing with a shake of his head.

"Obviously, I thought you were in danger." I wanted to keep Lucy talking, learn anything I could about Ella. "Then I noticed something in the ransom video that led me here."

I didn't mention the boys. Didn't reveal I had friends on the grounds. That was my ace. I was counting on the Virals finding me.

One way or another.

"We weren't *in* any trouble!" Tears leaked from Lucy's eyes. "Everything was according to plan until now. Peter, what are we going to do?"

Her brother halted. Rotated to face her.

I tried to catch his eye, but he avoided looking at me.

That made me very, very nervous.

"I'll call him," Peter told his sister.

"We're not supposed to!" Lucy shot back.

Peter's arms flew up. "You have a better idea? We've been stuck in here a week! I have no idea what's going on!"

Peter pointed at me without looking. "This . . . *changes* things. We have to . . . I have to . . . think. Make the right decision."

I didn't like how that sounded. Who did Peter have to call?

Steeling my nerve, I took a shot. "You're calling your stepfather. Rex Gable."

Peter finally looked at me, unable to conceal his disgust. "You're an idiot."

Storming to the back of the room, he opened a door I hadn't seen and disappeared.

I whirled back to Lucy. She was staring into space.

My muscles tensed.

I can take her. I'll pummel this bitch and escape while Peter is out of the room.

But what about Ella?

This might be my only chance to learn where my friend was being held.

"Help me understand." I spoke quietly, not wanting to upset the jittery girl before me. "Why did you pretend to be kidnapped, Lucy?"

She palmed the tears from her eyes. "Just shut up."

"Did Rex Gable make you do this?"

Lucy laughed bitterly. "Peter's right—you're a moron. Sticking it to our stepfather is the whole point."

My mind struggled to process this information.

"The ransom," I guessed. "You want his money."

"*Our* money!" Lucy practically shouted. "It's bad enough he married into my *mother's* fortune. That fat pig isn't getting mine!"

"I don't understand." I didn't understand.

"Why would you?" Peter walked briskly past me and whispered into his sister's ear.

She nodded, seemed to calm slightly.

Keep them talking.

"Rex Gable was stealing from you?" Trying to make sense of things.

"Might as well have been." Peter dropped into the other chair. His whole demeanor had changed—Peter was relaxed and composed, but it didn't put me at ease.

Who had he spoken to? What had they decided?

Where the hell are the boys?

I'd sent Hi to check the riverfront. Shelton and Ben would be down by the cemetery.

How long before they came looking for me?

Ella. Get information. Help your friend.

Choosing my words carefully, I tried again. "Rex Gable has money that belongs to you?"

"The bastard controls our trust fund." Peter stretched his legs with a grunt. "As *trustee*—what a joke—he decided that some of *our* funds are needed for general household expenses."

"Because the stupid sonuvabitch already pissed away his own

money!" Lucy stamped her foot like an irate toddler. "Our mother's *entire* nest egg—gone. All to pay his ridiculous gambling debts. It's not right! And now he's after *our* inheritance, as if we wouldn't notice."

"Every cent in that trust belongs to Lucy and me." Peter spoke with total conviction. "Our *real* father left it for us, held in trust so our ditzy mother couldn't squander it. But somehow that weaselly buffoon got himself appointed the trustee."

"It's bad enough we have to live in his house like hostages." Peter's fingers clenched into fists. "I won't let that con artist waste my inheritance on his own problems, all while pretending it's for *our* benefit."

"So you faked your own kidnapping." Things were starting to make sense. "Rex Gable would have to pay the five million in ransom from your trust."

"That's the idea," Peter said dryly.

"And yet," Lucy spat, "here we are."

It made a sick kind of sense. I even felt a little sorry for them.

Until I thought of Ella. Now I understood why there was never a second ransom demand. She wasn't part of the scam.

Where *was* Ella? She'd been missing for almost two days.

Had she figured out what was happening? Learned of the twins' scheme?

A scary possibility occurred to me.

Had Ella been silenced for what she discovered?

"How long have you been in this barn?" I ventured carefully.

"Forever." Lucy ran a hand across her face. "It's a nightmare." Then she chuckled without humor. "I mean, it's been seven days, and we have a freaking *VCR* for entertainment. Wanna watch *Dirty Dancing*? I've seen it thirty times since Monday."

My mind raced. Should I ask about Ella directly?

I had a second jarring thought.

The dark form that watched us through the Gables' basement

window. My midnight attacker on Morris Island. I knew in my bones that neither had been Peter.

The twins were working with someone. Who?

I tried to be casual. "Who shot the video?" Hoping they might reveal their accomplice.

"You'll meet him soon enough," Peter checked his watch. "He's on his way here. Now."

He. The man from the beach? The bastard who snatched Ella?

I *had* to find out who it was.

"That *stupid* video!" Lucy spat. "So unnecessary."

"Let it go," Peter groaned. "It doesn't matter."

"It does matter!" Lucy's finger shot toward me. "It's the reason she's here."

"We *needed* a ransom video." Peter was clearly aggravated by his sister's complaints. "The police wouldn't take us seriously, otherwise. I've watched the clip a dozen times. There's no way she used it to track us. You can't tell where it was shot!"

Keep them talking.

"How did your stepfather get a copy before the police?" I asked.

The twins' eyes met. Then both looked at me.

"How do *you* know that?" Peter demanded.

"We haven't tipped the police to that yet," Lucy said on top of him.

"It's in his Gmail. Rex Gable had your ransom tape at least twenty-four hours before the cops."

"Because *I* planted it there," Peter snapped. "Along with dozens of suspicious calls on his cell phone. But we weren't gonna nudge the authorities toward Rex until after . . . everything."

His voice hardened. "How do *you* know about it, Tory Brennan?"

"I hacked his email." Fighting to keep my voice steady. "I told you, I was trying to help."

"We had *everything* mapped out!" Lucy was standing with her arms crossed. "The email. The video. The fake blood puddle."

"The stain in your basement was fake?" That got my attention. "But it reacted to Luminol. Bleach was used to clean it, obviously, but the underlying substance triggered as well."

I didn't mention my dog claiming he smelled blood.

Peter's eyes became saucers. "We used horseradish sauce, plus a little blood at the edges. Then we cleaned the spot with bleach to confuse the issue. But how in the world could you—"

I pounced while Peter was thrown. "What did you do with Ella Francis? Why take *her*?"

For a moment, both twins simply stared at me.

"What are you talking about?" Lucy finally managed.

Peter actually grabbed my arm. "Ella Francis is missing?"

There was something new in Peter's eyes. Uneasiness. A touch of panic.

I opted for a straightforward approach. "Ella Francis disappeared several days after you did."

Watching Peter closely, I added, "A zodiac card was left on her bed."

Peter immediately shook his head. "Impossible. Ella has zero to do with this."

Lucy spoke through clenched teeth. "Screwing with our heads, Brennan? It's not gonna work. No one else was abducted. *We're* not even abducted! You can't BS your way out if this one."

I stared hard. "You really don't know?"

Peter was still gripping my shirtsleeve. He thrust his face within inches of mine.

"Think carefully about continuing to lie, Tory. I'm all out of patience."

I ripped my sleeve away. These idiots didn't know where Ella was.

Which meant I was done playing along.

"Someone kidnapped Ella Thursday night." I rose, causing Peter to shoot up beside me. "She's been missing more than forty-eight hours. A zodiac card depicting Cetus was left on her bed. I'm *not* making this up. And I'm through with the two of you. Now tell me who else is involved in this ridiculous plot. *I'm* all out of patience."

Peter's face twisted in anger. "You don't tell us what to do! I don't think you appreciate your situation here, Brennan. We're in charge, not you. You better watch your—"

Both hands on his chest. Full shove. With white-hot rage exploding inside me, I didn't need my flare power to knock this bully down.

Peter landed on his butt, then scrambled backward. Awkwardly regaining his feet, he stared at me in shock. Lucy covered her mouth.

My hands found my hips. "I don't think *you* appreciate the situation. Your jackass game is over. Ella Francis was kidnapped, whether you planned for it to happen or not. Now you'd better tell me who you're working with, or I'm going to *beat it out of you*!" My voice had risen to a shout. "You spoiled, self-centered, psychotic, awful people!"

Peter's eyes darted to his sister, then back to me. "You're crazy!"

"I'm much worse than that." Smiling without a trace of warmth. "I suggest you don't test me on this point."

Deep within, I felt the wolf crack an eyelid.

I didn't drop the leash. Not yet. But I let my primal essence stir.

These two morons were going to tell me what I wanted to know.

One way or another. Consequences be damned.

Peter took a single step toward me.

I grasped the invisible veil that held my powers at bay. Prepared to discard it.

Outside, the padlock rattled. Clicked. Hinges screeched.

All heads turned as the barn door swung open.

CHAPTER 41

It's true," the man said. "Unbelievable."

I ran to meet the bulky figure slipping through the door.

Finally, a bit of luck.

"Detective Hawfield!" My finger shot back toward the disheveled twins. "They *faked* the whole thing! They don't know about Ella, but they're working with someone, and . . ."

I trailed off.

So stupid.

I backpedaled from Hawfield as the pieces slid into place. "You."

"What's she talking about, Fergus?" Peter's voice had an edge. "If you've gone off script, I'm going to be *very* upset."

Detective Hawfield closed the door behind him. Crossed his arms. Sighed.

"How did she find you?"

"Who knows?" Lucy spat. "Ask *her.* We haven't left this dump since you brought us here."

Hawfield stood between me and the door. The twins blocked my path to the window. I tried not to panic, fully aware that the danger level had just risen dramatically. Hawfield's service revolver—a Heckler & Koch HK45—gleamed from its holster.

Come on, Virals. Where are you? Time to track ol' Tory down.

Edging away from the detective, I cursed myself a fool.

How did I miss the signs?

"You're the leak." The words slipped out before I could stop them.

"That I am," Hawfield replied, absently hitching his belt. "We needed media pressure to move the money along. Rex Gable is one tight son of a gun."

"What's this talk about Ella Francis?" Peter glared at Hawfield with evident distaste.

"Collateral damage." Hawfield shrugged. "She knew things that didn't work for us. I took care of it."

My blood turned to ice. *Ella!*

"You don't make decisions like that!" Peter shouted. "You don't make decisions at all!"

Hawfield said nothing.

"You're our *employee,* Fergus." Lucy's words dripped with scorn. "This is *our* plan. *We* call the shots. Leave the thinking to those who are good at it."

"You're only to do as you're told," Peter seethed. "Nothing more or less. We're paying you enough for that."

"I did what was necessary." Hawfield's voice was light, his face devoid of emotion. "Same as we'll have to do with this one. Can't have loose ends running around, telling tales."

Peter tensed. His gaze dropped to the floor.

Another step back.

Inside, I prepared. The cage around my powers began to weaken.

No way was I going down easy.

"What do you mean?" Lucy looked to her brother, confused. "What was necessary?"

Peter glanced in my direction, eyes full of doubt.

"Don't worry yourself." Hawfield's hands met behind his back. "I'll handle the messy stuff. I can take care of both girls at once, as soon as payment is received. We'll need them until then, however, as insurance policies. I'll stick this girl in with the other one."

My heart leaped. *Ella must still be alive!*

Lucy seemed to finally grasp what she was hearing. "You're talking about *killing* her. And Ella Francis, too?" Once more, her eyes darted to her brother. "Peter, he's lost his mind!"

Peter stared at the floorboards. A single vein was pumping in his neck.

"They shouldn't have stuck their noses in this," he mumbled. "It's their own fault."

"We don't have a lot of options," Hawfield said.

I kept very still, thinking furiously on how to escape.

Ignoring Hawfield, Lucy hurried over and grabbed her brother's arm. "Peter, what are you saying? Use your head. No one was supposed to get hurt. You *promised*. We'd fool Rex and take our own money. But now—" she choked on her words as their enormity sank in, "—you're talking about . . . *murdering* . . . two people we know!"

Peter ripped from his sister's grasp. He took a few steps, keeping his back to me.

"What are we supposed to do?" Voice shaking. "Super cop over there already kidnapped Ella. It's done. We can't undo it!"

Peter spun, jabbed an unsteady finger my direction. "Tory's standing right here! She knows *everything*. How do we deal with that? You think she'll agree to forget the whole thing?"

"I'll keep your secret," I lied immediately. "Just let me go."

Hawfield snorted.

"You're just saying that!" Peter roared at me, before turning on his sister. "Do you want to save our trust fund or not? Because right now, there's no other way . . . no path around . . ."

His entire frame shuddered.

"Things are too far gone," he finished, practically whispering.

Hawfield nodded grimly, one hand dropping to the butt of his HK45.

Lucy stared at Peter in disbelief. "Of *course* there's another way! We shove Tory in with Ella, take the ransom, and bolt. We can tell the police where to find them later—that might even buy us more time to escape. Who cares what happens after we blow town? We're gonna disappear anyway!" Her hands flew up. "We don't have to kill anyone!"

"You're planning to disappear by pretending to be *dead*," Hawfield countered. "A ruthless double-cross by the kidnapper, after payment was received. Everything changes if the police know what really happened. They'll hunt you down as fugitives."

Peter shook his head, suddenly unsure. "Maybe Lucy's right. We could try—"

"And I think you're forgetting about me." Hawfield's voice grew colder by the word. "*I'm* not planning some tropical getaway. I have a life here, and a position of respect. I won't be abandoning them after getting my cut. And both girls know I'm involved."

Hawfield gave a tight shake of his head. "No, you'd best leave this part to me. I'll make sure there's nothing hanging out there to worry us. We'll get our money. The plan will proceed without any more speed bumps."

Peter waved a dismissive hand. "I don't remember asking your opinion, Fergus."

Hawfield stiffened at the rebuke.

"Let's call it off," Lucy said suddenly. "We can just leave. Stick Tory and Ella on a deserted island somewhere and get out of town. Wait for the whole thing to blow over."

Peter's eyes met the identical pair belonging to his sister. Something passed between them. Then, slowly, he began to nod.

"Things got too crazy." His gaze flicked to me. "No one was supposed to get hurt. We just wanted what was ours, that's all. I think I lost my mind a little."

"It's okay," I said, trying to make his feel comfortable. "I understand. I'll tell the police what happened."

"You're not telling the police anything." Hawfield's face was granite.

"Enough, Fergus." Lucy sneered at the detective. "It's over. We're not killing our classmates for money like a bunch of psychopaths. I always knew you were too simple for this scheme. Where *is* Ella, anyway? Do you have her in that awful cell?"

For a moment, Hawfield said nothing. But something changed behind his eyes.

I inched toward the door.

Abruptly Hawfield laughed, startling everyone. The guffaws lasted for at least ten seconds, before trailing off into breathy chuckles. He wiped his eyes with thick, hairy knuckles.

The twins rolled their eyes. They didn't get it.

But I did.

Not good.

Hawfield removed his gun from its holster and addressed the twins. "You two really are impossibly stupid, you know that? I guess it was just a matter of time."

Peter strode toward the detective. "Now listen to me, you cretin. I've about had it with—"

Hawfield whipped the gun across Peter's face, knocking him to the floor.

Scarlet ropes flew from Peter's nose. More blood ran between his fingers as he lay on the hardwood, clutching his face in agony.

Lucy screamed. Dragged her brother away from Hawfield.

I tensed, preparing to sprint, but Hawfield aimed the HK45 at me.

Muscles frozen, I stared into the terrible black emptiness of the gun barrel, imagining what the bullets inside could do to my flesh.

Hawfield spoke calmly. "I've let you children think you're in charge long enough. Since you don't intend to be sensible, I'm done pretending." The detective snorted. "Did you think this was some rich kids' game? That you could just pack up the pieces if things turned ugly?"

All levity left Hawfield's voice. "There's no 'calling it off.' I want my money, and I'm going to get it. And I have no intention of spending the rest of my life in prison because you two didn't have the stomach to finish the job."

"We won't help you," Lucy hissed. "I'll tell the police everything."

From his knees, Peter nodded, sending blood spatter onto his knees.

Shut up, you two!

Hawfield sighed. "That's what I figured. Which means you'll have to go as well."

"What do you mean?" Then Peter's voice cracked. "We had a *deal*, Fergus. Detective Hawfield, I mean. You get a million dollars just for helping!"

The detective smirked. "You know, I think I knew this would happen from the start. I doubt I ever really planned on splitting the money. From where I'm standing, *five* million bucks sounds way better than one."

Lucy began to sob.

Peter seemed astonished, at a total loss for words.

I knew what I had to do.

"I can dig four holes as easily as two," Hawfield continued matter-of-factly. "That's a lot tidier anyway. No loose lips to sink my ship, so to speak."

His placid manner was terrifying. Hawfield felt no remorse at the prospect of murdering four teens for ransom money.

He'll do it. He'll kill us all.

I risked a look at my watch. Astonishingly, I'd only been inside the barn ten minutes.

Where the hell are the Virals?

Hawfield noticed my glance.

"You fools!" He stormed to the window. "This girl didn't come out here alone. Those boys must be around, too!"

Whipping the shade aside, Hawfield peered out the window.

The hand gripping the gun hung at his side.

No more time. No second chances.

My eyes slammed shut.

Please don't fail me now.

I called for the wolf.

For the other Virals.

For all the power that lay inside me.

SNAP.

CHAPTER 42

Power infused me like a river of molten lava.

My limbs burned with energy.

I didn't wait to test my limits. To see if my powers would cooperate.

Eyes shining with golden light, I fired forward, slamming into Hawfield from behind.

The force of my bull charge propelled him against the wall.

The gun dropped from his fingers. Skittered across the floor.

Unfortunately, my blitzkrieg attack had actually shoved the detective halfway through the window, blocking the best route of escape.

I scurried backward, a growl slipping from my throat.

At the same time, I tried to contact the Virals.

"You little hussy!" Hawfield wheeled his bulky frame, eyes darting for the HK45.

The pistol spun to a stop at Lucy's feet.

She picked it up and immediately handed it to Peter, who had risen at her side.

Peter aimed at Hawfield, a cold smile on his bloody face. "How are things now, you stupid redneck?"

"Peter." My golden gaze never left the detective. No one was looking at me. "Be careful. He's dangerous."

Hawfield was eyeing the gun in Peter's hand, his face blank.

"He's a buffoon," Peter said lightly, enjoying the turn of events. "A pawn in our game, nothing more. I can't believe we relied on him. Now, toss me those cuffs, then—"

Hawfield strode directly for Peter.

"Don't move!" Peter screeched, backpedaling. "Stop! I swear I'll shoot!"

Peter's finger jerked. Nothing happened.

Hawfield snatched the HK45, then backhanded Peter to the ground.

Lucy screamed as she retreated to the desks lining the wall.

"You have to disengage the safety," Hawfield explained, demonstrating as he spoke. "Otherwise, the weapon can't fire."

He pointed the barrel at Peter. "You were saying?"

"Fergus, please!" Peter held up both hands in supplication. "We can work this out. You can have half the ransom! Or *you* take four million, and we'll split the one."

"The time for deals is past," Hawfield said. "Make your peace."

I shot forward again, but this time, the burly detective was ready.

Hawfield swung the weapon toward me, stepping back to absorb any body blow.

But the detective didn't know what I could do.

What a flaring Viral can do.

I ducked past him, racing toward the furniture along the far wall. Hawfield spun awkwardly. Springing atop a desk, I pivoted, ignoring Lucy's panicked shrieks.

I faced the detective again, now in position. "Try to keep up."

"Enough of this mess." Hawfield leveled his pistol. Closed in slowly.

Faster than thought, I launched myself out into space, hands grasping a rafter beam.

Swing. Tuck. Release. I flipped in midair and landed smoothly behind him.

Hawfield spun again, trying to aim, but I was already moving. Grabbing the flagpole, I couched it in one arm like a lance and charged, jamming the eagle headpiece into his gut.

Crack! Crack!

Both shots flew high.

The air exploded from Hawfield's chest with an audible *oof.*

The detective collapsed, the HK45 jarred from his fingers.

A scarlet blossom spread from where the headpiece had pierced Hawfield's shirt.

Hawfield stared at me a beat. Two. Then he scrambled for the gun.

But I was too quick.

Moving with canine speed and grace, I kicked the weapon across the barn, then slammed my heel down on his hand. Hawfield howled in pain.

I almost pitied his predictable, glacial movements.

He was a plodding dinosaur. I was lightning made flesh.

Glancing over my shoulder, I saw the twins huddled together, frozen in shock. My flaring ears easily detected their panicked breathing and thundering heartbeats.

"Get out of here!" Watching the detective. "My friends are somewhere outside!"

Peter started, as if waking from a dream. "Incredible! How did you—"

"Just go!" Back to the twins so they couldn't spot my irises. "Find Hi, Ben, and Shelton. I'll deal with this clown."

But Lucy shoved her brother toward the back of the barn.

"The tunnel," she hissed. "The boat should still be at the dock, we can take it. Let's go!"

"No!" I shouted, but couldn't risk turning to face them. "Check the woods. My friends can help us!"

Too late.

I heard a door slam behind me, followed by footsteps pounding down stairs.

Whatever bolt hole was back there, the twins had taken it. They were gone.

Detective Hawfield had risen to his feet. I streaked toward the window, pulled the drape back into place. Then I slapped off the light. The room became shrouded in gloom.

Darkness. Advantage Tory.

"You're quite the gymnast." Hawfield's voice floated across the chamber. "Come try that trick again."

"You're not much without a gun," I taunted, slinking from shadow to shadow.

Hawfield was trying to circle, but I could hear every scuff of his boots. Could see his hulking form without difficulty.

Hawfield barely looked at me, eyes searching furiously for his HK45.

I mirrored his movements, keeping the tent in the center of the room between us.

The gun was behind Hawfield, against the baseboard of the opposite wall.

He was closer, but couldn't see it.

Keep his focus on you. Away from the weapon.

"You lost, Fergus." My hunch was right—his clenching jaw revealed how much he hated that name. "The twins are gone. They're probably calling your buddies in blue right now."

"Not a chance." Still circling. "They're running for the hills."

Hawfield's sweat permeated the air. Heavy. Earthy. Sour. Metallic.

I knew those odors. My flaring nose could easily decode them.

Fear. Anger. Worry.

Hawfield was off balance. I had to keep him that way.

I neared the window. Hawfield tensed, no doubt expecting me to dive for it. He'd try to grab me before I scrambled out. That or locate his gun, then hunt me through the woods.

Run? Then what? How would I find Ella?

Hawfield would kill her immediately, then disappear forever.

No. *I* needed the gun. With it, I could prevent Hawfield's escape.

I could *force* him to tell me where Ella was.

An ugly snarl curled my lips.

And I would. This monster wasn't going to hurt my friend.

Suddenly, Hawfield stopped moving.

"Your eyes." His voice was taut. "What's wrong with them?"

Whatever it takes.

"You made a mistake, Fergus." I forced a low chuckle. "I'm not your average girl."

I gave him the full force of my lupine gaze.

Hawfield staggered backward. "Demon!"

Then he surprised me.

Trampling the tent, Hawfield barreled right for me.

I leaped to the side, ducking his outstretched hand while extending my legs into a split.

My foot caught his.

Hawfield tripped. Flew headlong into the wall with a bone-jarring crash.

As he lay in a dazed heap, I hurried to retrieve the gun.

By the time the detective sat up, I had him in the crosshairs.

"Thanks for showing me how the safety works."

The detective rose to one knee, lung billowing. He spat a bloody glob into the corner.

"Just get out of here," he fumed. "Go now, before I lose my temper."

"I don't think so." I clasped the gun two-handed like Aunt Tempe had taught me. "My friends will be here soon. You're going to tell us where Ella is."

"You're alone." Hawfield rose unsteadily. "If your pals were here, they'd have come by now. I was wrong after all." He took a step toward me. "You're just a nimble girl with strange eyes. You don't have what it takes to pull that trigger."

He took another step.

I pulled back the slide on the HK45. "Try me."

Hawfield froze. Our eyes locked. One heartbeat, then he took a step back.

Suddenly, my temperature skyrocketed. Sweat erupted all over as my senses lurched into overdrive. Information poured into my brain.

Scents. Smells. Sounds. Impressions.

I felt each Viral pause where they stood. A blast of thoughts nearly wiped my hard drive.

Tory?

Tor, where are you?

Hey, you oka—

Too fast. Too much. I staggered.

Sensing my body was about collapse, I tried the only thing I could think of.

Closing my eyes, I reached out to the other Virals.

The flaming cords thrummed like lines on a ship in a storm. I couldn't grasp them. Couldn't harness the connections.

Something untethered with an explosion of black.

SNUP.

A flash of red exploded in my mind. Pain seared across my forehead.

I felt myself falling, My eyes opened to see the hardwood rising to meet me.

Hawfield was above me, holding the gun. He lifted my dead weight, then flung me over one shoulder.

I tried to resist, but my mind was Jell-O. I couldn't remember how my limbs worked. How to make sounds. I was carried, helpless, through the barn door and out into the trees.

A police car. An open trunk.

Falling. The slam of a lid. Screeching tires.

Then my eyes rolled up and I slipped away for good.

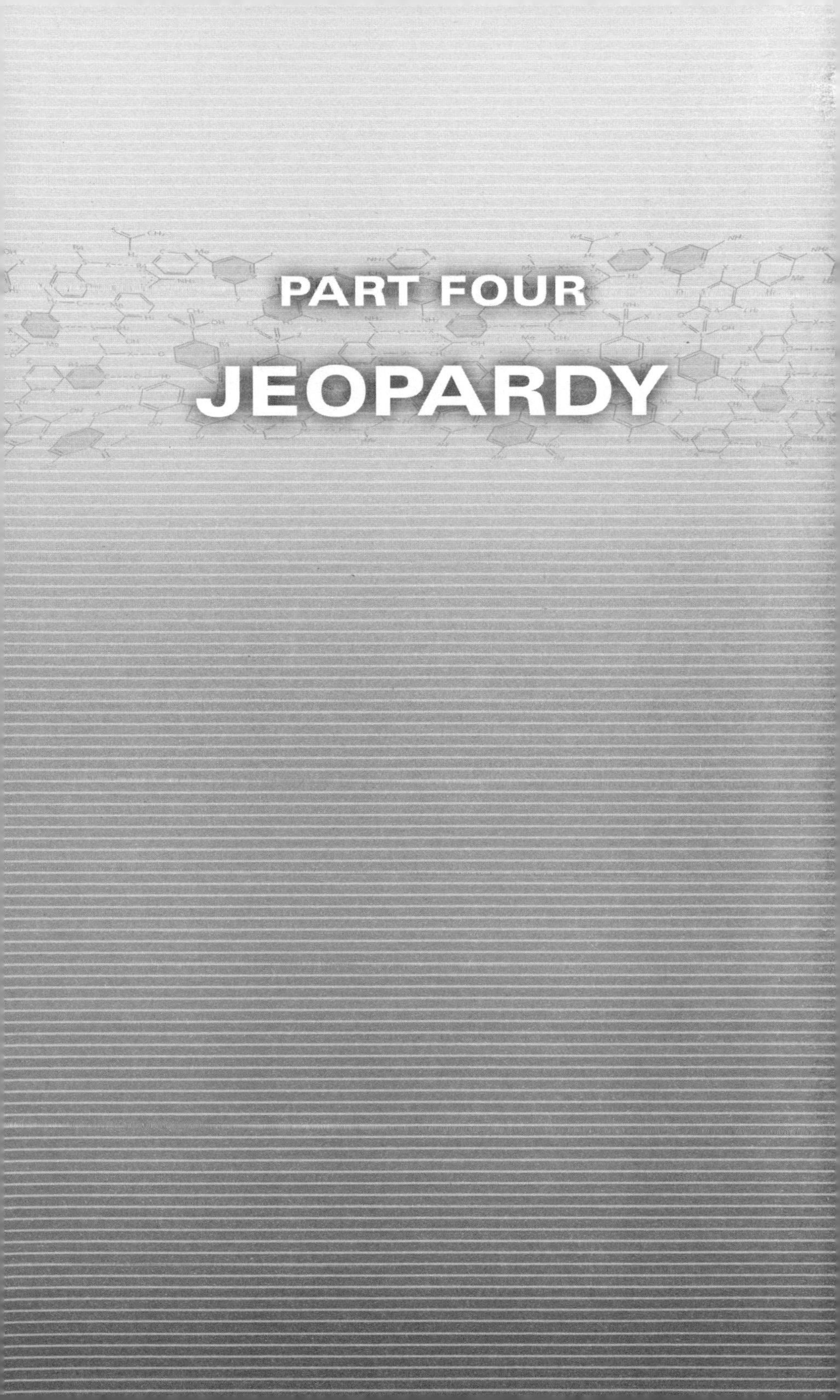

PART FOUR
JEOPARDY

CHAPTER 43

I heard Hi shouting from a hundred yards away.

"What's that fool done now?" I muttered, digging a rock from my sneaks. These retro Jordans might look cool, but they were light on padding.

Adjusting my glasses, I ran in the direction of his howls. Ben and I had already scouted the phosphate mine, and were just finishing a circuit of the old cemetery.

Not my favorite assignment. Freaking graveyards. Next time Tory wants some ancient crypts inspected, *she* can have the job.

"Come on, Devers." Jogging over to join me, Ben cocked his head toward the riverbank. "Sounds like Hiram's about to wet himself."

We found Stolowitski down a ten-foot mud slick, gripping a clump of vines for dear life. His lower body was submerged in the fast-flowing Ashley River.

"About time!" Hi yelled. "Get me out of here. I think I lost a shoe!"

"What in the world?" I almost broke down laughing.

"Where's Tory?" Ben dropped to his butt and scooted down the incline Hi had obviously failed to notice. Halting ten feet from the water's edge, he considered how to get closer without following Hi into the river.

"How should I know?" Hi grumbled, red-faced. "We split up. She was headed for the old barn. *Go check the dangerous riverbank, Hiram. There might be secret caves.* No one said anything about fifty-foot cliffs!"

"You let her go alone?" Ben scolded, slowly working his way down to where Hi was beached. "That defeats the whole purpose!"

"I'm *aware* of that, Benjamin." Hi tried slinging a leg up onto the riverbank, but it flopped back into the roiling current. "But she'd figured out you sent her away from the mine on purpose. *You* try telling Tory what to do when she's pissed."

"I'll pass." But I shook my head at Hi anyway. He looked like a giant fishing lure.

Ben wrapped one arm around a low-slung willow branch, then extended a hand toward Hi, who stared at it dubiously. I shuffled clockwise to get a better view.

"Don't drop me," Hi pleaded. "I can't swim all the way back to the marina."

"Relax." Ben planted his feet and steadied himself. "On three. One. Two—"

Hi leaped too early, but Ben was ready. Locking arms with Hi, he dragged him up onto dry land, then pushed his portly frame back upslope.

"Just carry me," Hi wheezed. "Be my knight in shining armor."

Ben kicked his rear. "Keep moving, you dope."

Hi collapsed at the top, then pointed to a knobby root at the crest of the slope.

"Him," Hi informed me solemnly. "That's the one that got me."

"We waited on the path for like ten minutes," I said, cleaning dirt from my lenses with the tail of my shirt. "Ya'll didn't show, so we checked the graveyard real quick. Where you been?"

"I've been floating in the drink for at least that long." Hi was pulling off his drenched socks. One shoe was definitely AWOL. "Tory must've heard me yelling. I think she's punishing me for colluding with you guys."

"Wait." Ben straightened. "No one's seen Tory since we split up?"

"There's nothin' up this way," I pointed out. "That's why we sent her to the barn in the first place."

"Then where is she?" Ben rose, scanning the tree line. "Could she have doubled back?"

"And left Hi to drown?" I felt a hand rise to my earlobe. "No way. She'd have come right by here."

I glanced at Hi, sitting in a puddle on the grass. "You been shouting the whole time?"

"Like an opera singer," Hi confirmed, squeezing river water from his socks.

I was about to say more when it happened.

A slap of cold jolted my system.

Strange buzzing filled my head, like a fax machine attempting to connect.

Ben's eyes went wide. Hi popped to his bare feet, then crouched like a hunted animal.

Suddenly, I knew what was happening.

Tory was flaring.

"It's her!" I whispered, unsure why I'd dropped my voice. "She must be in—"

Something brushed against my mind, making me dizzy.

A blast of heat filled my chest.

BEN! HI! SHELTON! I NEED—

The message abruptly ceased.

Tory!

I tried sending thoughts back, sensed Hi and Ben attempting the same.

Brief contact, then my mind recoiled as if struck. The connection was gone.

Hi staggered against a tree trunk.

"Tory!" Ben shouted, spinning in a wild circle. "Where are you?!"

My brain seemed to spin inside my skull. Then I was on my knees, vomiting in the tall grass. When the world finally righted itself, I felt hands beneath my armpits, holding me up.

"You're okay, buddy." Hi's voice cracked. "Shake it off. We have to find Tor."

Ben was pacing, frantic, at a loss for what to do.

"The barn!" I gulped, straightening my glasses. "That's where she was headed!"

Ben took off without a backward glance. Hiram and I followed, racing through the brush and into deeper woods.

"No shoes!" Hi yelped, hobbling away from a pinecone. "Worst birthday *ever*!"

Ahead, I heard an engine rev.

Squealing tires.

Then the sounds of a car tearing through the mud.

We caught Ben at the barn, which was no hollow wreck after all.

Oh damn. This looks new.

A window had been smashed. The door stood ajar. Ben raced inside, only to reemerge seconds later, firing over to a set of sloppy tire tracks.

Ben screamed in anger and frustration.

And I knew.

Tory was gone.

⬡ ⬡ ⬡

"I'm telling you, she's been taken!"

Ben slapped the intake desk, causing everyone to jump.

"Take it easy," I whispered, fingers tugging at both ears. "We won't help Tory by getting locked up ourselves."

I imagined Moms bailing me out. Nearly lost my lunch.

The duty officer rose, his face a thunderhead. "Another outburst like that, son, and you'll get your own special room to cool down in. Understood?"

"Yessir," Hi answered for Ben, who was hovering close to tilt. "We're just worried about our friend. She's been missing for at least an hour."

The officer spoke with forced patience. "She's only been gone an hour?"

"Tory was with *us*," I answered quickly. "In the middle of nowhere. No ride of her own, no other way home. We were doing . . . something important. She wouldn't have run off alone."

The officer rubbed his chin. "You're the same kids who came in here yesterday, right?"

I nodded, nervous, not liking where this was going.

"And you don't have any *proof* your friend was kidnapped? You didn't *see* it happen?"

Ben's mouth opened, but I clamped his arm.

"No, sir." *But she didn't just bail without telling us!*

That settled it for the cop. "We've been warned that you four like to tell fantastic stories. Always have something crazy to report. I'm sorry, but without more, I can't help you. Hawfield's orders. We'll call your parents, and they can sort this out."

Ben tensed. I cringed, anticipating an explosion. I kept a grip on his forearm, though my glasses nearly slid off my nose.

"Is Captain Corcoran available?" Hi asked.

I tried not to cringe. *Hiram, why?*

"He might be," the officer answered warily.

"Great." Hi smiled as if the issue had been settled. "Carmine and I go *way* back. Since his Academy days. We'll just pop by his office and fill him in on the new info."

"Now hold on a—"

"Officer—" Hiram's eyes dropped to a shiny silver name tag, "—Shinn, is it?"

The cop snapped a curt nod.

"Great work down here, Shinn. You're a credit to the intake desk. On the ball. I can tell you're heading places."

Hi leaned forward and lowered his voice conspiratorially, forcing Shinn to bend closer as well. "Thing is, Captain CC made us *promise* to bring him any intel we might learn about the Zodiac kidnappings, no matter how trivial. I'd hate to upset such a powerful man by failing to follow his orders, wouldn't you?"

I coughed into my hand, hiding a smile. I saw Hi's play now.

Corcoran was our last chance. Hi knew the captain—and his sour attitude—and was hoping young Officer Shinn did as well. We had to get past this stupid desk.

With a world-weary sigh, Shinn pointed toward the elevators. "Top floor. No stops."

Snagging Ben's arms, Hiram and I hustled him from the desk.

⬡ ⬡ ⬡

"What did I do in life to deserve you kids?" Corcoran grumbled.

I kept my mouth shut, though I felt the exact same about him.

Ben planted his fists on Corcoran's desk. "Tory's been *taken*, Captain. Do your job!"

Corcoran pointed to the chair Ben had vacated. "Sit your butt down, you little cuss. Or else you're out of here. I'll not be scolded by some whippet who can't even shave."

Ben dropped back with an exasperated grunt. I could tell he was nearing the edge.

We all were.

Tory had been snatched, miles from here, by who we couldn't even guess.

And we had no idea how to get her back.

This is the worst.

"Think what you like about us personally," Hi said, "but we've got history together, Captain. Without us, you wouldn't be sitting in that cushy chair at all. You know we wouldn't be here unless we truly believed Tory was in danger."

Corcoran bristled at Hi's mention of the past, but refrained from comment.

I added my voice. "We told you everything we know. Just tell us if you can help."

Corcoran crossed his meaty arms. "Fine. I'll look into it."

"How?" Ben pressed. "What are you going to do?"

"Honestly, boy, I have no idea." Corcoran's forehead wrinkled as he considered options. "If she was grabbed in the woods, as you say, then I don't rightly know where to start. You've given me nothing to go on."

Ben threw his hands up. "You're the *police*! There's has to be someone you can—"

He stopped dead. A faraway look entered his eyes. Then, "Thank you for your time, Captain. Please do what you can."

Ben popped up and strode for the door, motioning us to follow.

I glanced at Hi, who shrugged. Baffled, we hurried after our friend.

Half rising from his desk, Corcoran called to our backs. "Don't do anything stupid, you hear?" But we'd already disappeared down the hall.

Ben mashed the elevator button, then pushed it again and again.

My patience only lasted until the doors closed. "Well? What the heck was that?"

"We made a mistake." Ben stared at the lit arrow, willing the car to descend faster.

"How so?" For once, Hi passed on a pithy quip.

"We came to the wrong place." I saw a glimmer of hope in Ben's eyes. "But if we hurry, we'll still have plenty of daylight."

"So where are we going?" I couldn't help but ask.

"To the one person who'll know where Tory is. Or how to find her."

CHAPTER 44

I awoke in semidarkness.

Blink.

Blink blink blink.

A cool hand was stroking my forehead.

"About time," said a familiar voice. "I was starting to worry."

Lurching upright, I grabbed the dim form hovering over me.

"Ella!" Wrapping both arms around my friend. "You're okay!"

"I wouldn't go *that* far." She hugged me back just as fiercely.

Eyes adjusting to the gloom, I took in my surroundings. Packed earth floor. Dank, moldy stonework. A single lightbulb burning beyond a line of rusty steel bars.

Bars I knew had been forged by Philip Simmons.

Like a bad dream.

I'd joined Ella in the ransom video cell.

"How long have you been here?" I whispered.

"Two days, best I can tell." Ella's long black hair was tied in a make-shift braid. Bits of leaves and twigs poked from the messy tangle. Her face was pale, her eyes red and puffy. I could tell she'd been crying.

"It's hard to say." Ella gestured to the gaping emptiness above our heads. "The light never changes down here, but that bastard feeds me every once in a while. A bucket comes down on a chain. I think we're at the bottom of a well."

Reality crashed in, full force.

I'd been kidnapped by Detective Hawfield.

At the crucial moment, my powers had betrayed me.

What about the boys?

"Was there anyone with me? Did Hawfield mention my friends?"

Ella shook her head. "He brought you alone. That was the first time I'd seen him since he shoved me in here. You were *totally* out. I've been trying to wake you for a while. For a moment, I . . . I thought maybe . . ."

I grabbed her hand, squeezed tightly. "I'm fine. And we're getting out of here."

"I'd like that very much, Tor." Her voice faltered. "I'm pretty scared."

Rising, I gave her another quick hug. "Don't worry. We will. I promise."

Releasing my friend, I surveyed the murky chamber. "What is this place?"

"An actual dungeon," Ella replied with disgust. "Used to punish slaves who got out of line. We're near an old plantation, I think. But deep in the woods, a few miles away."

She must've read my surprise.

"He talks too much," Ella said. "Hawfield explained the cell's origin when he dumped me in here. I think he was trying to freak me out." She shuddered, rubbing her arms. "It worked."

I tested one of the steel bars. The inch-thick metal didn't budge.

"Have you seen the twins?" I asked.

"No." Her eyes grew troubled. "I don't know what he's done with them."

"Oh, they're fine." Bitter words. "Though I wish they weren't."

Seeing her expression, I explained what had occurred earlier in the barn. How the twins had duped us all, then been double-crossed.

When I finished, some of the fire returned to Ella's eyes.

"Those spoiled brats!" She yanked her grungy braid. "How could they be so stupid?"

"The twins got away, but I doubt they'll help us. Those two will just keep running and never look back."

"They better run *far*," Ella hissed. Then she hiccupped, fighting back tears.

"How did you end up in here?" I asked, trying to distract her.

"The bastard tricked me," Ella said acidly. "It's my fault, I guess. I saw Rex Gable Thursday night. He came into the Flying Tomato, drinking scotch with his golf buddies. He just sat there, laughing and joking, without a care in the world. It *infuriated* me. So I called Detective Hawfield and told him what we suspected. Oops."

Her eyes found mine. "Tory, I told him about you, too. What we saw at the art gala."

"It's okay," I reassured her. "How could you know? Just tell me what happened."

"Hawfield told me to meet him in the parking lot, and not to tell anyone what I suspected. Or that I was meeting with the police." Ella groaned in frustration. "Like an idiot, I did exactly as instructed. I took a break, snuck outside, and met him alone. Ten words into my story, I saw his arm swing, and suddenly I was on the gravel. Next thing I know, he's pushing me down a tunnel that led here."

She covered her mouth. "Tory, I'm so sorry. I led that bastard to both of us."

"*Shh.*" I pulled her close again. "Don't you *dare* blame yourself. *He's* the monster."

Something crunched.

Our heads whipped in unison.

I heard a throaty chuckle. "Aw, how touching."

Hawfield was standing on the other side of the bars, wearing jeans and a red polo. He wiped both hands on his shirt, then powered an electric lantern. With the added light, I could see a narrow opening in the wall behind him.

The way out?

"Two songbirds, trapped in a cage," Hawfield gloated.

I glared at the detective. "You're a psychopath."

"If it makes you feel better," Hawfield said lightly, "I was tracking *your* movements long before this girl called me. But that cinched it—I wasn't ready to pin the whole song and dance on Rex Gable just yet. Hadn't fully covered my tracks. That steak needed a bit more time to marinate, and you two poking around and spreading rumors might've upset my apple cart, so to speak. Couldn't have it."

Ice prickled my spine.

"You were tracking me?"

"Ever since you broke into the Gable house." An expression of true bafflement twisted his features. "Gotta admit, that shocked me. I sat there and watched you and those boys do it, with no idea what you were thinking. You even found the fake bloodstain. Amazing! I won't pretend that episode didn't rattle me. It *did*. I ended up keeping our CSI boys away from that spot while I considered how to deal."

I felt Ella's startled glance. No time to explain. "But we didn't learn anything that night."

Hawfield stepped forward and casually leaned against the bars. His lantern sent shadows dancing up the walls.

Ella and I retreated across the cell.

"See, that's what *I* thought, too." His confusion seemed genuine. "But, next thing I know, I get a call from the witch over in Folly Beach, and she's telling me that the *same four teens* were asking questions about my zodiac card. Who told you about Ophiuchus, anyway?"

Answer him. Trade information.

"We stole a photocopy from the DA's desk."

Hawfield nodded in appreciation. "The fat kid. By the window. Ballsy."

"Why would Clara Gordon call you?" I ventured, hoping to keep Hawfield engaged.

The more he talked, the less he could do . . . unpleasant things.

"Oh, I put her on alert," Hawfield absently scratched his cheek. "All the other psychic astro-quacks, too. I wanted to know if anyone started asking questions about lost zodiac signs. Good thing I took the precaution, too."

It made sense. Hawfield was a more careful planner than I'd thought.

"After that doozy," the detective went on, "I told Bolton's headmaster that you kids were officially 'persons of interest' in the Gable case. That helped me keep tabs as well."

He smiled wide. "Paugh said you girls were close. A fact I took note of."

I shook my head in disgust. "All that work, just to steal some money."

Hawfield snorted. "A *lot* of money. And it *was* work."

"You're sick," Ella hissed.

He waved off the comment. "You were easy to bag, but damn, Brennan, Morris Island might as well be on Neptune. It's near impossible to invent an official-sounding pretext to get out there. I had to go special ops."

The beach. My shadowy attacker.

Thinking of Coop, my temper sparked.

"How's the leg, Detective? Or did my wolfdog bite you in the ass, instead?"

His smirk vanished. "That rabid mongrel should be put down. Maybe I'll see to that, when I'm finished here." The grin returned. "I missed you on the beach, but then you walked right into my arms at the plantation, didn't you? That silly rock. I was careless there. Nearly wet myself when you brought it downtown, but it all worked out in the end. Crazy backflips notwithstanding. You're an agile little imp, I'll give you that. Almost had me in the barn, until you lost your nerve."

My nerve was fine and dandy. It was my brain that short-circuited.

"Why zodiac cards?" Ella's voice sounded small and weak.

"You mean my pals Ophiuchus and Cetus?" Hawfield chuckled. "Seemed like just the kind of occult, hippie mumbo jumbo that would rile the media, but couldn't possibly lead back to me. I have an old book on the stars that my daddy gave me, along with a set of cards he bought at a garage sale. Those two fit the bill."

He laughed, louder this time. "Lost signs! Deadly portents! Just the kind of New Age hooey to get reporters in a lather. Of course, I had to spoon-feed the knuckleheads every step of the way. Journalism is a dying art."

Clever.

Wincing inwardly, I thought of all the time we'd wasted trying to decipher the meaning behind those zodiac cards. Pointless.

"Dropping Ophiuchus by the Gable house was easy." Hawfield sniffled in the damp air. "Planting Cetus at the Francis place took a little more doing, but I pulled it off. But I'm all done with cards now. Don't think I'll bother with Dr. Howard's condo."

The sound of Kit's name on Hawfield's tongue infuriated me.

Did my father even know I was missing? What would the boys tell him?

"You've been sabotaging these cases from the beginning," I said.

No wonder the investigations were inept.

The CPD was being led around by the nose.

Hawfield watched me with amusement. "Of course, Tory. Kinda stands to reason, since, you know, *I'm* the kidnapper. And I've got my bases covered. My colleagues won't trust anything your friends have to say. I've left specific instructions to ignore those boys. They're considered highly unreliable."

"Bastard."

The Virals didn't know who not to trust. And I couldn't get a message to them.

Ella inched closer to me. "So now you're doing this alone?"

"I'll still pin everything on Rex." Rueful shake of the head. "That man doesn't have a friend in the world. Gambling debts up the wazoo, plus the whole trust fund angle with his stepkids. He's the perfect fall guy."

A flaw in his plan occurred to me. I seized on the idea.

"Lucy and Peter are loose. They could blow your cover with one call. There might not be a dollar in ransom coming your way."

"True." The affability drained from Hawfield's voice. "But I doubt the twins are ready to face the music yet. They'll go to ground and keep quiet. For a little while, at least. Long enough for me to collect the dough, I think. But I won't be able to stay in town after all."

The detective shrugged. "Disappointing, but five million bones should salve my wounds. I planned for this eventuality, too. Gotta cover every angle, I always say."

Then his expression hardened, like an invisible mask slipping into place. "You girls are my insurance policy. Double coverage, so to speak. If the twins blab, I've still got *your* lives as leverage. For a bit, anyway."

His last words chilled my heart.

"You'll regret this," I whispered.

"Maybe." He turned to leave. "But not as much as you, I expect."

CHAPTER 45

I'd never driven so fast.

"Slow down, Blue!" Shelton shouted at me, flopping sideways in the backseat as we swerved onto Folly Road. "We won't help anybody if we crash and burn!"

Reluctantly, I reduced speed.

My heart was in my throat. I was close to panic.

Tory was missing.

A lunatic might have her caged like an animal.

My knuckles whitened on the steering wheel. The Explorer accelerated once more.

We had to get her back. *I* had to get her back.

If something happens to Tory . . .

I stomped on the gas, forcing the negative thoughts away.

Find her. Find her find her find her.

"I take it we're heading home." Hi was staring at the passing landscape, his face a sickly green. He didn't do well with speed. "You gonna tell Kit?"

"Not Kit." I swerved to pass a slow-moving truck. "We need the mutt."

"Cooper?" Shelton's head poked between the front seats. "Why?"

"We get the wolfdog." *Swerve.* "Flare." *Accelerate.* "Find Tory." *Pass.*

I swung back into our lane. A bus flew by. Horns blared.

"Great plan." Hi's fingers were imbedded in the armrest. "If we're alive to attempt it!"

The miles roared past, but not fast enough for me. Reaching Folly Beach, I turned left and shot toward Morris Island, crossing the bridge, only slowing as we approached our complex.

Wheeling my Explorer into its usual spot, I spun to face Hi and Shelton.

"Here's the thing." This might be a tough sell. "We can't tell Kit anything."

"His only daughter's been kidnapped!" Shelton shouted.

"Then how do we get Coop?" Hi asked at the same time.

"We have to sneak him out somehow." I tried to explain, though long speeches aren't my thing. "Look, if we tell Kit that Tory's been abducted, we'll have to tell him *everything.* Then he'll march us back to the police, where we'll have to repeat the whole story all over again. After that, our parents will never let us out of their sight, which means we'll be no help to Tory. And they won't know where to look anyway!"

"But *we* don't either," Shelton said glumly.

"Coop will." My voice was more confident than I felt. "He and Tory have that crazy bond. Some mental connection. We all do, but not like those two. The wolfdog will know where to go." *I hope.*

Hi was nodding. "Flaring together, maybe we can sense Tory's location."

"Exactly." I pinned Shelton with a hard look. "But if we tell her father, we'll never get the chance."

Not that I'd let Kit stop me. Nothing is going to stop me.

Shelton hesitated, then, "You're right. But if this fails—"

"We go straight to Kit." I pushed my hair behind my ears and tied it off with a rubber band. "I'm worried Corcoran might've called him already."

"Doubtful," said Hi. "The way the cops just reacted, I doubt they'll help at all."

"More reason to do this ourselves." I took a deep breath. Wiped sweaty palms on my black tee. "You guys ready?"

Two shaky nods. Best I could expect.

Exiting the SUV, we slunk toward Tory's unit. I didn't really have a plan.

Turns out, I didn't need one.

The door to the garage was unlocked. Kit's 4Runner was gone.

Relieved, I hurried to the flower pot where Tory hid an extra house key.

Not many secrets on Morris Island.

Opening the interior door, I was instantly steamrolled by eighty-five pounds of furry beast.

Coop exploded into the garage, bouncing like a live wire. He whined, growled, and pawed the ground, clearly in distress. Then, baring his teeth, the wolfdog fired outside.

"Stop him!" I shouted, clawing dust from my eyes.

"Stop him!?" Hi spread his arms. "How? That's like stepping in front of a freight train with teeth."

Emerging from the garage, I saw Coop's tail as it disappeared down the road.

"Damn!" I didn't know what to do. It's not like we could force him to join us. Not that much dog, all riled up.

Think, Blue! Tory's counting on you!

But I blanked. Felt close to melting down.

Tory was the one who made plans. Not stupid me. Right then, I just wanted to smash something.

Shelton grabbed my sleeve. "Let's flare, quick! Maybe we can call him back."

I nodded swiftly, grateful for a course of action. Closing my eyes, I called out the beast.

In the beginning, I'd struggled to light a flare. Even a year later I still needed to be angry. But after months of secret practice sessions—pushing myself, testing my limits—summoning the wolf had become second nature. Seductively easy. Flaring felt as natural as breathing.

A single thought of some monster hurting Tory . . .

SNAP.

I felt the familiar rush. Relished the surge of energy that came with it.

My senses exploded with supernatural intensity.

How can Tory think this is bad? How could anyone deny themselves this pleasure?

I glanced at Hi and Shelton. Both had switched on.

"Now what?" Hi asked. "This is the part where Tory does her thing."

"She talks about glowing lines." Shelton was still panting. "Connecting us, in her subconscious."

Squeezing my lids tight, I tried to imagine what Tory described. Tried to picture Cooper. Tory. Me, Shelton, and Hi. The Virals, together as one. Linked. Body, mind, and soul.

Nothing happened.

Whatever Tory could visualize, it didn't work for me.

Frustrated, I screamed Cooper's name in my head. Imagined chasing him down.

Didn't feel a thing.

"This is stupid." My fingers curled into fists. "How can I summon a dog with my mind?"

"Coop-er!" Hi cupped his hands and shouted into the wind. "Yo, Coop! Here boy!"

Without a better idea, I joined him. Shelton added his voice as well. The three of us called and called, hoping our Hail Mary would connect.

I was about to give up when a gray streak shot from the brush. Coop raced over, favoring his forepaw, bristling from head to tail.

The wolfdog stopped a few paces away. Flashed gleaming white teeth.

Hi backed up a step. "Easy now, killer. We're family, remember?"

The wolfdog was clearly agitated.

It occurred to me that we'd never flared near the mongrel without Tory present.

Unexpectedly, Coop sat. Then, tipping back his head, he unleashed a full-throated howl.

My eyes widened in recognition. "He knows."

I met Coop's golden eyes with my own. Willed him to understand.

Come with us. Help us find her.

Coop cocked his head. Whined. Then he rose and trotted to my Explorer. Pawed the door.

Despite everything, I smiled. "The mutt's in."

"Okay, great." Shelton's hands rose. "But where do we start?"

I looked at Coop. He barked. Scratched at the handle a second time.

The image of a forest popped into my head.

A sending from Coop? From Tory? Some trick of our flare power?

I didn't know. But suddenly, I was certain what to do. "Back to Drayton Hall."

Surprised, Hi and Shelton started to speak at once.

I cut them off. "We go back to where we lost Tory's trail. Let Cooper track from there."

"The kidnapper *drove* away," Hi pointed out. "There won't be any trail to track."

"Not one we can see." I was already moving toward my car. "But maybe the dog has other methods."

I opened the door. Coop leaped inside and settled in the passenger seat.

Turning back to Hi and Shelton.

"You two have a better idea?"

CHAPTER 46

I had a decision to make.

Ella was huddled at the back of our cell, head against the wall, staring at nothing.

I approached the steel bars. Moving down the line, I tested every one. None wobbled or shifted. I wondered how twentieth-century steel had made its way down into a nineteenth-century slave pen. Decades ago, someone must've restored this horrible prison to its original condition.

I didn't want to think about why.

Glancing up into the gloom, I saw a chain hanging fifteen feet off the ground.

"That's how he lowers the bucket," Ella had explained bitterly. "Food comes down every twelve hours. Like we're freaking livestock."

I can make it. Flaring, I can reach that loop on the end.

But not without showing Ella something I'm not allowed to share.

What choice do I have? Am I supposed to take my secret to the grave?

Because, no mistake, that's where this was headed.

I didn't tell Ella what Hawfield had said in the barn. How he intended to "take care of the problem." Why terrify her? Why take away her hope?

Given what I knew, I couldn't hold back. Not with our lives on the line.

"Ella?"

My friend looked up. "Yeah?" Weariness dulled her voice.

"I think I can grab that chain." I pointed into the dim emptiness above. "Climb up."

Ella shook her head. "I tried myself a half dozen times. You can't reach it, not even if you climb the bars first."

"I'm going to try. Can you keep watch?"

"Sure." Ella's voice carried zero optimism. "But it might be better if I stood below to catch you. Or boost you. Or something."

"No. I don't want to be surprised if Hawfield comes back."

"Okay." Ella rose and walked to the bars. "But while I think you're a born soccer player, there's no way you can jump *that* high. Unless you've got moves I haven't seen."

Maybe one or two.

Assuming I don't just black out instead.

I shoved the unwelcome thought aside. There were no other options.

"I have to try. Keep lookout?"

Ella nodded, peered through the bars to where we knew the entrance to be. "All clear."

Come on, DNA. Don't fail me now.

Eyes closed. Mind clear.

SNAP.

As if answering my prayers, the power unfolded easily.

My senses awoke. Amplified. Power flooded my limbs.

For the first time in days, I didn't have to fight to stay upright.

I *flared,* strong as ever before.

No time to celebrate.

Gauging angles, I took two running steps toward the wall. Leaped.

My sneakers hit the stones four feet up. Legs flexing, I pushed off with every fiber of flare strength I could muster, propelling myself backward, outward, toward the center of the room.

I catapulted across the cell. Body soaring, I twisted in midair like a diver, hands flailing toward the black quadrant of space where the chain should be.

Nothing. Panic jolted me. I was going to fall, and hard.

Then my fingertips brushed metal.

I clawed the slippery links.

My left hand slipped free.

But the right one stuck, my fingers wrapping the wet steel in a death grip.

I spun wildly, one-armed, my body pirouetting across the chamber. The metal links cut cruelly into my palm. My shoulder screamed, the bone nearly ripping from its socket.

The hold began to slip.

Arm muscles burning, I propelled forward, throwing my left hand back up onto the slick chain. With both hands in place, I shifted my weight, easing the strain on my joints.

Panting, I held on tight, my momentum carrying me in lazy arcs above the stone floor five yards below.

"Anytime, Brennan." Then Ella glanced over her shoulder. "Holy crap!"

She scurried beneath me, staring up in shock. "You did it! How in the world?"

"Beginner's luck," I grunted, keeping my eyes slitted to tamp their golden glow. "I'm gonna climb up, and see if there's a way out."

"*Go go go!*" Ella bounced with sudden energy. "Then, for the love of God, come back!"

Gathering my strength, I began to haul my body upward, a few links at a time. After five exhausting pulls, I'd ascended high enough to wiggle a foot inside the loop.

I paused, hanging in the fetal position. Breathless. My arms were overjoyed at the unexpected respite. I knew that without the added flare power, I'd never have made it that far.

"Great job, girl!" Eyes blazing, I could make out Ella clearly, fifteen feet below.

I prayed she couldn't see me just as well.

Concentrate. The job isn't done.

Hanging like a spider, I cast my hyper-senses out in a net.

Water was dripping from somewhere high overhead. Looking straight up, I could make out the moldy wooden planks sealing off the ancient stonework. Flaring, I could see how misshapen the boards were, twisted and swollen from years of exposure to sunlight and water. Trickles of illumination filtered through the rotting wood.

A covered well. That must open to the outside.

But the distance was another thirty yards, minimum. I couldn't climb all that way. We were much farther underground than I'd thought.

A cocktail of dank, musty odors filled my nostrils. Mold. Wet stone. Rotting vegetation. I shut off the rancid flow before my stomach emptied.

My fingers burned. The rusty chain bored into my palms. Flare sensitivity was making the ascent doubly painful—my nerves were on fire—but I needed the extra power to keep going.

I couldn't reach the walls—the chain I dangled from was centered in a shaft at least ten feet across. Harnessing my flare vision, I studied the stonework, searching for some other way—*any* way—out of this terrible well.

There.

Ten feet above me, a rectangular hole cut into the stonework.

“I see something,” I called down to Ella. “A way out, maybe.”

“Okay!” Ella’s voice echoed loudly in my enhanced ears.

“I have to get higher.”

Taking a deep breath, I gathered my strength for the treacherous assent.

I can do this. Ten more feet.

Reach. Grab. Pull.

Reach. Grab. Pull.

Three more lunges brought me level with the opening.

It was a fetid, black maw, with no hint of light. I glanced up again. The chain ran through a small opening in the wooden boards, but the top seemed forever away.

A look back at the dark gap in the wall.

Neither option was appealing.

Gassed, I opted for crawling over climbing.

Shifting my weight, I kicked out with both legs. Began to swing the chain across the shaft.

Back and forth.

Back and forth.

Slowly, my momentum brought me near the lip of the opening.

Timing was everything.

On the next upswing I flung myself forward, launching my upper body into the crevasse.

My knees cracked against the wall below, skinning painfully as I worm-wiggled into the tunnel mouth. There I paused, gasping for air while I rubbed my bruised and abraded limbs.

“I’m in some type of tunnel,” I called down. “I’ll see where it leads, then come get you.”

“Be careful!” Then, with a slight quaver. “Please hurry back.”

“I will, Ella. I promise.”

Rising on all fours, I began crawling down the passage.

Grimy stonework passed beneath my hands and knees. I traveled as fast as I dared, flare senses on maximum.

For the first twenty feet, the tunnel sloped gently downward. Then the grade steepened, the passage dropping into a black pool of shadows even my flare vision couldn't pierce.

The floor became covered in a slick wet moss that came loose under my fingers. Wet leaves coated the tunnel's sides, along with a layer of something sticky I didn't want to identify.

I inched down the incline cautiously, testing the greasy surface as I descended.

A loud bang sounded ahead.

Behind me, the chain rattled.

I froze, ears probing, but silence quickly reasserted itself.

Distracted by the noises, I failed to place my next hand with care.

My palm slipped. In an instant my body was tumbling forward. I plummeted down the shaft, unable to halt my headfirst plunge along on its filmy surface.

Seconds later, I rolled from the chute onto more wet stone. Scrambling to my feet, I examined the dark chamber in which I'd been deposited. The room was the same dimensions as the prison from which I'd escaped. But no endless well above, no line of bars across.

Wiping muck from my hands, I attempted to get my bearings.

My instincts told me I'd fallen back to the same depth as the cell holding Ella.

Find a connecting tunnel. Free Ella. Then get the hell out of here.

Straining my flare vision, I spotted an opening at the other end of the chamber. I squeezed through, found myself in a smooth, brick-walled tunnel running in both directions.

A flash of light.

"What the hell?"

I spun toward the voice.

Hawfield was ten feet away, holding his lantern, a stunned expression on his face.

"Damn gymnast!" Hawfield charged, one hand reaching for his gun. His massive bulk filled the narrow tunnel.

I fled in the opposite direction.

"There's nowhere to run!" Hawfield bellowed.

Boots pounded behind me.

Reaching a T intersection, I shot to the right, with no idea where I was going.

Crack! Crack!

Stone chips flew as bullets tore through the space I'd just vacated.

Oh my God oh my God oh my God!

Searing heat rose in my chest. Haloes appeared at the edge of my vision.

No! Not now!

My senses began to overload. I stumbled into another crossroad, cut left.

Footsteps echoed a few paces behind me.

Shock waves traveled my nervous system.

Disoriented, I tripped, landing heavily on the ground.

Rolling, I saw another chute to my left. Cold air drifted from its mouth.

"Game's over, honey." Hawfield loomed above me, sucking in wet, panting breaths.

The detective pulled the slide on the HK45.

Click.

With a last gasp, I scurried for the hole in the wall and shimmied into the adjacent room.

"Get back here!" Hawfield growled.

I rolled sideways as the gun barrel appeared in the opening.

Crack! Crack! Crack!

A deafening roar filled the chamber.

Somehow, my flare hung on by a thread.

I covered my ears, tried to block out the gunshots reverberating in my brain.

Through a cloud of pulverized stone, I spotted salvation.

Stairs. Leading up.

I took them at a dead sprint.

Behind me, I heard the detective force his way through the gap.

"Give it up, kid!" Hawfield craned his neck. "I'll chase you down like a dog!"

The stairs were high and incredibly steep, with a tiny square of light at the top.

Reaching the apex, I felt a light breeze on my face. Heard a sparrow's call.

Ignoring sounds of pursuit, I slithered through an old trapdoor and exited a small cave.

Fresh air. Blinding sunlight.

Tall trees surrounding me, staring down with solemn faces.

I wavered a moment, frozen in indecision.

What about Ella?

No choice. I couldn't do anything for my friend without ducking Hawfield first.

I'll be back, Ella. I swear on my life.

Picking a direction at random, I bolted into the woods.

CHAPTER 47

Hiram, look out!"

Too late. The leash jerked from my fingers.

"Oh, crap!" I stumbled, nearly face-planted on the pavement. Caught a lone glimpse of Coop's hindquarters disappearing through a line of magnolias.

Shelton smacked his forehead. "Nice job, Stolowitski. He's loose!"

"Told you it wouldn't work!" I shot back, rubbing my wrenched shoulder. "When has Coop ever agreed to my authority?"

Ben held his tongue, but his golden glare spoke volumes.

We were back in the Drayton Hall parking lot. Less than two hours had passed since Tory went missing there, but it felt like a million years.

I wiped sweat from my forehead, could feel my cheeks blazing scarlet. "Hey, next time *you* try to restrain that monster. Coop must weigh eight hundred pounds! It's like walking a grizzly bear."

Shelton rolled his yellow eyes. "What now?"

"What else?" Ben took off after the wolfdog. "We follow!"

"Great. Running." With a groan, I lumbered after him. "Worst birthday ever!"

Ben had driven back to the plantation like an aspiring NASCAR champion. Coop selfishly took shotgun, staring intently ahead, seemingly in agreement with our chosen route. Shelton and I sat in the back, staring out our windows like a couple of weirdoes. Mesmerized. Neither of us had ever ridden in a car while flaring.

So many things to see. To hear and smell. A constant sensory barrage.

I wanted to take the whole world and eat it.

Ben glanced at us once, in the rearview, and chuckled. I guess he'd done it before.

But after twenty minutes of breakneck speed, my canine DNA decided to sledgehammer my brain. Turning onto the plantation's long driveway, my flare suddenly spiked like hot monkey fever, then nearly fizzled out completely. I broke out in cold sweat, nose burning, vision strobing, ears ringing like a hot microphone. It's a miracle I didn't mess my shorts.

Beside me, Shelton winced and rubbed his temples. The car swerved momentarily as Ben gritted his teeth, his face gone paler than a Twilight vampire. Even Coop reacted, shaking his head as if to fend off a swarm of bees.

The wackiness passed as abruptly as it started. I nearly coughed up a lung, but my other body parts seemed to function okay. I was relieved, but more than a little spooked—Tory's recent blackout was fresh in my memory. I wasn't anxious to lose consciousness and roll into a ditch or something. Not if I could help it.

In any case, our Viral telepathic jump circle refused to engage, probably because we didn't have the slightest idea how to engage it. Without Tory, we three bozos were flying blind. No, worse than that—we couldn't even locate the airplane. It was during our last failed attempt that Cooper yanked my arm from its socket and bolted for the hills.

So Shelton and I bombed after Ben, through the magnolias and onto the humongous lawn fronting the manor house, in hopeless pursuit of an enraged runaway wolf hybrid.

Flaring, I spotted Ben easily, fifty feet ahead, dashing eastward across the acre of grass. Coop was thirty yards farther up, bounding at full speed toward the woods on the opposite side.

"Wait!" Shelton pointed the other direction. "The barn's that way, on the *west* side of the grounds!"

"Coop doesn't seem interested!" I shouted as we ran. "What's this way?"

As I spoke, Coop reached the tree line and disappeared among the shadowy trunks.

"Coop's headed for the edge of the property." Shelton attempted to shrug while sprinting. "Far as I know, that's empty forest. The handout doesn't list anything."

"Super." Panting. Wheezing. "I'm excited."

Though my mind is a steel trap, I'm not exactly built for long distance pursuit. I carry a bit too much weight in the . . . everywhere to be an effective cross-country runner. Yet with my powers unleashed, I felt light as a feather. Strong. Fast. Agile. Nevertheless, I was still puffing and blowing a Clydesdale by the time we reached the woods.

Ben waited at the edge of the forest. "The mutt never broke stride. I think Coop knows where he's going."

"Maybe he's tracking her perfume?" I gasped hopefully, turning my head to eject a lethal snot rocket.

Shelton waved at the silent grove before us. "But how do *we* track the wolfdog?"

Ben stared at the snugly massed jumble of trees, as if trying to extract an answer by sheer force of will. Finally, "Follow me." He jogged into the gloom.

I glanced at Shelton, who was looking at me.

"Deserted forest," he said. "No idea where we're going."

I nodded. "A psychopath might be hiding inside. I'm a terrible hand-to-hand fighter."

Shelton shook his head. "This is my life now."

"Hey, at least it's not *your* birthday. Worst one ever, by the way."

His fist came up. I dapped it with mine.

"For Tory," Shelton said.

"For Tory." All joking shelved.

Squaring our shoulders, we hustled into the woods.

⬡ ⬡ ⬡

"Hi!" Shelton hissed. "Hear that?"

"Of course I do." I spoke just as quietly. "My powers are maxed out right now. I can hear your freaking heartbeat."

He nodded, eyebrows up. "Same here."

Then Shelton whistled lightly to catch Ben's attention up ahead.

When Ben turned, Shelton tapped his ear.

Ben nodded impatiently. He brought two fingers up to his eyes, then pointed them left.

"What does that mean?" I muttered, taking a private moment to adjust my sagging shorts. "Look that way? Go investigate? I'm not an army ranger here."

Hearing me, Ben covered his face. Then he whispered, "Just watch my back."

"That's what I've *been* doing." But I zipped my lips at his exasperated glare.

We'd all heard the barking.

Coop? The yips had sounded like Tory's wolfdog, but honestly, it was impossible to tell.

Ben crept forward through the trees. This stretch of forest was particularly terrifying—tall, skinny oaks, with little understory in between. Yet the trunks were tightly packed, limiting how far one could see. The effect was a sensation of being exposed on all sides, while simultaneously feeling hemmed in and surrounded.

I hated it. Beside me, Shelton looked close to passing out.

A furious baying erupted just ahead. Something large crashed though the trees.

Ben froze, unsure how to react. Then he arrowed directly for the commotion.

"Go *toward* the sounds?" Shelton squawked. "That's a classic horror movie mistake."

"Too late now!" Steeling my nerves, I fired after Ben. Shelton trailed a step behind.

The noise rose, a sudden cacophony of barks and whines.

Definitely Coop.

Then Ben yelled at the top of his lungs.

Adrenaline flooded my system.

I vaulted a fallen log, circled a clump of willows, and stormed into a small clearing.

Coop was rolling in the leaves, pinning someone beneath his massive bulk.

Ben dove on the tangle with a voice-cracking whoop.

Raising both fists above my head, I unleashed a primal growl, preparing to launch my full weight onto whatever I didn't recognize and pummel it with my eyes closed.

Ben saw me coming, held up a hand in alarm.

"Hi! Stop!"

I skidded to a halt, eyes wide, lungs pumping. "What!? What's going on!?"

Coop rolled to his feet, began licking the person at the bottom of the pile.

It was Tory.

CHAPTER 48

I began breathing again.

Hiram had stopped his blind charge and wouldn't crush me. Thank goodness. Pushing Cooper aside, I got to my feet. Felt a huge surge of warmth.

I was no longer alone.

The Virals had found me.

Ben was beaming, unable to hide his relief. He turned quickly, wiping his glowing eyes. Shelton darted forward and crushed me with a hug.

Coop was dancing and bucking, his tail wagging so hard he had trouble keeping balance.

My boys. My heroes.

"How?" Ben asked simply.

"My wolfdog found me." Catching him, I hugged Coop tight. "I was totally lost, hiding behind this log. He appeared like a guardian angel. Where are we, anyway?"

"The woods south of Drayton Hall," Shelton said. "A mile from the river, maybe twice that from the barn where you disappeared."

So close. We barely traveled at all.

My elation quickly evaporated. Ella was still locked in that terrible cell.

I scanned the group. Noted with satisfaction that everyone was flaring.

"*Hawfield* is the kidnapper." I waved for the boys to huddle close. "The twins faked their abduction, and were working with that jerk to rip off their trust fund."

"Faked?" Blood rushed to Ben's face. "They made the whole thing up?"

"Holy crap!" Shelton reached for an earlobe. "The *cop* did it?"

"Why would they steal their own money?" Hi wondered.

"I'll explain everything later," I said. "What matters now is Ella. Hawfield took her to keep her quiet. I found the twins hiding in the barn, but they took off. Hawfield showed up, and my flare bugged out. Then he locked me up with Ella in the cell from the video."

"So you confronted the twins alone, without waiting for us?" Ben couldn't keep the anger from his voice. "After making us promise not to do anything like that?"

"We can discuss my impulsiveness another time—"

"Oh, we *will*," Ben assured me.

"—but right now, *Ella* is all that matters. That cell is somewhere in these woods. Deep underground, at the bottom of an old well. I flared and escaped, but ran into Hawfield and had to leave Ella behind."

My voice broke.

I'd left her there, alone in the dark.

Ben's hand found my shoulder. "You had no choice. But the pack is here now. We'll find Ella, and deal with that dirty cop, too. Just lead the way."

Ben's words stiffened my resolve. Reaching up, I squeezed his hand before he released it.

Shelton's eyes darted around the clearing. "Hawfield's in these woods?"

"Armed. He's taken a few shots at me already."

"Then he's toast." Ben's tone was glacial.

The boys looked my way. Cooper sat at attention, his total focus on me.

Hi gave a shaky thumbs-up. "Do your thing, Tor. Stir the drink."

I nodded. "Let's join hands. Coop in the middle."

We formed a circle around the wolfdog.

My eyes closed. I pushed all doubts away.

The flaming cords sprang to life, a fiery lattice connecting the five of us.

Centered on Coop. The nexus. Our touchstone.

The disturbance was gone. The lines seemed frozen in place, awaiting my command.

Working by instinct, I expanded the cords, then untethered my consciousness and sent it racing through the channels.

My perception flicked from person to person.

Hi. Ben. Shelton. Coop.

I'm here.

My eyes opened. I saw the boys staring at one another in wonder.

Without quite understanding how, I flashed to Hiram. Looked out from his eyes.

I saw a redheaded girl covered in grime, face pinched in concentration. She smiled.

It's working. We can trade.

I felt Shelton's anxiety as he took a peek through my eyes. *I'll never get used to this.*

Amazeballs. Hi stepped forward and poked Ben in the chest.

Ben slapped Hi's hand away. Grinned wolfishly. *Everyone ready?*

For what? Shelton sent.

Hunt.

My gaze dropped to Coop, standing in the center of our circle.

We hunt, the wolfdog sent. *As Pack.*

Coop laced the sending with the concepts of friendship, family, and trust.

Kneeling, I kissed his doggie snout. *I couldn't have said it better.*

⎔ ⎔ ⎔

Gun drawn, Detective Hawfield stalked through the woods.

The barking had come from somewhere just up ahead.

Late-afternoon daylight angled through the trees—blinding sunbeams alternating with lengthening shadows—making it harder to see.

But he'd be damned if he was giving this chase up.

That meddling, terrible, unbelievable Brennan girl.

She was some kind of evil spirit.

How in God's name did she escape that cell?

The Francis kid had still been inside. She'd screamed for Brennan to run, obviously unable to flee herself. He'd thought about dealing with her right then and there, but decided to wait. He might still need a hostage.

Because, right then, all of Hawfield's plans were in shambles.

The twins were gone. Out of his reach.

Brennan was somewhere loose in these woods.

He was supposed to receive the ransom tonight. If the twins kept their mouths shut just a few more hours, he could still pull this off. He could *win.*

But Tory Brennan threatened everything.

That she-devil *had* to be found. And dealt with.

Hawfield checked his HK45. Seven rounds in the cartridge, plus one in the chamber. Another clip was strapped to his ankle.

More than enough for one little girl.

This time, no prison cell.

Something rustled in the brush to his left.

Hawfield froze. Brought the pistol around.

He wasn't worried. One teen, alone in the woods. He'd catch her eventually. They were miles from anywhere, and Brennan didn't know where she was to boot.

No one would hear him take care of this problem.

I just have to find her.

A twig snapped.

Hawfield spun, trying to locate the source. Game roamed these woods. He didn't want to give away his position wasting some deer.

A silver streak shot from the bushes dead ahead.

Something huge bounded to within a dozen feet of where he stood.

Hawfield found himself face-to-face with a wolf.

The beast growled, saliva dripping from his massive jowls.

Hawfield fired reflexively, but the animal had vanished into the sea of gray trunks.

"Jesus!"

A wolf! Here, in the Lowcountry.

Then he went cold, one hand dropping to the lacerations on his leg.

Was that the animal that attacked him on Morris Island? Brennan's maniac pet?

Hawfield raised his weapon, scanning for more predators. Wolves rarely hunt alone.

Silence. Stillness. As if he'd imagined the creature.

Hawfield chuckled darkly. "Go find the Brennan girl, you mongrel."

Leaves crunched to his right.

He turned.

Brennan stood in plain view, twenty feet away.

She glared. Made no move to run.

The girl's eyes had that same yellow tinge. Unnerving, but Hawfield had been in tough spots before. Some creepy teenage waif wouldn't get under his skin.

"Freeze, and I won't fire." Hawfield inched closer, looking for a clear shot.

Brennan stepped behind a trunk.

Hawfield sped forward, determined to finish this once and for all.

Snapping branches. Hawfield glanced to his left.

The wolf was charging his flank, on a direct collision course. As he watched, the beast coiled and sprang.

"Holy—"

Hawfield spun, backpedaling. A root caught his ankle and he crashed to the ground.

Crack! Crack!

Bullets ripped into a tree trunk twenty yards away.

No other sounds. The creature was gone.

Hawfield clambered to his feet. The first tinglings of fear gathered in his massive belly.

What's going on?

Movement in the corner of his eye.

Hawfield swung his weapon. Squinted through the patchwork shafts of light.

One of those boys!

Ben Blue.

For a second, the detective could only stare in astonishment. By the time he thought to shoot, Blue had darted behind a fallen log.

This was bad. Brennan's friends were in the woods, too.

I might be outnumbered.

A whistle behind him.

Hawfield pivoted.

The fat kid smiled, waggling his fingers before slipping from sight.

Hawfield's rage exploded. "Think you can toy with me, you punks?"

A hungry growl was his only warning.

Riiiip!

Searing pain tore through Hawfield as a furry gray rocket slammed into his side. Before he could blink, his attacker bounded into the bushes.

"Ayyyeeee!" Hawfield collapsed in a heap, one hand grabbing his backside.

Crack! Crack! Crack!

Slugs tore into the space where the beast had vanished.

Blood ran down Hawfield's pant leg. He felt a hot wetness pooling in his shoe.

The dog. Those boys. They found this place somehow.

Hawfield spotted the black kid on a log, ten feet ahead. He grinned, then disappeared behind a row of prickly pears.

The fat one followed close on his heels.

Ben Blue darted between the oaks to his left, sliding from his field of vision.

With cold dread, Hawfield realized the kids were closing.

Tightening the noose.

They're playing with me. And that's the same wolf from Morris Island.

Then Brennan stepped from the trees right before him.

Arms crossed, she stared down at him with glowing, inhuman yellow eyes.

"What are you?" Hawfield asked hoarsely.

A cold smile curled her lips. "Your worst nightmare."

Hawfield snarled. Arm jerking up, he fired wildly.

Crack! Crack!

Click.

Too late, Hawfield realized his mistake. His hand had barely moved for the second clip when a drop of hot liquid struck his forehead.

Hawfield looked up.

Stared directly into a pair of canine jaws.

CHAPTER 49

"Easy, boy."

I stepped from behind a cluster of oaks.

Cooper's eyes flicked to me, but he didn't move away.

Hawfield's neck was a centimeter from the wolfdog's gleaming incisors.

Hold. I sent. *Nothing else.*

Coop growled, clearly in disagreement, but he eased back a few inches.

Hold.

The boys raced from the forest. Hi pulled the empty HK45 from the detective's fingers. Shelton ran to my side, unsure what to do.

Ben walked directly to Hawfield and kicked him in the stomach.

"Ben."

"Yes?" His eyes never left the detective.

"Just search him, please."

Ben ran rough hands over Hawfield, freeing the handcuffs from his belt and the extra clip strapped to the detective's ankle. He tossed the latter to Hiram.

Hi immediately walked both weapon and ammunition over to me. "Yours."

I ejected the spent clip from the HK45, slammed the new one into place, then worked the slide to chamber a round. Then I held the weapon loosely at my side, barrel pointed at the ground.

"I'm terrified of you right now," Hi said, wide-eyed. "And in love. Take me shooting with your aunt Tempe next time."

Intensely aware of Coop's proximity, Hawfield hadn't moved a muscle. He seemed almost hypnotized by the wolfdog's gaping jaws.

"Remember Coop, Detective?" Ben stroked the wolfdog's head. "You two have met once before. I don't think he likes you."

Coop growled low in his throat, causing Hawfield to recoil.

Power down, I sent to the other Virals.

Ben shot me a hard look. *He's not secure.*

We can't let him see any more, I answered. *Cuff him. I have the gun.*

"She's right." Hi turned away. Shelton quickly followed suit.

SNUP.

The power fled, but I didn't stumble.

Something had changed. With the flares. Within me.

My powers had . . . righted themselves somehow. The lines were unclogged. I can't describe it any better.

Ben cuffed Hawfield tightly, then stepped back, his irises fading to dark brown.

I clicked my tongue for Coop to stand down.

The wolfdog snarled at Hawfield one last time, then complied, retreating a few feet and dropping down on his haunches. Coop was still favoring his injured forepaw.

I stepped forward. Placed the gun barrel against Hawfield's cheek.

"Is Ella okay?" I asked softly.

"Yes." Terror filled Hawfield's eyes.

"Quickest way to her cell?"

"The stairs." Voice anxious to please. "The GPS coordinates are in my pocket."

Ben rifled Hawfield's pants, found a slip of paper, and handed it to Shelton. He began punching the numbers into his iPhone.

"Let's hurry." Rising, I looked to Ben. "Should two of us stay and watch him?"

"No splitting up," Ben said firmly. "Not again. We'll drag this sack of crap with us."

And we did.

Following Shelton's lead, we cut through the forest, pushing and prodding the detective along with us. Daylight was fading to dusk, giving the forest a sinister, spectral aspect. I couldn't wait to get out of there.

Hawfield didn't resist. Answered my questions without expression.

At the cave mouth, I told the boys to wait. Ordered Coop to sit.

Alone, I hurried down the stone steps, through the crawl, and into the tunnel. Following Hawfield's instructions, I located a hidden niche with both a key and extra lantern.

The cell was through the last opening on the left. I raced inside.

Ella was standing by the bars, having seen the light approach. Spying me, she burst into tears. "Oh thank God!" She reached a hand through the barrier. "I thought it was him again."

I met her fingers, hugging my friend as best I could. "Told you I'd come back."

Locating the lock, I inserted the key and opened the cell door. Ella stumbled out.

"Let's get the hell out of here." She was holding back sobs.

I wiped away a few tears of my own. "I couldn't agree more."

Hand in hand, we hurried from the chamber, ran the whole way back to the surface. Emerging in the failing light, I felt a sudden elation. A sense of fulfillment.

We'd done it!

We rescued Ella. Bagged the kidnapper. Foiled the twins' awful scam. Even when things looked darkest, we'd kept our cool, using our brains and special skills to solve a crime the police never would have. A total Virals victory.

"Let's head back to town." My voice carried a distinct twinge of satisfaction. "I'm sure Detective Hawfield is anxious for a chat with his coworkers."

My reference to police seemed to snap Hawfield from his funk.

"Release me," he demanded calmly. "You have no idea who you're dealing with."

Ben shoved Hawfield in the back, propelling the detective down a short incline. "We're dealing with a criminal. Nothing more."

I followed a pace behind, gun in hand, Coop by my side. Taking no chances.

At the bottom of the slope, Hawfield made his move.

The detective spun, catching Ben with a shoulder that knocked him sideways. His hands were suddenly free. I saw the glint of a second key as it fell to the dirt.

Coop charged. Leaped for the detective's throat.

Hawfield caught the wolfdog, then crushed his injured paw with one meaty hand. Coop yowled in pain as Hawfield tossed him to the ground.

I gaped like a simpleton. Hawfield moved impossibly quick for a big man.

Shoot him.

But I hesitated for a split second, unprepared in the moment to actually take a life. Hawfield charged me. Slapped the HK45 from my grip.

The weapon flew backward, landing in an uneven pile of leaves.

Shoving me aside, Hawfield ran to the gun. Picked it up. Turned with a smile.

"Amateurs."

He raised the weapon. Took aim right at me.

My heart stopped beating.

Creeeeeak!

Hawfield glanced down at his feet as the ground beneath him sagged.

A look of horror spread across his face.

CRACK.

Hawfield danced left, but his movement only increased the ripping and snapping sounds.

CRACK. CRACK.

Hawfield's mouth formed an O.

SNAP.

With a ponderous groan, the ground gave way completely.

The detective disappeared in a whoosh of swirling leaves.

"Noooooo!"

His scream lasted a three count, then ended with a sickening thud.

Hi crept to the edge of a black, gaping hole where Hawfield had been standing.

He looked down. Whistled.

"That's pretty deep." Hi cleared his throat. "I . . . uh . . . don't think anyone could've survived that."

"What just happened?" Shelton's voice had risen ten octaves. "Did the earth open up?"

Shaken, I looked at Ella. She nodded grimly.

"It's an old well," I said. "Capped by rotting boards. Hawfield must've walked right on top of them, and he wasn't a small man."

I used the past tense. Knew the detective was dead.

Ben glanced nervously at the forest floor. "Are there any more of those?"

"I don't think so." Gently tugging Hiram back from the edge. "The cell Hawfield used is at the bottom of this shaft. The bastard just landed in his own cage."

○ ○ ○

It took forty minutes to get back to the parking lot. The sun set as we walked, forcing us to rely on Hawfield's lantern.

Hi and Shelton helped Ella along, offering encouragement when her steps faltered.

Reaching pavement, we stopped, somewhat at a loss.

"*Soooo.*" Shelton scratched his head. "What now?"

Against all odds, I snorted in amusement. "Honestly, I have no idea."

"We just solved a quadruple kidnapping." Hi shrugged. "That's a good day, right?"

I nodded, but felt empty inside. A man had died.

An awful, evil man—one who'd fully intended to kill me. But it felt wrong to celebrate. A part of me was actually upset.

Ella read my mood. "I don't feel sorry for that maniac. He was going to kill us both. Hawfield got what he deserved."

"Truth." But Ben's eyes gave him away. He was troubled, too.

I was about to respond—with what, I have no idea—when flashing lights appeared in the distance.

"Crap, cops!" Then Hi did a double-take. "Wait, cops! That's *good* this time!"

"Why are they out here?" Shelton asked. "Did anyone call them?"

Everyone shook their head.

"The gunshots?" Hi ventured. "Maybe some old lady lives in a shoe around here."

My mind cleared. The police's unexpected arrival clarified what to do.

"You three need to leave, *right now.*" I whistled for Coop, then snagged his collar when he approached. "Take the SUV and go. I'll stay with Ella and handle the fallout."

"Out of your mind," Ben said immediately.

"I'm serious! You *especially.* There's no reason for the cops to know you were here."

"But how?" Hi waved at the driveway. "That cruiser is coming down the only road."

"There's a back way off the grounds," Shelton said quickly. "Farther down this access road. We *could* drive away without anybody knowing."

"I'm *not* leaving Tory to face this alone," Ben insisted. "Get serious!"

The flashing lights grew closer, red and blue beams reflecting off the forest canopy overhead. A single police car was creeping down the driveway. Would reach the lot in moments.

"She's right." Hi stepped to Ben. "You can't afford more bad publicity. Not again. Not right after the Gamemaster thing. And if you're going, Shelton and I might as well bolt, too." He turned. "No offense, Tor, but it makes the most sense for you to stay with Ella."

"None taken. I completely agree."

"I won't tell anyone you guys were here," Ella promised. "Not one word."

Ben wagged his head in disbelief. "You're all nuts."

I turned to Ella. "Can you give us a minute alone?"

She nodded, strode a dozen yards across the parking lot. Arm-wrapping her body, she watched the cruiser's cautious approach.

Shelton and Hi began to fidget, no doubt counting down the seconds.

I spoke softly. "The cops will eat you alive, Benjamin Blue. You have to go."

Ben tensed, ready to argue.

"Detective Hawfield *died.* This is going to get serious. It's way too much heat for you. *Please* be sensible."

Ben hesitated. Then his shoulders slumped.

"Maybe you're right." Deep breath. "But you're taking away the *other* possibility, too."

"I don't understand." I glanced over my shoulder at the approaching vehicle. "What other possibility?"

He smiled wanly. “Ben Blue, The Hero. That kinda would’ve been nice.”

I paused, at a loss for words. My heart broke for him.

“But that’s okay.” Ben dug keys from his pocket. “After all, we’re Virals, not heroes. And that’s fine. Plus, I’m not really the hero type.”

He turned to leave.

Impulsively, I grabbed Ben’s arm. Pulled him close.

Smashed my lips against his.

The kiss only lasted a second, but also an eternity.

Then I stepped back and shoved Ben toward the Explorer.

“Of course you’re the type.” I was grateful the darkness hid my blushes. “Now go.”

Ben stared, stricken, thunderstruck. Hi and Shelton watched, wide-eyed with shock.

“*Weirdest* birthday ever,” Hi whispered.

“Go!” I shooed them with both hands. “Hurry!”

Their paralysis broke. United in purpose, the boys piled into the SUV. I pushed Cooper in after them, ignoring his whines of protest.

Ben cranked the engine. Wearing a goofy grin, he spun the tires, then raced down the access road with his headlights off. The Explorer quickly vanished from sight.

Ella hurried back to my side. “What’d you say to convince him?”

My lips quirked. “I opted for surprise instead.”

Ella looked at me curiously, but let the comment slide.

I took a deep breath. “You ready for this?”

Ella flashed a shaky smile. “Absolutely not. Stay close.”

So we waited, holding hands, as the cruiser finally pulled into the lot.

The car rolled to a stop. The door opened. A familiar figure heaved himself out.

“Great day in the morning! It’s true!”

I almost smiled.

Inside, my wheels were spinning.

Maybe.

I strode to the car. “Hello, Captain Corcoran. How’d you end up at Drayton Hall?”

“Expert police work,” he shot back. “What in the world are you doing here? Not being kidnapped, I see.”

“Saving my life!” Ella said hotly. “No thanks to you!”

Recognizing her, Corcoran started. “Aren’t *you* supposed to be kidnapped?”

“Everyone relax.” I squeezed Ella’s shoulder, then turned my full attention on Corcoran.

“Let’s talk, Captain. We have a *lot* to tell you. Most of which you aren’t going to like.”

Corcoran frowned. “I’ve got enough problems already.”

“Sorry, but things are about to get worse.” I forced a smile. “But I’ve got a proposal that might interest you.”

CHAPTER 50

Police headquarters was in an uproar.

Microphones and portable lights had been set up on the front steps. Captain Corcoran stood in the glare, fielding questions from the media.

His face was grave, but I could detect the glee hiding behind Corcoran's carefully neutral expression. This was his moment.

I stood with Ben, Shelton, and Hi at the back of the throng.

Kit had taken Coop for a rest stop.

No one paid any attention to the four of us.

Corcoran had taken the deal.

"The Charleston Police Department has solved the Zodiac kidnappings," Corcoran announced loudly. "Ella Francis has been returned to her parents, safe and sound. Peter and Lucy Gable are also uninjured."

A reporter with poufy brown hair and scarlet press-on nails pushed forward. "Is it true that a member of our police force was the Zodiac kidnapper?"

Corcoran glared at the woman. "I can't comment on that at this time. I will say that a veteran detective in the Major Crimes Division was killed during the rescue of Ella Francis. His involvement in the case is currently under investigation."

A white-haired man with a strong voice called out. "Was Detective Fergus Hawfield the Zodiac kidnapper? Where are the Gable twins?"

Corcoran's face reddened. "We aren't going into specifics on the front steps, Harold!"

A roar of voices erupted in response. Questions flew at the captain.

"He's not enjoying himself as much now," Hi observed. "What a douche. When the press learns what Hawfield did, they're gonna bury this department. Corcoran wanted to be the face of this debacle?"

"He didn't mention *us.*" Light glinted off Shelton's lenses. "That's good enough for me."

"Corcoran will survive," Ben commented sourly. "He always does. We crack the case, *he* gets to be the hero."

My head whipped to Ben. Was that bitterness?

I saw no trace. Ben was smiling, relaxed for the first time in days.

Maybe months.

I thought back to my impulsive kiss in the parking lot. Felt my ears burn.

"Ella's gonna play ball?" Shelton asked. "Keep our secret?"

"No question." I zipped my Windbreaker, shutting out the cool night air. "She won't mention we were there."

"And Corcoran will stick to the script?" Hi shook his head. "The guy's not a rocket scientist. Or a rock scientist. He's dumb, is what I'm saying."

"True, but he's *very* ambitious." I fervently hoped that was enough. "Corcoran will say he tracked Hawfield to the woods, tricked him into emptying his gun, then chased him onto the covered well. Then brave Captain Corcoran entered the slave pen and rescued Ella. She'll go along with all of it. For our sake."

"Lying to the police." Shelton shivered. "I can't believe she agreed to that."

I watched Corcoran attempting to field questions without answering them. His face was flushed, his hairline damp with sweat. His eyes darted like a hunted animal.

Enjoy the spotlight, Captain.

"Ella's a friend," I said. "She knows what we did for her. And since there won't be a trial . . ."

I trailed off. None of us liked talking about Hawfield's death.

The detective had threatened to kill me. Had tried to on at least three occasions. In the end, his own actions had led to his demise. That and a few planks of rotten wood.

If he'd consented to being arrested, he'd still be here.

Hawfield had been every bit as cold-blooded as the Gamemaster.

The man deserved zero pity, especially from his intended victims.

And yet . . .

A hand on my shoulder.

"It's not our fault," Ben said quietly. "You shouldn't feel bad."

I reached up, covered his hand with my own. "I know. But I do."

Shelton's voice startled us apart.

"So the *Gable twins* called Corcoran?"

I nodded. "Corcoran said he got the call around four. Lucy and Peter were at the airport, although Corcoran didn't know that at the time. They told him pretty much everything—that the kidnapping was a fake, about Hawfield's involvement, even the cell's location."

Hi snorted. "We're lucky Captain Crunch took them seriously."

"It wasn't luck." I smiled. "Corcoran thought the call was a prank—but then he remembered you three, in his office, screaming about me being abducted in the same woods. He was still skeptical, and thought maybe *you guys* were the pranksters. So rather than risk any embarrassment, Corcoran kept the tip to himself and drove out to Drayton alone for a quick look-see. If he hadn't, we'd all still be filling out reports."

Hi straightened, as if a thought had just occurred to him. "The *twins* saw you, Tor! If they ever get caught—and tell the police their story—you'll be implicated."

"I know. But they're on the run. Corcoran said they flew to London, then on to Prague. The authorities still want to charge them, but with Hawfield having 'solved' the Zodiac kidnappings, the police aren't going to start some international manhunt for two spoiled kids. Except for Hawfield, no one got hurt, and the ransom was never paid. If the twins stay out of South Carolina, they'll probably never face any charges."

"I hope they stay abroad forever," Ben said. "Losers."

"It won't be a disaster if they do talk," I said, hoping I was right. "The twins saw me confront Hawfield in the barn, but they ran before the detective took me hostage. There's nothing linking me to the cell, Ella's kidnapping, or Hawfield's death. Plus, Lucy and Peter had nothing to do with Ella's abduction. Corcoran buys that—why else would they have called and ratted out the dirtbag?"

Hi pursed his lips. "The twins could be charged with what? Extortion? Lying to the police? Inventing a kidnapping? Accessory to assault?"

"Nothing to sneeze at." But I frowned. "Those idiots could actually wiggle their way out of trouble, if they stay away long enough, then negotiate a surrender. Corcoran says he'll stay on their case, and it's *definitely* in his interests to keep my name out of any statements the twins might make. I think I'll be okay."

Corcoran's voice boomed from the speakers. "How? Keen police instincts, that's how. Investigating alone, I was able to locate the place where Ella Francis was being held, overcome her abductor, and free the poor girl."

Camera flashes strobed. Corcoran adopted a stern, manly countenance, pausing to allow the photographers to get his good side. Unintentionally, his gaze fell on me.

The captain quickly looked away, his expression souring.

I hope they use that *face for the morning papers.*

"What a buffoon." Hi covered his eyes. "I can't watch. He's taking credit for *everything.*"

Footsteps behind me.

Kit's hands fell on my shoulders. Ben edged slightly away.

"We need to get home, kiddo." He spoke gently. "Coop's in the car. I'm glad you were able to come down and see your friend, just give me a little warning next time. Whitney and I are thrilled Ella's safe and sound. And the Gable kids, too, I guess. Although, I *swear.*"

"It's Corcoran." The captain leaned over the podium to instruct a reporter. "*Captain* Carmine Corcoran. C-O-R-C-O—"

Kit shook his head. "This guy again?"

Then Ben tugged my elbow. Nodded to his left.

"Kit?"

"Yeah?"

"Can you pull the car around? I'll be there in a sec."

Kit's gaze flicked to Ben, then he nodded. "Five minutes."

As my father strode away, Shelton and Hi both unleashed dramatic yawns.

"Welp." Hi stretched his arms over his head. "I'd better go check on various things that aren't right here. You coming, Shelton?"

"Oh, you know it." Hiding a smile. "Stuff to do. No time to waste."

They hurried off together, chuckling quietly.

Thanks, guys. This couldn't be more awkward.

Ben was looking at me, a soft smile on his lips.

Panic.

Despite the cool night air, I started to sweat.

"Chill out, Brennan." Ben seemed more at ease than I'd ever seen him. "I just wanted to tell you something. I think I know what was wrong with our flares."

"What?" Completely thrown. This was *not* what I'd expected.

"Why the powers went haywire." His face grew serious. "For months now, ever since we stopped talking, I've been holding something back. I was flaring all the time, but mostly because it made me feel connected to you. And Hi and Shelton," he added quickly.

"Ben, I'm *really* sorry that—"

"Don't be." He shook his head. "You had every right to hate me. Lord knows I hated myself. What I did was unforgivable."

"I never hated you. Not for a minute."

He smiled at that. "Thanks for saying so. But the point is, while flaring, I was also walling myself off. Protecting my feelings. Distancing myself from the pack. I think I *fought* the connection, on some level." He tapped his head. "At least up here."

I considered his words. "You think that messed with our flares?"

He nodded. "I don't understand it, either. But when we were in the woods, all five of us together, it was the first time I really let go. And look what happened."

I thought about Ben's theory. It made an odd kind of sense.

Could the problem have been as simple as Ben refusing our Viral connection?

"We don't understand these abilities," I said slowly. "Maybe accepting our place in the pack is necessary for the group to function."

But for some reason, I was skeptical. Ben's resistant mind-set might've negated the group's ability to link minds, but why would that make my flares *backfire*? And what about the odd feelings I kept getting? They didn't seem connected to Ben at all.

Ben shrugged. "All I know is, when I stopped fighting it—and lowered the barriers I'd built inside my head—the power flowed easily. Our minds merged."

I grunted in frustration. "There's so much we still don't know. It makes me crazy!"

"We'll get there. Our pack is whole again."

I looked at Ben. Noticed the light reflecting in his brown eyes.

Whoa, boy.

"Whole," I agreed.

Beep! Beep!

"Tory!" Kit called from behind the wheel of his 4Runner. Coop's massive head was hanging out the back window. "Time's up. Let's skedaddle."

I descended two steps.

Stopped.

Shot back up.

Wrapped Ben in a bone-crushing hug.

Startled, it took him a moment before he hugged me back.

Then, face flushed, I raced down to join my family.

EPILOGUE

Monday

Shielding my eyes from the sun, I peered down the street.

No sign of him.

"He didn't say anything to me," Hi repeated. "And if Shelton were sick, I'd be the first to hear about it. At length."

"Maybe he overslept?" I suggested. "We had a pretty eventful weekend."

Hi shot me a skeptical look. "And missed the boat to school? He's *never* done that."

Hiram and I were standing outside Bolton's gates, uniform jackets off as we drank in the morning sunshine. The sky was a perfect azure blue, as if celebrating the end of the last week's madness.

"Did you text Ben?" I asked. "Would Shelton be with him?"

"Shelton was home last night, and Ben went back to his mom's place in Mount Pleasant. Neither said anything about missing school. I *knew* we should've checked on him before leaving the dock."

"Don't get jumpy." Though I was starting to worry myself. "We caught the kidnapper. There must be some explanation."

Hi was about to reply when a voice called down the block.

"Guys!" Shelton was sprinting toward us with something in his hand. "Check this out!"

"See?" Hiding my relief. It'd been a long week, and I was done with surprises.

"Where you been?" Hi demanded.

Shelton jumped to a stop before us. "I did it!"

My eyes narrowed. "Did what?"

"Cracked the encryption!"

I stepped closer. "Seriously? You opened the B-Series files?"

"Well, no. But I *did* figure something out." He pushed his specs up the bridge of his nose. "You're not going to like it."

My patience slipped. "Shelton, what did you find?"

Shelton waved for silence as a gaggle of classmates passed through the gate. None gave us a second glance—our Gamemaster celebrity status was already old news. The whole town was talking about a crooked cop, the scheming Gable twins, and Ella's terrifying ordeal. The new scandal had erased any interest in our tired story.

Ella was staying home for the week. I didn't blame her. The last thing she needed was to be surrounded by stares and whispers. She needed to rest and recover.

We'd texted constantly that morning. My friend was tough as nails, and her biting sense of humor was returning. I knew she'd be okay.

After the students passed, Shelton spoke quickly. "That encryption is impossible to break, but I remembered something Chang did. How he'd been able to determine which server held Karsten's old files."

"Okay." Waving for him to continue.

Shelton smiled like a Keebler elf. "Well, the same type of info was hidden in the metadata on the files we downloaded at the aquarium. I was able to track down which server can access them."

I could never follow his computer-speak. "So you can access the B-Series files?"

"No." His head shook impatiently. "But I know *where* we could. Just like with Karsten's data stick. It's the same technology."

"You'd better not say the aquarium again." Hi ran a finger across his throat. "If we go back there, they'll feed us to the orcas."

"Nope. Different place." Shelton caught my eye. "Got a guess, Brennan?"

Something in his expression told me the answer.

Naturally.

"Chance."

"Candela Pharmaceuticals," Shelton confirmed. "User name: Chance Claybourne. The B-Series files are stored on a hard drive somewhere at their corporate headquarters."

My head dropped. Then shot back just as quickly.

"Screw it." Voice grim. "Let's go. Now. Text Ben."

"Seriously?" Shelton glanced at Hi, who shrugged. "We're gonna skip class *again*?"

"I'm done tap-dancing with Chance Claybourne," I vowed. "We're gonna solve this mystery, once and for all."

⬡ ⬡ ⬡

Candela's main office is located on Bee Street, in Charleston's busy medical district. The gleaming black monolith rises thirty stories, towering over the surrounding neighborhood.

We huddled in the shadow of a building across the street.

"I thought Candela was headquartered on Cole Island," Ben said.

"That's a production facility." I pointed at the skyscraper before us. "This is the corporate headquarters." A glance at Shelton. "That's what we want, right?"

"I think so. At least, this is where Chance's office should be. Candela's website lists this address for upper management in research and development."

"There's nothing on Cole but that factory," Hi added. "Security out there is probably through the roof. No chance we bluff our way into *that* setup. Our only shot is here, where they don't actually make drugs."

I nodded my agreement. "We have to sneak into Chance's office. From *his* computer, I'm sure we can access any files he controls."

"So what's the plan?" Ben asked.

"Go inside. Look around. Improvise."

"Brilliant." Hi stroked his chin. "Quick question: Is having *no* plan the same as having a *terrible* plan, or are those different categories?"

"Just follow my lead." Nervously smoothing my uniform. "Unless you think of something better."

The lobby was spacious and cold, with marble floors and twenty-foot ceilings lit by white globes. A half-dozen elevators stood across from the entrance.

Striding purposely, I headed directly for them.

A pair of security guards eyed us curiously, but made no move to intercept.

One elevator was standing open. We hurried inside.

I pressed a button at random. Floor 20. Why not?

The doors closed. No one spoke as we ascended. What was there to say?

I watched the illumination move from floor to floor, without stopping. 14. 15. 16.

The car slowed. Stopped. The doors opened.

Beyond them stood a mousy grandmother carrying a giant stack of files. Thick glasses hung unused against her lilac sweater.

"Oh!" She started. "My goodness! I didn't see you there."

"No problem at all." Hi smoothly took the lead. "Could you point us toward Chance Claybourne's office?"

"Claybourne?" The woman blinked. "The young one? Isn't he with special projects?"

Hi nodded, smiling patiently. "That's our man. To the left, or right?"

The woman cocked her head like a parakeet. "I'm sorry, sir, but that department is on the twenty-seventh floor. Not down here in accounting."

"Of course, my mistake." Hi stepped back into the elevator and pressed 27.

The old woman moved to join us, but Hi held up a hand. "Terribly sorry, but this car is full. Have a nice day!"

The doors closed on the befuddled senior.

Ben chuckled. "Not bad, Stolowitski."

"I do my best."

Reaching 27, I stepped from the elevator and started down the hall. This floor was nicer, with plush carpet underfoot and gleaming oak doors lining the walls. I tried to look confident while striding the corridor, scanning nameplates from the corner of my eye.

We'd nearly completed a full circuit before I finally spied Chance's office.

A corner suite, of course.

I stopped, then poked my head inside. Was immensely relieved to find the room empty.

We all scurried in, closing the door behind us. Hi shut the blinds.

The office was enormous, with floor-to-ceiling windows composing the two outer walls. Bookshelves and file cabinets lined a third. Near the door, a black couch and chair combination surrounded a glass coffee table. Farther in, a polished wooden desk held a single LCD monitor.

"Get to work," I whispered to Shelton. "Chance could be here any second."

Shelton moved to the computer and inserted his flash drive.

"Excellent. He's already logged in, and the putz didn't password protect his screen saver."

As Shelton began tapping keys, Ben, Hi, and I moved behind him to watch the monitor.

I couldn't follow the commands, but he navigated the system with ease.

"They're using Windows Eight, so I'm familiar with the OS. And this computer is accepting my flash drive as native. And look here." Shelton tapped the screen. "Under the heading 'Special Project—PX.' *Voilà.*"

A folder labeled "B-Series."

My pulse quickened. "Can you access the files now?"

Shelton clicked. The folder opened, revealing at least two hundred subfiles.

I chewed my lip, scanning the list. "Try . . . that one."

My finger speared a PDF entitled "Brimstone—Project Goals and Parameters."

Shelton opened the file. A two-page document filled the screen.

The header proclaimed:

CONFIDENTIAL AND PROPRIETARY.
THE INFORMATION AND OPINIONS CONTAINED IN THIS REPORT ARE THE EXCLUSIVE INTELLECTUAL PROPERTY OF CANDELA PHARMACEUTICALS, INCORPORATED. VIOLATORS WILL BE PROSECUTED TO THE FULLEST EXTENT OF THE LAW.

"Whatever." I began reading the document.

By the time I'd finished, my knees were shaking.

"Oh my God." Shelton covered his mouth.

Ben kicked the base of the desk. "That idiot!"

Hi was wide-eyed. "Man, this is as bad as it gets."

I didn't speak. Couldn't tear my eyes from the awful report.

My mind raced, trying to assess the implications.

Finally, I had to say the words out loud. Didn't want to believe them.

"Chance ordered new tests for Parvovirus XPB-19. He's resurrecting Karsten's experiment, but on a larger scale."

"Moron!" Hi shot both hands through his hair. "He doesn't understand the consequences!"

Suddenly, the door swung inward.

Chance stepped inside, holding a sheaf of papers.

His sleeves were rolled up, his tie loosened. Chance's pricey Italian shirt was stained and wrinkled. He looked like he hadn't slept in a week.

Chance paused in the doorway, taking in the four of us crouched behind his desk.

We stared, unable to muster a defense. The jig was up.

Caught red-handed. We're toast now.

Then Chance did the last thing I expected.

"Good." Wearily, he closed the door behind him. "You're all here. Saves me the trouble of having to find you."

Tossing the papers onto his coffee table, Chance collapsed on the couch. He rubbed bloodshot eyes with his palms.

We stood in a clump. Frozen. Clueless what to do.

"You might as well sit." Chance gestured lamely. "It's not like I didn't know you were here. Security alerted me the minute you walked in. They've had your descriptions for months. I hear you spoke to Delores in Accounts Receivable. Next time, be polite and share the elevator."

Dumbfounded, I did the only thing possible.

Slowly, expecting a trap, I walked over to the chairs. The boys trailed behind me.

I sat. So did Hi. Shelton and Ben remained standing behind us.

Chance hadn't moved, remained slumped on the couch like a dead man.

Then abruptly, he straightened. Tension filled his frame.

His gaze roved the group. "I guessed right about you four, didn't I?"

No one answered.

Chance spoke without emotion, as if discussing poetry at a Starbucks. "What happened when you caught the supervirus? Were the effects solely physical? Or did it change the way you think as well?"

"Let's get out of here, Tory," Ben urged. "Now."

"I know everything, Benjamin." Chance spoke simply, without threat or rancor. "I have Karsten's old files. I've determined that Coop was the sole carrier. And I have no doubt you were infected. I've seen what this bug can do."

"Yes."

All eyes on me.

"Yes," I repeated, looking directly at Chance. "We caught the supervirus. And, yes, it has had . . . effects on us. We call ourselves Virals now."

Shelton gasped. Hiram's eyes nearly shot from his head.

Ben shifted uncomfortably, his knuckles whitening on the sides of my chair.

"We have to bargain." I spoke to my friends, never shifting my gaze from Chance. "The B-Series is too dangerous to ignore. And Chance knows too much already."

Chance nodded slightly, but didn't speak.

I leaned forward. "What do you want from us, Claybourne? Why are you pursuing this so hard? Why revisit illegal experiments with a canine virus?"

Chance inhaled deeply. A single tear leaked from his eye.

"I knew I wasn't crazy," he whispered.

I sat back, some of my anger evaporating. "Is that what this was about?"

Chance glared from across the table. "Try questioning *your* sanity for a while. See how much you like it."

Fair enough.

"But you *can't* continue these tests." My voice grew pleading. "This experiment you ordered—Brimstone—you have no idea what you're getting into. Trust me on this. You have to kill the project."

Chance looked out the window. For a long moment, he didn't reply.

Finally, "Too late for that."

My tone sharpened. "What do you mean?"

Chance continued as if he hadn't heard. "These changes you spoke of. You're talking about special powers. Extraordinary gifts, right? I know. I was there. I saw what you can do. It's amazing."

"Those *gifts* might be killing us," I shot back. "We barely control them. This isn't a game, Chance. The supervirus won't transform you into some kind of real-life Green Lantern. You're playing with fire. You might be toying with a new plague."

His voice changed. "You're saying the virus could be dangerous? Deadly?"

"That's *exactly* what we're saying," Hi said. "How are you still not getting it?"

"You don't want any part of this, Chance." Shelton's face was granite. "No lie."

"Stop what you're doing," Ben warned. "Now."

Chance ran a hand across his mouth. It trembled.

"What are you so worried about?" I caught his eye and held it. "What's happened?"

Chance met my gaze for a beat. I saw real pain. Guilt? Fear?

He jerked his head away, once more staring out the window.

"It turns out, you guys are right." Chance barked a hollow laugh. "I shouldn't have ordered those experiments. I started Brimstone months ago, before I appreciated the danger."

Icy fingers ran down my spine. "Chance, what did you do?"

He stood, then studied each of us in turn. "You think this virus may be killing you?"

"It's possible. We don't know anything about it, really."

I wasn't sure where this was going.

Chance nodded, as if he'd made a decision. "I'll help you. I'll put all of Candela's medical resources at your disposal. We'll find out exactly what the virus has done to your DNA, and whether there's any possibility of treatment."

Ben stepped toe-to-toe with Chance. "We don't *want* your help, Claybourne. Never did."

Chance ignored Ben completely. "I offer this service in exchange."

I rose. Pulled Ben back a few paces. Took his place before Chance.

"In exchange for what?"

"Your help. I think I've made a terrible mistake."

Suddenly, the odd feeling returned, stronger than anytime before, boiling up inside me like a hundred million suns. I staggered, eyes widening in shock.

For the first time, I could sense a pattern. Could trace the mental connections firing from my subconscious. Energy pulsed from me. Pushed outward. And was flowing toward . . .

Chance.

Impossible.

But it was true. Unbidden telepathic tethers were snaking from my brain and enveloping the boy standing rigidly before me.

Stunned, I reached out a shaky hand. Grabbed Chance's arm. He didn't resist.

As my fingers made contact, the sensation amplified, like touching a third rail. An overwhelming feeling of kinship bloomed inside my mind, its tendrils whirling faster and faster, like a cyclone gaining steam. Then the impression slowly faded into oblivion.

"You," I breathed, unable to manage more.

Chance looked away, but shivers racked his frame.

"The feeling. It's a reaction to . . . *you.*" I stared at Chance. "How? Why?"

Chance's last statement hit me like a sledgehammer.

I could barely speak the words. "What mistake, Chance? What did you do?"

Chance hesitated. Looked from Ben to Hi to Shelton to me. Then he smiled sadly. "You're not the only Virals anymore."

Chance's eyes ignited with molten red light.

ACKNOWLEDGMENTS

Exposure would not have been possible without the tireless effort of our super-editor Arianne Lewin at G. P. Putnam's Sons. Thank you for knocking this story into shape. We'd also like to thank our excellent publicist, Elizabeth Zajac, for getting us from place to place, alive and mostly in one piece. Additional ovations, of course, go to everyone at Penguin Young Readers Group. You guys make it all happen. We are forever in your debt.

More plaudits go to Don Weisberg at Penguin and Susan Sandon at Random House UK. You saw the potential of the series first, and we thank you for believing in Tory and her crazy pack. We also must must *must* thank Jennifer Rudolph Walsh and the folks at William Morris Endeavor Entertainment for everything that they do. You connect all the dots. We appreciate the results.

Last, but certainly not least, an emphatic thank-you to our loyal readers. You are the point of everything that we do. Cheers!

Kathy REICHS

ONLINE

Be the first to hear Kathy Reichs' news and find out all about her new book releases at

www.kathyreichs.com

Join the official Facebook page at
www.facebook.com/kathyreichsbooks

Follow Kathy on Twitter
@kathyreichs